Praise for Charles Sheffield:

"Sheffield's uncommon vision and storytelling skill will keep you on the edge of your seat."

—*David Brin*

"Charles Sheffield is one of the very best hard science fiction writers in the world."

—*Kim Stanley Robinson*

"Charles Sheffield has the scientific grounding of a Clarke, the storytelling skills of a Heinlein, the dry wit of a Phol or Kornbluth, and the universe-building prowess of a Niven—and he may have a better take on psychology of spaceborn humans than anyone else in the field."

—*Spider Robinson*

"One of the most imaginative, exciting talents to appear on the SF scene in recent years."

—*Publishers Weekly*

Praise for TOMORROW AND TOMORROW:

"[Sheffield's] speculations on humanity's exotic future are fascinating—his cosmological explorations are based on ideas at the forefront of modern astrophysics. This is science fiction in the grand tradition: ambitious, elegiac and ultimately satisfying."

—*San Francisco Examiner-Chronicle*

"Sheffield clothes the most advanced speculations of modern science (all elegantly laid out in a factual appendix) in alluring forms of danger and beauty."

—*Washington Post Book World*

"Sheffield's *Tomorrow and Tomorrow* shares Verne's spirit of scientific adventure that has taken men and women to the bottom of the sea and the other side of the moon and will someday take them to the end of the universe. . . . This is truly a love story of the ages."

—*Orlando Sentinel*

Also by Charles Sheffield

TOMORROW AND TOMORROW

AFTERMATH

Charles Sheffield

BANTAM BOOKS

New York Toronto London
Sydney Auckland

AFTERMATH
A Bantam Spectra Book/August 1998

BOOK DESIGN BY GLEN M. EDELSTEIN

Library of Congress Cataloging-in-Publication Data
Sheffield, Charles.
Aftermath / by Charles Sheffield.
p. cm.
ISBN 0-553-37893-7 (trade pbk.)
I. Title.
PS3569.H39253A69 1998
813'.54—dc21 98-12325
CIP

Published simultaneously in the United States and Canada

Bantam Books are published by Bantam Books, a division of Bantam Doubleday Dell Publishing Group, Inc. Its trademark, consisting of the words "Bantam Books" and the portrayal of a rooster, is Registered in U.S. Patent and Trademark Office and in other countries. Marca Registrada. Bantam Books, 1540 Broadway, New York, New York 10036.

PRINTED IN THE UNITED STATES OF AMERICA

FFG 10 9 8 7 6 5 4 3 2 1

To Nancy, who believes everything I tell her.

ACKNOWLEDGMENTS

When I'm in the process of writing a book, I can't imagine what I might do to improve it. And when I'm done, I hate going back to make changes—even when they are changes for the better.

So I would like to thank those readers of the first draft who dragged me weeping back to the keyboard and helped me to create the finished work: Andrew Dansby, Anne Groell, Sharon Keir, Nancy Kress, Penny Wilson, and Eleanor Wood.

PROLOGUE

From the secret diary of Oliver Guest.

Entry date: June 14, 2026

The day I died: July 6, 2021. I remember it like yesterday.

I woke up a little after seven, though it might be more accurate to say that in the final night of dreams I never slept. Sometimes I was with my darlings, all my darlings. They were the same age at the same time, as they had never been in life. They would be fourteen years old forever. I would see to that.

But I traveled into nightmares, too, whenever my thoughts drifted forward half a day to imagine my final minutes. No Death Row, of course, and no march to the scaffold, not in these enlightened times; rather, we would stroll together, I and the observers and reporters and admirers and guards, to the Chamber of Morpheus.

What wonderful things words are. Three-quarters of a century ago the suicide flights of the Japanese Air Force became the kamikaze, the Heavenly Wind; today the death cell and sleep without end become the Chamber of Morpheus.

But back to reality. I woke around seven on the morning of my last day, and by eight they were at me again.

This time it was a short, neatly dressed man with a dark beard and a balding, wrinkled brow. He entered the room where I struggled to swallow coffee and toast—this condemned man, at least, ate no hearty breakfast—and he began, "Oliver Guest—"

"Do I know you?"

"We have never met, no. I am Father Carmelo Diaz."

"I specifically said, no priests. I was promised no priests."

"I know. It is not as a priest that I come here."

An obvious falsehood. A true priest can no more decide to be a nonpriest than a fish can decide to live out of water. But he went on with something of greater possible interest, "I carry with me an offer from the Governor."

"Let me see it."

He shook his head. "Although I have the offer with me in writing, I would rather first discuss it with you orally."

"No. Let me look at it. Then maybe we will talk."

With apparent reluctance, he reached into an inside pocket and handed over a thin packet of papers. Official state seal. Governor's official letterhead, and below it a certification that Carmelo Diaz was empowered to meet with Oliver Guest and negotiate on behalf of the state. And, finally, an outline of the terms of the offer.

While I was reading, I felt sure that Carmelo Diaz's eyes were in constant motion, flickering from me to walls, to floor, to ceiling, and finally—irresistibly—back to me.

I didn't have to watch Diaz to know this. I had seen the same behavior in a hundred visitors. They were intrigued—and some offended—by the apparent opulence of my living quarters. The furnishings were massive, immovably attached to the floor, and finished in soft and expensive leather. The walls, all the way up to the ten-foot ceiling, were covered in rich dark red velvet. Shoes sank deep into the pile of the soft carpet. The lamps, all ceiling inlaid, could dim or brighten at the touch of a button.

Less obvious—not obvious at all to me, until I did my own experiments—was the room's harmless nature. Harmless, in the specific sense that a person in the room would find nothing to permit self-damage or self-slaughter. Left to explore the room, as I had been free to explore it, any visitor would finally conclude that everything was innocu-

ous with the exception—the eyes of Carmelo Diaz, ever and always, came back to me—of the occupant.

I had no pen, of course, to sign anything. Nor would he have. Guards would be brought in to provide a writing instrument if we reached some kind of agreement.

That was a large if. I folded the three sheets of paper and handed them back to Diaz.

"A model of vagueness, if you don't mind my saying so. The state wishes me to give certain specific information. If I provide it, then certain vague concessions will be offered to me as a quid pro quo."

"It was written that way at my request." Given the setting, Carmelo Diaz seemed too much at ease. I wondered if he had been here before, dealing with others on the threshold of the Chamber of Morpheus. The innocent blue eyes in that rounded Celtish skull told me nothing. Apparent innocence itself meant less than nothing, and all first impressions based on appearances alone are likely to be deceiving. I, for instance, have features and build that appear somewhat coarse, even loutish, while my nature is both sensitive and finicky.

"No two humans are identical," he went on. "Your needs and wishes do not match those of the next man. You and I need room to maneuver, a freedom to negotiate."

"Freedom is hardly a term that I would apply to my situation. Can you offer me freedom?"

"You know that I cannot." There was a certain blunt charm to Father Carmelo Diaz. I could imagine that, under other circumstances, he might make a fine dinner companion. It must be one factor in his presumed successes.

"So what can you offer me?"

"Why don't we first confirm what the state asks of you?" And, when I said nothing, "It is really very little. Your trial provided overwhelming evidence that you murdered fifteen people. We wish to know if there were more."

"What makes you think there might be?"

"The chronological pattern. There are anomalously long gaps between cases five and six, between eight and nine, and between twelve and thirteen."

"Perhaps I was busy with other matters. I had to

earn a living, you know. A man can't just go on having fun all the time."

It was said to test him, and I was pleased to see that he did not wince.

"Do you have other suggested victims?" I went on. "It is hardly useful to propose gaps, unless you have people to fill them."

"I suspect that you, Dr. Guest, know these statistics far better than I do. But let me state them for the record." It was his first suggestion that we were being recorded, though I of course had assumed it.

"Confining ourselves to this population area alone," he went on, "an average of thirty thousand fourteen-year-olds run away each year. Most return home in due course, but close to one-sixth of them remain unaccounted for. Of those, let us assume that only one child in a thousand possesses that standard of physical beauty which satisfies your apparent need. There would still be a suitable candidate, every couple of months, whose permanent disappearance would be indistinguishable from all the rest."

The thing I liked about Carmelo Diaz was his matter-of-fact manner. No weeping and wailing and accusations from him about the "poor, helpless doomed children." No suggestions that I was the devil incarnate. It made me wonder if, deep inside, he carried the same needs. He was deliberately, and successfully, matching his speech patterns to my own.

I didn't let any of this influence me. I learned, long ago, how easy it is to find in others a false resemblance to oneself.

"That's all you are asking?" I said. "If there were others?"

"Well, not quite." He hesitated. "You chose such beautiful children, such models of physical perfection. We would like to know who the others were, and where their bodies can be found."

So far it had all been one-sided. Time to change that. "You have told me what you want," I said. "Now tell me what you can offer in return, were I to give it to you."

"If you provide the names of the others whom you killed, and tell us where their bodies are hidden, I will seek a reduction in your sentence."

And then, of course, it was my turn to smile. "A reduction. Very fine. Father Diaz, I am thirty-six years old. What would be your estimate of my life expectancy?"

"Fifty years. Maybe as long as seventy."

"Very good. I agree with that. But I was sentenced to fifteen consecutive sentences of forty years each. That's a total of six hundred *years of judicial sleep, a coma during which I will age at my normal rate. I will not live to serve even two of those fifteen sentences. So what are you telling me? That you can commute the total to twenty years? That you can arrange for all the terms to be served concurrently?"*

"I can do neither one."

"So what can you do?"

"I can try to arrange for you to be placed in abyssal rather than judicial sleep. I can make no absolute guarantees, but at the reduced body temperature your rate of aging will decrease." He paused. "Or so I am told."

I felt almost sorry for the man. They had sent him to me so inadequately briefed.

And then my sense of caution cut in. He was too *innocent, too poorly informed.*

"Father Diaz, how much do you know about my professional line of work?"

"Very little." He was sensitive, exceptionally so, and his voice suggested that somewhere in the last few seconds the conversation had turned, and he knew it. "Before your arrest you were a medical doctor. One, I gather, of high reputation."

"Perhaps. But not as a physician who treated sick patients. I have always been in research—and my particular line of research is in life-extension procedures. Although my primary thrust is not the study of abyssal sleep, I have done work in that field. I can assure you that the rate of aging of a subject in abyssal sleep, under optimal circumstances, is reduced by a factor of at most three. Even in AS I would die of old age before my sentence was one-third over."

His eyebrows raised, and he looked not at me, but up at the ceiling.

"That is AS as you know it today," he said at last. "But in twenty years time, or thirty, who knows? Do you not have faith in science? Science advances."

"And sometimes, it retreats. As you say, who knows? In twenty years, civilization itself may collapse. In thirty years, the world could be unrecognizable."

I make no claim of prophecy with those statements. I was just making conversation, keeping my mind away from the subject of the close of day and the beginning of endless night.

Father Diaz, a Jesuit by training if ever I saw one, did not allow himself to be diverted. "Science advances," he repeated. "You are a logical man, Dr. Guest. You understand the odds. On the one hand, we have possible progress in AS that grants you a chance—albeit a small one—of living through your entire sentence and beyond. On the other hand, without some kind of negotiated settlement you face mandated judicial sleep until your body expires of natural old age."

On most matters I was, as he said, a logical man. I was also a man with no alternative offer. At the very least, I would see this through the next stage.

I nodded. "Let us obtain writing materials."

"There are others?"

"There are. Three, as you surmised. I will provide you with names, and with locations, and with dates."

I had my own agenda. Father Diaz was tolerable company. If he left, I would be open to invasion by others more doubtfully acceptable.

I gave him what he had asked, names and places and dates. He stayed, as the hours wore on. At my request, a chess set was brought in and we played three games. One win, one loss, and one draw. A fair reflection, I thought, of the result from our other game.

We ate a simple lunch of cheese and onion sandwiches. I, to my surprise, had a fair appetite.

And then, sooner than I thought possible, two o'clock was approaching.

"Do you propose to stay to the end?" I asked.

He nodded. "Unless you have an objection."

"No prayers, then. No last-minute attempts to save my soul."

"I cannot save another's soul. Only the person can do so."

It was the closest he had come to priest talk, and a good thing, too. He seemed resigned to the fact that I was not about to discuss the logic of my choice of victims.

"We must soon be going," Diaz continued. He gestured toward the door of my room, where a face was visible at the grille. "It will be better if you leave this room voluntarily, and are able to walk without assistance or coercion."

"Certainly."

I was, in fact, preternaturally calm. In retrospect, a sense of the unreality of events had surely overtaken me. Who can accept the idea, viscerally rather than intellectually, that this is to be the last conscious half hour ever, in a universe destined to endure for tens of billions of years? Carmelo Diaz had promised to do his best on my behalf, but I put no stock in his success—either intellectually or viscerally.

We walked, side by side but far from alone. All the way along the corridor, with its dull gray walls and infrequent locked doors of bright blue, others paced before and behind us.

No one spoke. The whole building was as quiet within as it would be without. Judicial sleep, which killed no one until they expired of natural causes, had ended the long rhetoric about capital punishment. No one would be outside, chanting their scripted slogans.

Actually, I am not sure there would have been any sad songs for me, even in the good old days of Sparky and Slippery Sam. So far as most people were concerned I deserved the electric chair or the lethal injection—probably both. After my capture I had followed the news reports. I was a child killer, the worst one in decades.

All a perversion of reality, and quite unfair.

The door of the Chamber of Morpheus stood open. It was flanked by guards, all unarmed. Should I prove violent, no one wanted to kill me accidentally and destroy the notion that this was a civilized and even kindly proceeding.

I walked forward and sat down on the soft black cushions of the room's single chair. Leg and arm braces clicked into position. Everyone remained at a respectful fifteen feet, until at last one woman moved forward to stand in front of me. Much to my surprise, I recognized the Governor.

"Do you," she asked, "wish to make any final statement?"

I shook my head.

"I am told that you were a man with great gifts, Oliver Guest," she went on. "You had the power to do great good, and you did great evil from choice. Your punishment does not begin to match the dreadful nature of your offense. God have mercy on your soul."

She stepped back to join the ring of people, while I wondered what that was all about. Then I had it. We were just two months away from elections. For Governor Jensen this was just another media opportunity. Her comments made a brief nod to the scientific community, pointed out that she was strong on law and order, and reassured the religious that she was one of them.

It was tempting to speak my thoughts—what had I to lose? But beside her, Carmelo Diaz watched intently. Without Governor Jensen's blessing, there was no way he could keep his end of the bargain.

On with the show.

I survey the room. Even without a special reason for knowledge I would be familiar with this chamber. It is a nightmare from everyone's childhood. I stare at the big clock. One fifty-five. The gray circular wall and the white sky of the ceiling is as distant to me now as the remotest galaxies. Above me, a silver hoop slowly descends to encircle my seated body at midchest. Everything is done automatically, without human involvement.

"He who is without sin among you, let him first cast a stone." So no one will be responsible for what comes next. The cool injection carrying me to the undiscovered country is controlled by the Chamber of Morpheus's central computer, a device close to human in intelligence but untroubled by human doubts or conscience.

One fifty-seven. Most condemned prisoners, I had learned, close their eyes as the hoop settles into position. I stare, unblinking, as the green syringe extends itself and sits waiting by my upper left arm.

One fifty-eight. Everything can begin, I am ready.

But procedure must be followed. I watch the slow sweep of the second hand, marking the countdown to the end of the universe. There ought to be music, the sound of trumpets or perhaps a Dies Irae. *But music is not permitted in the Chamber of Morpheus. Instead there is total silence, the audience hushed and rigid.*

Twenty seconds. The end of the needle, so fine that it fades to invisibility, touches my arm. I flinch. The descent into judicial sleep is supposed to be painless—but on whose testimony?

The clock readout reaches two o'clock—and moves past it. Five seconds. Ten. I sit a little straighter, convinced that something has gone wrong and the journey to Lethe is delayed.

And then I realize that the injection was made exactly on schedule. I had not felt it, but I am moving, expanding, ascending on pink clouds of glory. The chamber, far below me, fades out of sight.

The forever sleep has begun.

IN THE BEGINNING

First Strike. February 21, 2026; Kimberleys Plateau, Western Australia.

It was evening, but it was not dark. Would darkness ever come again?

Wondjina crawled from the shadow of the rocks and peered north and west. No clouds were in the sky, and the Sun was on the horizon. Soon it should be night, cooling the desert and bringing longed-for relief.

But there would be no night; soon, again, would come the Rival.

Wondjina turned to face south and east. A hint of pink was already on the skyline, warning that the Rival was alive in the heavens and about to rise in the cloudless sky. If Wondjina were to find water it was best to seek it at this time, in the cooler hour before the Rival usurped the Moon and evening turned again to day. It must be done quickly. Thirst was all through him, weakening his muscles and stiffening his joints.

He made his way to the dried-out riverbed and walked along it, seeking patches of sun-seared grass. Under the grass, deep in the gravel, he would find the water that fed their roots. There, and nowhere else.

For twelve days, the Rival had risen as the Sun set. Between them, Sun and Rival seared the land and drew off every hint of surface moisture. Without dark there could be no night, without night there would be no midnight fall of dew. And the deep waters were running dry.

Wondjina took the trowel from his waist sling and started to dig in the gravel of the watercourse. From time to time he laid down the tool, picked up the hollow reed, and pushed it deep. He sucked hard on the other end.

Nothing, and still nothing. Every day, the reed had to be pushed deeper. Dig again, dig harder. Finally, after ten minutes of hard effort, a few mouthfuls of warm, brackish liquid.

He straightened and stared again to the south. The Rival had lifted above the horizon. Now it was a dazzling blue-white point too bright to look at. There was no circle of light, like the Sun's disk, but when the Rival was high in the sky it threw down its own intense spears of heat.

This torment could not last. Or if it did, Wondjina's family would not be here to see it. They would leave, heading away to seek help from lowland strangers.

Wondjina would not leave. He was old, and he would live or die in the homeland. But he could not survive like this. Hunger and thirst gnawed within him. Midsummer was long past, and the Sun was on its annual journey north. Heat should be lessening, rain should carry in on the west wind. But not this year.

Twelve days ago the Rival had appeared in the night sky. Darkness became a memory. The heat steadily increased, a dry wind blew from the south. No animal moved across the red sands. Even the tough, leathery grass had wilted.

Wanderers through the homeland brought word of other changes. Lake Argyle, the great water far to the north, had dried completely for the first time in many years. Far south, the Ord River ran low in its course. The Rival's presence was felt, north or south, as it was here. You could not run from it, any more than you could escape by flight from the Sun itself.

Wondjina, the family's living memory of older times, knew what must be done. The answer was not to flee. It was to ask the spirits of cloud and rain to bring relief.

Ask now, ask tonight. The family was determined to leave tomorrow.

He squatted onto his haunches and rubbed the wrinkled skin of his knees. Everywhere was reddish, powdery dust, worse than at any time in his long memory. He opened the woven bag, took out the necklace of dried bones and the bright-stained sections of emu shell. Let the youngsters speak of new ideas, of their belief that the Rival was nothing more than a star suddenly grown great. What did they know? Not one of them could recite a history of the family, not one had learned the modes of address to the spirits of autumn rains.

First, there was the choice of site. Level and high and on the open plateau, where the Rival would always be in sight.

Wondjina began to ascend the course of the dried-out streambed. He climbed slowly and carefully, leaning on his iron-wood spear for support. Hunger had weakened his limbs, but he must husband his strength for the ceremony. The Rival lay directly ahead, its southern fire striking matching points of light from sharp-sided pebbles in the watercourse. Was it imagination, or did the intruder tonight flame brighter yet, putting the vanished Sun to shame?

A slender gray-green lizard darted from under Wondjina's feet, scrambling uphill. Instinct drove his spear, guiding its fire-hardened point through the wriggling body. He leaned and grabbed in one movement.

He ate the lizard whole. The tip of the long tail, hard and scaly and indigestible, was the only rejected fragment. Crunching the delicate bones and allowing cool blood to trickle down his throat, Wondjina felt strength enter his body. He had seen no animal life for three days. This lizard was a clear omen, a gift from the spirits of the rains. It said, the time to begin was here.

He reached the plateau and advanced to its southern margin. The desert land dropped away ahead. Far off, rolling dunes marched to the horizon. On his left the land rose to the distant hills, fading into the continental interior. Above, creeping higher in the sky, the Rival burned in Heaven. It threw the shadow of Wondjina stark behind him.

He laid out the pattern of eggshells and bones, slowly and carefully. The heat was fierce, sucking sweat from his body as soon as it appeared. His grizzled, tight-coiled hair was warm to his touch. The brief respite of evening was over.

Now, then, or never.

He removed his breechclout and pouches and smeared the red ocher and white pipe clay on his body. Then the weaving dance began, turning steadily from right to left, following the line of shells and bones. The chanted invocation to the spirits of rain and cloud came without conscious thought. He had not spoken those words for many years—how many? He did not know—but they came easily.

The Rival rose higher in the sky, moving toward its own

noon. The naked figure danced on and on, a solitary black mote on the great plateau. Danced, as his energy slowly faded. Danced, as his legs weakened. There had been a sign that he was to begin. There must be a sign that he was permitted to stop.

Nothing, though his legs were beginning to buckle. The dry south wind blew, and the Rival pierced his body with its daggers of heat. He decided that he would dance until he died. If his life was demanded as the condition of succor, he was willing to give it.

When the change came he at first noticed nothing. It was hot as ever, the wind blew still. Only when he stumbled and fell from sheer exhaustion, then made the effort to regain his feet, did he see it.

A new line of hills rose above the southern horizon. He stared at them for seconds, before his tired brain told him that what he saw was impossible. Not hills. Clouds. As he watched they crept closer, changing from that single indistinct line to lofty mountains and dark feathery canyons.

Not just clouds. Rain clouds.

Wondjina whooped in triumph. Rather than trying to stand up, he fell forward and lay prone. With his left cheek on the dry, gritty ground, he gave thanks. He watched the steady advance until the wonderful moment when a rearing thunderhead swallowed up the Rival's fire. The wind fell to nothing, then came back as veering random gusts. The air was no longer lung-searing hot.

As the first drops of rain spattered the parched soil, he stood up. Now it was time to rejoin the family. Later he would tell them how at his plea the cloud spirits had saved them—even if they did not want to believe it.

He left the eggshells and bones where they lay, a tribute to the spirits. The rain was changing from a shower to a downpour to an astonishing cloudburst. He cupped his hands in front of his mouth, turned his face upward, and drank.

The family would not be where he had left them. When rain came like this after a long dry spell, there was only one place to be. Wondjina hurried toward it. Soon he had left the graveled watercourse and was traversing the side of the hill, still heading downward.

The slope ended at an oval pan of clay, forty yards across and a hundred long. The dry surface of Lake Darnong was a mosaic of deep cracks, half an inch across. Rain hissed down onto the flat clay bed and vanished immediately into the fissures of the thirsty earth.

The whole family, thirteen people plus the four dogs, stood

waiting. Everyone was smiling and holding woven collection bags. The cracks in the clay foamed and bubbled.

One of the dogs saw it first. She darted forward. Two seconds later she was back with a muddy frog wriggling in her jaws. And then they were everywhere, the whole soaked surface alive with frogs awakened by water from their estivation and wriggling up to feed and mate.

Family and dogs ran forward together. Wondjina followed, more slowly. As he walked onto the slick clay, already covered by half an inch of water, he turned to stare triumphantly south. The Rival was hidden by dense clouds, but it must still be there. It had lost. Wondjina and the cloud spirits had won.

Much later, as day followed day of remorseless rain, Wondjina realized his error. The whole landscape was changing, vanishing, washing away in great mud slides and borne off on torrents of rushing water. It became cold, colder than any winter, and white flakes fell from the sky.

Chilled and shivering, Wondjina crouched beneath a useless shroud of cloth. He had been wrong. The Rival had not been conquered. It had been challenged, and now it was showing its strength. The cloud spirits had not brought the rain. The Rival had brought the rain and storm, not to save the family but to destroy it. Stay or go, it made little difference now. Wondjina's world was gone, and it would not return.

Wondjina, cold and despairing, died on the sixth day of the rains. He never knew that the Rival, burning fierce above the clouds, had yet to reveal its full power.

Second Strike. March 14, 2026; Suborbital.

The weather on takeoff from LA was as freakish and wild as Tom had ever seen it. Strong gusts at random, from every direction. Blame events in the Southern Hemisphere for that. But once you were above the atmosphere, the weather problems all went away. The six-passenger ship flew itself—or rather the automatic pilot made the decisions. Human pilots were a passenger courtesy, about as necessary to this flight as feathers. Which was fine with Tom Wagner, because it left him free to entertain his special VIP, the woman who had been brought aboard incognito and at the last moment.

"No, ma'am. You won't see the supernova from here." She was sitting next to him, and he leaned across her to point south. "It's thataway. But we're flying a great circle suborbital between LA at thirty-four degrees north and Washington at thirty-nine degrees. What you want to see is down at sixty degrees south. To get a peek at it we'd have to go a lot higher than a suborbital flight."

Janet Kloos stared south anyway, taking her cue from his pointing finger rather than his words. She looked to be in her late thirties, but Tom knew she was a fair bit older than that. As he recalled it from the last campaign, the Vice President was pushing fifty. Apparently political life agreed with her.

"And it can have these terrible effects on the weather," she said. "Even from so far away."

"Yes, ma'am. It certainly can." Her words confirmed his first impression. Janet Kloos was a certified pilot, qualified to fly a ship like this one. Her naive questions about the suborbital jump had been for Tom's benefit. She wanted him to feel comfortable, and the easiest way was to make it clear that in spite of her status, he, not she, was in charge here.

Which was fine with him. Know-it-all passengers on the flight deck were the hardest of all to deal with.

"It will get worse before it gets better," he went on. "According to the forecasts that I've seen, the effects should peak in another couple of weeks. After that it will gradually dim, and then things ought to head back to normal."

"Not in some places." She stopped staring south and leaned back in her seat. During this portion of the suborbital trajectory the ship was close to a free-fall condition. "I see the State Department reports, and I'm not giving away secrets when I tell you that we've been lucky. There are major storms crawling up and down South America from Tierra del Fuego to Panama. Australia is waterlogged. South Africa's being washed away into the Atlantic and Indian Oceans, fifty percent of the topsoil already gone. There's never been anything like it since they started keeping records. The East Indies, too. The Sulawesi trade delegation back in LA were just telling me that they cannot possibly make their export shipments. They can't even feed themselves."

Tom nodded, but he was hardly listening. He cast his eye quickly over the banks of instruments—all normal—and then stared north. If there was nothing to see to the south, there was plenty to look at in the opposite direction. It was an aurora, and like none that he had ever seen. He checked their height. Eighty miles, close to maximum and right in the middle of the main altitude of auroral activity. Soon they would reach apogee and begin their downward glide. That was a shame, because the display was worth watching from this vantage point for as long as you could.

He caught her attention and pointed to the left. In the north, the sky was on fire. Streamers of pink and red and yellow-green trailed across the starlit heavens.

"Aurora borealis," Tom said. "Northern lights. The strange thing is, I've heard nothing from the solar observatories about a big flare."

"It's absolutely gorgeous. I've seen the aurora before, on transpolar flights. But nothing like this.

"Ahhh!" She had suddenly gasped. Tom came close to doing the same. Overlaid on the trailing wisps of the aurora the whole sky had lit with an intense flicker of blue.

"What is it?" Janet Kloos had been leaning over Tom for a better look at the aurora, but now she sat straight. "It's everywhere, in front and behind and overhead. What's causing it?"

Tom did not answer. When the flash of blue came he had felt a tingle through his whole body. In the next moment he thought that he had gone blind. He was staring at the instrument panels, and seeing nothing. At the same moment as he stabbed the controls for a general systems reboot and circuit breaker reset, he heard a warning whir of gyros.

"What is it?" Janet Kloos said again. He noticed a harder note in the Vice President's voice.

"I don't know. But we've lost the computers, main and auxiliary. I'm trying to bring them back up."

Trying, and failing. All the lights on the panel and in the cabin had died, that was why he had at first thought that his sight had failed. But lights were not the worst problem. Tom knew every control, even in the dark. He was working the correct switches. The trouble was, nothing responded. Lights would not come on, servos sat lifeless. When he pulled on the control stick it responded sluggishly. It felt as though the hydraulics were working, but every electric amplifier had failed.

The ship was slowly turning, dipping at the nose. Tom knew the cause—there had been a slight forward pitch at the moment when the controls failed, and it was continuing. He would have to correct it manually.

"Can you fly it like this?" Janet Kloos, thank God, had her fear under control. Tom was not sure that he could say the same for himself.

"Sure. But I may need you to take the dual controls and give me a hand. I'm feeling a lot of resistance."

For the moment that didn't matter. The problems would start in another few minutes. At that point they would be flying at more than four thousand miles an hour, returning to the atmosphere. The angle for reentry had to be just right. The automatic pilot normally took care of that, but it was dead.

How could it fail, with triply redundant logic and servos at every stage? But it had. The flight had become his responsibility, to work the hydraulic controls himself with no power-assist.

The door in the rear of the cabin opened. "What the hell are you doing up here?" It was a male voice, slightly intoxicated. "You've switched all our goddam lights off. Oops." He was peering at the turned face of Janet Kloos, pale and greenish in the glimmer of the aurora. "Ms. Vice President? I'm sorry. I hadn't realized that you were on board. Can we get lights back there?"

His smug expression suggested that he had known very well who was in the cabin. He had come forward to complain on a dare or a boast—"See, I went up there, and I told the Veep . . ." He had no idea that there was real trouble.

"Return to your seat, please." Tom guessed that the SEAT BELT sign was not working, along with everything else. "We have an electrical problem. Tell everyone to buckle up until we're sure it's fixed."

As he spoke he was working the attitude controls, getting a feel for the level of resistance of the mechanical gyros. He could correct their attitude, with a good deal of physical effort. But that was only the beginning. For a landing—any landing, anywhere—he needed engine power. Without thrust the suborbitals had the gliding angle of a lead brick. He had already tried for a preliminary one-second engine burn, without success. He couldn't ask for ground assistance on possible landing points, because the communications circuits were dead.

The ship's environment was still close to free fall, but the nose was steadily turning farther downward. Tom hauled on the control to work the gyros and begin to bring them level. As he did so he caught sight of the forward view. The ship had tilted far enough that he could see the Earth beneath. They were past the midpoint of their high arc.

It would be ten o'clock at night below, local time. They should be seeing, even at this altitude, the scattered patches of light that signaled urban development. Tom saw nothing below but total darkness.

"Where are we?" Janet Kloos was working the controls with him. She knew, thank God, exactly what to do. "The last time I looked at the locator display we were over Nebraska."

The locator display was dead, along with everything else. But Tom understood the implied question. Nebraska still had lots of wide-open spaces where you might not find a city for a hundred miles.

"We're past Nebraska, ma'am. We're over Iowa, or maybe Illinois."

"So where are the cities? There must be a large-scale power failure down there."

Before Tom could answer—and what could he answer?—a pinprick of bright orange suddenly blossomed below, then as quickly died.

An explosion—of an aircraft, out of control and smashing into the ground at high speed?

In silence, he and Janet Kloos worked the controls together, bringing them back to an even keel. When the angle of attack felt right and he sensed a faint hint of atmospheric lift from the ship's stubby wings, he turned again to the instrument panels. The computers refused to come back on-line. The communications circuits were dead. There must be plenty of fuel—they had started from LA with full tanks—and the ship's reactor was presumably still working, since it did not depend on electrical power. But all that became irrelevant when the engines would not fire. The ship was a dead lump of metal and plastic, racing through the upper atmosphere.

Janet Kloos was holding the ship's angle exactly as Tom had set it. She said, "I've never done an unpowered descent. How much speed do you need to avoid a stall?"

Tom's respect for the Vice President increased. Her thoughts were running on the same lines as his own.

"About four hundred. These suborbitals weren't designed to glide."

You could land a ship like this at four hundred. Tom had done it, himself, in training—during daylight, with assistance from the automatic pilot, and with a long, clear runway awaiting his arrival.

It was night, there was no automatic pilot, and the land below was dark and unknown.

Tom thought, *We're going to crash, and I have the Vice President on board.* And then, in a flash of grim humor, *Vice President? Hell, we're going to crash with* me *on board.*

The ship was racing down through the atmosphere in its long arc of descent. Tom, with no information except the feel of the controls, guessed that they were already around twenty thousand meters. The buffeting from wind currents was no more than usual, and the faint glow of frictional heating and ionization looked familiar and normal. As the descent continued, that glow faded. It would have been easy to imagine that everything was under control.

Janet Kloos was not fooled. She had released the dual controls. Now she was leaning forward and to the right, staring down at the ground. "Where are you going to put us down?"

The question of the moment. A four-hundred-mile-an-hour landing speed sounded like nothing compared with suborbital speeds ten times that, but a normal touchdown was at less than one-fifty.

"Do you see anything down there?" Tom's question didn't sound like an answer to hers, but it was.

"I'm beginning to. The aurora helps. Now that my eyes are used to the darkness, I'm beginning to see outlines."

And so was Tom. In every test that he had ever taken, his sight had been judged exceptional. Especially in low lighting. Owl eyes, one tester had said. But owls didn't land at four hundred knots.

The terrain below was gradually appearing as faint contrasts between dark gray and total black. Since their trajectory had not changed, they should be descending toward the suborbital field fifty miles west of Washington. If he could direct them in to that, they had at least a chance.

He glanced at the backup altimeter. That ought to be working; it used air pressure rather than computed absolute position. But it was too dark to see. His guess was that they had descended to around five thousand meters. They had maybe four minutes more flying time.

Below he saw rugged terrain, ranges of wooded hills. The Shenandoahs? If so, they were getting close. He could hear the sound of rushing air on the streamlined body. That was unusual; during a normal powered descent it was masked by the noise of the engines. Should he say something to the passengers? If so, what? And how could he do it, with no cabin address system?

They were descending fast. Tom saw a broad river valley, and for a moment he had hopes. Then the hills were back, rushing closer beneath them. Their slopes seemed covered with soft, gray feathers. It was easy to imagine that you could land on that downy surface, and it would serve to brake your movement. Tom knew better. At four hundred miles an hour, those soft, pliable branches would chop the ship into small pieces.

He gripped the control stick more tightly. Janet Kloos reached over and placed her hand on his. "We're not going to make it, are we?" she said quietly.

"I don't think so." Tom tried to match her calm. "Not unless something opens up in the next few seconds. It's all trees down there."

The banality, the *normalcy,* of their comments struck him. Last words ought to be epic and memorable, even if there was no way to record them. Were the flight recorders working? Probably not, since everything else had failed.

Her hand was still on his. The sound of air on the ship's body had risen to a scream. The topmost branches of the forest streaked by a few meters below. In the final moment before the world ended, Tom had enough self-control and curiosity to think a final question: *What killed us?*

Third Strike. March 17, 2026; Bathurst Island, Canadian Arctic.

The oil rig could be worked by hand, but the cold was extreme and after the first day no one suggested it.

Early on the morning of the third day, Cliff Barringer called a meeting of the four-man crew.

"We've all been talking for the past couple of days in bits and pieces. I want to get organized and make some decisions. Nothing's working right, but I have no idea why. The good news is that we're in no danger, and we won't starve."

"Or freeze," Judd Clemens said. He was the oldest of the group, with thirty years of Arctic experience behind him. "Dahlquist says we're sitting on the world's biggest oil and gas field."

"We are." Dahlquist was the odd man out, a lightly built and nervous geologist half a head shorter than the others. "All the groups who have leases in the basin agree. The seismic data and chemistry indicate more light crude in the Sverdrup Basin than the Saudis ever had. But we shouldn't be burning it—good quality hydrocarbons are too precious for that."

"So we take a little drop, give us some light and keep our asses from freezing to the ground." Barringer jerked his thumb toward the homemade lamps and the two oil stoves. "You want to turn those off, you do it over my dead body. Look, I don't want to talk morality. I want to review the situation and make some decisions. The communications equipment is down, we've not heard a word from outside, and the rest of the group are two days overdue. What do we know, and what do we do?"

"We're still getting paid, aren't we?" Big Eddie Hansen was frowning. "I mean, we're here. It's not our fault if the equipment's no good and the others don't come."

"Suppose they don't arrive until midsummer?" Cliff Barringer addressed his question to all of them, not just Big Eddie. "How long are we willing to sit on our duffs and wait? You may be more patient than me, but I want to know what's going on. When I turned in at nine o'clock three nights ago, everything was working—"

"Later than that," Clemens interrupted. "Me and Eddie was outside watching the aurora. We come in at about half-ten when it clouded over, and everything seemed all right then."

"So it happened sometime during the night. But when we got up, half our stuff was useless. I want to know why."

"A lot more than half, I think. Radio and television communications. Computers." Dahlquist began to tick items off on his fingers. "Snowmobile. Rig pump controller. Hut thermostat. Fuel cells. Clocks and watches. Fluorescent lights. Electric oven. CD player—"

"Enough," Barringer interrupted. "What *is* working?"

"Everything mechanical. Oil stoves, and oil lamps, and the thermometer and can opener and hand pumps and the manual rig. Batteries still work. Everything *simple*. Nothing that uses electronics or elaborate controls."

"Electronics? The snowmobile has a simple two-stroke engine—"

"—with an electronic fuel injection system." It was Dahlquist's turn to interrupt.

"All right. Look, you said all this yesterday. The question is, what can we do about it?"

"About the equipment? Nothing. We have no way of repairing electronic equipment. It'll have to be heli-lifted south."

"Which assumes that the helicopter arrives, when all we know is that it's way overdue. If we knew what was causing this—"

"You know my suggestion. All this forms some strange sort of side effect of the supernova."

"That happened down in the Southern Hemisphere," Clemens said, in the tones of a man with little interest in any event south of the Arctic Circle.

"It did." Dahlquist became defensive, as though this was now regarded as *his* supernova. "The star that blew up is at sixty degrees south."

"About as far away from us as you can get." Clemens proved that he knew a little more about southern events than he pretended. "It's produced weird weather around most of the world, but nothing here. And it started over a month ago, and it's nowhere near as bright now as it was. So how could it cause trouble *now*?"

"I don't know."

"Look, you two." Barringer wondered why he could never hold a decent meeting. The talk always seemed to run off down side alleys. "I'd like to know what caused the trouble, too. But I'd like a hell of a lot more to decide what we're going to do right here in this camp. And I don't want a debate. I want to make some suggestions."

That produced at least a temporary silence. Barringer waved his arm around, indicating the walls of the prefabricated hut. "You could probably run right through the walls if you wanted to, but it won't blow away and it's thermally insulated. So option one is to sit in here and wait 'til we all go crazy with each other's company. I don't like that. So here's my idea. We know that BSP has leases northwest of here, and Amarillo has leases to the southwest. They must have test crews, too."

"They do," Dahlquist said. "I talked to them a week ago, about interpretation of the seismic."

"Do you know where their camps are?"

"Pretty well. They're both fifteen to twenty miles away from us. I can give you a heading."

He did not say "compass heading." Bathurst Island sat almost on the North Magnetic Pole.

"We can manage twenty miles," Barringer said, "even without the snowmobile. It's time we compared notes with the other groups. If we're the only ones with troubles, great. They'll help us. If we're all in the same boat, then we'll help each other. So I say we draw lots, to decide who—"

"Me." Judd Clemens had his hand already in the air. "I want to go. I know how to travel easily over snow, I've done it often enough."

"And me." Big Eddie Hansen raised his hand.

Barringer stared at him. "Do you know how to move on snow?"

"Better than you do. And like you said, I'd go crazy sitting here waiting for nothing."

"He'll be fine," Clemens added. "Me and Eddie know the land and we work together good. All right?"

"Just give me a minute." Barringer had been thinking of two trips, one man to BSP and one to Amarillo. But what Judd Clemens said made a lot more sense. If BSP was affected, so almost certainly was Amarillo. And two men could help each other if one got into difficulties. "All right."

"When can we go?" Clemens asked.

Barringer glanced out of the thick plastic window. It was still a few days short of the equinox, so at this latitude the sun never rose above the horizon. From about ten to two in the afternoon, a strange half-light reflected off the clouds. Today it was calm outside, with no breath of wind. "It looks good to me right now. What do you think?"

"Perfect." Clemens stood up. "Come on, Eddie. Let's get suited up and our snowshoes on, and we'll be off."

"Where'll we go, Judd?"

"Amarillo. They eat better than at BSP. With luck we'll be there in time for dinner."

In five minutes they were pushing out through the multiple layers of thermal plastic that covered the flimsy door of the hut. In one more minute, Judd Clemens was back.

"Here." He handed the rifle that he was carrying to Dahlquist. "I thought I'd better test it to make sure this fired, before we lugged it all the way to Amarillo. You can add it to the list of things that doesn't work. See you tomorrow, early afternoon."

He pushed his way out again, while Dahlquist sat down and examined the weapon.

"Odd. I would have thought that this—oh, I think I see. It's the laser range finder and the target follower, they are controlled by a little ballistic computer. When that's out of use, there's a safety feature that stops the gun from being fired."

"Could it be bypassed?"

"I think so. With a bit of tinkering." Dahlquist laid the rifle down. "I'll take a look at it later. At the moment I have three weeks' worth of well logs to look at—and no computer to help."

Barringer took the hint. He put on his own suit and went outside. The area around the camp was flat and featureless. Bathurst Island was a bare, eroded, and glaciated sheet of rock, with nothing but the small island of Ellef Ringnes between its jagged shoreline and the North Pole. A big change from Indonesia, or the tall offshore rigs east of the Falklands.

The snow around the prefab hut was about a foot and a half deep. Its thin crust showed the marks of two pairs of snowshoes, heading off to the southwest. Judd Clemens and Big Eddie Hansen were already reduced to two blurry dots on the horizon. They had moved much faster across the snow than Barringer could ever have done.

He turned to go back inside. Clemens, and Big Eddie, too, might be at home in this land, but they were not real oilmen. Oilmen roamed the world. They would never stay a life in one place.

A full day passed with no sign of Judd Clemens and Eddie Hansen. Barringer was not worried. The weather held fine, and visibility was good.

On the second day, about noon, he went outside again. He wanted to look for the others, and also Dahlquist was getting on his nerves. The geologist was prone to confusing a discussion of neutron well logs with conversation.

The weather was changing, but not in any threatening way. The temperature was up, and a thin fog lay on the land. It was not enough to confound, and anyway Judd Clemens was a seasoned Arctic traveler with a good sense of direction. But where the devil were they? They must know that he was itching to know the situation at the Amarillo camp.

About ten o'clock on the third morning, Dahlquist suited up to take the short walk over to the rig. "Be back in about an hour," he said.

Barringer nodded. Yesterday's feeling of irritation with Dahlquist was still there.

By one-thirty the geologist had not returned and there was

still no sign of Clemens and Hansen. Barringer put on his own snowsuit, feeling more annoyance than alarm. He had fried ham steaks over the oil stove for him and Dahlquist, and eaten some himself. The rest was cold and spoiled, and he was damned if he would start over when the other man came back.

The air outside was warmer and perfectly still. Yesterday's fog had thickened. The dark oil rig, about fifty yards from the hut, stood misted and indistinct.

Barringer walked in that direction, crunching through frozen snow and calling Dahlquist's name. His voice was swallowed up by the still air. He came to the drill site and circled around it. On the far side, about five paces beyond the rig, he saw a ragged piece of windproof cloth. It was bloodstained. Two steps away he noticed a long smear of blood leading away from the rig. The surrounding surface of the snow was trampled and broken.

Barringer did not follow the line of the long blood smear. He backed away toward the hut, nerves jangling. When he turned he saw what he ought to have noticed earlier: paw prints in the snow, ten inches across. They led toward, and wandered around, the hut.

He ran for the door with its hanging sheets of thick plastic. As he opened it and went through, he turned. A white shadow was approaching through the fog, silently and at great speed. He scarcely had time to close the door and snap the bolt into position.

The building shook. Barringer backed away across the hut and snuffed the oil lamp. In the darkness, he waited. Ten seconds later a tall form reared up against the window. He saw great curved claws on the window's edge, and a long head reaching for the roof. At last the beast dropped to all fours. The nose quested, sampling the air for a few moments, then the animal turned and loped away across the snow. Barringer thought that he made out two more shapes, outlined eerily against the swirling mist.

He had seen polar bears before, from a distance. Judd Clemens had pointed them out. He said, "You have to pity them. For twenty thousand years they ruled this land. Everything they saw was either their own species or it was prey. Then we came along and took over."

Took over with our helicopters that could seek them out, our power sleds that could outrun them, and our guns that could kill from half a mile away. But without those aids, Nature's balance tilted back the other way. No need now to pity the bears.

In the dark hut, Barringer groped his way to where Dahlquist had sat. A full-sized polar bear weighed half a ton. It was ten feet from nose to hindquarters, and it could run faster than any human. The wicked claws would rip the walls of the hut like tissue paper.

Had Dahlquist found time to do his "bit of tinkering," enough to make the rifle work? Barringer was about to find out. Then, and only then, would he have an idea of his own possible future.

1

March 21, 2026.

Art Ferrand woke just before dawn. The only bedroom of the house faced due east, and he lay at ease until he could watch the disk of the rising sun neatly divided by an east–west line of fence running down the middle of the yard.

Day 41, and the vernal equinox. In a normal year, at this latitude and altitude, the crocuses would be about ready to flower.

But this was not a normal year. Yesterday, the tulips and azaleas had been in bloom in the front yard.

Art rolled over and climbed carefully out of bed. Gingerly, he put weight on his right leg. Some aches and pains were easing, but some would be with him forever. At sixty-two, lost cartilage did not replace itself even with the telomod treatment. His knee was probably as good as it would ever be, and that wasn't so great.

He leaned on the windowsill and peered south-southeast, down the slope of the hill. That way, line of sight but much too far off to be seen, lay Washington. What did the city look like now, on Day 41? It was hard to picture—and hard not to try.

The little house sat at fifteen hundred feet on the edge of the Catoctin Mountain Park, woods above and steep fields below. He noticed that the red Maryland dirt of the fields was hidden by healthy green. Another anomaly. Like the flowers, the grass was a month and more ahead of schedule. The sky was as it had been for the past three days, with clouds coming in slowly from the south. If today followed the same pattern, afternoon would be overcast and evening would bring heavy rain.

Most people would say the house was little more than a log

cabin. There was the bedroom, its small bathroom fed by rainwater collected as runoff from the sloping slate roof; and there was the other room, on the west side, a combined kitchen/living room/library/storehouse, with a little porch where Art could sit and watch the sunset.

He had come here on February 22, when most people still regarded the event of Day 1, February 9, as nothing more than an astronomical oddity, on a par with a bright comet. No, less than that. The Alpha Centauri supernova, like the star system that gave rise to it, was never seen in the Northern Hemisphere. An invisible event, trillions of miles away, might be something to excite the scientists. For everyone else it seemed to have no connection with the real world of jobs and day-to-day worries.

Art was a consultant specializing in networks and feedback analysis. As one of the increasing number of people with no permanent job, he had more offers than he could use. He took work when he felt like it, and found plenty of time to listen to the news reports and range the science web. He was also free to go wherever his instincts told him.

The astronomers had certainly been excited. There hadn't been a naked-eye supernova in the Milky Way since the seventeenth century, and now here was one that in celestial terms was close enough to spit at. Not only that, according to current accepted theories of stellar stability, Alpha Centauri could not go supernova. That led to lengthy and intense debates among the astronomers. To Art, it all suggested that a better theory was definitely overdue. As one lady analyst said, defensively, astronomy was not a field in which you could create experiments to test your ideas. The universe was your laboratory. You had to wait for Nature to come up with a test case.

For a few days, Art watched the images flowing down from the spaceborne observatories and listened to the discussions, hard to understand, of the energy that was being released. One figure, of all the discussions of billions and trillions and quadrillions, jumped out at him. The Alpha Centauri supernova was currently ninety percent as bright in Earth's sky as the midday sun.

Of course, said the commentators, that would last at most a month or two. Then the star would dwindle rapidly in brightness to its original level and probably less.

President Steinmetz had chimed in, offering reassurances. The supernova would have major effects, he said, on climate; but those would be felt in the Southern Hemisphere. Art was a lifelong weather buff. At his home in Olney, less than twenty miles from the White House, he had listened. Then he downloaded scores of weather maps and satellite images, and tried to decide what a ninety percent increase in incident solar radiation, all in the Southern Hemisphere, would do to the Earth's lands, oceans, and atmospheric circulation patterns. It was summer below the equator, a double summer.

It didn't take more than a couple of days for Art to realize that he had no idea what was likely to happen. Worse than that, the dozens of analyses made by the professionals all seemed to come up with wildly different answers. President Steinmetz was a smart man, but his principal job today was to soothe an alarmed public.

On Day 14, February 22, the supernova was reported to be as bright as ever. Art packed into his solar electric van the hundred kilos of possessions that really mattered, locked up the house, and headed for the vacation house in the Catoctin Mountain Park.

He had agonized over whom to tell, and what to tell. His sister, his neighbors, his colleagues at Syncom? "Get out while you can." They would, very reasonably, ask, "Why?" He had no good answer. Suppose nothing much happened? Suppose all the heat from the supernova caused a few big thunderstorms, and nothing more? He'd have put a lot of people to a lot of pointless trouble—if they took any notice of him, that is. To some of his friends he was already the man who had cried wolf.

Worry about what you *do, boy. Then you'll be way ahead of most people.* His grandfather had told him that, over and over, half a century ago. Art could hear him still. Finally, twenty-seven days ago, he had headed for the mountain cabin. He would return to Olney as soon as he was sure that his worries were pointless.

Seven days ago, on March 14, the problem of going home had become orders of magnitude more complicated.

Art went across to the gas stove, lit a burner, and set a kettle on top. While the water was heating he turned on the radio. Most people didn't seem to understand what survival was all about. It wasn't that you abandoned modern amenities, like health monitors and web wandering and silver bullets. It was that you made sure they ran independent of external supplies, like the little radio with its built-in fifty-year battery of doped fullerenes; or else you made sure that you could do without them if you had to. When the electricity failed, you went to gas and oil for light and heat. When those ran out, you turned to wood and tallow candles.

They would never run out, at least in Art's lifetime. The

whole of Catoctin Mountain Park was his for the taking. He couldn't use one-hundredth of the fallen trees and broken limbs within a mile of the house, brought down by the screaming winds of the previous three weeks. There was wildlife aplenty.

But some things, even if you could do without them, you would sure miss. Art dumped boiling water on freeze-dried coffee, sniffed the aroma with pleasure, and added a spoonful of creamer. You could buy milk easily enough, if you were willing to walk half a mile down to the farm. But how long would that last?

His supply of coffee and creamer would be enough, at a guess, for three or four months. Long before that, he had reasons more urgent than food to be back in Washington.

Over on the table, the ancient and bulky radio was scanning its entire frequency range, seeking a signal above background strength. He had dragged it out of storage six days ago, and found to his surprise that it still functioned once he had cannibalized the now-useless new radio for its fullerene batteries. They built things to last when that old radio was made. On the other hand, it lacked sensitivity and an automatic signal tracker. Once or twice while he sipped his coffee a faint and scratchy voice surfaced out of a mass of static, then to his annoyance it quickly lost itself.

Even so, here was the first suggestion that services might be creeping back.

Art knew the precise moment when they went away. Just after eleven o'clock on the evening of March 14, the wind was rising and he was speculating on the chances of another severe storm. He was gazing out of his bedroom window at the cloud patterns when the sky lit with a shimmering blue discharge like an intense aurora. Within seconds, the bedside light went out and the hum of the refrigerator stopped.

By the light of a gas lantern, Art confirmed his suspicion. Electrical power was gone. The refrigerator was nothing better than another storage cupboard.

The next morning he discovered that he had to deal with something worse than a simple power outage. His DNA sequencer was dead. His car would not start. The telcom produced no dial tone. His computer, even on battery power, was lifeless, as were his personal secretary and calculator. Since then he had been reduced to making notes of schedules and dates and anything else he wanted to organize, and doing his rough calculations with pencil and paper. God help anybody under forty, who with rare exceptions knew nothing of the hand methods.

Art waited. It took another day or two to realize that all aircraft had disappeared from the skies, and that traffic on the road beyond the fields was nonexistent.

He didn't have an explanation for any of this. Extreme weather around the globe could be expected to damage many high-tech systems, but you would expect them to degrade gradually and gracefully, just as they were designed to do when individual components or subsystems failed. Instead, everything had happened all at once, in that single flicker of violet-blue. It was damnably annoying. Just when you most needed a broad-band communications system to tell you what was going on, that failed along with everything else.

And if *he,* way out here, was uneasy without electricity and cars and airplanes, what the hell must be going on in the cities of the world, where lives depended on police, buses and trains, hospitals and schools? What about food supplies, and running water? Unlike Art, city folk could not go hunting in the woods above his house, where deer and wildlife were always plentiful.

He pushed away his bread and honey, losing interest in breakfast. His own advantage might only be temporary. Deer were plentiful, but would they remain that way? Others, less lucky than him, could head north at any time and disturb his snug little haven in the park. They might be armed, and dangerous. And if people were hungry now, that was surely going to get worse as the year wore on. Winter had ended abruptly halfway through February. With mid-March like boisterous late May, who knew what July and August might bring? Meanwhile, he was not willing to venture far afield to satisfy his curiosity. The woodchuck that came out of the hole first after the danger seemed over was not the one most likely to survive. Until planes were flying again and cars passed regularly along the road beyond the fields, curiosity as to what had happened would wait.

But he was willing to venture near afield. In fact, it was close to a requirement. If he missed his exercise, even for a single day, that right knee stiffened. Indoor stretching and flexing would do at a pinch, but nothing was as good as a gentle walk for a mile or so along the dirt track that followed the line of the woods, followed by a return over the humps and tussocks of the fields.

The telomod was working, no doubt about it. Two years ago it was all he could do to hobble from car to house. The question was, had the treatment gone as far as it could go?

And then, the second question, one that he was almost unwilling to ask: Where, how, and when (if ever) would he receive the next treatment?

Art left his cup, plate, and knife on the table. They were pretty clean and he would use them again later in the day. He did make a concession to his old standards and wash his hands and face, easier now that his beard was fully grown. Baths were a once-a-week luxury. He had plenty of wood for fuel, but even with wild torrents of rain filling the cistern every day or two he had to be careful with fresh water. A person might carry water for bathing from the stream that ran downhill about a quarter of a mile west of the house. But that person, Art had decided after one trip with a bucket, would need to be a hell of a lot more fastidious about personal hygiene than he was. And he for one was not about to stand outside buck naked in the cold rain to take a shower, no matter how dirty he got.

He turned off the radio, which was still interrupting a continuous crackle of static with the occasional tantalizing hint of human speech. As a matter of course, he checked the electrical power, telcom, and computer. Nothing. The little DNA sequencer received his special attention. If he had the power to restore just one device or service to working order, he would gladly continue without electric power and communications and everything else. Just give him back the ability to analyze, simply and quickly, the structure of the chromosomes of his own body.

Outside, the van still formed an inert mass of plastic, metal, and composites. Even the battery, which ought by now to have been amply recharged even with the weak solar flux of mid-March, was dead. Art wasted no time on it and began to walk southeast, toward a midmorning sun now sporadically hidden by broken cloud.

Already, the temperature was at the upper limit of comfort. In a single day he could see a change in the plants. The buds of the rhododendrons flanking the dirt path were almost fully open, and farther off toward the woods on the left he saw a new mass of faint pink. It was wild rose, blooming far before its season. Instead of pleasure, the rush toward summer created in him a powerful uneasiness, a sense of events removed from their natural course. What came next? Was Alpha Centauri finally fading in the southern skies? The astronomers had so far done miserably on predictions, maybe they would be wrong again.

When he reached the dirt road he found it puddled and sticky from the rain of the previous evening. Today he went in the opposite direction from usual. He moved off left, to the higher ground at the fringe of the woods, and picked his way through tree roots and low brush. So far as he was concerned it didn't matter how much clay he had on his boots, but he knew he would be exposed to a different philosophy when he reached his destination.

After three-quarters of a mile the track took a sharp turn right and down, toward the state road that ran across the lower edge of the hill. Art did not follow it. Instead he kept going east along a less traveled and even muddier trail, just wide enough for one car or van. His goal was already visible, where the track forked and a pair of small houses stood less than fifty yards from each other.

He turned toward the one on the left, and the dogs from the right-hand house ran out to greet him before he was halfway there. They made one identifying sniff and wagged their tails frantically.

"Not today," Art said. "Got nothing for you. Down, fellas."

The dogs had drawn their own conclusion from the smell of his pockets. They followed him until he was twenty yards from his destination, then wandered away toward their home.

"Thank God for that," said a voice from the doorway. "I've had to shoo his damn dogs out of here twice—and he doesn't do a thing to help. He sits there and laughs. Come on in. Wipe your shoes."

The speaker was a bit shorter than Art, who did not consider himself a tall man. He had thin white hair, gnarled arthritic hands, and a smiling leprechaun's face. He watched closely as Art wiped his boots on the rough matting just inside the door.

"Good enough?" asked Art.

"Good enough." They shook hands formally, though they had known each other for close to two decades. "The usual? With water?"

"Might as well. With water."

He took the glass from Ed O'Donnell's hand. It was not yet eleven in the morning, but as Ed explained, in his house they kept "Catoctin Mountain Time." It was always the appropriate hour for a drink.

Art took the ritual sip, and nodded. "Very fine. Better than the last batch."

The still was in a small shed behind the house, where it had sat for the near twenty years since Art bought his own house and became Ed's second-nearest neighbor. Ed's nearest neighbor sat on a metal-framed chair near the window, holding his own drink. He was a tall, well-muscled man, wearing shorts that revealed a long clean scar running from the front of his thigh to well below the right knee.

"Cheers, Art." The glass was raised.

"Cheers, Joe." He settled into a similar chair opposite.

"This goddam stuff is going to kill all of us."

"Hey, something has to." Ed chimed in across the bar that separated them from the kitchen. "I don't see you refusing to drink it. Bambi burgers all right, Art?"

"Fine. Unless you have salmon?"

"Saint's days and bonfire nights only."

Art took his cue from the conversation. Clearly, no one wanted to talk about personal worries. Ed had grown kids and a brother in Idaho. Joe had two sisters and their children in Atlanta. There could have been no contact with any of them since March 14. Ed and Joe were making a deliberate assumption: no news was good news. Let's hope they were right.

"So what the hell's going on with you." Joe Vanetti rubbed his scarred and swollen knee and turned to Art. "Figured things out yet?"

"I don't know. But I was lying awake thinking about it last night. I got another idea."

"A new one."

"More like an old one. You know that blue sky flash seven days ago, when all the power went out?"

"I didn't see it."

"You know him," Ed called from the kitchen. "Nine o'clock, and he's asleep."

"Well, it happened all right. I saw it, Joe. It seemed to be in the upper atmosphere, way above the clouds. At the time I wondered if it had anything to do with the supernova."

"We asked you that," Joe protested. "And you told us it couldn't have. You told us that the supernova can't ever be seen from here."

"It can't. But it might still have an effect. I remembered something from forty years back. You would still have been in the Air Force, Joe, you might recall it better than I do. Do you remember when everybody worried about a nuclear war between the United States and Russia?"

"The Soviet Union it was, back in those days. God, do I remember." Joe, close to eighty, had entered the Air Force at eighteen. "We used to have these nuclear war drills. 'In the event of a nuclear attack, descend into the basement. Place your head between your legs, and kiss your ass good-bye.' I was scared shitless, I just knew we were going to blow each other to hell. We were so on edge, we'd start a war by accident."

"Then maybe you remember something called EMP."

Joe scowled. "Something technical. And it came later. That's all I remember."

"He's a mine of information," Ed said from the kitchen. "Thank God we never had a war with him running it."

"Do you remember EMP, Ed?"

"Hey, Art, be reasonable. I was a software developer."

"Which means he don't know shit about anything," Joe said. "So what's EMP, Art?"

"If you had a big nuclear war, all this radiation would hit the atmosphere, and it would cause a great pulse of electricity and magnetism—an electromagnetic pulse. And that would play havoc with electronic equipment down here on Earth."

Ed was carrying in three loaded plates. "Here we go. Venisonburger medium with bun and no onion. Venisonburger rare with bun *and* onion. And venisonburger medium with onion and open top. You're on your own for helping yourselves to drinks." He set the plates on the table. "But there was no nuclear war."

"Right. But there was a supernova."

"Are you telling me that's like a nuclear war?"

"Not really. But an EMP was supposed to make a big blue flicker in the sky, like the one we saw. If the supernova caused an EMP . . ."

Joe had taken a big bite, and he spoke with his mouth full. "I thought radio waves and things like that traveled at the same speed as light."

"They do."

"So how come we had the supernova a month and a half ago, but the electricity and television and everything else only went haywire last week? Wouldn't the radiation get here at the same time as the light?"

"Ought to. I don't know why it wouldn't."

"And if what you say is true, how come everybody else hasn't figured this EMP thing out?"

"I feel sure a lot of people have. But how could they spread the word? You said it, radio's gone and TV's gone, and the web is down. There's no way to tell anybody anything."

It seemed like a good time to stop talking and start eating. Art bit into a piece of onion, one of those homegrown in Ed's kitchen garden and hanging in strings on the kitchen wall. It was as hot as any he had ever tasted, and he took a drink to help it down. The combination of hot onion and moonshine took his breath away. His idea had seemed brilliant when it came to him late the previous evening. Now the others were pointing out that it raised more questions than it answered.

After a few minutes of silent chewing, Ed wandered through to the kitchen again to put a pan of water on the old stove. It occurred to Art that although Ed would never describe himself as a survivalist, most things in the house worked just fine without utilities piped in from outside. There were advantages to buying a place nearly eighty years old and not bothering to replace fixtures as long as they still worked halfway decent.

"Where's Helen?" he asked.

"Down the hill, at Dr. Dennison's place." Ed brought a jar of brandied plums through and set it on the table. "She says once a year's enough to sit and listen to three old farts going on at the world."

"She said 'old farts'?"

"If you'd heard her, you'd know that's what she meant."

"She sick?"

"Just the usual. Arthritis. At least old Dennison's honest, he told Helen that her arthritis is general wear and tear, and there's not a lot he can do."

"There's not a lot any of 'em can do." Joe cracked the top of the jar and spooned plums and brandy on the same plate that had held his venisonburger. "Goddam quacks. Remember what they told you three years ago, Art, that you had only a few months to live?"

"I'm not likely to forget it."

"But you're alive. How many of them are dead?"

"I wish I knew." There was a long pause. Joe's question had, almost by accident, forced them to consider the outside world. None of them looked at the others. Then Art said, "Give medicine credit, Joe. The telomod treatment saved my life."

"Ah, they just feed you that scientific bullshit so they can increase the bill. You'd have got better anyway."

There was no point in arguing with Joe. He was past the age where you could hope to change his mind. But he was wrong. Art knew, without a shred of doubt, that the treatment at the Institute for Probatory Therapies was the reason he was alive to eat lunch today. He had seen the scans. His body had been riddled with metastatic carcinomas before the telomods went to work.

"Doctors, they're no different from other scientists." Ed picked a plum out of the jar with his fingers, transferred it to his mouth, and spoke indistinctly around it. "Take the supernova. All the theories, and the government making statements about what was supposed to happen. The weather after the supernova didn't match any of 'em."

"A couple of people's predictions came close."

"A couple, out of hundreds. So why do we pay taxes, to get rubbish like that?"

"You don't pay taxes, Ed. You boast about that."

"Why should I, when the country's going to hell?"

"Of course it is," Joe said darkly. "With that Jew in the White House, what do you expect?"

Art shook his head. Joe was an old friend, but on certain subjects you had to ignore him.

"He was your choice, Joe," Ed said. "You voted for him."

"I know I did. But look at the choice I had. Either that Heebie, or that *woman*."

"He's not biased, you see. No, not him." Ed addressed Art as though Joe Vanetti were not present. "You'd never guess his second wife was Jewish."

Art did not bother to reply. He didn't need to, because the line of conversation was on a well-worn track. On cue, Joe said, "She certainly was, the bitch. Hey, do you know why Jewish divorces cost more?"

He looked at them expectantly. Art had heard the joke a hundred times, but it was Joe's punch line. He and Ed remained silent.

"Because they're worth it," Joe went on. "But I don't think I'll marry again."

"No?" Ed poured brandy from the jar into his glass, drank some, and pulled a face. "Phew. I was in rare form when I made that lot. So what will you do, Joe?"

Within two years of buying the place on the mountain and meeting neighbors Ed and Joe, Art had learned the rules. If you wanted to be accepted you didn't step on someone else's joke, no matter how often you had heard it. The other two had been playing the game forever, and for this bit he was a member of the audience.

"I won't marry," Joe said. "I'll just find a woman I don't like, and give her a house."

"Does Anne-Marie know that?"

"Not from me she don't."

"I can't see why that woman puts up with you." Ed turned to Art. "She's twenty-five years younger than he is, she's good-looking, and she has her own place. She doesn't need an old wreck like him. She could get somebody handsome, like me, only I'm married. Why does she bother?"

Art had been asked the question, so he was now in the game. "You have to know how it works, Ed. As far as you and I are concerned, Joe here is a poor old crock with hardly enough strength to stagger from his place to yours. He'd never get back home from here without your brew. But as far as older women are concerned, any single male under ninety who's not actually terminal is an eligible bachelor. They outlive us, so there's not enough of us to go around."

"It's not like that with me and Annie." Joe was complacent. Among male friends, insult was the only acceptable expression of affection. "She says I'm dynamite."

"She means you're always going off at the wrong time, I'll bet. I don't see you walking over to her place, now that the truck don't work." Ed had the bottle in his hand. "Another? One for the road."

Art shook his head. "Not me," Joe said. "Your liver will be in a museum when you die, Ed. It won't need to be pickled, neither. And I don't need to walk to Annie's place. She knows I've got the gammy leg. She'll be up here about five."

"How would you be knowing that? You using telepathy?"

"No. Telcom." Joe took the bottle. "Maybe just a drop after all. I think this batch is better than the usual bat piss."

Neither he nor Ed seemed to realize the significance of what he was saying, but the words jolted Art's nervous system into overdrive. He could feel his heart racing.

"You made a telcom call *today*?"

"Sure." Joe was pouring a closely calculated measure of liquor, and he did not look up. "Tried this morning before I came over, and got a dial tone. First time for a week. So I talked to Annie, and she said she'd be over. Stands to reason, things had to come back to normal before too long."

"Ed?"

O'Donnell went across to the chest where the communications unit was sitting and pressed a button. He shook his head. "Not my telcom. Dead as Lincoln. Never a light on the board."

"Told you that was a piece of junk when you bought it." Joe stood up and went over to stare at the unit. "You had a perfectly good phone already."

"Couldn't get a replacement when part of it busted. You know that. Goddam companies, always pushing what you don't want." Ed lifted the headphone. "Got a tone, though. Sounds funny. Here." He held the set out to Art. "You're the communications wizard."

Art took the headset and listened. It was a dial tone all right, but behind the rhythmic pulse was a strange and distant singing, the sound you might get if you had no in-line amplification and were placing a call to the Mars expedition. He performed the standard repertoire of tests and obtained no response. He examined the program board more closely. The unit was relatively new, certainly no more than three years old.

"I think you're out of luck, Ed. The control chips are blown."

"Figures. The warranty ended in January. The bastards."

"I don't think you can blame the company." Art turned to Joe. "My unit's newer than this one, and it's dead, too. Could I make a call on yours?"

"Out of region?"

"Yes."

"Sure you can." The question had been automatic—Joe would have been outraged if Art made any move to pay. "Now?"

"Anytime that's convenient."

"Now's as good as any." Joe stood up heavily, favoring his leg. "Otherwise this old bugger will want us to help him with the clearing up."

Ed said nothing, until the other two were at the door. Then he shook Art's hand, ignored Joe, and said, "Help the poor man, will you, in case he falls over. When Annie says she's coming over, all the blood runs from his brain down into his pecker. I'm still not sure it's enough for action." And when the other two were twenty paces away, "Hey, Joe. Helen's been telling me to ask you this. Do you love Anne-Marie?"

Joe turned and gave him the single sideways glare that said no sane male ever asked another man a question like that. O'Donnell laughed and retreated into the house. Joe and Art continued their slow progress, limited by two bad right knees.

If it had been up to Art he'd have walked faster, no matter how much it hurt. He was desperate to try that call. It was pointless to explain why to Joe. A lot more depended on it than his friends would be willing to believe.

2

The dogs came to meet them midway between the two houses, wagging their tails wildly and rearing up on Joe with their muddy paws while he cursed and tried to push them away.

"Down, Rush," he said to a large white mutt. "I've got nothing for you out here, you silly bugger. *Down,* I said, until we get home."

It was the best diversion that Art could have hoped for. While Joe was feeding the dogs in the back of the tidy and well-organized house—whatever Anne-Marie was coming over for it wasn't to do cleaning—Art went straight to the telcom set. It wasn't merely old, it was antique. An actual telephone. There was no store-forward, no video plugs, no conferencing, no min-rate path finder, and pathetic internal storage. A bit more primitive, and you'd be back in the era of analog signals and rotary dials. But when Art picked up the handset he heard a treasured pulse tone, though again it was overlaid on a background hiss like interstellar space.

Another side effect of Supernova Alpha?

A dial pulse was a good start, but no more than that. Art held his breath and hit buttons.

He had spent a lot of time in the past week, trying to remember and write down the thirty-odd numbers that he needed. In the past he had relied on his personal secretary to store them, despite his preaching to others—"We've become too dependent on interconnected technologies. One day the information system will be hit and come down like a house of cards. We'll have a devil of a time putting it back together."

Do as I say, not as I do.

His half sister's number was firmly in his head. He called that first, though she was not the reason for his awful feeling of urgency. The attempted connection to her California number produced a series of strange clicks that ended in the odd, open silence of a lost line.

He was not much worried. Carol was superwoman. Her competence at everything she touched made Art feel inferior during their once-a-year visits. Carol would manage to land on her feet. She always did.

The group's numbers were much more guesswork. He had written down seven that he was sure of, and half a dozen more where he was within a digit or two of the full eighteen (though a miss was as good as a mile when it came to percom numbers). He had given up on the rest. If he could get through to just one, they would start to network.

By the sixth dead end he was starting to sweat. Some of it might be a delayed effect of Ed's lethal white lightning, best followed by a walk to let your brain clear and your kidneys recover from the insult. But mostly it was the conviction of problems on the way. That feeling had started the second he realized that his DNA analysis box was out of action.

He kept trying. Joe, who had finished feeding and cursing the dogs, came into the room and watched him in silence.

"Bad news?" he said at last.

"No damn news at all. I think we only have a local piece of the network up. That explains why you could reach Anne-Marie's old handset, and I can reach fuck all."

He was stabbing at the soft screen as he spoke, convinced that he was wasting his time. It was a shock when, after another eternity of clicks and snaps and whistles, a voice said, "ID, please."

It was the standard reply of a screener, verifying the caller's acceptability before the machine would take a message. But if Art's ideas were right, everything using microchips had failed when that blue flash filled the sky—and smart screeners were on the list.

"Dana?" he said. "This is Art Ferrand. It's you, isn't it, not the screener?"

There was a moment of background crackle and hiss. Then, "Art. God, I'm glad to hear from you. The line came back, but I haven't been able to reach anyone with it. The screener doesn't work, nor does the API controller."

"I think the national grid is down. We're patching in to each other through old equipment—you can practically hear electrical relays opening and closing. Where are you?"

He did not recall where she lived. Their contacts had been electronic, plus the quarterly meetings at the Institute for Probatory Therapies.

"Not where I usually am. Arlington was looking bad, mobs and looting and fires. I got scared."

Art knew that without being told. The old Dana Berlitz was sassy and sexy and full of life. The woman on the line was all nerves.

"I left two days ago," she went on. "I'm out with my sister Sarah in Warrenton. Where are you?"

"Up north, beyond Frederick. I ran for it early, over a month ago. You drove?"

"Drove?" Her voice was steadying. "You really are out of it. The cars stopped working a week back. There was this funny sort of blue flash, up in the sky—"

"I know. We had it here, too. I think it was everywhere. All the equipment with microchips in it is useless now. Trouble is, that's just about everything in the world. How did you get to Warrenton?"

"The hard way. On my bike, fifty-seven miles door-to-door with that lousy saddle I always swore I was going to replace, not a car on the roads and it rained all the way. I won't try to tell you what my ass felt like when I got here." She laughed—a good sign. "Sarah took one look at it and slapped on a big skin patch. You ever had one?"

"Never needed one."

"I don't recommend it. The first few hours while it was bonding, it wriggled whenever I sat down on it. Cheap thrill." She laughed again, but in her next words the worried tone was back. "Art, do you have your sequencer with you?"

"Of course. I don't go anywhere without it."

"Is it working?"

"Dead as Lincoln. The sequencers are full of microcircuits."

"What are we going to do?"

"That's why I've been so keen to get in touch with you and the rest of the group. How are you feeling?"

"So far, fine—except for the sore backside. My last genome scan was normal, but I'm worried about how long it will last. I was supposed to be reevaluated when we met again in six weeks."

"Me, too." Art didn't know as much about the details of Dana's disease as he did about the condition of some of the others in the program. It was cancer, of course, and she had been hit young. She had been in the program longer than Art, but she was still only forty-three; in Art's eyes that made her practically a child. He knew that she had a grown-up son, which meant she'd married—or got pregnant—very young. But she never spoke of him, or of any male in her life, which was amazing in someone so attractive and friendly.

In your dreams, Art Ferrand.

"Look, Dana," he went on. "We have to find out what's going on with the program. Probably everything is fine, and the doctors are in the same position as we are, just not able to reach people. But I won't risk that. You may think I'm overreacting—"

"Overreacting? That's what my first doctor told me, when I went to him with a lump in my neck. That asshole cost me a whole month. You're not overreacting, Art. I'm on a knife edge, and I'm sure you are. Unless we have a way of checking the condition of our telomeres and making the right adjustments, we could be dead in a year of new cancer or premature old age. My question is, what do we do?"

"We keep trying to contact others of the group, today. But unless we find out from one of them, directly, what the situation is at the Institute, I'm heading there tomorrow. I won't be happy until I see Dr. Lasker and Dr. Chow and Dr. Taunton in person, and know that they can keep the program going even if the usual equipment is dead. I'll call you and let you know what I find—assuming the line still works."

"Forget it. Art, I was worried before you called. I know you'll do your best to get to the Institute, and I'm sure you'll try to let me know what you find. But I've worked so hard to stay alive, I'm not willing to sit and hear things secondhand. Where do we meet?"

"I don't know. The usual place, the Treasure Inn, where we stay for our group sessions? If it's open."

"When?"

"You'll probably need three days. Any of the others we reach, we tell 'em the same thing, the Treasure Inn three days from now. But what about your sore rear end? There's no cars, and you can't ride all that way."

"Let me worry about that. How are *you* going to travel? You've got farther than me to go, and you have that bad knee."

"I'll get there. Try and reach some of the others. I'll see you in three days."

"Cross your fingers. Good luck, Art."

"Good luck, Dana." Art closed the connection, and found Joe staring at him calmly. He had been listening to Art's end of the conversation with obvious interest.

"Well," he said, "that was a new one. Who is she?"

"Dana Berlitz. Part of my treatment group."

"And I'll bet I know which part of you she's treating." Joe Vanetti did not smile. He was a big man, tall and broad and slow-moving. It was hard for Art to imagine him as he had been in his thirties. According to Ed O'Donnell, in Joe's Air Force days he had been a heartbreaker who cut a broad swath through the Washington female population.

"But what are these telly things of yours that need fixing?" Joe went on.

"Telomeres are the end pieces of chromosomes. In ordinary people, they shorten as you get older. In cancer cells, they don't. Dana and I had a treatment to shrink our cancer cell telomeres, but we don't want our other telomeres shortened too much or we'll get old real fast. It's like a tricky balancing act, and we need to keep checking that nothing's going haywire. Our interest in each other is purely professional."

"Sure it is. I'm not deaf, I heard how you spoke to her. You're soft on her. Just remember to keep your pants up."

"It's nothing to do with sex. But I'm going back to Washington."

"I know that. Ed and I were talking about it this morning, before you got here."

"How could you? I only just made up my mind I had to go."

"All the same, we knew it. We've seen it before." And now Joe did smile, the slow, self-satisfied grin of a man who has seen his predictions come to pass. "You arrive up here, see, and you tell us the world has gone to hell. First it was the Lascelles virus, that airborne thing that would kill the lot of us."

"It would have, if they hadn't come up with the viral phage and released it."

"Maybe. Point is, they did and nothing happened. I bet your neighbors in Olney gave you hell when you got back, sending them running for the hills the way you did. Then there was Scarlatti, going to vaporize Washington."

"He tried."

"Sure he tried. Lots of people try things. Point is, he failed. And now there's this Supernova Alpha thing, and from what I hear that's fading away, too."

"This is different."

"So what me and Ed figure," Joe went on, as though Art had not spoken, "we figure this. Every couple of years the craziness down there in Washington gets too much for you, and you head up here for a jolt of sanity. You ought to stay, and when you get a few more years on you, you probably will. But you're young, you still got this feather up your ass to save the world—not that most of it's worth saving. So you're going back, one more time. But tell me this. The cars don't run, and the buses don't run, and the trains don't run. So *how* do you think you'll go? Your knee's near as bad as mine."

The question of the hour. He couldn't ride a bike such a distance, even if he had one. If he walked, Joe was right, his knee made it close to impossible and the journey would take weeks.

"Damned if I know. Got any ideas?"

"Nothing special." Joe sat down, rubbed at his scar, and stared into space. "But here's a thought, for what it's worth. Did you know that Annie keeps three horses on her place?"

3

March 23, 2026.

"There is a tide in the affairs of men, which, taken at the flood, leads on to fortune."

Saul Steinmetz raised weary eyes from the daily briefing package and stared at the cloth text hanging on his wall. His mother had embroidered it for him when he was nine years old.

There ought to be more, an addition that read: *"But sometimes it lands you at a raw sewage outlet."*

Like now.

During the past eight hours he had met with twenty-three senior officials of the executive branch, with six Senators, and with the heads of the nation's three biggest conglomerates. He had made decisions on how to finance the federal debt; how to pay the military when electronic transfers had ceased to exist and the public was suspicious of paper money; how much to draw down the government grain and dairy stockpiles; and where and how to send food supplies. He had discussed protocol for U.S. embassies overseas and foreign embassies here, approved Army manpower allocation to preserve and in some cases reestablish the inland waterways, and ordered a red-alert status at the Mexican border.

Saul had done all this, yet felt that he had done too little and usually too late. Decisions based on incomplete information were one thing, a fact of political life. Decisions made with *no* information were another. How could you manage the world's largest and most complex economy, when everything was interlocked and you had no idea of the status of key components? It was blindfold chess, played with imperfect knowledge of the initial position.

For the thousandth time in the past weeks, he turned toward the holographic projection unit in the corner of the office. For the thousandth time, the volume sat empty. How long before information services got the Persona back in operation? Or would they never do it, given the general collapse of data services?

A movement outside the window caught his eye. He stared, stabbed at the interoffice controller, then realized that he had tried it twice already today. In spite of optimistic promises it too was still not repaired. He raised his voice. "Auden!"

Auden Travis appeared so quickly that Saul wondered if the aide spent his days and nights lying outside the door of the Oval Office, although his elegant clothing denied that.

"Yes, Mr. President? Sir, it is working now, actually."

"Outside?"

"Just a few lines. But we can patch you to anywhere in the country."

"Good. That's not what I need at the moment, though. Is General Mackay in the building?"

He hardly needed Travis's nod. With external systems down, the only way to get access to the President was by staying close. Auden wasn't the only one willing to spend his nights and days on the threshold. Did they realize, any of them, how little real power he had now?

"Shall I get her, Mr. President?" Travis was studying and perplexed by the changing expressions on Steinmetz's face.

"If you please."

When Auden was gone Saul turned his attention again to the briefing documents—handwritten, most of them, though one or two had been hammered out on an ancient typewriter. Somebody must have been rifling the Smithsonian collections for anything that worked.

Last night he had asked for a summary of the situation around the world. What he had received was patchy, even with the best available sources, but he could see enough to extrapolate a pattern. The places where technology was the newest and most advanced had been hit the worst. Total system breakdown there had caused the loss of food, water, and power. Deaths in the hundreds of millions to billions were reported for the Golden Ring countries, the Sino Consortium, and the Federation of Indian States.

Reported, how? Probably through the ham radio net. Some of the amateurs had held on to their old equipment, and been back on the air within days.

South America and the southern part of Africa had a different problem. They did not have so complex a technological infrastructure to lose, but the vast weather changes produced by Supernova Alpha more than made up for that. They were tottering on the brink of government collapse.

Countries with new technology built on top of an older one had managed the best. Europe and North America still had the skeletons of despised and ignored old communications, power, and transportation systems, sitting underneath the slick and glossy fabric of today's—or yesterday's—advances. It was depressing, to sit in the middle of chaos and be told that you were one of the lucky ones.

The report said nothing about Australia, where a recent craze for everything new must have combined with the most severe storm systems; but the absence of news from Australia told its own story.

Of course, the weather patterns in both hemispheres were not based on observation. They were based on computer predictions, and the computer models relied on historical weather data. God knows how good or bad they might be today. Saul turned in irritation to the unit where the global weather was normally updated every half hour from metsat data. The display was dark—and even dusty. Nobody had mentioned it to him, but the cleaning services must be in as much chaos as everything else.

He turned as a perfunctory knock on the door preceded General Grace Mackay, hurrying along ahead of Auden Travis. The Secretary of Defense—intense, dark-haired, and skeleton-thin—had a cadaver's smile on her tired face.

"I think we have some good news, Mr. President."

"About time. Tell me something I want to hear." Steinmetz gestured to dismiss Travis. The young aide went reluctantly.

"We thought we had lost the comsats, the metsats, and the micro-positioning system," Mackay said. "Now we are convinced that they are still alive and functioning."

"You could sure as hell have fooled me." Steinmetz waved to the blank displays. "Where are they, General?"

"The problems are in the receiving stations. We hope to have a couple back on-line in the next forty-eight hours. You'll have your weather pictures again, and if anyone can do ground-based transmission the comsats will give us global communications."

"Can anyone?"

"Not for a while yet."

"Then I won't hold my breath waiting for incoming calls. Anything else?"

"A confirmation that's not so good." Grace Mackay had been in military and government a long time, much longer than Saul. She knew that a boss didn't like to be told only of problems or setbacks. Saul suspected she would save some good news for the end.

"The former Vice President's body has finally been located in the Blue Ridge Mountains. We have an updated number for cabinet-level deaths and casualties in Congress."

Saul made the customary mutterings of regret. He had known that the Vice President was doomed only minutes after that ominous blue sky flash nine days ago, when he had stood at the window in his darkened office and watched planes in approach patterns for National Airport drop from the sky like heavy fruit.

Vice President Janet Kloos had been riding a six-passenger suborbital, in transit from California, where a new trade deal with Sulawesi called for official presence. Saul had intended to go himself until the last few minutes. It could so easily have been him. The selection and swearing-in of the new Vice President, Brewster Callaghan, now on the West Coast, made one thing very clear: no one was irreplaceable. Everyone was expendable. But Janet had been a terrible loss.

Saul wasn't nearly as sorry to lose thirty-odd people from Congress. Half of them hated his guts, and the rest hated Brewster Callaghan. *A thousand friends have less weight than a single enemy.*

General Mackay was standing, quietly waiting. He had noticed it in his first few days in office. Other people's time was his, while his time was his own. If he was late getting to an event, that event wouldn't start until he arrived. It must be especially hard on someone like Grace Mackay, because a four-star general had her own powers to keep most people waiting.

"That's not why I told Travis to go look for you." Saul pointed to the window. "Do you know what I saw out there?"

"No, Mr. President."

"Well, nor do I. It was an aircraft and it was heading for a landing at Andrews; but it looked like it came out of Noah's Ark. Fixed wing, fixed engines, and no vertical takeoff boosters." He waved to an armchair. "Let's sit down, General, they're not playing the National Anthem. Was that thing the Air Force One substitute you've been promising me for the past few days?"

Grace Mackay sat down very carefully on the edge of the seat.

Steinmetz watched her hands. He had seen the reports based on her secret monitors as recently as two weeks ago, just before the EMP hit. Saul was assured by his intelligence office that the cabinet members had no idea they were being observed, but he had his doubts about that. In any case, what did it matter if Saul knew that his Secretary of Defense ground her teeth every night as she slept? That she was married, but had engaged in sex only once in the past four months? She needed doses of powerful prescription drugs just to keep going. Grace Mackay wouldn't die in office—she wouldn't be allowed to—but three years after that she could well be a goner.

Yet she would fight like the devil to keep a job that was killing her.

So how much would President Steinmetz endure, to achieve and hold on to *his* position? And how worn and exhausted did *he* seem to others? Saul thought he knew, but chances were he put the estimate for himself way too low.

It was the worst time in history to be President. If you had an enemy and started a war, you had a fair chance to make heroic decisions and big speeches and come out looking a hero. But what sort of credit did a man receive for dealing with a natural disaster? None at all. You couldn't win. People who lost possessions or family would blame you no matter what you did. They'd say you had offered too little and too late. Nobody would remember the good work.

General Mackay was ready and waiting, examining Saul's face. Sick or well, drunk or dry, she had the instincts and techniques of a great briefer and communicator. She spent as much time establishing what her audience knew and didn't know as on providing information.

"What you saw was a C-5A," she said when she was sure that she again had Saul's attention. "It's half a century old, and it looks primitive. But it can be flown without computer support or smart sensors or pilot neural meshing. For the time being, that plane, or another like it, is likely to be Air Force One."

What Grace didn't add, because Saul already knew it, was what happened when you tried to fly a modern plane without the help of its PIP—Pilot Interaction Package—and other goodies. Five top test pilots, each confident of being able to fly anything that could get off the ground, had died proving they were wrong. Others were still clamoring for their chance when General Mackay ended the effort. Test pilots were a breed unlike any other—but so were politicians and generals.

"Do you have a cutoff date?" Saul asked.

"About 1980. With any big aircraft later than that it's going to be marginal. We are still looking at the low-cost end of commercial planes, we may be able to use some of them. And it's not just stability and control. By the end of the last century the microchips were handling fuel injection and stall protection and everything else."

Everything else. And everything meant *every* thing.

Grace Mackay was head of a department whose guns and lasers could not fire—the chips in their targeting and range-finding and loading and release circuits had become in an instant brainless dots of fused gallium arsenide. The planes would not fly without the help of superhuman data reduction speeds and reaction times. The ships, bristling with dead weapons for both defense and offense, sat in port or floated out of control on the oceans of the world. The manned platforms in low Earth orbit, so far as anyone could tell without direct communications, had become chilly sarcophagi.

They had been designed, all of these, with the luxury of triple redundancy. If one microchip, by some rare misfortune, were to fail, then two others remained to accept sensory data and provide control commands. As for the idea that all three might fail, at the same moment—that was unthinkable.

Saul reminded himself that as Commander in Chief of the same organization, he had swallowed that official line of logic. How many *Titanics* did it take before the lesson sank in permanently? Probably, it never did. Every generation had to learn for itself.

Saul knew how tired he was. At fifty-six, he was sure he had less energy than his ninety-two-year-old mother. He pulled himself back with an effort to Mackay, silently waiting and watching.

"I'm sorry, General. I rely on your judgment completely. What you feel is safe for me to fly, I fly."

"Yes, sir. Give us several more days, if you please. I'm working with the civilian agencies to define a network of suitable landing fields and en route handoffs. Of course, for the time being everything will be on visual flight rules."

"Fuel?"

"Not a problem. More diesel oil and kerosene than we know what to do with."

"Unless we have more break-in problems."

Grace Mackay had finally heard something to put surprise on her drawn gray face. "Seriously? People are stealing aircraft fuel?"

"It looks like it. You can't really blame them. Diesel fuel and heating oil are the same thing. The power grid is still down, and in the north-central states the emergency distribution system of heating oil isn't working as it's supposed to. No, that's the wrong way to put it. The distribution system isn't working *at all.* We're operating under martial law. Looters are in danger of being shot. But before the blackout North Dakota was reporting fifty below. People are stealing because if they don't take what they need they'll freeze to death—and we don't have a broadcast system to *warn* them they may be shot."

Saul paused. He was doing what a good communicator never did. Unless there was a secondary reason, maybe to reassure someone or to drive home a point extra hard, you didn't tell somebody what they already knew. With the head of civil law enforcement vanished in Florida and presumed dead, Grace Mackay had been a key player in justifying martial law.

"Sorry, General. You know more about most of this than I do."

With others present, she would have made at least a formal disclaimer. Between the two of them, she just smiled. "Too damn much, Mr. President. May I offer you a piece of better news?"

"I can use all you've got."

"Data bases. We've been assuming that all the civilian data bases were wiped clean by the pulse."

"They were. I've had fifty reports coming in from all over the region."

"But the intelligence data bases were protected. They are in Prospero-rated environments, sitting inside Faraday cages, and the pulse didn't get to them."

"So?"

"Well. I'm a bit embarrassed to tell you this, because the Secretary of Defense has final responsibility for what's stored in the MMCIDB—the Merged Military Central Intelligence Data Base. It turns out that a whole lot of stuff found its way in there that shouldn't have, and I didn't know about it. They've got FBI files and population demographics and tons of personnel records."

"My God. And I've been telling the House Minority Leader for two years that she's paranoid about illegally stored and classified records. I owe Sarah an apology."

"Mander? I thought she was dead. She was on one of the earlier lists."

"I know. Her version is that she worked late, fell asleep in her office, and missed her ten o'clock flight. I think she missed it because she was shacked up. Either way, she has plenty of luck. What do you think you can do with the MMCIDB records?"

"Too soon to know. But there's a good deal of computer power locked up in those Prospero environments, and there are probably others in different parts of the country that we haven't been able to reach yet. I think we have a shot at reconstructing many of the civilian data bases."

"Good work, Grace. That's the best news I've had all day—not that most of today has been too brilliant." Saul leaned back and rubbed at his eyes so vigorously that he knew he was making them bloodshot. "But I'm glad I've got this job—for a damned silly reason."

He yawned and she waited. It was the end of a long day, and when he called her Grace she knew he was letting down his hair and indulging himself.

"Three years ago, Grace, I was in the top one hundred people of the country for personal wealth. Can you imagine that?"

"Frankly, sir, I can't. I can believe it, but I can't imagine it."

"That's a fair answer. But do you know what the other ninety-nine people are probably doing, those that are alive? They're sitting and wondering if they have anything left to count. The markets are closed, the economy has collapsed, none of the usual measures of wealth mean much anymore. And you know what, Grace? I just don't give a shit about money, mine or anyone else's. I'm too busy wondering if we're going to come out of the other side of this thing as a country, or if I'm the last President of the United States."

"I feel sure that you are not, sir. We will survive." She stood up. "Will there be anything else? I would not ask that question, but I have a meeting and eight people waiting for me down the hall."

"A few more minutes. They're probably enjoying the chance to relax." He waved her back to the chair. "I had the Deputy Science Adviser in here this morning. What do you think of Dr. Vronsky?"

"I am told that he has a very fine scientific mind, Mr. President."

"No need to be so cautious, we're not being recorded. Hell, if I *wanted* to record us I doubt if I could do it. My question is, do you understand what Vronsky says?"

"Usually. But he's not as clear as Dr. Chafets."

"I'm glad to hear you say that. I picked poor Doc Chafets as my Science Adviser because he knew exactly how much to dumb it down for me. Now he's dead, and Vronsky may be supersmart but he can't lower himself to my level. Yesterday he was trying to tell me about some big problem coming up in fifty or sixty years' time. Fifty years! And here I am worried about making it through tomorrow."

"Sometimes his explanations are beyond me, too, sir."

"And you have advanced degrees in physics and engineering. Think how he sounds to *me*, Grace—I know the media say I was a child prodigy who graduated college when I was fifteen, but what they don't tell you is that after that I went into real estate investment and didn't even go back for my diploma. I listen to Vronsky, and I don't understand. So I ask him questions, but his answers make me more confused."

"Yes, sir. If there's any way that I can help. . . ."

"That's what I'm getting to, in my not-so-subtle way. I want you to explain some things about Supernova Alpha."

"I'll do my best. What kind of things?"

"Why didn't people warn me about the pulse? Hell, I had briefings on everything from clouds over the Sahara to supermonsoons to calving of the Antarctic ice cap. It sounded more like a case for humanitarian relief than the collapse of this country. No one said a word about an electrical pulse that would knock everything sideways. I still don't know why the damn thing happened—or why it didn't happen at the same time as the supernova."

"Right." Grace Mackay sat perfectly still for a few moments. "According to Dr. Vronsky, he did mention the remote possibility of the electrical pulse to you, weeks ago. He says its delay was inevitable. But it was an accident of geometry that it happened at all."

"That's exactly what I'm getting at. Accident of geometry? What the hell is that supposed to mean? I don't get any of this."

"May I start with basics, sir? You know what a supernova is?"

"If I didn't know that by now, we might as well give up. It's the explosion of a star."

"A very violent explosion. When a star system goes supernova, it can shine a hundred billion times as bright for a month or two."

"But Vronsky said that according to theory, Alpha Centauri was the wrong type of star. It couldn't go supernova."

"Mr. President, *can* and *can't* make sense when you're talking about the future. We're talking about the past. It did. Time for a new theory. But here's what the astronomers tell us happens in a supernova. First, you get a runaway fusion reaction inside the star, and the outer surface blows off into space. That's what we see. People in New Zealand and Australia noticed it first—it was early evening—and they watched it get brighter and brighter until it was like a second sun. That's when the climate people started modeling the effects on the weather, and warned us to expect extreme conditions up here in the north as well as down south."

"You can speed it up, Grace. I've heard this much."

"I'm sorry, sir. I'll keep it short. When the star's outer layers blow off, they form a spherical shell. The shell is opaque to short wavelength radiation, so for a few weeks the X rays and gamma rays created in the fusion explosion stay bottled up. You've got billions of hydrogen bombs going off in there, but what you see at this point is just the bright outside of the shell."

"That's what we had until the middle of March."

"Yes, sir. But as the shell expanded it became thinner. And it wasn't of uniform thickness. Finally part of the shell was weak enough for high-energy radiation to get through. There was a huge squirt of X rays and gamma rays, all coming out at the same time. The 'accident of geometry' that Dr. Vronsky mentioned was that the beam of radiation came in our direction. It hit Earth on March 14."

"Why didn't it kill everything in the Southern Hemisphere? X rays and gamma rays are deadly."

"They are. But our atmosphere is opaque to most of those wavelengths and the radiation that got through hit the open Pacific Ocean and Antarctica. It did no direct damage to heavily populated areas."

"Keep going. I know this is going to end up bad, but I don't see how."

"The radiation absorbed by the upper atmosphere had enough energy to strip electrons from gas atoms. Enormous numbers of them. Electrons are charged particles, so they moved along magnetic field lines and kept building up their energy until finally—all at once—they produced a huge pulse of electromagnetic field. And *that's* what wiped out the microchips."

"All the chips?"

"Every one on the surface of the Earth, or close by in space. The pulse travels as well through vacuum as through air. But there's an inverse square law effect, so the farther away you are from Earth's atmosphere, where the pulse originated, the less power the pulse will have. That's why the manned platforms and the polar metsats are dead, in low Earth orbit, but the geosynchronous metsats and comsats in high orbit are working fine—if only we could receive from them."

"All the microchips. And it's hard to find equipment *without* a microchip somewhere inside it. I assume there's no way the chips can be repaired?"

"No, sir. They'll have to be replaced. And it's going to be a long job, because the production plants that make the microchips depend on their own microcircuits to do it. We face a difficult bootstrapping operation. Until the factories are up and running, we'll be relying on technology from the last century."

She paused. Saul Steinmetz had closed his eyes, and sat slowly nodding his head. "Do you have any more questions, Mr. President?"

"Yes. Why me, God? Why did it happen when I was President?" He opened his eyes and smiled at Grace Mackay. "I don't expect you to answer that. I'll be seeking answers from a higher authority. Thanks for the explanation."

"My privilege." She stood up, turned smartly, and marched toward the door.

"One other thing," Saul called after her. "You say that distance helps. What do you think the chances are for the Mars expedition?"

She turned in the doorway. "I've been afraid you would ask me that. I think they could be alive, and their ship in good working condition."

"In another few days they'll be back in Earth orbit. The plans for their visit to the White House were on my calendar before any of this started."

"Yes, sir. They are scheduled to retrofire and return to an orbit around Earth on March 26. The trouble is, I see no way to bring them down. The members of the Mars expedition are probably still breathing, Mr. President. But they are dead."

4

Regardless of opinions back on Earth, Celine Tanaka did not feel dead. She felt very much alive.

Stupid was another matter. How could all the Mars crew have missed something so obvious? Logically, they ought to have known about Supernova Alpha before anyone else. After all, space was all around them, their only scenery. They should have noticed anything happening in it.

After the fact, Celine tried to justify their oversight. First, they had been on the way home for seven months, and scenery that never changes—or changes too slowly to notice—loses its charm. Second, although no one on board would mention it, they were all thinking ahead to the return to Earth. Their place in history had been secured by the Mars landing, but at the time the aerobraking problems on the way down and the loss of one unmanned lander had occupied everyone's attention. The return from the Martian surface had been uneventful but equally tense. Only on the way home, with nothing to do but wait, could you give way to the sense of anticipation and excitement.

So Supernova Alpha had begun its change when everyone aboard the *Schiaparelli* was off guard. Celine, as head of instrumentation, did notice the apparent malfunction of one of her star trackers. It was reporting a photon variation above threshold. Since the trackers' target stars were chosen as stable stellar references, the tracker obediently noted the anomaly and turned itself off to prevent damage. But Celine saw no reason to investigate the problem immediately. There were four other working star trackers, and in any case spacecraft attitude control was not important during this phase of the mission. A fix could be made anytime in the next few weeks. She thought she would do it at the end of the work period.

In retrospect, that was less than totally conscientious. But no one else on board—except maybe Zoe—would have acted any differently.

Ten minutes after the star tracker went off-line, Ludwig Holter wandered into the instrumentation center. He had the face of a wicked elf and the slight build to match, and Celine noticed that he moved with a free-fall grace and economy of effort that three years ago would have seemed impossible to all of them.

"Celine, I'm picking up a report from Canberra of anomalous short-period variation in the brightness of Alpha Centauri. Do we have anything looking that way?"

Although he was German, his English was better than her Philippine/Hawaii mixture. Celine glanced at the big board. "Only one of our navigation star trackers, and it's off-line for checking. None of our scopes is observing in that direction. Want me to switch into the DOS, see if it's taking a look?"

The Distributed Observation System was a complex of forty-eight telescopes in Earth orbit, all tightly controlled to observe a common target. The *Schiaparelli* had been designed to receive the DOS output data stream, though the crew rarely did so.

Ludwig scowled from beneath blond bangs. "Nah. I'm sure DOS is booked up weeks ahead, and it takes hours to switch targets. Can you put our big scope on it?"

"Sure. Wilmer is using it right now for super-cluster observation, but as soon as he's done we'll take a peek."

"When?"

Celine pulled a face. "You know Wilmer."

"Not as well as you do, lady."

"I should hope not. He scheduled three hours, but he often runs over. Want me to ask him if we can jump in?"

"Not worth it. Wait 'til he's done, and let me know if you find anything interesting. I'm going to rest for a while." Ludwig drifted away, heading for the second of the three interlocking modules that made up the ship.

Celine was not surprised by Ludwig's comment. It was perfectly in order to take a midday nap. The ship would awaken him if any emergency occurred. Since an emergency was defined as a situation on board the *Schiaparelli*, there was by definition no emergency.

Wilmer Oldfield took advantage of Celine's indulgence and

made use of the ship's biggest telescope for even longer than she had expected. It was another six hours before he handed instrument control back to her. She fed in the celestial coordinates for Alpha Centauri, and as a matter of routine took a look to make sure that target acquisition had been correctly performed.

By that time, Alpha Centauri had brightened by seventeen magnitudes. Celine gave the blazing point of light on the display one glance, noted its still-increasing intensity, and immediately buzzed Zoe.

"Zo? You there? We've got something I think you'll want to take a look at."

"What?" Zoe Nash was the head of the Mars expedition, and she sounded half-asleep. It was a rare condition for her, but in this phase of the flight home lethargy seemed more virtue than vice.

"It's Alpha Centauri," Celine said. "It's superbrilliant. I think it's becoming a nova, even a supernova. More than a thousand times as bright as usual."

"Really?" Zoe became more lively. "I do want to take a look at that. Everyone else will, too. Make a general announcement, will you?"

"Sure."

Celine alerted the ship's general intercom, made sure that the scope would remain locked on Alpha Centauri, and headed aft. The ship had been designed with high redundancy, so that any one of its three sections could at a pinch become a stand-alone unit able to make the journey home. A much overcrowded journey, to be sure, and one with little margin for error if all seven expedition members were present; but the crew would reach Earth orbit alive. The price paid for that triple security was the difficulty of transition from one section to the next. Celine grumbled to herself as she squeezed through a narrow passage with an airlock at each end. Small-boned and thin as she was, it was still hard going. When she reached the observation chamber at the far end of the ship's third section, every other expedition member was already there.

She surveyed the group, wondering where to place herself. In the front row, pushing each other for extra space, were Zoe Nash, Wilmer Oldfield, and the chief geologist—and areologist—Reza Armani. Behind them were the other three crew members, Alta McIntosh-Mohammad, Ludwig Holter, and computer specialist Jenny Kopal. Celine had hardly seen them all in one place since the return ship left the surface of Mars.

Reza in particular had almost disappeared, gloating over his collection of Mars samples like a demented miser. Celine worried sometimes about his attitude, he seemed close to irrational on the subject. True, five of the samples did contain dormant bacterial life-forms of enormous interest. Wilmer Oldfield and Celine herself had performed the genome scans. The forms were DNA-based, but their sequences were nothing remotely like any Earth organism. Reza had stood by all through the work, glowering at Celine and Wilmer as though they might attempt theft of his treasure.

The observation chamber had not been designed to accommodate all the team at once. Celine was not going to get the best viewing position, no matter what she did. She squeezed in, peered over Alta McIntosh-Mohammad's shoulder, and gasped. Direct observation was quite different from looking at something on a screen. There was no question which star was Alpha Centauri. Although still showing only as a white point of light, it was brilliant enough to cast shadows inside the chamber.

"It looks brighter than it did just a few minutes ago," she said.

"It is." Wilmer recognized her voice and spoke without looking around. "Celine, did you get a reading for a number of magnitudes increase?"

His accent was the strongest in the whole international group. He was Australian, and he had bemused Celine at their first meeting by insisting that what he spoke was standard English.

"Yes, I did," she said. "It was seventeen, when I last looked."

"Then if it's a supernova—which I think it may be, even though it shouldn't—it's just getting going."

"What do you mean, *shouldn't*?" Zoe Nash was a short and stocky woman of mixed Ugandan and Turkish descent. She was right where an expedition leader ought to be, up at the front of the group. She was also, because of the shortage of space, squashed by the others against the observation window.

"Alpha Centauri is a double-star system," Wilmer said, in his relaxed drawl. "Double stars can become a Type Ia supernova, but only if one of the two stars is a white dwarf. Alpha Centauri doesn't qualify."

"Then I guess Alpha Centauri doesn't know that," said Zoe. "It's not a good day to be an astronomical theorist. Hey, give me some air, folks." She wriggled around to face Wilmer Oldfield. "What do you mean, just getting going?"

"If this is a supernova, the increase in brightness will be as much as a hundred billion. We are still far short of that."

"Are we going to be safe?"

Celine listened for Wilmer's answer with special interest. In addition to being in charge of instrumentation, she was also the expedition's physician. The medical supplies and equipment were adequate for "normal" emergencies, but a supernova didn't qualify.

"Safe?" Wilmer blinked his eyes and rubbed his stubbly beard as though such a question had never occurred to him. Celine's guess was that it hadn't. He was a super scientist and a sweetheart, but sometimes he seemed on a different wavelength from normal people.

"I dunno," he said after a moment. "But I can work it out easy enough. The bigger star of Alpha Centauri is pretty much a look-alike for our sun, same spectral type but a little bit brighter. It's about one and a third parsecs away, so that's about two hundred seventy thousand times as far as the sun is from Earth. If it becomes a hundred billion times as bright as usual, it will look a hundred billion divided by two hundred seventy thousand squared as bright as the sun. So there you are."

He paused, as though that was the end of the story. "Translation, Jenny," said Zoe. "Do the calculation, would you, for people like me. How bright will it be?"

"One hundred billion divided by two hundred seventy thousand squared is one point thirty-seven." Jenny Kopal was in charge of computers, and the common view was that she had a personal one inside her head. Celine found it easier to ask the dark-haired Hungarian for the answer to calculations rather than keying it in herself.

"That's *bright*," Reza said. He giggled. "Sell Sunscreen 100, you'll make your fortune."

"Well, that could be off a factor of two, one way or the other," Wilmer added. "But Reza's right, Alpha Centauri as seen from Earth will be bright, maybe as bright as the sun. Of course, that's only for a month or two, then it goes dim again."

Except for Wilmer, the group in front of Celine moved in concert, edging away from the chamber window.

"Are we in danger?" Zoe asked.

Wilmer shrugged. He had the long limbs and wide shoulders of an outdoorsman. That, combined with his Australian accent, had Celine in the first months of their acquaintance expecting him to talk about wombats and wallabies rather than quantum field theories. "I don't see why," he said at last. "We can handle solar radiation. We have the inner shielded area in Section One, in case of big solar flares." He looked thoughtful. "Course, when the gas shell of the supernova expands, a big slug of gamma rays will break out. We have no idea which direction they'll emerge. But we have enough shielding to handle that, too. The big problem is going to be the high-energy particle flux. That will carry a lot more energy than the visible light or the gamma rays. It'll be an absolute killer."

Zoe came bolt upright. "And you say we're not in danger!"

"We're not. The light and gammas travel at light speed, but the particles are much slower—five to ten percent of light speed. It will take them fifty years to get here."

The group relaxed again.

"Fifty *years,*" Zoe said. "I don't care about fifty years. I was worried about fifty minutes or fifty hours."

Wilmer shook his head. "No worries. We will be fine."

"*We* will be fine." Alta McIntosh-Mohammad was the *Schiaparelli*'s chief engineer, Scottish-Indian and taciturn. Whenever she spoke, the rest had learned to listen. "But what about *them*? Back on Earth. Will they be all right?"

"Wilmer?" said Zoe.

There was a much longer silence, during which Alpha Centauri visibly increased in brightness second by second. Celine thought of her mother and stepfather, now on a field trip in central Kalimantan. They were very resourceful, they would be fine. Wouldn't they? And her brother Hiroshi should certainly be safe enough, on the west coast of Canada. But Wilmer's lengthy pause was worrying, and the appearance of the rest of the crew suggested that they were having the same thoughts as Celine. She could see uneasiness on every face, tight-lipped control, and a reluctance to look at each other.

"That's a much harder question," Wilmer said at last—not what Celine was hoping to hear. "You put another illumination source, maybe as bright as Sol, down at sixty degrees south. It will have a hell of an effect on temperatures and global weather. In the long run, you'll see some ice melt and sea-level rise. But for good quantitative answers you need the best models on atmospheric circulation patterns. We don't have anything like that on board—though you can bet they're hard at work down on Earth."

"I hope bad weather won't screw up our landing plans," Zoe said. "The last thing we need is high winds and storms. I suppose if we have to, we can sit it out in orbit."

With hindsight, Celine would realize that Zoe had still been seeing Supernova Alpha as a problem for Earth but at most a minor inconvenience to the expedition. And everyone had taken their cue from the leader of the party. So after another half hour of watching they one by one wandered away, leaving the observation chamber for their own quarters.

Wilmer and Celine were the last to go. He was simply fascinated by the supernova and wanted to see as much of it as possible; Celine had her own reasons. She wanted a quiet place to think, and the observation chamber was as good as any.

Competition for the Mars expedition had been incredibly fierce. Each of the winners had multiple capabilities and would have multiple duties, but everyone knew that competence was only part of the picture. Politics was the other variable, beyond a candidate's control. The selection committee somehow had to achieve a mixture of crew members both competent and internationally balanced. Every crew member also had to be both vitally important and totally expendable. If someone died on Mars, there could be no sending home for replacements.

So in Celine's mind, Ludwig Holter satisfied continental European pride, handled all communications, and in a pinch took over the computers. Alta McIntosh-Mohammad pleased Britain and the Federation of Indian States and was chief engineer, while Reza Armani was American-Iranian and served as backup pilot in addition to his role as areologist. Zoe Nash herself knew all the communications systems and represented both Africa and Asia Minor. And Jenny Kopal, Hungarian with a strong dash of Russian, had spent enough time with Celine to be fully familiar with the *Schiaparelli*'s major command and control instrumentation.

Celine still wondered how she herself had been lucky enough to survive the final cut. Perhaps it was pressure from the Eastern lobby, with a little Hawaiian help. She knew she was hardworking and pretty bright, but the others of the crew were more than that. They were spectacular.

And in that company, the stand-out oddity was Wilmer. Everyone admitted it; they were highly competent, but he was a *real* genius. No one on board approached him as a pure scientist—and not one of them wanted him anywhere near when they were doing their jobs. He was as clumsy as you could get, and equipment fell apart in his hands. He was also the odd one physically. The rest were below average height and weight, Wilmer was tall and deep-chested and rangy.

Their special capabilities and redundancies had all made sense, even before they headed for Mars. Only when they had been traveling for a few months did Celine conclude that the faceless selection committee back on Earth had employed yet another set of criteria. The crew were matched not only in technical skills, but in personality types. They had been paired, she suspected, before they ever left Earth. The group was not particularly highly sexed, but unless people are actually neutered or drugged into an asexual stupor, couplings are bound to occur. Reza Armani and Jenny Kopal had paired off early, followed a month later by Ludwig Holter and Alta McIntosh-Mohammad. Celine thought them unlikely duos. Reza, for example, had a deep mystical streak and sometimes seemed both illogical and half-crazy. Jenny, in contrast, was a cool and objective atheist. But of course they hadn't consulted Celine before sleeping together. And she could imagine the reactions when she and Wilmer began to share quarters: Whatever does he/she see in her/him?

Zoe Nash had no one, man or woman, and seemed content with that. She was five years older than the rest, who were all within a year of each other, and maybe she saw them as her children. And maybe they liked that. They had lots of respect for each other, but of all possible losses Zoe's would be the hardest for everyone to take.

The personality types were varied in one other way that was hard to define, although Celine had pondered it often enough. Zoe was certainly the authority figure. Reza was the class clown and cut-up king, sometimes far-out enough to make Celine wonder how he had passed the psychological tests. But what were the rest? She could never decide, with one exception: Celine herself was the expedition's worrywart, a Cassandra who could always imagine a dozen ways that things might go wrong. Unlike Cassandra's, though, her own dire predictions had never come to pass.

Yet.

And that, she suspected, was why she remained in the observation chamber with Wilmer, and stared at Alpha Centauri. She was worried, and not sure why. He hardly seemed to know that she was there, until she said, "Wilmer, we talked about what the supernova might do to Earth. Could it do anything to the rest of the solar system?"

"Nothing to worry us. It will melt the ice surfaces on the moons of the outer planets, but as Alpha Centauri dims they'll freeze over again."

"What about the sun? There will be a lot of extra heat, all pouring into one side of it."

"It's a lot by terrestrial standards. In solar terms, it's nothing."

"It couldn't cause big solar flares, or anything like that?"

"I doubt it. Even if it did, Section Two of the *Schiaparelli* is well shielded against that sort of thing. We'll have plenty of notice, we'll just retreat there for as long as necessary. We're safer here on the ship than we would be down on Earth."

Celine could see why Wilmer was so good as a partner for her. No matter what happened, he stayed calm. And he could usually give her a sound, logical reason why her worries were groundless.

This time, though, she had the awful conviction that she would be right, and he would be wrong.

Supernova Alpha brightened and brightened. The crew of the *Schiaparelli* was in the best possible position to observe it. Four weeks after the first brightening—and one week before the change—the expanding gas shell around the star was big enough to show a visible disk to the on-board telescopes. From the second day, Celine had tuned their communications antennae to receive images from the DOS in Earth orbit. They all watched the fiery sphere pulsate and shiver under the force of explosions deep inside it. Wilmer did inverse calculations to determine the energy release from the observations. The numbers he quoted, in his dry, matter-of-fact way, were enough to make Celine shiver.

"If there were planets orbiting Alpha Centauri . . ." Alta said gloomily, when she, Celine, and Wilmer were together in the main galley of the *Schiaparelli*. She was the expedition's number two pessimist, right after Celine.

"Then you would be quite right to employ the past tense." Wilmer nodded to a display, where Alpha Centauri was now constantly displayed. "If they were ever there, they're cinders."

Celine didn't say anything. But after they had finished eating she went again to Section Two. There she checked that the quarters they would retreat to in case of a big solar storm were fully furnished with supplies. Then she did what she had done every day since the first blossoming of Supernova Alpha; she examined sequences of visible-wavelength images of both Alpha Centauri and of Sol, looking for changes in either.

Of course, she didn't see anything. The huge pulse of gamma

rays from Supernova Alpha, when it finally came, was invisible to human eyes.

The instruments, however, had sensitivity to everything from hard X rays to long radio waves. They caught the leap in the ambient gamma-ray level in the first fraction of a second, extrapolated the upward curve, and sent a warning bellow through the whole ship.

The crew had been well trained. *Better to overreact than underreact.* They headed at maximum speed for Section Two. Celine, in a bizarre way, felt vindicated. She had expected trouble, and here it was—and thanks to Celine they were ready, food and water fully stocked, extra instruments installed so they would know exactly what was going on outside.

Not much space, of course. They were in an emergency shelter, not a luxury hotel. But Celine sat bug-rug-snug and not unhappy between Wilmer and Ludwig, watching the gamma-level readout.

It was calibrated so that a level of zero equaled the mean solar gamma flux with a quiet sun. The current level—sixty-three—only meant something if you knew that the readout scale was the base-e log of the gamma intensity. That was easy to deal with if you knew, as Celine did, that e^3 is about equal to twenty. So an increase of three in readout value was equivalent to a factor of twenty multiplier in actual gamma-ray level. Readout level sixty-three then meant that the current gamma flux was $20^{63/3}$ of the usual value. 20^{21} was rather more than 10^{27}. Space outside the shielded compartment of the *Schiaparelli* was hot, hell-hot, with the gamma-ray burst from Supernova Alpha.

And still Celine, who would conclude in retrospect that she was an idiot, thought they were sitting pretty inside their shield. She hadn't even bothered to include a display showing anything of what was happening back on Earth. It was Ludwig, sitting with his miniature ear-link tuned to open communications channels, who after a few seconds grunted, sat upright, and said, "What the hell is going on?"

Nothing special, according to Celine's displays. She turned to him. "What do you mean? What do you hear?"

He had his control unit on his lap, scanning frequencies. He shook his head. "I don't like this. I was monitoring S-band, low data rate ground-to-space vocal. Then it went dead—and now so has everything else. I'm getting nothing at all, not even video or general communications uplinks from Earth."

It was Wilmer, on Celine's other side, who stirred from an apparent trance and said, "Check space to ground."

Ludwig said nothing, but his fingers stabbed at another section of his lap set. After a few seconds he glanced across at Wilmer. "Weird. Nothing going down from *low* Earth orbit, voice or image or computer bit stream. But for the geosynchronous metsats, higher up, it's business as usual. Do you want me to look at their image data stream?"

"Yes. But not what's being sent out now. Do you receive and store past data?"

"Some. It's a moving window. We store metsats for the past twenty-four hours, that's all."

"That will be ample. Tap us in to fifteen minutes ago, and run a display."

Zoe was finally taking an interest. She had not actually been listening, but she reacted to Wilmer's and Ludwig's tone of voice. She leaned forward toward them. "Hey, what's going on? How long before this gamma surge fades, and we can get out of here?"

Celine glanced across at the readout: forty-two. "It's fading already," she said. "It's down by twenty-one from the last value I saw. That's a factor of more than a billion. If it keeps going like this, we can all leave here in a few minutes."

"I'm going to borrow your display, Celine," Ludwig said. "Here's the metsat images."

Alpha Centauri vanished. In its place came the familiar and comforting sight of Earth as seen from geosynchronous orbit, thirty-five thousand kilometers above the surface. They stared in silence at the great globe, half lit by sunlight, half in darkness. Without knowing how to give a name to it, Celine could see a *strangeness* to the cloud patterns. Instead of broad bands or hurricane swirls, the clouds had an unusual north–south streaky structure, as though the equator—that already imaginary entity—had disappeared.

Peculiar, yes. But menacing? Not really. All seven of them sat watching in silence. At last, as Zoe was saying, "All right, I've enjoyed as much of this as I can stand," it came.

A blue glow started at the South Pole and shimmered north. Like a gas discharge in a fluorescent tube, it moved until it enveloped the whole Earth. And then, while they stared and wondered if they were seeing what they thought they saw, it was gone.

Wilmer leaned back against Celine. "We're screwed," he said.

"Dead unlucky, the geometry must have been just wrong. I knew it was a possibility, but I never thought it would happen. Ludwig, check the time codes on the data streams. I bet data loss in and around Earth began coincident with that high-atmosphere free electron phenomenon we just witnessed."

"What will it do?" Reza asked. He had the least electronic background of anyone on board.

"If it was as strong as I think," Wilmer answered, "it will have knocked out a lot of electronic gear down on Earth. Anything with microchips in it is probably dead."

"Well, doesn't that mean . . ." Reza said.

He was asking more questions. Celine could hear him, but his words didn't even register with her. If everything containing microchips no longer worked, then the planet would be plunged back to a pre-electronic age; except that the world of 2026, unlike the world of 1926, depended on electronic devices for every phase of living.

And there was more. Equipment in low Earth orbit would also be affected. That included the space stations—stations on which the Mars expedition had been depending for its safe return to Earth.

Celine thought again of her parents and her brother. They were probably not in situations critically dependent on electronic technology. They were all right.

But she was not. The chances of survival of the first Mars expedition had suddenly dropped by many orders of magnitude.

Sure, they should be able to fire retro-rockets to match speed with Earth. Sure, they ought to be able to park the *Schiaparelli* in Earth orbit. But the most difficult part of the journey home, the final reentry, would still lie ahead. And for that reentry, they needed resources that no longer existed.

5

As Grace Mackay was leaving Saul's office, Auden Travis popped back in the doorway. "You have no other meetings on your calendar this evening, Mr. President—"

"And plenty to do. I'll eat right here, if you could pass the word."

"Yes, sir. But I was about to add, you have two people still waiting to see you, Dr. Singer and Ms. Silvers. Also, we have more working lines. South Carolina is patched in—"

"Good."

"—and Mrs. Steinmetz is on the line. It's not one of her better days, sir. She is referring to you as Ben."

"Bring Dr. Singer in, and tell him to take the other headset. Then put Mrs. Steinmetz on the line. I want Dr. Singer to hear her. I'll see Ms. Silvers last, and she can eat with me. Order for two."

"Very good, sir."

Was that a faint look of distaste on Auden Travis's handsome face as he left? Better that, Saul decided, than the knowing smirk that a heterosexual aide might offer.

He sighed—*Why me, God?*—and picked up the old-fashioned headset as Dr. Forrest Singer entered, nodded, and moved to the other working telephone.

"Hello, Mother." Saul waited. When there was no reply, he went on, "How are you feeling?"

"They're not feeding me right." The voice on the other end of the line came through faint and scratchy, with odd breaks between the words. "And they have different people giving me my bath and cleaning my rooms."

"I'll talk to them, Mother. I'll make sure it gets fixed. We have trouble lots of places, because of the supernova."

"Oh? Well, you know that's nothing to do with me. I can't do anything about that. What are you doing, Ben? Are you meeting any nice girls?"

"This is Saul, Mother. I'm very busy. Too busy to think much about meeting girls."

"Why haven't you been calling me? I don't think you've called for a long time. I don't know when you last called me."

"I'm sorry, Mother. They've had a lot of trouble with the telephones. I'll try to call more often."

"You ought to take a break, you work too hard. Make them fix the food better here. They'll listen to you, they don't seem to listen to me at all."

"I'll tell them, Mother."

"And make sure you take a break from work sometimes. Go down to the temple, have a social life."

"I'll try, Mother. It's hard to get out at the moment, there's so much going on here."

"How's Tricia?"

"I guess she's fine. But I haven't seen her for ages."

"You need to meet some nice girls."

"I know. I'll keep looking, Mother."

"Girls like Tricia. Don't you be going with any of those dirty Washington women. You don't need those, the world is full of nice *respectable* girls."

Saul made the translation. For respectable, read Jewish. For Jewish, read Tricia Goldsmith—who was not in fact Jewish.

"I'd like to meet a nice girl, Mother. But right now I have to make sure you get better food, and have your rooms cleaned the way you like them. So I'm going to get off the phone this minute, and tell them to give you special attention."

"Not special attention, just the way it's supposed to be. I'm sure we're paying enough. We need to get our money's worth."

"I know. I'll take care of it, right now. And I'll call you tomorrow. I love you, Mother."

"I love you, too, Saul. You're a good son. I'm proud of you."

"Good-bye, Mother."

As Saul removed the headset he found he was gripping it so hard that the knuckles on his left hand were white. He glanced over at Forrest Singer. The doctor shrugged.

"I see no signs of further deterioration. She started out confusing you with your father, but by the end of the conversation she knew who you were and she got your name right."

"Before all the troubles started, I had a report dropped off on my desk about a new treatment at the Institute for Probatory Therapies. Telomod therapy? It sounded promising. I was wondering if it might help Mrs. Steinmetz."

"I recommend against that, very strongly." Forrest Singer, it always seemed to Saul, spoke as though the two of them were equals. Saul possibly held the slightly inferior position in the doctor's eyes. Saul was the President of the United States, true; but Forrest Singer was an M.D.

"First," Singer went on, "the treatment you refer to is in the earliest stages of testing. It is quite likely to cause unpredictable and possibly catastrophic side effects. And even if telomod therapy were able to improve your mother's health or longevity, it could do little or nothing for her mental state. Is there any value to turning back the physical clock, if we cannot do the same for the mental one? Hannah Steinmetz's mind will remain as it is today, that of a ninety-two-year-old lady with moderate dementia. Telomod therapy might recondition the glial cells of the brain, but too many neurons are already dead for restoration of mental functions."

Forrest Singer sounded very sure of himself. Unlike Saul, he didn't have to deal with the choice of guilts that went with doing something, or of doing nothing.

Which was the greater sin? To allow your mother to sink steadily to incontinence and total mindlessness; or to arrest the progress of her condition, and subject her to years of miserable dependence on others, illuminated by an occasional faint flash of memory and the knowledge of what she once was.

"I am always happy to advise you concerning your mother," Singer went on. Saul knew that was not true, but it was the socially acceptable lie. "However, Mr. President, my principal reason for coming here as your personal physician is to discuss your own health."

"I feel fine." Another socially acceptable lie.

"You are, for a man of fifty-six with your lifestyle and the unusual stresses of your job, in good condition. Early symptoms of osteoarthritis are still present, and I have sent to the White House kitchen a menu with somewhat different supplements designed to reverse that. I do not think you will notice any changes in the food. As usual, I am recommending a decreased consumption of alcohol."

Singer smiled, though with little evidence of humor. "But as usual, I doubt that my recommendation will have any effect on your behavior. Principally, however, I am here to discuss with you the series of tests we have been conducting for the past few months. They were interrupted just over a week ago, when the equipment failed. However, I had already drawn my main conclusions. First, in sexual terms you are physiologically normal, unremarkable in any way."

"You might find another way to put that."

Saul smiled as he spoke, but Singer still looked puzzled. At forty-eight he was somber and literal-minded, and Saul's guess was that he had been equally somber and literal-minded at twenty-one. He was also thoughtful, meticulous, and the best diagnostician Saul had ever met. Saul had long since accepted the fact that his own body was now public property. For two years, everything from his bowel movements to a spot on the end of his nose was grist for the media. But they wouldn't get the information from Forrest Singer. The man would freeze-dry them if they touched on anything that he considered protected by the doctor-patient relationship.

After a moment the physician continued, "I find your general activity level for your age to be above average, though well within the normal bounds of variability. Furthermore, all the chemical and ionic levels within your body are satisfactory."

The physician sounded as though he was imparting news, but nothing so far was a surprise to Saul. He nodded. "So, put it together and what have you got?"

"You have a conclusion which supports my original suspicion and, I would suppose, your own. You are impotent; but it arises from psychological rather than from physical causes. That you have become so since taking the oath as President is unlikely to reflect a coincidence."

"I agree." Saul knew that Forrest Singer was not the man to appreciate the irony of the situation. Here he was, President, a position that many of his predecessors had regarded as providing an endless sexual free lunch with more offers than a man could possibly accept. And most of them had been *married*. He was healthy, long-since divorced, reluctantly celibate—and surrounded by willing young women. There were groupies for sky guys and groupies for media stars, but a President presented a special challenge. For while you could count astronauts and rollers in the hundreds, the country had only one President.

"So what's your advice, Doctor?"

"Normally, I would recommend that a man in your situation should make opportunity follow desire. By this I mean that when next you feel strong sexual arousal, you should seek to act on it immediately. However, your position as President makes that course of action rather difficult."

Saul stared at him. Forrest Singer didn't joke, and he wasn't joking now. *When next you feel strong sexual arousal, you should seek to act on it immediately.* That certainly had the potential to enliven a White House dinner party.

"As it is," Singer went on, "I recommend that you do nothing, and continue to live as normally as possible. Eat more. Drink less alcohol. And try not to worry about your condition, which can only make it worse."

"I've certainly got plenty of other things to worry about." Saul turned to stare out of the window. "Thank you, Doctor."

"It is, as always, an honor to serve the President."

"And ask the lady waiting outside to come in, would you."

Saul was being a little petty, and he knew it. He didn't want Auden Travis ushering Yasmin Silvers into the Oval Office and standing there until he was told to go away. Yasmin was newer to the White House than Auden, and he surely resented her frequent meetings with the President.

Saul was still facing the window. It was dusk, and the emergency lighting system of the White House did not include the grounds and outside streets. Washington was darker than it had been in a century and a half. The glass of the window was like a mirror. Saul saw his own reflection and recognized a resemblance. He was an inch shorter than Grace Mackay, and he had a scholar's stoop where she was all straight-backed military, but they shared the gaunt, spectral look of people too preoccupied to think much about food.

Tonight, he would eat everything that came regardless of appetite. And, in spite of Forrest Singer, he would drink whatever he felt like.

In the glass he saw Yasmin Silvers silently entering the room. She was of medium height, with a smooth and controlled walk that reminded him of a prowling cat. *A cat may look at a king.* Could a cat stalk a President?

He turned, to admire the skin that he had seen only faintly in the reflection. Her mixed Asian and Hispanic descent had given her a flawless ivory complexion, with a hint of darker color. The hands that held a brown folder were long-fingered and delicate, their trimmed nails painted a startling silver. She gave him her usual knockout smile.

"Good evening, Mr. President."

"Hello, Yasmin. Sit down and make yourself comfortable." He went across and opened the long credenza. "I took the liberty of ordering dinner for both of us, so we can talk while we eat. I don't know about you, but I've had nothing since eleven this morning."

"Thank you, sir." Maybe she took his remark as a criticism, because she sat down and at once opened the folder. "I would not trouble you so late, but a new item has come up for rapid decision and action. It involves Internal Affairs." She shook her head as he held an empty glass toward her. "Not for me, sir. Not until we are finished with business."

If she was hinting that he ought to do the same, then she had too much damned cheek. Saul mixed a strong brandy and soda with no ice and walked back to sit at the other side of the coffee table.

"I've read briefing documents today until my eyes are dropping out. I'll look at what you have later, but can't you tell me about it?"

"Yes, sir. I can state the problem very simply. What are we going to do about judicial sleep?"

"I wasn't planning to do anything. With our infrastructure down and nearly out, judicial sleep isn't high on my list. Let's get food and power and water and communications and transportation back, then we'll worry about the criminals."

Saul had been elected as a Centrist Party candidate, in favor of severe punishment for criminals but opposed to capital punishment. It was a highly popular part of his platform. Yasmin Silvers surely knew that.

And she was nodding vigorously, a tress of sleek hair falling over one eye. "I'm not referring to the late Secretary of Internal Affairs's revised rules for sentencing, sir. Those can certainly wait. But we have nine hundred and thirty thousand people in judicial sleep."

"Do you have a list of sentences?"

But Saul was stalling while he thought through the options. He knew all he needed to know about the criminals; they were iced down for anything from five years to one thousand.

"Not with me, sir. I can get it for you if you need it."

Saul nodded. The perfect solution: JS, judicial sleep. No one was put to death, so it avoided all the old arguments about capital punishment. If new evidence came along to prove you innocent, you could be awakened. If you died while in the coma, well, tough, but it would be of natural causes.

And there was another factor, maybe the most important one of all. JS was cheap. No need for guards. No need, in fact, for any supervisory staff. Although one or two supervisory staff could be found at every JS facility, they were there only to provide the right public image of a caring and careful government. The smart monitoring and servicers took care of everything—drugs, nutrition, medical tests, and treatments—without ever finding it necessary to awaken their charges.

Storage space was minimal. A two-by-two-by-eight darkened cubicle per prisoner, and who needed more? Certainly not the iced-down occupants, whether dreaming or dreamless. Certainly not the public, paying for the upkeep and begrudging the expense, though it was only a hundredth of the cost per inmate of an old-fashioned prison. Not even those sentenced were likely to complain. If they didn't know it before they were caught, they soon learned the degree of public intolerance of criminals. Icing down was pleasant compared with some of the citizen proposals.

Judicial sleep was the perfect solution. And like all perfect answers, it was fine until you ran into the snags.

"Do you have the JS prison sites?"

"Right here, sir."

Rather than offering a written list, she had taken the trouble to mark the locations on a map of the country. Saul took it and spent a few minutes in silent study.

"Is it all right, sir?" she said at last. "I had to do it in rather a hurry."

The eagerness for approval. Maybe that was the best part of being President, everyone around you sought to please. It was also the most dangerous part. When people constantly tried to guess what you would like to hear, necessary bad news might never reach you.

"It's perfectly all right, very good in fact," Saul said, and watched her glow. "The map is invaluable. It also tells us what we have to do."

"Sir?"

"I'm afraid so. The JS support systems are sure to be packed with microcircuits, so they won't be working. That suggests we ought to wake everyone at the prisons, otherwise they may die. But once awake, they will need food and shelter. Remember that a big percentage of those placed in judicial sleep are there because they were violent criminals. Whatever they needed, they took. JS doesn't change someone's personality. It's all our police and military can do to keep things reasonably quiet as it is. And most of the sites are within fifty miles of major population centers. Do you want to be remembered as the person who unleashed a million desperate criminals on an innocent and unprepared citizenry?"

"No, sir. Of course not."

"Well, neither do I. Think politics for a moment. If we do nothing, I can say that all our resources had to be devoted to improving the situation for law-abiding citizens during a very difficult time. That is a safe statement, and it happens to be true. On the other hand, if I revive those in judicial sleep, and even *one* of them commits a crime of violence, I will be blamed as much as if I did it myself."

"I understand, sir."

But her eyes were downcast, and her lips trembled. Saul focused, and made one of those leaps of understanding that had brought him the presidency.

"Who is it, Yasmin? One of your family?"

"Yes, sir." She raised lovely tawny eyes to his. "You know."

"I didn't, until a moment ago."

"I didn't conceal it, it's in my personnel record. My younger brother."

"What did he do?"

"He stabbed my uncle, after my uncle had raped him. Raymond was sentenced to seven years. He has been in judicial sleep for three."

"Surely in a case of rape, self-defense or extenuating circumstances—"

"My uncle is Senator Lopez."

And now she said it, Saul remembered. Yasmin's application for a job as a White House aide had come with a strong push from Nick Lopez. The sexual tastes of Senator Lopez were one of Washington's poorest-kept secrets.

"Yasmin, how long can people survive in judicial sleep if the support systems are not working?"

"I asked several people over at Justice about that, sir. There is no agreement, but the answers range from one week to three weeks."

"I see. And already it has been a week."

"Yes, sir. Nine days, actually."

She was still staring at him with those big, doomed eyes. Saul stood up and turned away. "As I'm sure you realize, Yasmin, although a presidential pardon can be issued for almost any offense it is impossible for me to consider one in this case. My own supporters would say—correctly—that I was betraying the principles upon which I was elected. So that's a no-no. Do you know where your brother is located?"

"Yes, sir." A hushed, dead voice. "Raymond is in the Q-5 Syncope Facility, about forty miles south of here. I know the exact location."

"That's a strange choice. Q-5 is usually reserved for murderers and terrorists dangerous to the state."

"Raymond was described at the trial as 'a severe and continuing danger.' He isn't that."

"I believe you. I see Lopez's hand at work again. But, Yasmin, you have been working far too hard. Dangerously hard. You are in such poor condition that I, personally, fear for your life."

"Sir? I'm feeling fine. I'm not—"

"Shh. Listen to me. With your life threatened, the law permits as an act of charity the temporary return of a sentenced criminal from judicial sleep, in order to offer final comfort to his loved ones. I am going to order such a return. But you must understand that it can be only temporary. Your brother will return to serve the remainder of his sentence—as soon as the national emergency has ended."

There was a gasp, then a long, pregnant silence. Watching their reflections in the window, Saul saw Yasmin approaching him from behind. She stood so close that he could smell her perfume mingled with the odor of her skin. He saw ghost arms in the dark glass, rising to embrace him.

When next you feel strong sexual arousal, you should seek to act on it.

Yasmin was willing and wanting and waiting, longing to express her gratitude. She was almost thirty-one, old enough that no one could accuse Saul of taking advantage of a child.

Would he have performed the same favor for Yasmin's brother if she were not young and beautiful?

Saul had never been beautiful, and at the moment he could not believe that he had ever been young. But he knew the answer: never. It was not just, but the beautiful of the world enjoyed special privileges. And they were special targets.

He took a step. Forward. Away from her. To a safe distance.

He turned, and saw agony and indecision on her face. He could read that expression. She wanted to embrace him, but she was afraid that a sexual advance on the President in the Oval Office would be some form of lèse majesté.

"I think that it is time that we had some food." Saul spoke slowly and carefully, enunciating each word with special precision so that no emotion would show in his voice. "While we're being served, I'll sign an order authorizing your brother's revival from judicial sleep on family grounds. You have my permission to take action on it personally."

"Yes, sir. Thank you, sir." Her face was losing its darker tinge of blood. "I will act on it personally."

"Very good. While we're waiting for our food, let's review the general food availability and distribution data."

And someday, perhaps I will learn to act, too.

6

When hard times come to the party, dignity is one of the first guests to leave.

Art sat on the thinly padded seat of the orange tractor, drove at a sedate six miles an hour along the shoulder of the fast lane of I-270 South, and tried to think less-clichéd thoughts. It wasn't easy when you were dressed like a clown. He wore a long purple raincoat, beneath which heavy sweaters and thick trousers swaddled his body. On his feet he had knee-length rubber boots, borrowed from Joe and two sizes too big. A blue baseball cap with a long peak, held in position by a knotted orange mohair scarf, protected his face and head from driving gusts of rain.

It would be nice to complain, but who would he complain to? The road was total chaos, a tangled mess of new cars and trucks, billions of dollars abandoned where they had died ten days earlier. Not only cars, either. The puttering old tractor had passed dozens of bodies, pulled off onto the shoulder of the road and left to the mercy of the crows that patrolled the highway in search of roadkill. The only clear route was on the same left-hand shoulder, so he had often been forced to leave it and snake his way through the obstacle course of dead vehicles.

He was not sorry to see the rainswept road empty of living people. Three hours earlier, as the downpour started, he had heard shooting off to his left. Not hunting. Hunters didn't use rapid-fire automatic weapons. Someone had managed to strip the smart microcircuits out of a modern machine gun and make the result work. Art patted the bag at his side. The old handgun that Ed had offered him—no, forced on him—was still there, along with a dozen clips of ammunition.

"Sure you won't need this," Ed had agreed. "So you can just return it when you get back here. Same with the maps. They're pretty out-of-date, some of 'em, but I still use 'em." And, as Art stared at Joe, steaming triumphantly uphill on the little tractor, Ed added, "You can bring that back, too. Never forget one thing, Art. Second-class riding beats first-class walking, any day of the week."

Art couldn't argue with that. He knew he would never make it on foot, with a bum knee and fifty-odd miles or more to go. The previous day's experience with Annie's horses had been less than encouraging. He had spent three hours staring at the rear end of two of them, trying to persuade the horses that his idea of a destination was superior to theirs. A tractor, even a slow and ancient one, was a gift from God.

He slung the waterproof bag of food and supplies over his shoulder, said, "See you, then," and climbed aboard.

"Watch that clutch when you use reverse," Joe called as Art began his stately progress down the gravel and dirt road. "Wish we were going with you."

The funny thing was, he meant it. Radio and television were dead, but as long as power was off everything in the big cities had to be a total disaster. And Joe and Ed, like anyone with an ounce of curiosity, wanted to *see* the chaos and destruction with their own irrational eyes. Even Art had the urge, though if it weren't for his need to know about the telomod treatment he'd have made curiosity secondary to safety.

The deep boom of an explosion, far off to his right, brought Art sharply back into the present. It was early evening, beneath sullen skies, and the flash created a bright splash of white in the dusk. He had started soon after midday, and already he was within the thirty-mile ring development zone that girdled Washington. Law enforcement ought to be better here than farther to the north. Based on what he was seeing and hearing, it was worse.

Should he just keep on driving, as long as he could? The tractor had no lights. But if he stopped, where would he sleep? He could drive off the road and stretch out by the tractor, but it was getting chilly and the rain seemed ready to go on all night. One thing for sure: no matter what he did, he was going to feel terrible in the morning.

It could be worse, Ferrand. You could be walking. And it could be even a lot worse than that.

One of the most haunting things that he had ever read was in an old book, *The Worst Journey in the World*, about Captain Scott's expedition to the South Pole. The group who made the final run to the Pole were half-starved on the way back, working on difficult terrain, in temperatures twenty to forty degrees below freezing. Scott's diary entry showed that Evans, a desperately sick member of the party, became comatose one afternoon and died the same evening. That same morning, Evans had been trying to pull a sled.

Why was he pulling? Because he had no choice.

You're getting old and soft, Ferrand. Here you are, riding in comfort. You have warm clothes and dry feet, and plenty of food. Keep going another few hours, you'll be at the Treasure Inn having a drink with Dana.

Art wiped raindrops from his face and peered at the road ahead. There was more than enough light to see where he was going. Most of it formed a faint reddish glow, reflecting from the low clouds. With electric power still off, that glow did not come from streetlights. Parts of the city to the south were burning. It was a bad omen for the success of his trip.

The tractor rode easily and quietly on its big balloon tires. At Art's fuel-conserving speed of six miles an hour, the sound of the engine was muted to a deep purr by its efficient muffler. He found himself drifting; in no danger of falling asleep, but hunched over the wheel, pursuing random thoughts, and allowing the faint gray strip of the road's shoulder to guide his way.

Minute after silent minute, mile after uneventful mile. The rain was heavier, but the gusty wind had dropped to nothing. The highway was a graveyard of abandoned cars and trucks. Time had frozen, until at last a rattle of gunshots brought Art back to full attention. The shooting didn't sound close, but it made him realize that he had no idea where he was. The high overhead highway exit signs were unlit, and the lower and perhaps more readable ones sat off by the right-hand lane. His watch had become a useless bracelet on March 14, so he didn't know how long he had been traveling. His stomach, an unreliable guide, suggested nine o'clock.

He steered over to the slow lane and watched for exit signs. One came into view after another quarter of an hour. He whistled when he was at last close enough to read it. He didn't need to pull out a map to tell him where he was. It was time to leave the main highway, and he was less than two miles from his destination. He had promised himself a nightcap at the Treasure Inn with Dana Berlitz, a fantasy just to keep him going. Now it seemed like a real possibility.

He took the curved exit ramp and trundled out onto Montrose Road. At the traffic light at Seven Locks he turned south. The signal wasn't working, and he had yet to meet anyone else on the road.

That changed within two minutes. Traveling in the opposite direction along the road, lights off, a dark car swept up to and past Art almost before he knew it was there. From the glimpse he caught of its elegant lines and long hood, it was a real antique; maybe a Rolls-Royce Silver Ghost, or perhaps a classic Lagonda touring model, a full century or more old. It was traveling at least seventy miles an hour.

As usual, the very rich would find a way. But now wealth had to be measured by actual possessions, birds in hand. Bank accounts mean nothing when you have lost electronic storage of records.

Much of the missing information would probably never be recovered. Too late to do anything about it, but this could be an excellent time to owe lots of money.

The main highway from the north had seemed odd only because of its emptiness. Seven Locks Road was far more unnerving. This was a rich residential area. To right and left he ought to see the cheerful glow of curtained windows and floodlit driveways. Instead he saw the dark bulk of seven-bedroom ghost-town houses, silent and grim. In places he drove through a rank, rancid odor that the rain could not hide.

But at last, a hundred yards ahead, stood the Treasure Inn. It was hardly visible from the road. No lit VACANCIES sign tonight. No lit anything.

Art throttled back to a slow walking pace and eased into the far corner of the parking lot. He turned the engine off and sat still for half a minute, listening. The inn, like everywhere else, was dark and quiet. It might mean that no one was here; or it might mean that someone was here and didn't want it known.

He slid off the tractor seat and stood for a minute, cursing his knee and stiff joints. As soon as he felt able to walk he set off around the parking lot, moving slowly and cautiously. It seemed deserted, until at the back of the lot he caught sight of a motorbike pushed deep into a thick hedge of forsythia.

He felt the engine. Cold. He crouched low beside the rear wheel, rummaged in his bag for a box of wooden matches, and cautiously lit one. The license tag had expired—*really* expired. It was for 1996, thirty years ago. But it was a Virginia plate. That was encouraging. To get here he'd have tried to ride anything, including a magic carpet. Dana and the others would be no different.

He stood up slowly, one hand on his stiff knee. Assuming that Dana had arrived on this bike and was at the inn, he still had a problem. How was he going to find her? Shouting her name didn't seem like a smart idea.

He was still straightening when he felt a hand grip his shoulder from behind. Before he could turn a soft voice said, "Shh. It's me."

"Christ! You'll give me a heart attack."

"Not so loud! Follow me."

Art's night vision was lousy. She was just a moving part of the darkness, but he blundered along after her in his too-big boots.

"How did you know I'd arrived?" he whispered after forty blind steps.

He heard an amused snort from in front of him. "Are you kidding? I could hear that thing you were riding when you were a quarter of a mile away. Let's hope no one else realized where you stopped. Come inside, we can talk normally once the door is closed."

He sensed the opening in front of him, held his hands out to make sure of the location of the doorjambs, and stepped inside. He still couldn't see a thing, but presumably she could. He kept moving, heard the door close behind him, and stood sniffing.

"What have you been doing in here?"

"Nothing you wouldn't do if you could. It's the oil." She moved around him and he heard her walk away. Eight steps, ten steps. A long pause, and then suddenly he could see.

He was in the bar of the Treasure Inn. Dana was standing at the counter, holding a jar with a flame at the top. "Vegetable oil burns all right," she said. "It just doesn't smell too good."

"You brought it with you?"

"Just the oil and the wick." She gave Art the smile he remembered, one that lit up the room better than the makeshift lamp. "I figured I'd find a jar or a can or something to put them in. Welcome to the Treasure Inn." She followed his look. "Yeah. I'm sorry I can't offer you a drink."

Art was staring across the counter, where on his previous visits hundreds of bottles had stood on the shelves in neat rows. Now there were just half a dozen—all empty. It was worse than that. The pump handles had been torn off, the mirrors smashed, the countertop marked with what seemed to be blows from an ax. He turned to examine the broken window blinds.

"It's all right," Dana said. "We face the hedge at the back of the parking lot. I checked, you can't see the light unless you're actually in the lot."

"Someone did a real job on this place."

"Yeah. They didn't just clean the place out. I don't know why, but they tore it to pieces, too."

"You don't remember the Turnabout riots in '07?" Art sat down on one of the bar stools, as though taking the weight off his leg. Suddenly he felt weak and fragile. "You ought to remember, you're certainly old enough."

"That's not very gracious, you know. I feel like an old woman tonight, but I don't need people telling me."

In the dim light, with her fine jawline and high cheekbones, Art thought she looked about twenty-one. He said nothing, and she went on, "I saw coverage of the riots, of course I did, but I was out of the country and I had other things on my mind."

"You were lucky. I was right here. Too much so. What were you doing?"

"The Great Rush."

"Antarctica? I was thinking about it only today. What the devil were you doing down there? You don't look like a prospector."

"I wasn't. I was twenty-four, divorced, trying for something exciting." She saw Art's doubtful expression. "No, I wasn't a hooker. There were lots of them there, but I was just a supplier's secretary. Two years, and it wasn't as much fun as I thought it would be. I made a fair amount of money, though—the prices were outrageous, and the merchants who supplied the goods and equipment did a lot better than the prospectors. But I missed the riots."

"Something best missed. If you'd been here at the time, you'd understand this." Art waved his arm around the ruined room. "You see, the first wave comes in and takes out anything worth taking—drinks mainly, in this case. I'm surprised they didn't take the chairs, but they don't look as though they'd burn. When the second wave comes in, and doesn't find anything worth having, they get real mad. So they smash the hell out of everything. And any more waves do the same thing, over and over. Get in their way, they'll kill you without even knowing who you are. This place got off easy. The Turnabouts would have set fire to it, sure as sure."

"They didn't just take the drinks." Dana pointed to the door that led through to the kitchen and dining room. "I hope you've eaten. They cleaned out every last bit of food. Even salt and spices."

"I've got food." Art patted his waterproof bag. "Did you eat?"

"Enough. I brought my own, too. I don't want any more."

"Well, maybe you'll join me in a drink." Art opened his mouth, then stopped and shook his head. "Either I'm way over-tired, or I'm going crazy. I was going to ask you if there was any ice."

"No power, no refrigeration, no ice. But never mind ice. I told you, there's no drink in this place."

"There is if you brought your own." Art opened his bag, reached inside, and with the air of a magician taking a rabbit from a hat pulled out a quart plastic bottle. "Anything to drink out of?"

"I thought you were kidding. Wait a minute." She went off through the door to the dining room, taking the makeshift oil light with her. Art had brought half a dozen candles from his mountain house, but he wasn't willing to waste one. Sitting in the darkness he unscrewed the plastic bottle top and took a small sip. He grimaced at Dana as she came back holding two measuring cups and a larger metal pan.

"I don't look gift horses in the mouth, Dana, but this isn't one of Ed O'Donnell's better efforts. We'll need water."

"Are you telling me that stuff's homemade?" She put the pan and cups down on the counter. "I don't know if I'm that desper-ate. But water, we have. I brought a bottle with me. There's a big tank down in the basement, too. I filled the pan earlier and it looks fresh, but I don't know if it's safe to drink."

"Boil it, and you can drink any water that doesn't actually taste poisonous. Let me have those." Art took the metal pan, dipped a measuring cup in to fill it halfway, and topped the cup from the plastic bottle. He took a trial sip, nodded, and handed the cup to Dana.

She stared at it suspiciously. "I thought you said you had to boil the water."

"To kill bugs and bacteria. But alcohol does the same th[illegible] just as well."

"So long as it doesn't kill me." She sniffed the liquid [illegible] measuring cup and wrinkled her nose. "How long ago [illegible] made?"

"You don't look for vintage labels on drink tha[illegible]

plastic screw-top bottles." Art made his own mix, using the same proportions of moonshine and water. He raised his cup. "Come on, Dana, I'm not using you as a test animal. You may not need this, but I do. Here's to ruin."

"We already have that. Here's to us." She raised her own cup and took a medium gulp. "Maybe I do need this. It's been quite a week. You never called me after that first time, you know."

"I sure as hell tried to. All I got was dead lines. I did reach two others, just yesterday. Morgan Davis and Lynn Seagrave. They said there was no chance they could make it, they're off across country and no transportation systems are working. But they told me they'd try to network some others." The drink was burning its way down through his digestive system, leaving a trail of pleasant heat behind it. "How did you make out? Any luck?"

"If you want to call it that. I tried a hundred times, but I only reached one person."

"Who?"

"Seth Parsigian."

The warm glow inside Art faded. "That figures. Did he say he'd be able to come here?"

"More than that. He's here already. He arrived before I did and left this." Dana handed over a piece of gray paper. On it, in meticulous block script, were the words: I WILL RETURN BY MORNING. I AM TAKING A LOOK AROUND.

"How did he get here?"

"I have no idea. Until you arrived my bike was the only thing in the parking lot. But you know Seth, he finds ways."

"Right. He was probably chauffeured here in a stretch limo." More from uneasiness than hunger, Art rummaged in his bag and came up with a loaf of Helen O'Donnell's home-baked bread and a slab of smoked ham. He hacked off pieces of both and handed them to Dana. Despite her claim to want no food, she took them and began to eat.

"We have to be logical about this," Art went on. "You may not like him much—"

"I don't like him at all."

"And I certainly don't care for him. But if anybody in the world can find a way to keep the telomod treatments going, it's Seth."

Maybe it was the feeling that the old world was ended. Maybe it was closeness and candlelight. But Art knew that he and Dana were breaking two unwritten rules of the treatment group. You said nothing to anyone of what you thought or knew about other members; and you kept your emotional distance from all of them. He and Dana were closer today than they had ever been in the three years he had known her. There was a protective logic at work. When Art joined, the group had forty-two members. Five of those had died, horribly, when the treatment failed and cancers ran riot all through their bodies. You knew what might happen to you, but you didn't want to be too near when it happened to someone else.

He tore off a piece of bread, bit savagely into it, and said, "So what makes you so down on Seth?"

"Nothing specific, just impressions." She avoided Art's eyes as she went on. "Look, I want to live, and so do you. We've fought hard for the right; but there are limits to what we'd do. I wouldn't sacrifice you to save myself, and I hope you feel the same about me. Seth probably regards that as weak and wimpy. I believe he wants to live so bad, if it would help his treatment he'd kill his own mother and serve her up for breakfast."

They went on eating and drinking in silence for a while. Art thought that Dana agreed with him, and he was surprised when she at last added, "I believe that Seth is much worse than you think. But he's here, and he may be the only other one of our group who ever shows up. You have to be ready to work with him."

"Oh, I'll work with him, don't you worry. In our situation we can't afford to get into fights among ourselves. I'll work with the devil if I have to. But if you don't agree that he's ruthless, why are you so negative about Seth?"

"Part of it's personal. You'll probably claim that it's a woman thing, but I don't like the way he looks at me and talks to me."

"He comes on to you?"

"Not in the usual way. If it were just that, I could handle it. Guys have been hitting on me since I was twelve years old. I mean, most guys. I don't mean you. You've never come on to me at all."

Could that be a hint—at a most improbable time? But Art only said, "Of course not. I'd be afraid to. How does he look at you and talk to you?"

"Speculatively. Like I'm a piece of flesh. Like, if I could just get you alone, where no one was likely to come along and interrupt . . ." She held the empty measuring cup out to Art. "I don't know what was in this, but I'm talking crazy. Forget what I just said. Pour me another."

"Catoctin Mountain Park legal limit: one per person."

"Really?"

"Yep. Trouble is, no one ever says what it's one of." It wasn't really a joke. He was pleased out of all proportion when she laughed, put her hand on his arm, and said, "I don't need to worry about Seth. I won't be alone, will I? You're here, too. I'll be all right."

"That's true, ma'am." Art filled the cups again. He tried to do it slowly and carefully, but his hand trembled. Mary hadn't been alone, either. He had been there with her, and what good had that done? She had only wanted to make a video for her own use, she would have given up the camera willingly.

But he tried not to think too much about Mary. Usually, except alone and late at night, he succeeded.

"Are you feeling all right?" Dana was staring at him with a worried look on her face.

"Tired, I guess." Art screwed the cap slowly back on the bottle and offered a cup to Dana. "It's been a long day."

"It sure has." She took the cup and slid off her stool. "Come on. Bring your bag, and we can talk as much as you like tomorrow. I'll drink this as a nightcap."

"Where are you going?"

"To bed." She picked up the lamp. "We don't know when Seth will get back, but I'm not going to sit up waiting."

"There are still beds here?"

"A few, in the upstairs rooms. I guess they were too much trouble to haul away and not worth smashing."

She led the way out of the bar, through the ruin that had once been the hotel restaurant, and up the stairway. The banister had been broken off, but the carpet was intact. Art, climbing painfully to the top floor, heard the rattle of hail or heavy rain on the roof above the landing.

"Listen to that. I'm glad I'm here, and not out in it."

"I'm glad you're here, too." She paused at one of the doors. "I'm in the next one along, so you may as well take this room. I checked it out earlier. The water's off, but the toilet will work—once."

"It will be fresh water in the tank. I don't want to waste it."

"That's your option. I'm going to use mine in the usual way. I'm not ready to give up completely on civilization. You say you have candles and matches?"

"Yes."

"Do you want to light one before I go?"

"No. It's all right. I'll manage."

"All right. Good night, then."

She continued to the next door, entered, and closed it. Art stood hesitating in the dark corridor for a few seconds. Finally he went and knocked on her door. "Dana?"

"What?"

"Do you have a gun?"

The door opened. She raised the lamp and stared at him. "I do not. I never learned how to use one. I'd be more danger to myself than anyone else."

"Well, I have one. Knock on the wall or come into my room if there's any trouble."

"I don't think there will be. But thanks." She closed the door again. Art headed into his own room, lit a candle, and stared around him. A bed with a mattress, but no pillow, sheets, or blankets.

He had real trouble sleeping without a pillow. If he took off his thick sweater, he could fold it up and put it under his head. But it was going to be a cold night, he'd need all the warm clothing he could get.

So he'd manage without a pillow. What did he expect, room service?

Art placed his gun carefully down by the side of the bed, where he could reach it in one movement. He blew out the candle, stretched himself on the bed, and pillowed his head on his hands. He was still trying to make himself comfortable when he heard a knock on the door.

"Yes?"

"Are you decent? I'm coming in."

Dana entered. She was in a thin white slip, and with the oil lamp held high she was a vision from another century. She carried a pillow under her arm, which she held out to Art. "Here. I found three of these in the back of the closet."

"Thanks." Art admired her dancer's legs and curved hips, wondered at the way she was dressed, and said, "Pillows. That's just what I was wishing I had. Are you going to sleep in that outfit? You'll freeze."

"I brought flannel pajamas and a few sweaters."

"Good."

She stood for a moment as though waiting for him to do or say something more. At last she nodded and said, "Good night, then."

She left. Art heard her door close, and the click as she locked it—something he hadn't bothered to do to his. He got up again, made his way to the door, and turned the lock. As he fumbled his way back to the bed he realized what all this reminded him of: one of the old farces, set in a hotel or a country house, knocking on bedroom doors, full of confusion and mistaken identities.

Except that he, Dana, and Seth Parsigian—if he returned—were the only people staying at the Treasure Inn. There would be no middle-of-the-night shenanigans. It was time to go to sleep, if he was to be good for anything in the morning.

He settled into bed again, much more comfortable with the pillow against his cheek. And he wondered. Was he the world's most stupid man? Dana had been wearing pants when he arrived at the Treasure Inn. You don't wear a slip *underneath* pants. And you don't put flannel pajamas and multiple sweaters on over a thin slip. Which meant she must have put the slip on in the past few minutes, before she came into his room, and she would take it off again before she went to bed.

Or was there a completely different explanation, which he was just too tired to see? Art gazed at the invisible ceiling, tried to think, and at once drifted off.

As always in the past ten years, he was a light sleeper. Sometime in the middle of the night he came awake, abruptly and uneasily. While he stared up into total darkness, the sound came again. It was the scream of something or someone in terrible pain.

Should he go and make sure that Dana was all right? But the sound was far away, nowhere inside the hotel. He could not even place a direction. Without a watch he had little idea of the time.

He lay and listened. The scream did not come again. The drum of rain on the roof had ended, and now the night was totally and unnaturally silent.

At last, waiting for a dawn that never seemed to arrive, he fell into the unsatisfying half sleep of present nightmares and old, happier memories.

7

Art woke to the faint sound of voices. It felt early, but when he opened his eyes the ceiling and walls of the room were strangely bright. He rolled out of bed, tested his arthritic knee gingerly before putting his weight on it, and limped over to the window.

Snow. Thick, large-flaked snow, falling steadily and already deep on the ground. No wonder everything was so bright.

What was the date? Almost the end of March. It was unusual in this area to have snow so late in the year, but not unheard of. Ten years ago snow had fallen in April. But not snow like this. Not a dense whiteout that reduced visibility to forty or fifty yards, covering plants that had been seduced by early warmth to a late spring stage of growth. If this year's harvest had been a question mark before, it was now a guaranteed disaster.

Art went across to the toilet and used it, but he did not flush it. He closed the lid and opened the tank, leaned over, and sniffed. It smelled fresh. He rubbed cold water on his face, dried himself using the sleeve of his sweater, and closed the tank.

He could no longer hear the voices. Still in his stockinged feet, he picked up his waterproof bag, opened the door, and headed downstairs. The person he would most like to have seen was Morgan Davis. Morgan was only in his early forties but he had lost all his hair before Art met him, either naturally or as a by-product of some dubious treatment preceding the telomod therapy. His smooth, well-shaped skull and even features combined with a thoughtful way of speaking and an urbane manner to suggest a distinguished Chinese elder. Everyone in the treatment group recognized his authority. If Morgan were here, Art would certainly be glad to hand over his own role in major decision making.

No such luck. Morgan was far-off in Arizona. The only people in the dining room were Dana—fresh-faced and lively, her light brown hair pulled back from her face—and Seth Parsigian.

At every previous meeting of the treatment group—which Parsigian insisted on calling the Lazarus Club—Seth had been groomed and coiffured and impeccably outfitted in expensive business suits. Now, dressed in dark gray pants and a slick black overcoat three sizes too big, he squatted over a tiny gas stove. His black hair had been trimmed to an uneven stubble, marked and furrowed by the scars of past surgery, and now it was wet with flakes of melting snow. Somehow, amid all the rain of the past weeks, Seth had acquired a heavy tan. He glanced up at Art with alert, dark brown eyes and grinned.

"Hey there, big boy. Slept well, eh? You must have a real clear conscience."

The old incongruity, Middle Eastern looks and polished manner combined with a West Virginia good-old-boy accent, had vanished. Art felt that he was seeing Seth clearly for the first time. Here was the real man, poised, primitive, and confident, crouched over a pan of snow melt.

"No one else made it?" Art spoke to Dana, but it was Seth who answered.

"Anybody with any sense will be holed up someplace, 'til it's over. It's real rough out there."

"The weather?" Art recalled the agonized scream in the night.

"That, too." Seth jiggled the pan impatiently. "Come on, you. Boil."

"You brought the stove with you?" Art put down his bag, opened it, and felt around inside.

"Let's just say, I came across it. I knew from bein' here yesterday there was plenty of propane, a couple of five-hundred-gallon tanks of it down in the basement. Too heavy to haul out, I guess, without equipment."

Art, with a mixture of satisfaction and regret, pulled the jar of coffee crystals from his bag and handed it to Dana. Seth saw it, and his eyes gleamed.

"Now we're smokin'. Where'd you scrounge that, boy? I've not smelled coffee for a week."

"Let's just say, I came across it. Here's sugar, too." Art felt an odd reluctance to mention to Seth his hideaway up on Catoctin

Mountain. Yet he knew he would have no hesitation in giving details of the place to Dana, or even in taking her there. "What were you going to do with the hot water?"

"Boil rice. I got me a fifty-pound bag. White rice, I'm afraid." Teeth gleamed in the dark face. "Not nutritionally balanced, you know. Maybe we'll all get sick."

"Sick *again*," Dana said. She put the jar of coffee crystals down on the floor, straightened up, and began to pace around the ruins of the dining room. "Not if I have anything to do with it. I've been too close to death once. I don't care what you two do, but I'm heading for the Institute. Snow or no snow, I have to find out what our chances are."

Seth stared up at her from where he squatted. "Hey, girl, easy. There's a whole lotta day left yet."

Art stood up and went over to Dana. "Of course we're going to the Institute," he said gently. "We didn't come all this way *not* to go. But you need to travel on a full stomach. First you have something to eat and drink."

"I'm not hungry."

"I believe you. Before I entered the telomod program, my old doctors tried multiple drug antimetabolite chemotherapy. Did they do the same to you?"

"Sure they did. It didn't work, though—nothing worked. I tried the telomod as a last resort."

"Same with all of us. Right, Seth?"

"Too damn right."

"So, Dana, do you remember what the chemo did to you?"

"Of course I remember. I'll never forget. It didn't help with the cancer, but it stripped the lining of my mouth and throat and esophagus. They were raw. I couldn't swallow."

"You couldn't eat. So what did you do?"

"You know what I did. The same as you did, the same as we all did. I ate. I cried with every swallow. It took me two hours to force down a milk shake. But I ate. I knew I'd die if I didn't."

She walked back to where Seth was still sitting patiently by the stove. He had made a pan of coffee, and another pan was heating more water. "Here. You'll need this with the rice." She handed over a blue container of salt. "You're right, Art, of course you are. But we're so *close*. The Institute is less than a mile away. I thought of going there last night, but it was dark by the time I arrived and it was raining hard."

"Raining, then snowing," Seth said.

Art sat down on the floor opposite Seth, stretching his stiff leg out in front of him. "You went there, didn't you?"

Dark eyes gleamed. "Now why'd you think a thing like that?"

"If you hadn't, you'd have an itch inside worse than ours. You'd be keener than Dana to get out of here and over there."

"That easy to read, am I? Well, maybe I'll surprise you yet." Seth dumped a measuring cup of rice into boiling water and threw a pinch of salt in after it. "But you're quite right. I went over to the Institute late last night."

Art sipped sweetened black coffee. He felt his whole body beginning to wake up. "What did you find?"

"Nothing worth mentionin'—or I'd have mentioned it already. The Institute was the way it ought to be at night. Locked. I tried the doors. Dead bolts. I tried the bells, and they didn't work. No surprise, the automatic guards and security systems aren't functioning. I didn't try shouting, and I won't try shouting today. Were you thinkin' of shouting?"

Art shook his head. "No way."

"So why not?"

"Just listen. It's completely quiet outside. We're strangers here, but it shouldn't be this quiet without a good reason. Where are the people, and what are they doing?"

Seth raised himself from his crouched position, walking about the room to stretch his legs and leaving Art and Dana to make sure that the cooking rice did not boil over. "Where are the people, eh? You been livin' in the city the past week and a half?"

"No. Far from it." Again, Art felt a reluctance to give details to Seth.

"Well, if you had you'd be able to take a good shot at answerin' your own question. Maybe you can anyway."

Art said nothing.

Seth was over by a window, staring out at snow that fell as heavily as ever. After a moment he went on, "I'm in the shipping business—or I guess I should say I used to be. 'Til eleven days ago Supernova Alpha was givin' us wild weather, but nothin' that the system couldn't handle. Shipments from South America and South Africa were spotty an' gettin' worse, but the freight monorails were bringing supplies in regular from anywhere on this continent. Some folk were even sayin' it was no bad thing if food stockpiles were comin' down. The recom ag protocols can grow strawberries on a salt heap, so they say, and we've had gluts an' more and more long-term storage for the past decade. Be nice to pull 'em down a bit.

"Then, twelve days ago, March 14, Day of Infamy 'cept we had nobody to blame an' flame, Nature stopped playing around an' crapped all over us.

"When the gamma burst hit an' all the microchips went belly-up"—it was Art's first confirmation that what he had told Ed O'Donnell and Joe Vanetti was correct—"I knew we were in trouble, but I don't think anybody had any idea how much. I sure didn't. I mean, power went out, but we've had outages before. The Antifed blowout in '16 shut the whole damn grid down for eight days, how could anything be worse than that? Next day, though, I couldn't get a telcom working, or a van, or a credit machine. There were a dozen big holes around the city, where heavy lifters just dropped out of the sky. Nobody knew what the government was doing—if it still existed. I chose my place, stockpiled all I could, and went to ground. I might be there still, if Dana hadn't called. Though I have to say, I was gettin' awful itchy to find out what was happenin' at the Institute." Seth pulled back his sleeve to reveal three spots of light blue. "There's the reminder, my treatment session comin' up in six weeks—not that I need reminding, any more than you do. That's why we're here. It's why we're even *alive,* when logically we ought to be dead. Lazarus Club members might not like each other much"—Seth winked at Art, as though he knew more than he was saying—"but we can rely on each other for one thing: a strong interest in living.

"But what about the rest of the people? I don't mean the whole continent. I don't give a damn about that. I mean this city and the area around it. There's fifty million people here—no, forget that. Let's say, twelve days ago there *were* fifty million. It's been twelve days now without power. Twelve days since water came out of the faucets, twelve days since food supplies came in from outside, twelve days since a news broadcast system existed, twelve days since money or government could do anything for you."

"It takes longer than twelve days—" Dana began. But she stopped, and turned her head back down to the little stove.

"Longer than that, for people to die of starvation?" Seth walked to where Art had snagged a few grains of rice with his knife and was tasting them to see if they were cooked. "Yeah. It does. But it only took three or four days for some people to figure out that no one had any idea how long the problem would go on—we still have no idea, least, I don't. An' I live—lived—half a mile from the White House. Wouldn't you think it ought to be safe there, if anywhere could be? But by the sixth day I decided to get out. Too many corpses for my taste. An' I could hear gunfire around the clock. Most guns have smart circuits for automatic aiming and target motion compensation, so they won't work anymore. My guess was, for every shot I heard there must have been fifty people stickin' each other with knives or bangin' away with clubs and axes."

"So how did you get out of there?" Dana asked. "I mean, if it was so dangerous."

Seth grinned at her. "I'm not always the high-class gent you see today. I had to do a little slice-and-dice of my own before I was out of the city. No big deal, nothin' to get excited about. But I managed. That rice cooked yet?"

Art nodded to Dana. She began loading it onto flat pieces of hardboard made by breaking a ruined painting into three parts. The kitchens had been emptied of all the plates, and the hardboard fragments were her best approximation. The original picture had showed a group of pirates burying treasure. Art, turning his piece over before Dana loaded it, found he was looking at a bearded bare-chested man, a sandy strip of beach, and the prow and foredeck of a sailing ship in the background.

"So what's your answer?" he asked. "Where are the people?"

Seth took a load of rice and went back to the window. "What do you think, maestro? I already said my piece."

"I've not been close to things, the way you have, but nothing you've said surprises me. A lot of people are dead, maybe thousands, and everyone else is going to lie low until the government gets hold of things again, or folks become so starved and desperate that they think they have nothing to lose."

"Not far off." Seth was eating rapidly, with no sign of reduced appetite at the thought of heaps of corpses within twenty miles. "But you're too optimistic. I'd say you got a few thousand dead where there's big food warehouses and the pressures are less. In the inner cities, though, it's more than that by now. And the starvation and disease are just startin', not to mention rats and flies and polluted water and no food. Things are going to get a lot worse before they get better."

Art glanced across at Dana, wondering how all this talk of death was affecting her. She was nodding thoughtfully and eating as heartily as Seth. When it came to the crunch, she in her own way was as tough as anybody.

"From what I saw coming over here," she said, "you might both be optimistic. I must say, I didn't waste time stopping to look—the first sign of trouble, I was up to seventy miles an hour and long gone—but I saw plenty of dead bodies. And I passed through whole subsections in the suburbs where the smell was just awful. I only saw one cleanup group, and they were pulling a wheeled trailer by hand."

"Not today, though." Seth laid his emptied makeshift plate on the broad windowsill. "This snow is the best thing that could have happened to us. Nobody'll be outside who doesn't have to be. How long 'til you're ready to leave? We don't know how long it's goin' to stay this way, might as well take advantage."

"Two minutes." Art swallowed a final mouthful of rice, washed it down with coffee, and followed Dana out of the dining room.

"I don't know how you felt," he said softly, when Seth was safely out of hearing, "but I think he may have more to do with the number of dead bodies back in the city than he wants to admit."

She turned to him and dropped her voice. "I'd bet on it. There's something I ought to have told you last night, but I didn't because we've never talked about other group members before. Did you know that Seth was once put on trial for murder?"

"He told you that?"

"No, and I never asked him. When I first met him I remembered reading about it. He was accused of blowing up three of his partners on a boat off Cape May. They were planning to push him out of their business."

"He was acquitted; he must have been."

"Right. Good lawyer, tainted evidence. But that doesn't mean he was innocent."

"I'm sure he wasn't. You heard that 'a little slice-and-dice.' Did you see the gun in his belt when he stood up and his coat was open? I've never seen him wearing clothes before that looked anything like that—and his coat's too big for him."

Dana, who had reached the top of the stairs, turned to look down on Art. "Honey, you know my views on Seth. I'm not his number one fan, and I'll take you over him any day of the week. But last night he's not the one who arrived wearing somebody else's rubber boots. And I let *you* into my bedroom."

"That's different. Those boots were loaned to me by Joe Vanetti." But her point was valid. Seth might have friends, too, though he had the guarded, watchful eyes of a natural loner.

Dana, before she went into her room, added to that idea. "Forgetting the gun and knife and coat," she said, "I'll tell you one thing about Seth. I've never seen him look as much at ease anywhere as he does here and now. He seems *right* for this situation. He's at home. That's scary, but it may be just what we are going to need."

As Art went into his own room he wondered if he would be able to protect Dana from Seth if the need arose. He doubted it. He might be ruthless enough—he believed he could be—but Seth was better armed, younger, and fitter. Art pulled on the outsized boots. More agile, too. Could you walk through snow in these damned things, or would it all be hopeless floundering?

He donned the purple raincoat and the blue baseball cap, but drew the line at tying the mohair scarf over it. Instead he knotted it around his neck under his coat. The handgun went into the raincoat pocket, baggy and shapeless enough that one more bulge made little difference.

By comparison, Dana was a fashion plate. She wore a form-fitting jacket and pants of slick dark blue kevlon, black knee-high boots, and a jaunty black cap with built-in earmuffs. Art met her at the top of the stairs. He looked at her appreciatively but dubiously, until she said, "Fully thermal, though they don't look it. Don't worry, Grimaldi, I'll be a lot more comfortable than you will."

Her words were reassuring. Seth Parsigian's expression, when they joined him in the dining room, was not. Art wondered what Seth would have done had he not been there. And then he knew. Until they had been to the Institute, and determined the status of the telomod treatment program, nothing would sway Seth—or Art himself—from pursuit of the main purpose.

At stake was something more important than sex. At stake was life and death.

8

Seth led the way as they emerged from the inn. Since early morning a wind had arisen. Instead of falling vertically the snow formed drifts along the side of the building and had buried the hedge of flowering forsythia. Overhead, the sky glowed with a leaden, heavy light. If old weather patterns still meant anything after Supernova Alpha, more hours of heavy snow were on the way.

The highway was deserted. Snow piled against the wheels and doors of abandoned cars, while smaller humps by the side of the road suggested more ominous possibilities. Art felt no urge to investigate. He noticed that last night's sickly odor had vanished from the air, cleansed for the moment by the snow cover.

The bulk of the Institute for Probatory Therapies formed a faint gray outline through the swirling flakes. Its twenty stories loomed far above the surrounding buildings. Art recalled, with no pleasure at all, that the telomere research center was on the fifteenth floor. Even if they could find a way in, the elevators would certainly not be working.

"We can try the ground-level entrances again, like I did last night," Seth said softly. "But I think it'll be a waste of time. Our best bet's a fire escape. Dana, you're the lightest and the nimblest. If the two of us give you a hoist . . ."

"I get it. Then I'll be the one guilty of breaking into government property." But she sounded cheerful at the prospect, and as they approached the building she pulled a long, heavy wrench from the pocket of her pants.

"You had that thing with you last night?" Art asked.

"I certainly did." She gave him her sunniest smile. "Be prepared, as my old troop leader used to say. You only asked if I had a gun."

They had all been speaking in near whispers, keeping sounds to a minimum. As they moved around the Institute, looking up for the black metal filigree of a fire escape, Art realized that the silence was about to end. Entering the locked building could not be done quietly. The sound of breaking glass would carry far across the hushed landscape. Their only hope was that no one would decide to come and investigate.

The snow-covered bottom of the fire escape was at least ten feet above ground level. Art planted his feet firmly and braced himself with his hands on the wall of the building. Seth stood by his side, using his own interlocked hands to provide Dana with a first foothold. She went up easily, first to waist level, then to place one foot on Art's shoulder and the other on Seth's.

"I'm not quite high enough." Her voice came from above their heads. "I'll have to jump and grab. Are you ready?"

Art grunted assent. There was a sudden and painful increase in weight on his shoulder and a shower of dislodged snow. He looked up. Dana was hanging from the bottom of the fire escape, which swung lazily downward under her weight. He and Seth grabbed it as it approached ground level. As soon as her feet touched the ground, Dana stepped around the descending ladder and started up it.

"I'm past this," she complained. "You need a junior gymnast, not an old lady." But she was already two floors up.

"Go on." Seth gestured to Art. "It will swing back up as soon as we're off it. We don't want to leave anybody with a ready-made entrance."

Dana was up at the third floor, crouched by a window. Art hated heights, but he knew he would get no sympathy from the others if he stopped to explain that. He climbed, approaching Dana as she swung her wrench. The sound of breaking glass was incredibly loud. It went on and on, ringing out into the distance as Dana broke away the jagged edges of the hole she had made. Art, just below her, turned to stare out through the falling snow. It had eased off a little. He could see for maybe half a mile. On all that white plain, nothing moved. He followed Dana, scrambling carefully past the jagged edges of the broken window to land on all fours on top of a metal desk. The surface was icy to his hands, and his breath frosted the air. It was as cold inside the building as outside.

He climbed down, feeling his heart pounding. Was it relief at escape from outside danger, or fear of what they might find on the fifteenth floor? If the telomod treatment was no longer available, he and Seth and Dana were dead. Not dead immediately, not maybe for six months or a year, but dead.

Without a word, they left the room. It had been some kind of administrative center, with cabinets and lifeless terminals and blank displays scattered in among the broken file trays and desks. Useless junk, Art thought. Objects from a past age, which looters hadn't even thought worth stealing. Would they ever have value again?

No lights showed on the central bank of elevators, with their smashed-in doors. It was going to be stairs, then, twelve more stories of them. Art put his head down, ignored his knee, and climbed steadily in the lightless stairwell. It was a consolation, when they came at last to the fifteenth floor and emerged into the building's dim interior light, to see Dana and Seth panting as hard as he was. His daily walks on Catoctin Mountain were paying off.

"Now we find out," Seth grunted, and hurried forward. Dana went after him. Art, much more slowly, followed. He had given up hope of finding Doctors Lasker, Chow, and Taunton, the three key members of the telomod research group, here at the Institute. Now it was a question of discovering where they had gone, following them, and persuading them to continue treatments.

And then that was no longer the question. Art knew the truth before he entered the lab. Even in the freezing air, the scent of corruption filled his nostrils. He stepped forward, to where Dana and Seth stood in silence at the open double doors.

The lab had always been messy, but with the organized messiness of a medical research facility. Now it was a chaos of broken glassware, smashed electronic equipment, and overturned furniture. A pitched battle had taken place here, in among the long workbenches.

What had they been fighting over? Probably something as simple as food or fresh water. There were plenty of genome readers, scanning probe microscopes, and gas chromatography units, but the big jars of distilled water on the lab shelves had all vanished.

In any case, the reason for the fight did not much matter. And the outcome had been inevitable. With fists and improvised clubs against guns and knives, the staff of the Institute hadn't had a chance. It had been a planned attack, too, with assistance from someone on the inside, because the doors and windows of the Institute showed no signs of an earlier break-in.

Seth stepped forward and paced the cluttered space between two of the benches. He stopped halfway along. "Here's Dr. Mackerras," he said, softly and without emotion. "And here's Janina—she was the lab technician who gave me my treatment. I always liked her." He took two more steps and leaned over a body. "I think this is Dr. Chow, but his name tag's gone. And half his face has been blown away."

Dana and Art, without a word, separated and began their own inspection of the space between and around the workbenches.

"Dr. Rothstein," she said after a few seconds. "And Gil Senta—he was the first person to interview me, when I wanted to join the program. Here's somebody I don't recognize—probably from outside, he's dressed differently. Dr. Lasker is underneath Gil. Looks like she died of gunshot wounds. Three of them, in the head."

Art seemed to be the lucky one, if that was the right word for it. The aisle along which he walked was a jungle of shattered glass and twisted metal, but he saw no people. Then he turned the corner, and wasn't lucky after all. Four bodies, ice-cold when he moved them to see their faces, lay tangled together.

"Dr. Taunton is here," he said. He did his best to keep his voice neutral, as Seth and Dana had done. They would realize, without histrionics or explanations on his part, that his words spelled doom for all of them. Dr. Taunton was the third member of the triumvirate. The three leaders of the telomod treatment group were all dead, and telomod therapy still had a big experimental component. Even if living members of the Institute's support staff could be found, they lacked the knowledge needed to adapt treatments to changing circumstances.

Art kept walking the aisles. The damage to equipment, when you looked at it more closely, was not so bad as at first sight. Given good technicians—and electrical power, and spare parts, and working microchips—it might be made to work again. None of those things was available; but nothing was so complete a disaster as the loss of the top brains of the program.

Seth Parsigian had given up on his own inspection. He climbed on top of one of the workbenches and sat cross-legged amid the mess. His arms were folded, and he hunched forward with his head bowed.

"All right," he said as Dana and Art walked over to join him. "We got us a setback. Question is, where do we go from here?"

"They're dead," Dana said. She clutched Art's arm, hard. "All of them. Even if some technicians got away, they don't know enough to help."

"Maybe in some other city, on the West Coast . . ." Art said. But as he spoke he knew he was offering false hope. The telomod treatment group had drawn its members from all over the country. There were even a couple from Asia and Europe. Why would they come all the way to the Institute if the same thing could be found anywhere?

Seth picked up a long splinter of glass and fingered its edge. "No, no. It's hard enough to travel locally. We'd be chasing rainbows lookin' for another group someplace. Anyway, we don't have time for that."

Finally he raised his head, to stare at the other two. "We're down to long shots. How much risk are you willing to take?"

"Anything," Dana said at once. Art nodded agreement, but he was thinking: *Down to long shots? Wasn't this trip to the Institute* already *a long shot?*

"Any amount of risk," he said. "If I knew what to do. Do you have something in mind?"

"Oh, yes." Seth acted amused—there was a smile on his face, no matter how little it seemed to belong there. "How long since you joined the telomod program?"

"Nearly three years," Art said, and Dana added, "Closer to four for me—my anniversary is next month."

"That right? Me, I'm one of the old-timers—in the program near five years, started when they didn't hardly know what they was doin'. Got scars to prove it. And I got a lot more years to go, touch wood." Seth slapped the black bench top, which was hardened plastic. "I'm not about to give up."

Dana glanced at Art, a look that said, *Is Seth losing it? What's he talking about?*

"Back then," Seth went on, "Lasker and Taunton were already involved. Dr. Chow arrived four months after I had my first shot of telomerase inhibitor, two months after my tumors started shrinking and I began to think I might have some kind of chance. Old Chinaman Chow was a new boy compared to me. And 'cause I was one of the first, I heard some of the old history, back before my time. See, Lasker and Taunton knew what they were doing, but the techies round the labs told me they weren't the brains behind the project. The real genius, the spark who started things going here, he was somebody else."

"I never heard of anybody like that," Art said slowly. "And I think I've met most people around the Institute."

"Yeah. See, he was never at the Institute. He was a big-brain research scientist, doing his own thing at some ol' college. He never had a hands-on role in the application of telomod therapy, but he knew more about the basics than anybody. And I'd bet money—if money meant anything now—that you did hear of him."

"I'm sure I didn't."

"Me neither," Dana added.

"Ah. Neither of you ever heard of a man called Guest?"

"Never," Dana said, while Art stood staring.

"*Oliver* Guest? *Doctor* Oliver Guest?" Parsigian laughed aloud at the expressions of understanding and disbelief on their faces. "Ah, now you're gettin' there."

"Grisly Guest," Dana said.

"The child murderer," added Art.

"One and the same." Seth nodded casually. "From around these parts, too. Local boy makes good."

"But he worked on clone research, not telomod therapy," Dana objected. "The clone king. He knew more about cloning than anybody. At least, that's what they reported during the trial."

"He did telomods, too. A real broad-gauge maniac, old Oliver. You didn't hear about him from the telomod group, because he wasn't somebody the project was goin' to advertise when it went lookin' for grants and experimental subjects. His name was a no-no at the Institute. But I checked him out after I heard. He started the whole ball rolling for the telomod treatment. Without him our program wouldn't exist. Then he got a bit sloppy, and they nabbed him for his after-hours hobby."

"He was found guilty," Art said. "Fifteen children—"

"—eighteen, by the time they was all done. Found guilty, and iced down for six hundred years. He was under forty when it happened. Which means that he ought to be alive now, in that Q-5 judicial sleep place down south of here where they put the weirdo cases. Wake him up, and he can treat us. If we can get to where he is, through all the shit that's flyin' around since Supernova Alpha. *And* if he's alive, I don't know how quick they spoil when they're not bein' looked after. *And* if we can *control* him, so he don't add us to his little list. That one may be the toughest—I reckon he's one smart and crazy son of a bitch."

Seth pushed himself off the bench. Hot, dark eyes challenged Art and Dana. "See now why I ask you: How much do you want to live? How much risk you willing to take?"

How much do you want to live?

Art lay on his bed at the Treasure Inn, shivered in spite of his warm clothes, and tried to answer the question.

It had been on his mind as they struggled back from the Institute through a whiteout blizzard that reduced visibility to a few yards; on his mind as they cooked and ate rice and beans; on his mind as darkness descended early, and the chances of anyone else reaching the inn faded to zero. On his mind now, in the middle of a long night when he could not sleep and time seemed to have stopped.

How much do you want to live?

The faint creak of the opening door would not have awakened a sleeper. It brought Art to full alert and had him reaching for the gun at his bedside.

"Who's that?" He was ready to fire into the darkness.

"Dana." She spoke in a whisper. "I'm sorry, I didn't mean to wake you."

"You didn't. I can't sleep. What do you want?"

"Nothing special. I just didn't want to stay in my room. It's next to Seth's, and I could hear him prowling and prowling. I don't know if he ever sleeps."

"Everybody sleeps—even Seth. Maybe he feels as wound up as I am. What were you going to do here?"

"Nothing. Feel a bit less nervous, I guess. I was going to stretch out on the floor."

"No need for that. It's a double bed." He felt he had to add, "Don't worry, you'll be safe with me."

He heard a skeptical grunt in the darkness. "Sure. How many times have I heard that line? In another universe, before I got sick, before Supernova Alpha. Come into my bed, you'll be safe with me." The mattress dipped to the left under her added weight. "*You can trust me;* men have been saying that since I was twelve years old. It's one of the three big lies. Move over."

Art slid to the right, at the same time as a groping hand touched his.

"My God. You're *freezing*. No wonder you can't sleep. Here, this will help."

He felt a rough blanket laid over him, and a warm body moved against his. It was hardly a personal contact—there were layers of clothing between them. But it was oddly soothing.

Soothing. What did it say about your age and condition, when you found the midnight arrival of an attractive woman in your bed *soothing*?

"He's not really asking us, you know." Dana's voice was muffled against his shoulder.

Art didn't have to inquire who and what. "You're right. Seth's going to do it anyway, no matter what we want. The only question is, do we help?"

"It will be illegal—though I don't think there's much law enforcement at the moment. And it will be dangerous. The media didn't have anything good to say about Oliver Guest, but they agreed on one thing. He is brilliant, and he's ruthless. We'd be releasing a monster. Could we control him?"

"I don't know." Already, Art was feeling warmer and more relaxed. "Maybe we ought to think of it this way: If Seth brings Oliver Guest out of judicial sleep, are his chances of controlling Guest better if we are involved?"

"I think they are, but that's still not the real issue." Dana wriggled, the contours of her body fitting more comfortably against Art's. "I don't trust Seth—I do trust you, or I wouldn't be here—but he does have a way of asking the key question. For a chance to go on living, how far are we willing to go?"

"And what's your answer?"

"What's yours?"

"You show me yours and I'll show you mine. I think we need to wait and see."

"That's a cop-out." Dana snuggled closer and put her arm over Art's chest. "Let's not debate it tonight."

"Mm." With warmth came mental ease, and a desire for sleep. Art, who only a few minutes ago had expected to be awake all night, could feel himself beginning to lose focus, moving into the state where thoughts lose their sharp edges.

How much of human communication was done without words? He and Dana talked of making a decision, but he knew that their decision was already made: they would do whatever they had to do, within (and perhaps beyond) reason. They would seek out Oliver Guest.

And after that?

How much do you want to live?

A lot.

Maybe, in their own ways, he and Dana were no different from Seth Parsigian.

9

From the secret diary of Oliver Guest.

I have observed a characteristic pattern in those whose ways wander far from socially acceptable behavior. It applies equally to bigamists, confidence tricksters, thieves, and murderers. Thus:

At first, extreme caution is practiced. Every record is deleted, every step is double-checked, no trace of physical evidence is allowed to remain.

With continued success comes a change in attitude. Since I have not been caught, I am smarter than judicial control; therefore, I will not be caught. *So runs the false logic. Contempt for law increases. Behavior becomes more and more sloppy. The trail is no longer erased, physical evidence is left behind, the fruits of crime are introduced into the household. At last—often, it is true, after an amazingly long time—a final and fatal error is made; the authorities descend.*

Having noticed such behavior patterns I was careful to avoid them. I took nothing from my victims that anyone would ever be able to measure. No physical evidence of my avocation was permitted in my house. I never used the same collection procedure twice, since repetitive actions can lead to the development of a psychological profile.

Even so, I allowed for the possibility that I might one day become a suspect. In such a situation it was then predictable that my property would be searched. I made special provisions to insulate and isolate the subbasement level of my house, but even if that other lab were discovered, the work going on there had no apparent relevance to crime. It would seem to be an independent, if unconventional, research activity.

How, then, was I caught?

Attend, those of you with urges that you are powerless to resist. We are, every one of us, slaves to chance and the compulsions of our own natures.

My would-be nineteenth victim was a beautiful girl, just fourteen, with lustrous dark hair and skin, and startling blue eyes. LaRona lived in a filthy apartment, sharing it with five noisy siblings by different fathers and with a blank-eyed mother whose intelligence barely was able to correlate intercourse with subsequent birth.

I saw LaRona during one of my scouting visits to the poorest districts. I never went twice to the same area, unless of course I spotted a candidate there. After observing LaRona on a dozen separate occasions, twice walking past the open door of the apartment where she lived—empty boxes in the hallway, smells of grease and mildew and human excrement—I knew that I must act. I had in my collection nothing remotely like LaRona, no one with her coloring, her walk, or the lapidary quality of her jeweled eyes. It would be a kindness to remove such a perfect creation from so awful a setting. Foul play would probably never be suspected. Any rational investigator, examining the circumstances of LaRona's life in the apartment and her disappearance, would conclude that she had wisely run away from the intolerable.

I made my preparations.

Luring LaRona directly away from the apartment complex would be impossible. Mere survival there required wariness, and during my visits I had been careful to adopt clothing that fitted the setting. No one in her right mind would trust such a man with anything. However, the mother was once more pregnant by yet another transient father. And LaRona, the only remotely responsible member of the family, had taken it upon herself to make sure that her mother visited the nearest clinic for periodic examination and remedial medications.

My medical reputation was, if I say so myself, outstanding. An offer of pro bono services, which I explained to the clinic I did for one month each year, was welcomed. On my first day I examined the records for LaRona's mother. They were disgusting. I offered to take responsibility for all nonstandard clinical tests, and for the preparation and administration of tailored antibodies.

LaRona and her mother came in as scheduled. I explained to them—or rather to LaRona, since her mother appeared to understand nothing—that we had a problem with incipient Paget's disease. It would not affect her mother now, but if left untreated it would lead to chronic inflammation of the bones and their eventual softening. My diagnosis, prognosis, and proposed treatment were all completely accurate. I did not mention that Paget's disease is a problem for the elderly, and that the symptoms would not manifest themselves for many years. Nor did I offer my opinion that in view of the mother's lifestyle, her survival until she became elderly was highly unlikely.

LaRona listened to me with total attention and understanding. She was eye-achingly, mouth-wateringly beautiful. I longed to possess her forever.

Patience, *I said to myself,* patience.

LaRona and her mother would come to the clinic for six consecutive days. Her mother would be partially sedated for two hours. During those two hours I would administer the designed organism that would cure the disease. And in those same two hours, although it was not described in any treatment record or agreed to in advance, I intended that LaRona and I would sit and talk to each other.

We did. Slowly and awkwardly at first, but by the third day she was telling me of her dreams and hopes and aspirations. Shyly, she admitted to me that she wanted to become a physician. Just like you, she said. I doubted that. But incredibly, in that hellhole where she lived, she was observing diseases and attempting to make her own diagnoses.

While her mother lay snoring we wandered through the clinic together. I tested her. What did she think was wrong with that man's hand? Why did that woman's neck bulge so oddly? How would you treat it? She answered, I lectured, she questioned, I explained. Hours of bliss, and not only for me. She swooped on facts and theories and drained every drop of blood from them. It reminded me of my own youth, when new knowledge filled the world.

Our golden time had to end. On the sixth and final day of her mother's treatment, I went down to the basement lab of my home and prepared my collection kit. I emptied the back of my car. The next few hours were my unavoidable period of vulnerability, when a sharp judicial officer seeing LaRona and the collection kit together could correlate means and crime.

Mother was sedated for her treatment. Instead of ranging through the clinic, today I took LaRona into the little office allocated to me. She brought with her, faint but unmistakable, a delicate odor of gardenias. There was a medical research conference going on north of the city, I said. I was heading there as soon as her mother's treatment ended. Would LaRona possibly be interested in going with me? I could have her back by nine o'clock. I was careful to say, "back at the clinic." Dr. Oliver Guest, of course, had no idea where she lived.

She hesitated. "What about Mother?"

"She'll be all right. She knows her own way home, doesn't she?"

Neither of us suggested that her mother might like to go with us. Nor was I about to offer to drive Mother home. I had always been careful to take public transportation when visiting LaRona's district. There was no way that I would risk my car being seen there.

It was a foregone conclusion, as I had known it would be. To visit a medical research conference, LaRona would have agreed to send her mother home by parcel post.

Treatment ended. Mother was informed by LaRona that she wanted to do some shopping and would come home later. I was not mentioned. It was a dull day in February. As we drove away from the clinic it was already close to dusk.

Earlier in the day I had set our destination in the car's AVC system. Someone older and more sophisticated would have been suspicious of the place to which the vehicle took us, a parking lot for an entertainment center open only during the summer months. LaRona was too happy and excited to notice. She babbled on about what she had seen earlier in the day. While I had been busy providing

Mother with final—and, I suspect, futile—instructions for monitoring her own condition, LaRona had seen a human clone enter the clinic.

I listened with half an ear, and looked around carefully to make sure that the place was deserted. It was a popular venue for illicit sexual liaisons, but today no other car was present. I surreptitiously reached into the door compartment on my left-hand side, where the killing spray was ready and waiting.

At that crucial moment she asked, "Why is it more difficult to clone an organism from an adult than a fetal cell?"

Every rational brain cell told me to proceed, to use the spray, to perform the collection process. I needed only ten clear minutes and all evidence would be hidden away. But she was touching on twin passions of mine, clones and telomeres. I could not resist. With the spray can sitting in my left hand, I explained. A clone developed from adult cells would be born with its telomeres already shortened. It would have a reduced life expectancy. But telomeres are rebuilt in an organism's germ cells. Thus fetal cell clones are provided with long telomeres and gain a "fresh start."

She asked me two questions, both intelligent and searching. As I concluded my second answer, a police car drew up beside us. An officer appeared. He was black, very young. He politely asked me what we were doing in a deserted parking lot. I gave an honest answer. I was Dr. Oliver Guest, and I and my passenger were discussing problems of genetics. He nodded, but he said to LaRona, "How old are you, miss?"

"I'm fourteen." She was wearing the skimpy top and short skirt favored in her district.

"Thank you."

He moved back to his car. Even then, for the briefest moment, I thought they might leave. They were just cruising, and I was respectably dressed. But I heard his words to his woman partner: "Disgusting old fucker. Even if she is a hooker, she's still only a kid. People like him oughta have their balls cut off." And, returning to me, "I'm afraid that I must ask you to come with me."

"My car—"

"Your vehicle will not be moved or damaged." He

glanced down, wary for possible weapons, and saw the spray. "What is that in your hand, sir?"

Use it on him, LaRona, and his partner? Impossible. I would botch any attempt. Unplanned violent action is alien to my nature.

It was over, then and there. I knew it, even though I had told the exact truth and nothing was farther from my mind than sex with LaRona. But policemen are creatures of habit. They would inspect my car, from sheer routine. They would find everything, my whole collection kit.

It was a tragedy. LaRona would have been a star, one of the crown jewels of my collection. It was not to be.

She is presumably still alive. Thinking about her now, I wonder if she has achieved her ambition. She is almost twenty. Has that keen mind and fiery desire for knowledge lifted her from awful family circumstances, into formal medical studies?

I am curious, but only mildly so. As I say, she is now close to twenty. Much too old. Even were we to meet, she would no longer be of interest to me.

10

The snowfall had dwindled to a few random flakes. A cold night breeze blew from the north, and the curious odor that it carried made the waiting woman wrinkle her nose in disgust.

Muffled in a long black coat and with a black woolen scarf covering her face, she was sitting on the lower level of the great memorial. At the sound of footsteps she rose to place her back against the stone wall. Her gloved right hand slipped into her pocket.

The man approached confidently and quickly, saying when he was still ten steps away, "It's all right, Sarah. Don't put a bullet through me."

She relaxed as soon as she heard his voice, and removed her hand from her pocket to show a wicked ten-inch blade. "Knife, not gun."

"Very wise. Most of the guns don't work anyway." Nick Lopez made a careful survey of their surroundings. As the woman had done, he sniffed the air. "Pretty rank up here. This is the first time I've been outside the Federal Enclave in over a week. Now I can see why."

The air carried multiple odors, burning wood and paper and plastic mingled with the sweet reek of animal putrefaction and decay.

"It's coming in from the north. I gather it's much worse up there." Sarah Mander moved forward and turned to ascend the steps. "Apparently martial law isn't working worth a damn outside the Beltway. Good thing there are no media outlets. They'd be having a field day with the bodies and the burning."

"Still plenty of media types around, itching to do what

they've always done. That's one reason I felt I had to see you in a place without eyes and ears."

"I wondered why you dragged me out here." Sarah Mander paused in the shadow of the great seated figure and stood staring up at it. "What you have to say had better be good. I didn't enjoy the walk over, and I don't like the idea of walking back. And this place is freezing."

"Then I'd better get right down to business." Lopez moved closer. With his tall pompadour hairstyle he towered over the woman by nearly two feet. "You must be getting the same briefings on the House side as I hear in the Senate. How's it look?"

It was a question rather than the information that she wanted, but after a moment she nodded and said, "Four days ago I'd have sworn that this country was down and out. Power grid dead, information network destroyed, data bases vanished, no working infrastructure. Looting and rioting along the eastern seaboard, thousands freezing to death in Chicago and Minneapolis. Nothing much of Florida south of Orlando after the second hurricane, and lots of California wiped out by mud slides. Horrible. For a while I worried about outside attack, because all our weapons had turned to junk. Then I said to myself, who could possibly want our problems?"

"I can add to your list. I've heard of starvation and cannibalism in the Dakotas, there's nothing civilized in Houston or Kansas City after the second round of fires and floods, and tornadoes took out most of Oklahoma City. We've had it easy by comparison. But you said that was the way you felt four days ago. How about now?"

"Now?" Sarah Mander paused, her gloved hand at her chin. "You know, I really think we'll make it. We had running water for an hour this morning—no way you'd drink it, of course—and my staff reported a flicker of power for a few minutes in the electric grid. I heard people laughing in the Rayburn Building for the first time in weeks, and one of my aides actually used the words 'next year' in a report."

"It's the same on the Senate side." Lopez took a step closer to the statue. "So things are looking up. Which brings me to the main point. How do you see our chances with what we've talked about for the past year?"

Her laugh was humorless, muffled by her scarf. "Are you kidding? The country may recover, but our plan doesn't have a prayer now. It's the old story: in a time of crisis the power always swings back to the presidency. Any ideas of tilting control more our way died on February 9. We just didn't know it then. You'd better not have dragged me out in the cold and dark to argue that point."

Nick Lopez stood by the base of the great statue. With his height and coloring and dark cloak, he was like a carved icon himself. He nodded slowly. "I agree with you. The supernova changed the game. We don't have a chance."

"So why are we standing out here?"

"Every problem is also an opportunity."

"Nick, do you mind? Save the platitudes for the public appearances."

"Sorry. Only, this time the cliché happens to be true. I realized it yesterday, when I was listening to the acting chief from Navy describing loss of naval capability. Apparently the only branch that's working right is the submarines."

"I knew that. The deep subs weren't touched."

"But while old Rumfries was droning on I decided that although we may be in deep shit, every other country in the world is a lot worse off. This may not be the right time for a power struggle between branches of our own government, but it's one hell of a good time to show the rest of the world who's boss."

"Still smarting over last year's put-down at the Korean reception?"

She saw his teeth flash in the gloom. "Me? Worried by some half-assed ignorant wog who treated me like a teaboy? No more than you were, by your Indonesian visit and the words of the honorable Mr. Sutan concerning the place of women." He waited, watching her face change in the gloom, and at last added, "That was four years ago. Elephants and Sarah Mander. But I'm telling you, this could be payback time."

She was silent for half a minute, staring toward the city. New fires had broken out to the north, pillars of orange topped by dense black smoke that was blowing toward them. Finally she shook her head. "And I'm telling you, the President is more powerful than he's ever been. Are you proposing to take on Saul Steinmetz?"

"Not today, thank you. I don't much like him, but he's a tough son of a bitch. We don't do this without Saul Steinmetz, Sarah. We do it *with* him, with presidential consent and cooperation."

"You mean we try to talk him into it?"

"I mean exactly that. We pitch the idea of a Pax Americana—naturally, for the good of the rest of the world."

"But this country would have total domination. Nick, he'll never go along with it."

"Are you sure? Look at it from the point of view of Saul Steinmetz. You made it all the way to the presidency. Where can you go next? Nowhere but down, writing your memoirs and opening libraries and sinking into senility—unless someone can point out some new goal, something to make you unique even among Presidents."

"Suppose he did bite on it. What's to stop him forgetting who suggested the idea in the first place?"

"It could happen. That's our risk. It would be our job to find friends and recruits in the White House, just as an insurance policy. We should be able to do that."

"And our reward, if we succeed?"

"Pretty much what we ask for. It's not Steinmetz's habit to be stingy with his friends. I'm sure we could find positions of power and influence—abroad or at home. It's a new world out there, Sarah. We could probably do anything that we really want to."

"Anything?"

He did not answer, but followed her as she walked forward to the north boundary of the monument. Together they stared toward the restless, crippled city.

"I think so," she said at last. Her eyes reflected the smoky, ruddy glow of the distant fires. "You're right, it's a whole new world out there. If not this, then what? So. Who's going to make the call to the White House, you or me?"

11

So near and yet so far.

Celine stared at the mottled globe of Earth, hanging in front of her and seemingly close enough to reach out and touch.

The old Greeks had a word for it, just as they had a word for most things. It was hubris, an arrogance that defies the gods and invites disaster. According to Reza Armani, expedition mystic, in its journey to Mars the *Schiaparelli* had moved into the abode of the gods, the space between the planets; now its crew was to pay the penalty.

The added irony was that they had all discussed this possibility. Over and over, on the way to Mars and on the surface itself, they had agreed that the fatal *Gotcha!* had to be the one you never expected; otherwise, you built contingency plans to deal with it. A thousand things might go wrong on the way to Mars, landing on Mars, exploring Mars, rising from the surface of Mars, and returning from Mars. You had to prepare for all of them and make the tough decisions ahead of time. Only when you were finally in Earth orbit, in the hands of a reentry system and personnel honed to perfection by ten thousand tries, could you at last relax and feel safe.

Celine couldn't blame the others. She had gone along with the argument. Who could imagine that the reentry system, that whole gorgeous and intricate assembly of people and techniques and hardware and software, might vanish in one flash of free electrons and electric field surge? The *Schiaparelli* itself had never, even in its designers' wildest imaginings, been seen as a ship able to endure reentry through Earth's thick atmosphere. It would disintegrate fifty miles up.

"We have to make a decision pretty soon." Zoe Nash was seated next to Celine, studying her own displays. "It's a onetime choice. I think it will be an easy one, but we have to be sure. Ludwig?"

"No change." He was wearing an earphone and working a miniaturized control pad. To Celine, he looked more like a willowy blond elf than ever. The prospect of disaster was driving them all to their extremes. Zoe was more impatient and demanding. Wilmer was remote and thoughtful. Reza was increasingly strange, oscillating between the manic clown and the aloof mystic. Celine was not sure, but earlier in the day she thought Reza had been weeping. A bad sign, in a group whose time of real stress still lay ahead.

So what had Celine become? Indecisive, probably, to the point where she could see impossible problems in doing anything at all.

"I'm picking up only a few dozen signal sources from Earth," Ludwig said. "Normally I would expect hundreds of thousands. All the signals are weak, and so far as I can tell with our onboard equipment they are low frequency and omnidirectional. I'd say they're amateur radio signals. If we wait—"

"What about signals from space sources?" Zoe cut him off in midsentence. The *Schiaparelli*'s largest scopes were trained on the big international space stations, ISS-1 and ISS-2, and their images were showing on her displays.

"The high orbits are broadcasting as usual—I'm receiving regular signals from all the automated geosynchronous birds. My question is whether anyone down below is picking them up."

"Still nothing from the manned stations?"

"Not a peep. No output from the polar orbiters, either."

"We have to assume the worst." Zoe swiveled in her seat. "Anything in low orbit had its electronics wiped out by the EMP. Alta, give me a second opinion."

Alta was watching in glum silence. She had been studying the same images as Zoe. She took her time before she answered, while Zoe sat and fidgeted impatiently.

"The hatches are invisible on both stations," Alta said at last. She sounded to Celine like a robot, without hope or feelings. "Even at highest magnification, I can't tell if they are open or closed. I see no sign of interior lights, but of course they might be turned off to conserve power. I don't think the high data rate antennae are working. They seem to be pointing in random directions. I see two small single-stage orbiters in docking position at

ISS-2, and none at ISS-1. That's unusual. Maybe there were orbiters at ISS-1, there surely should be. But if they were secured electronically and not mechanically, after the gamma pulse they would have been released. They could be floating quite close to the station; a general sky scan to find them would take quite a time."

"Time we don't have." Zoe turned back to face the screens. "Assuming that the life-support systems failed two weeks ago and no one is presently alive on either station, the general condition of all systems must be deteriorating. We have to pick one and get over to it as fast as we can. I say we head for ISS-2. Any discussion?"

A thirty-second silence followed. Celine found that in itself depressing. The crew of the *Schiaparelli* had been picked because they were bright, innovative, and opinionated. When no one could think of a second option that was a very bad sign.

"One point," Alta said at last, and Celine found her hopes rising. "This is not exactly discussion, but it is something that you need to be aware of. Neither of the single-stage orbiters docked at ISS-2 is class three or better. Each one can carry only three people, four at a real pinch."

The others, without a word, turned and looked at Wilmer Oldfield. He frowned back at them. He outmassed the others by at least fifty percent.

Zoe gave a barking laugh. "Starvation rations for Wilmer, until we're down on Earth. However we arrange the groupings, we'll have to split up and ride home in two parties. Anything else? If not, we'll get this show on the road. Jenny. Trajectory and rendezvous?"

"Computed and stored." Jenny was like a computer herself, steady and meticulous and unemotional. "I allowed an arbitrary start time up to four hours from now."

"That's ample. Alta. Confirmed configuration?"

"I recommend we fly just Section Three over to ISS-2. That gives us more fuel for final maneuvering—but not enough to reach ISS-1 if we don't like what we find."

"Understood. Any final questions before we go ahead? Yes, Reza, what is it?"

"My specimens." He was in his most agitated phase. "The Mars life-forms. I realize we have a strict mass limit—"

"Forget it. No Mars samples. Just our bodies, and our personal effects."

"I refuse to accept that. These are small, they are light, and they are so valuable—"

Zoe cut him off. "I asked for questions, not arguments. They are valuable samples, and indeed we put great effort into collecting them. We will take them with us to ISS-2. If we can create a safe environment for them there, we will leave them until someone can come up from Earth and retrieve them."

"Suppose we *can't* create a safe environment for them?"

"That will be unfortunate. But, Reza, I assume that if it comes to saving you or saving the samples, it is no contest."

Reza paused for a long time. Celine thought he was about to get into a shouting match with Zoe. Jenny put a hand on his arm. He looked at her, and then again at Zoe. He cupped his chin and cheek in his hand in a classic pose. At last he said, "I'm *thinking.*"

Zoe glared at him.

She doesn't get the reference, Celine thought. *And Reza is way out of line. He ought to know that it's the wrong time for clowning.*

"No samples," Zoe said. "If we take nothing back to Earth except our own selves, that is enough. There will be other expeditions to Mars, but we are the first. And we are going home. We *are* going home. We have come too far and worked too hard for me to accept anything else."

Reza scowled, and for another moment Celine thought there would be an open mutiny. Finally he nodded, and so did everyone else. Celine felt that it was she alone, Celine (Cassandra) Tanaka, who deep inside whispered, *Perhaps.*

Jenny Kopal had programmed a careful approach to ISS-2, one that allowed ample time for close-up inspection. Every sensor on the *Schiaparelli*—as well as every human eye—was trained on the big station as it slowly turned against a background of stars.

Celine, Ludwig, and Zoe were already in their suits, floating at the open entrance to the *Schiaparelli*'s main hatch. There was no way to dock the Mars ship at ISS-2 without active cooperation from within the station. The first transition had to be an open-space maneuver.

That held no fears for Celine. She loved EVAs. An antenna repair on the outward trip to Mars, when the *Schiaparelli* floated eighty million kilometers distant from the home planet, had given Celine and Ludwig Holter the record for both the longest and most distant free space activity. That evening, in her excitement and exuberance, she had seduced Wilmer. He had said afterward, as though describing something as far removed from human control as a stellar flare, "I wondered when that would happen."

Today would be different, and depressing. Straight ahead lay the station, a dark irregular bulk that answered no queries and offered no signs of life. On the left, filling the sky, was an alien Earth. All the normal circulation patterns of the atmosphere had vanished, replaced by great streaks and whorls of cloud that curved across the equator. The surface beneath was rarely visible on the sunlit hemisphere that faced them; but the *Schiaparelli*'s onboard sensors had recorded south-to-north wind vectors of up to six hundred fifty kilometers an hour. That exceeded by a wide margin the highest speeds ever reported in Earth tornadoes.

"We have attained zero relative velocity." Jenny Kopal's calm voice sounded over Celine's suit radio. "Distance from ISS-2 is eighty meters."

"Hold there pending further instructions." That was Zoe Nash. "All right, no point in waiting. Let's go."

She led the way out of the hatch. Celine and Ludwig followed more slowly, drifting across toward the space station. By the time they joined Zoe she was waiting at a point between the two orbiters where a station entry hatch was located. She moved the airlock door a few inches with her suited hand, making it clear from her action that the hatch was not sealed. If the inner lock was open, too, the interior of a large part of ISS-2 would be airless.

Celine, moving abruptly from sunlight to shadow, felt a cold like death inside her. It could only be psychological, because her suit maintained internal temperature control. During the return journey from Mars they had talked often about the return to Earth space, and the joyful reunion they would have with the staff of the big stations when they docked there.

"The orbiter access external airlock is open." Zoe spoke for the benefit of those aboard the *Schiaparelli*. She had the hatch fully open and was moving inside. "The inner door of the lock is not sealed. No mechanical locks are engaged. ISS-2 appears to have been relying on electronic control. That was probably the case everywhere on the station."

The crew of the station are all dead. Celine added those words only to herself. Everyone on the *Schiaparelli* was capable of drawing the same conclusion without assistance.

Once they were through the inner airlock door, she and Zoe moved away in different directions. Zoe had assigned their duties in advance. Ludwig would remain outside and determine the condition of the two single-stage orbiters. Celine would head for the control room and decide what elements of ISS-2, if any, might be restored to useful function.

Zoe had reserved the most unpleasant job for herself. She would inspect the station's living quarters.

But unpleasantness was all relative. Celine, easing her way along the corridor that led to the deep interior and heart of ISS-2, had to push her way past four bodies. They rested against the corridor wall, contorted as they had been at the moment of their deaths. She made a brief inspection, enough to confirm that they had all died in the decompression that followed the failure of the ISS-2's locks.

It had not been a quick death. This corridor was a hundred feet from the lock, and the air pressure drop to a fatal level had been far from instantaneous. There had been time to reach a bulkhead with its own safety airlock, and learn that it too would not work.

Two of the people were holding hands. Celine shone her suit light on their uniform tags and noted their names: Ursula Klein and Lawrence Morphy. United forever in death. They must have made that final gesture deliberately, and if she lived she would find a way to record the fact. Had they also, the living man and woman who now formed freeze-dried and desiccated corpses, had time enough to realize that the cause of all their problems was a failure of the microchips throughout the whole of ISS-2?

Surely not. The fatal *Gotcha!* was the one that you never expected; no one had expected this.

Celine recorded the other two names also, and forced herself to keep going. The control room had its own share of horrors. Seven more corpses. Three people, all women, sat in chairs before the control board, where not a warning light glowed or a single display was active. The interior temperature of the chamber, according to Celine's suit sensors, was hundreds of degrees below freezing. ISS-2 was dead. Unlike its doomed personnel, the station might one day be brought back to life. But that resurrection would require the replacement of thousands, perhaps millions, of electronic components. Celine had no hope that she and her companions could perform such a task with the limited resources available on the *Schiaparelli*. So far as the Mars expedition was concerned, ISS-2 was a derelict hulk and would remain so.

She made a final inspection of the seven bodies in the control room, again noting from the uniforms the name of every dead individual. She did not know why she was doing it. Earth records would certainly contain identification of everyone on ISS-2.

She did it anyway, a bizarre gesture of final respect. Then with the presentiment of death inside her she drifted back along the corridor to the airlock.

There was no sign of the other two. Zoe must still be inside, while Ludwig was presumably in one of the two orbiters. Celine headed for the nearer, noting as she approached how small it seemed. She had been to orbit and returned from it many times, but always in vehicles ten times the size of this one. It looked like a toy, a single-person reentry pod. And this little bug was supposed to hold three or four of them?

Celine made a determined effort to avoid negative thinking. This orbiter would take them home, because it had to. She had seen ISS-2, and she knew there was no chance of waiting on the station for a possible rescue from Earth.

Ludwig was inside the orbiter. He had pulled the front off the control board, and was studying what lay behind it using the light of his suit. He turned when Celine's light added to his in illuminating the panel. "Well? What did you find?"

"What we expected." She did not want to go into details. "We will have to use these orbiters. Maybe we can scavenge materials from the station, and fuel. But no working electronics."

He scowled at her. "Marvelous. But not surprising. And not good, because the electronics are shot in both orbiters. The other one is a bit bigger inside than this one, but they have identical computers and identical control systems. We won't need fuel, because both orbiters have full tanks. But we do need control systems, and that's going to be a problem. Zoe's one of the best, but even she can't fly a reentry without controls."

"She's going to if she has to." It was Zoe's voice, thin over the radio link. "We all do what we have to do. You two stay where you are, I'm outside the station now and on my way. I'm afraid it's all bad news inside ISS-2."

"I don't think we'll be forced to a seat-of-the-pants reentry attempt." Ludwig did not press Zoe for details on what she had found inside the station, any more than he had asked Celine. "These single-stagers, thank God, are built simple. Most of the control surfaces don't use computers, they're self-adjusting on reentry to external conditions. And where they do need computers, they're designed so you can pull and replace the whole box."

"You mean we can use what we have on the *Schiaparelli*?" It was the first good news of Celine's day. "Suppose we need it there?"

"We won't." Zoe had reached the hatch and was trying to squeeze inside. "We can take anything from there, because we won't be needing the Mars ship at all. We're going home."

Celine, trying to move to let Zoe in, became even more aware of the cramped interior space of the single-stage orbiters. There was no way that she and Ludwig could admit Zoe. The padded seats would have to come out before a third person could get in. And what would a reentry be like, without cushioning against deceleration forces?

Stop thinking negative. Whatever it's like, it's better than the alternative.

Celine turned to Ludwig, who had removed the little cube of the control computer. He was staring at it dubiously. "This sucker is dead. I can replace it with a good one from our ship, but that's not the hard part. The tricky bit is going to be software. We need the right program routines."

"Routines which we don't have." Even Zoe sounded discouraged for a moment. "The *Schiaparelli* never expected to need a program for Earth orbit reentry."

"Routines which we *might* have," said a new and unexpected voice. It was Jenny Kopal. She, like the rest of the crew on the Mars ship, had been silently listening in on the discussion.

"How so?" Zoe, like everyone else, deferred to Jenny on all questions related to computer software.

"Back when we were setting up the *Schiaparelli* data bases, I was given a free hand as to what programs I could load. So I decided it was best to be generous—"

"Thank God for a program pack rat," Zoe said. "Jenny, I've seen you gloating over your master files like a mother hen. I never dreamed it would pay off this way."

"I thought it best to be generous," Jenny said calmly. "I loaded every routine in the data base that had a 'space use' descriptor. They didn't take up much storage. Even if—"

"I don't care how much storage they took." Zoe interrupted again. "The question is, do you have the programs to control reentry of these particular single-stage orbiters?"

"I don't know. I downloaded many thousands of programs. I'll have to establish a search with the appropriate parameters."

"Do that. How long will it take?"

"I can set it up in half an hour. The search will take longer—a lot of the files are on DNA backup storage. Very high packing density, but it has long access times. Maybe three hours."

"Do it. Ludwig, I want these orbiters ready to receive new hardware as soon as possible. Replace chips wherever we have substitutes on the *Schiaparelli*. Patch around them if we don't. And mark the places where the pilot has to take over control of the orbiters and fly them directly."

"Yeah. Right." Ludwig stared quizzically at Zoe, then turned back to the dismantled control panel. "Like me to make 'em go faster than light while I'm at it?"

"Save that for next time. Can you finish this in twenty-four hours?"

"Naturally. I'm Superman, remember?"

"Get this ship ready to fly in less than twenty-four hours, and I'll buy you a new cape."

Zoe backed out of the hatch. When Celine joined her she was hovering motionless, staring at the great bulk of Earth hanging overhead. Since entering the station, ISS-2 and the *Schiaparelli* had moved together in their ninety-minute orbit of Earth, and now they faced the nightside of the planet. Ship and station were in an orbit with an inclination of thirty degrees, and at the moment they were close to their northern limit. Celine knew that North America lay beneath them. No lights were visible. The great cities were in darkness, or obscured by heavy cloud. She wanted to believe the second explanation.

"Two days." Zoe pointed up toward Earth. "Two days at the outside, and we will be there."

She spoke with total conviction. Celine felt her own surge of confidence. She knew that Zoe as expedition leader and chief pilot might speak optimistically to boost the spirits of the rest of them. But it wasn't that. This was straight-from-the-heart Zoe Nash, Zoe sure that she could do it, Zoe knowing that nothing could stop her; Zoe able to make things happen so that nothing *did* stop her. That was why she was the expedition leader.

Zoe said she would be on Earth within two days. Therefore Zoe would, beyond a doubt, be on Earth within two days.

12

Sometimes you didn't know when you were well off.

Saul Steinmetz stared at the list in disbelief. For twelve days he had cursed the lack of telecommunications and satellite systems. Now they were creeping back to life, and his problems were worse than ever.

He was being swamped. According to the log in his hand, he had received—over an ailing and imperfect communications system—eighteen hundred and forty-seven calls in the past six hours. They had come from every state and almost every country. Each one requested, begged for, or demanded the urgent personal attention of the President of the United States.

Saul hit the intercom, and Auden Travis popped in with his usual promptitude.

"Auden." Saul waved the typed list, all eight feet of it. "Doesn't anybody in this place know the meaning of the word *priorities*? What am I supposed to do, answer these goddammed calls in order, first called, first served? I need a cut on urgency and importance. Take the fucking thing away and *organize* it."

Auden Travis was a handsome young man with clean features, a strong Roman nose, and curly brown hair. His sensitive mouth twisted with a look of pained embarrassment. Saul knew why. It wasn't the chewing-out, it was the cussing. Auden never swore, and he disapproved of it. Saul did not normally swear, either. But there were times when you had to do it to get the message across hard enough. This was one.

"Take this amorphous piece of shit out of my sight." He shook the list. "I never want to see it again."

Travis took the paper and vanished without a word. Saul

turned back to his desk and stared out of the window. People thought he was the boss and they asked him for help. They were wrong. Nature was the boss. You could plot and plan and scheme and schedule all the things you were going to do when the communications system came back on-line, and when service finally returned you couldn't do a damned thing.

Saul looked out onto a world of white. For the third day in a row, snow blanketed the East Coast from Maine to Norfolk and as far west as Indiana. The food convoys were stalled in eastern Kansas. Steam locomotives, equipped with snowplows, stood helpless in twelve-foot drifts. High winds had brought down more trees and power lines, closing roads that had only just been opened.

When would the snow end?

God knows, Saul thought. *But God's not telling.*

The Defense Department had at last managed to bring up a ground station and communicate with one of their own orbiting metsats. The succession of images proved one thing beyond debate: predictions made by the numerical weather models were garbage. A three-year-old could do as well drawing patterns with colored crayons.

The intercom buzzed, and Saul turned to it. "Yes?"

"Two things, Mr. President." It was Auden Travis again, speaking in an unnaturally low voice. "DOD has a working feed from one of their high-resolution birds. They don't have the use of the maximum data rate antenna, so the nature and number of images is limited. We only have Australia so far, but General Mackay feels that these images really deserve your attention."

"Fine. Can you pipe the pictures into this office?"

"Yes, sir. I'll do that at once. And one other thing, sir. The House Minority Leader and Senator Lopez are waiting in the outer office."

"Christ. You've made my day."

"I'm sorry, sir. I was given no notice of this. They just arrived. Together."

"I'm not blaming you, Auden. I'm sure you don't want them cluttering up your work area. Send the rabble in. If they want to talk to me they'll have to watch some pictures first."

"Yes, sir."

Saul turned to the big display that formed one wall of his office. The lights dimmed, the windows with their polarizing filters became opaque, and the first image blinked into existence. It was in simple false color rather than the derived hyperspectral presentation that Saul preferred. He could guess the reason. Three-band color could be done with a lower data rate. The people controlling the satellite had decided—rightly, in Saul's opinion—to opt for maximum coverage area. Anything really interesting would be caught in more detail on a later orbit.

The image had no vocal tags. Latitude and longitude tick marks were shown on the outer boundaries, and the words SYDNEY, AUSTRALIA appeared in small letters in the bottom left-hand corner.

Saul leaned forward. He had not visited Sydney for twenty years, but he had seen plenty of satellite coverage during the Queensland Secession War. What he was looking at was nothing like Sydney.

The great drowned valley that had created and framed Sydney Harbor no longer existed. In its place stood a deep brown smear, miles across, as though a giant ball had rolled over the land from west to east.

Saul heard the door behind him open and close. He ignored it and called for a zoom of the center part of the image. The effect was of flying in closer and closer, a small area viewed in exquisite detail. He should see individual roads and houses and cars, even people.

He saw nothing but an endless wasteland of mud. Sydney was gone. What had replaced it bore no more signs of human influence than the satellites of Neptune.

BRISBANE, AUSTRALIA. An open expanse of water and, miles to the west, a new coastline. The satellites used absolute latitude and longitude to pinpoint their images. Brisbane now lay beneath the Pacific Ocean.

Had any of the models predicted tidal waves, earthquakes, and massive sea-level changes? If they had, no one had presented those results to Saul. Perhaps they had been discarded, on the grounds that they were "implausible."

He stayed with it for a few more scenes. The whole southeast of Australia, judging from the images of Adelaide and Melbourne, had shared the same fate as Sydney and Brisbane.

Saul asked for an image of Canberra, which lay inland and on high ground. It should have escaped damage from the sea. Perhaps it had. It was impossible to tell, because the area was covered by impenetrable clouds. Their sinister tinge of dull red suggested that the surface beneath had been blown high into the atmosphere.

In his scan of the list of incoming calls, Saul had noticed nothing from Australia and New Zealand. Now he knew why.

He heard the creak of chairs behind him. Someone was increasingly excited or impatient. For the moment, he had seen enough. Saul killed the display, watched as a snowy vista gradually reappeared outside the window, and finally turned around.

"Good morning. Excuse me if I did not greet you earlier. I felt that I—and you—ought to examine firsthand what is happening around the world."

Saul knew that the smiles greeting him were as hollow as his own words. The two visitors made a splendid study in contrasts, proving once again that politics was flexible enough to accommodate every human strength and weakness.

Sarah Mander had an unlined, guileless face. Yet she was probably the most secretive person in Washington, man or woman. She was also cultured, witty, well educated, vengeful, racist, and anti-Semitic. It depressed Saul that conversations with such a witch could be so enjoyable.

Senator Nick Lopez was round-faced and brown-complexioned. The hair above his broad brow was set in a high, old-fashioned pompadour that resembled a frizzy black hat. Saul wondered where Lopez found a hairdresser willing to perpetrate such a monstrosity. Lopez had degrees in mathematics and law, but openly disdained "book learning." He was fast-talking, confident, and supernaturally bright, and after a meeting with him Saul always came away feeling that he had somehow been tricked, in a way that he didn't quite understand. Nick Lopez also had his darker side, one that would not be revealed in public.

"The House Minority Leader and the Senate Majority Leader visiting me *together*," Saul said musingly. "I'm not sure what the appropriate protocol is for such a rare combination of forces."

Sarah Mander smiled. "Count the spoons when we leave, I guess."

In spite of himself, Saul found he was grinning back at her.

"It's our dollar." Lopez made no attempt at small talk. "I guess we should explain why we came."

"And we'll be brief," added Mander. "You're a busy man, Mr. President. Two thousand calls to return."

Eighteen hundred and forty-seven. But that was twenty minutes ago, by now she was probably right. After the meeting he would learn where she had learned the number. But then it would hardly be worth knowing, since obviously she *expected* him to find out.

"Thanks for your consideration, Sally. Go ahead."

"Cheap shot, Mr. President. You can do better than that."

And she was right. It was a cheap shot. He knew she preferred "Sarah" and hated the more informal version of her name. *Sally Mander. Lizard woman.* She must have been taunted with jibes like that since she was a kid.

"Sorry, Sarah. I'm in a bad mood today and I feel stupid."

"Sure. Pull the other one. Nick?"

"This is only a preliminary meeting." Lopez picked up without hesitation. "We want to present an idea. I'm glad we saw those images, because they reinforce our point."

"Which is?" Saul sensed the change. The overture was over, the action had begun.

"This country has taken a real beating, but we will recover. And I think we'll be like a broken bone, stronger than ever when we heal."

"God, I hope you're right. I keep telling myself that, but then I look outside." Saul gestured to the window, where the snow fell constantly.

"It was in the latest weather forecasts, and it's not the *Fimbulwinter,*" Sarah Mander said. "It might last three days, but it won't last three years. It will end. I spoke with Science Adviser Vronsky early this morning. The supernova is fading."

"And about time."

"But other countries have not been so fortunate." Lopez ignored the others' comments, they were a sidebar to the main theme. "Australia, Micronesia, and South America are ruined. I don't know if they exist anymore. South Africa is silent, and the rest of the continent is chaos. United Europe has fragmented to its pre-Union nationalism. The Sino Consortium was about to walk all over us in trade, now the members are back in the Stone Age. The Golden Ring is broken, and their radio reports suggest a total collapse of central authority. Congresswoman Mander and I have compared notes. Outside of western Europe we cannot discover a single foreign entity that today deserves the name of *nation.*"

"I agree." Saul wondered at the line of logic. Nick Lopez was a dedicated isolationist, while Sarah Mander hated not just blacks, Hispanics, Jews, and Native Americans, but every foreign group that came into her sights. "What are you suggesting? I hope you are not proposing to resuscitate the foreign aid program. It ruined every country that ever received it."

As he was speaking, Saul realized that he knew quite well

where Lopez was going. His own mention of foreign aid was a way of marking time, thinking the idea over—and rejecting it.

"Foreign aid, never." Lopez's face in repose showed a natural easygoing good humor, part of his success as a politician. The fire and conviction that sat on it now was something that no voter would ever see. "Mr. President, we can offer something much better. We, the United States, are in a position to assume a more central role in the world. We have an opportunity that may never arise again, to assert global dominance. Our military has overwhelming superiority. Our food reserves form an invaluable asset. We will soon once more have working communications, a strong infrastructure, and a stable government. We cannot lose—and people everywhere in the world will bless us for rescuing them from barbarism."

"You paint an attractive picture, Senator. And a plausible one."

And who would lead that global empire? Saul knew the answer—and he felt the lure in his bones.

"With you as leader." Sarah Mander was reading his mind. She wore the inviting smile of a Siren. "President Saul Steinmetz. First President of—may I say it?—the United States of the World."

President Steinmetz. And, as a reward for their initiative and support, positions of global power and influence for Sarah Mander and Nick Lopez. After that, presumably, a voice in the succession.

"I'm not sure I'd look good on a gold coin." Saul, deliberately, moved the level of intensity down a couple of notches. He tapped his nose. "I'm very fond of this, but it's a bit too Semitic, don't you think? Remember, I'm the man who goes to temple and gets pointed out as 'that Jewish-looking guy over there.' Maybe in full face, rather than profile?"

He felt the relaxation. Since he did not reject their suggestion out of hand, they assumed he was thinking it over. They would not expect him to buy the idea at once—it was far too radical. And some of Lopez's words raised other questions that really needed thought. *Our military has overwhelming superiority.* Had Lopez seen the rough airborne beasts slouching toward Andrews AFB and National Airport? What was the basis for such an assertion?

"If anything is to be done we must go beyond generalities," Saul said at last. "We need a specific plan. Staffing levels, resources, schedules, approaches. Of course, we can't do anything concrete until our own crisis eases. And I will need full congressional approval."

The exchange of glances came and went in the flicker of an eye.

"Of course." Lopez stood up. "This meeting was no more than a preliminary discussion of principles. An enormous amount of work remains to be done. However, we think we can guarantee you the overwhelming support of both Houses."

In other words, we did our homework. But Saul could have guessed that. There had to have been the usual backroom quid pro quos, although he did not know the details and the stakes were bigger than usual. *You have my support, provided that my wife's family has control of Congo copper production?* Or maybe, *Offshore oil leases in Argentina, in exchange for three locked-in votes.*

Saul stood up, too. "Our surveillance systems will give us a more accurate world picture within a week. We'll know better then what has to be done. Why don't we meet again in five days?"

The usual handshakes—firm and brisk from Nick Lopez, while Sarah Mander clasped Saul's hand warmly in both of hers—and they were gone.

He smiled until they left, then sat and seethed. The witless bastards. A President had to be ambitious, sure, otherwise it would be the worst job in the world. He was certainly no exception. But every President also had an eye on posterity. What would people remember about you, a hundred or two hundred years from now?

Not, you hoped, that you had waited until the rest of the world was at a low point, then made a cheap power grab. Mander and Lopez were living in the wrong century. What they were proposing was some form of a Pax Americana. There was no way that such an entity could survive for very long, unless you were willing to grind the people of other countries into absolute servitude.

And probably not even then. It had been tried. You ran the risk of plagues of frogs and locusts and pools of blood, and the loss of your firstborn child.

Almost always, the moral high road was the right road, even if it was seldom the popular way.

Saul glanced at the portraits that lined the office wall.

He divided them into two groups: wrong but romantic, or right but repulsive. Sarah Mander would have told him in an instant the name of the book from which he had stolen the two categories. Nick Lopez might know, but he would deny the knowledge.

They both had a special interest in politics. How was a President usually remembered by the general public?

By trivia, some of them false.

You chopped down a cherry tree. You charged on horseback up a useless piece of real estate called San Juan Hill. You used a wheelchair. You were so fat you got stuck in the White House bathtub. You were as stingy with words as a miser with his gold. You recorded your own crimes—and kept the recordings. You rented bedrooms for one-nighters at the White House. You were shot in a motorcade, and set off the biggest conspiracy theory in history.

And Saul Steinmetz?

The first Jewish President, but the hell with that as a claim for immortality. Kennedy was the first Catholic President, Reagan the first divorced President. Who remembered them that way? No one.

Jewishness was merely an obstacle, a fence that he had already cleared on the way to the White House. What he needed was something as memorable as ending slavery, as important as bringing the nation out of the Depression. Suppose he put the country back on its feet now, and made it stronger and better than it had ever been? That might do it. His recent meeting would not make that job any easier.

He glanced toward the empty corner of the office where the Persona had once maintained its hologram, then he slid open a drawer of his desk and looked inside. A handsome face with long hair pushed Byronically back from the brow stared straight at him from the old painting. *The Presidents on the wall were your predecessors, Saul; but I am your spiritual Papa.*

Benjamin Disraeli had fought every one of Saul's battles, and won, to become the Prime Minister of the biggest empire the world had ever known. And he had done it in a century where *jew* was a verb.

If Disraeli were here, what would he be doing now?

He would be asking his universal question. What if?

What if Saul had given Sarah Mander and Nick Lopez a flat and immediate no?

They must have come prepared for such an answer. They would have alternate strategies able to neutralize or bypass Saul. For that to be possible, they needed a high-level insider within the White House itself. Preferably someone with detailed information on military strength and disposition.

The same question was in his head again: What did Sarah Mander and Nick Lopez know about the condition of the country's military machine that Saul didn't?

By definition, he could not answer that. Yet.

If Presidents had one common weakness, it was the disguised fondness for introspection. Saul roused himself and hit the intercom. When Auden Travis appeared—with his usual speed, and carrying a yellow folder—Saul asked, "Are we able to use hidden personnel tracers yet?"

"No, sir. Security says it may take months. We first need to build a factory to make the microchips."

"I was afraid of that. Is General Mackay here today?"

"I think so, sir. Would you like to see her?"

"No, I want you to make sure that she receives a piece of information, through as indirect a route as possible. I want her to be told that she is under surveillance."

"Yes, sir." Travis hesitated. "Do you want me to try to arrange for surveillance?"

"No. I'm not planning that at the moment."

"Very well, sir." Auden Travis, quite reasonably in Saul's opinion, looked baffled. When it was clear that Saul was going to say no more, Travis proffered the folder. "This is the list of calls, sir, reorganized in a suggested order of priority for action. Cases where the staff could not make a decision are marked with a star."

"Fine." Saul took the yellow folder, but still Auden Travis hesitated. "Is there something else I need to know?"

"I think so, sir. Thirty-four of the calls were from the same person."

"I suppose that's good. That many less to answer."

"Yes, sir. All those calls are from Mrs. Patricia Goldsmith. She said you know her as Tricia."

His face asked the question. Auden was a relative newcomer to his White House job, and it proved he knew less about Saul than he imagined. He must have looked for Patricia Goldsmith in Saul's contact file, and found her identified as a wealthy local resident and prominent socialite.

Saul opened the folder. "Did you speak with her yourself?"

"Yes, sir. On her thirty-fourth call. I thought I ought to find out what she wanted. But she refused to tell me any more than she told anyone else."

"What did you tell her?"

"That you have been terribly busy with numerous crises. That you are flooded with calls."

"What did she say?"

Auden Travis's face flushed a bright pink. "Something I prefer not to repeat."

"It's all right. I know how Tricia can be. Remember, quoting someone isn't the same thing as saying it yourself."

"I told her that I would pass on her message, but you were in an important meeting and could not be interrupted. She asked my name, and I gave it to her. She asked me how old I was. I said I didn't think that was relevant. Then she said that she had heard of me, but if I wanted to go anywhere in this job I must not block access to the President by his old friends. Sir, I don't do that."

"I know. I'm sorry, Auden. Think of it as the habits of the very rich. They are not used to being frustrated."

"Yes, sir. I try to treat this sort of thing as part of my job."

"It is, but it ought not to be. Don't worry, I'll take it from here."

As Travis left, Saul examined the ranked list of callers. Eight foreign heads of state, thirty-three congressional representatives, nine state governors, fourteen heads of government departments, eighteen heads of industry and major party contributors. They all needed to speak with him "urgently and immediately." And that was just the first page.

He flipped through the list, sheet after sheet. Everyone was looking to Washington. Judging from the message summaries, every caller had outstretched hands. Nick Lopez and Sarah Mander were right. A country with food and weapons and a working infrastructure had never been so powerful.

He came to the final page. There they were, Tricia's calls, right at the end, with her number and his staff's priority assignment. She had been assigned the lowest level. No one knew why she was calling. Nor, for that matter, did he.

Automatic call routing had died with Supernova Alpha's gamma-ray pulse. Saul went to his private line, one that could not be monitored by Auden Travis or anyone else, and entered the sequence by hand. He was half hoping there would be no reply, but it was answered immediately.

"Hello?" Tricia's voice was clear and high-pitched, a little faint over the noisy line but easily recognized.

"Hi." He felt breathless. "This is Saul."

"Saul! Mr. President! It's been *ages*."

Strictly speaking, that was not true. She and Saul had been at the same reception, just before Christmas. They had eyed each other from across the room. Very slim and taller than Saul even without heels, she stood out above the crowd. Her black hair was as sleek and stylish as ever, setting off a pale, flawless complexion and fine cheekbones. She was not with her new husband, Joseph Goldsmith, but even so she and Saul had kept their distance.

He said nothing now, and after a few moments she added, "Saul, are you there? How are things?"

"It's a mess—a mess all over the country. All over the world. We've been hit hard, but we are better off than most."

He had interpreted her question impersonally. With Tricia he should have known better. She laughed, the insider's laugh he knew so well.

"Now you stop that. You know what I mean. How are *you*?"

"I'm fine, Tricia. One thing about being President, people do coddle you. A better question is, how are you managing out at Highgates?"

As he spoke he glanced at an expanded metsat view of the local area. Highgates lay fifty miles to the west and slightly south, in Virginia horse country. Like the rest of the region, the four square miles of estate surrounding the forty-room mansion of Highgates was blanketed with snow.

"Well, it's hard to go anywhere." Tricia's voice was resolutely upbeat. "So for the past week I haven't tried. We have our own generators and our own wells and plenty of food. I'm learning to enjoy solitude. I can't complain. And you know me, I never do."

She was right. Tricia took misfortune in her stride, chin up and head held high. It was one of her best points. She complained about nothing—or about only one thing, which Saul was not going to mention.

"You are wise to stay home," he said. "I'm trying to bring services and systems back, but it's slow going. Staying at Highgates makes good sense."

"Oh, don't say that." There was a joking pout in her voice. He could visualize her dark-eyed face, as clearly as if they had a videophone connection.

"I'm planning a trip into Washington tomorrow or the day after," she went on. "I was really hoping I could stop by and say hello. You tell me you're fine, but I'd like to see for myself and make sure. You drive yourself too hard, you know. You're too busy with others to take care of your own health."

Getting from Highgates to Washington would be difficult, but Saul knew better than to suggest that to Tricia as an obstacle to their meeting. She would find a way.

"Tomorrow would be good. How about dinner? Here?" The words seemed to emerge from his mouth without the involvement of his forebrain.

"That will be perfect."

He regained some self-control. "It won't be just the two of us, I'm afraid. There have to be some other people present, and we'll be talking business."

Saul could do what he liked with his calendar. Tomorrow had nothing that could not be moved. He was testing, searching for information.

"That's all right," she said at once. "So long as we can both be there. About six? I know you like to eat early."

"That will be good."

"Wonderful. You know, I'm *really* looking forward to seeing you. Bye, Saul."

Before he could add anything, the line went dead. Saul leaned back in the padded chair, specially designed for his predecessor, and breathed deep. It had been two years and more since they had spoken to each other, but his heart was racing. He had not known what Tricia wanted when he placed the call to her, and he had no better idea now.

The list of callers was still sitting in front of him, open to the last sheet. He didn't even want to think about them, until he noticed Yasmin Silvers's name at the top of the page. How had he overlooked that earlier?

He knew. He had been focused totally on Tricia. The initials next to Yasmin's name showed that she had spoken with Auden Travis, but there was no message summary.

Saul touched the intercom. "Auden? I see Yasmin Silvers called. You spoke with her."

"Yes, sir. Should I come in?"

"No need for that." Saul detected a curiously cold tone to Travis's voice. Had the two of them been arguing? "What did Yasmin want?"

"It was an information call only, sir, that's why her message shows low priority. She had been heading south. She said that you had authorized her trip—to the Q-5 Syncope Facility at Maryland Point?"

"Quite right." Saul ignored the implied question, why? "I did. She ought to be there by now."

"She isn't. She was not able to travel, yesterday or today. She says the roads to the south are closed because of high snowdrifts."

"Where is she?"

"She is staying at a place called Indian Head. It's about forty kilometers south of here."

"What is it? The name is familiar."

"It is an old Navy weapons center—very old, I gather."

"Does she need help?"

"She did not ask for it, sir. It would also be difficult to provide it, because the roads from here are close to impassable."

"Very good. Thank you, Auden." Logically, that was the end of that subject. Yasmin Silvers was in a known location, and she was safe. Saul ought to get back to other matters, like the high-priority items on the list. But at some hidden level his brain was at work, linking Yasmin and Indian Head with the words and agenda of Nick Lopez. Whatever Mander and Lopez might be, they were not fools.

He walked over to the bureau in the corner of the office and pulled out a volume of large-scale maps of the local region. Finding a selected location in the atlas was harder work than the Query-and-Display system, with its instant map information for any point coded into the worldwide digital data base. But the Q-and-D was down, and would be until a version could be pipelined in from the intact Prospero-rated intelligence data center at Bolling Air Force Base. Maybe three more days, according to Grace Mackay. Meanwhile . . .

Saul found Indian Head. Naturally, the old Navy base was on the river. It stood at the point where the Potomac turned, broadened, and began a long sweep due south. It was easy to see how Yasmin had become stuck there. From Indian Head all the way to the deliberately isolated outpost of Maryland Point and the Facility for Extended Syncope, the only roads were second- or third-class highways.

And Auden Travis was right, too. With few plows available, the roads down to Indian Head would still be deep in drifts.

It would be difficult for Saul to drive there until the drifts were cleared. But other avenues lay open—if you were President.

He glanced over to the stately grandfather clock, imported a week and a half ago into the office. Three-thirty. There would be time enough.

He touched the intercom unit that sat on the bureau. "Auden? Please call Yasmin Silvers and tell her I would like to have dinner with her this evening at Indian Head. I have some matters that I need to discuss with her personally. And call General Mackay.

I want a vessel ready and waiting to carry me downriver to Indian Head. I will leave here one and a half hours from now."

He broke off the connection without waiting for a reply from Auden Travis. No matter how much the aide misread Saul's motives and disapproved of them, he wouldn't dare to say it. And it was just possible that he was not totally wrong.

An hour and a half. Saul walked back to his desk. The list of callers still sat there, staring at him accusingly. Eighteen hundred calls, an hour and a half to make them. Three seconds for each.

Saul closed the folder.

As one of his more easygoing predecessors was apt to say, before retiring for a couple of martinis and an evening of relaxation, "We have to be sure to leave some work for tomorrow."

13

By six o'clock it was already dark. Outside, the snow fell steadily. President Steinmetz had been sent safely on his way, after a hectic hour and a half in which Auden Travis had tried to do two days' work. Now Auden could take off his coat, roll up his shirt-sleeves, and catch up on some of his other duties.

The emergency power system of the White House had not been designed for extended use. A week and a half was well beyond its intended lifetime, and now and again the lights flickered and dimmed. Each time Auden stopped, sat back, stretched, and allowed himself a moment of rest. If the power reduction lasted more than a few seconds, he would have to find out what was happening.

It was during one of those moments of power reduction that Nick Lopez quietly entered the little office.

Auden, flustered, sat up and took his hands from behind his head. "I'm sorry, Senator. I didn't know you were still here."

Lopez just grinned. "I wasn't here. I left, and I came back. Any chance of a few more minutes with *el Presidente*?"

"Not tonight. He's on his way to Indian Head—by boat."

"Is he, now?" Lopez gazed at Auden shrewdly. Without being asked, he pulled up a chair and settled onto it. He moved easily, and with unusual grace. "May I ask why?"

"He has a meeting there with one of the staff." Auden was going to say no more, but Nick Lopez was staring at him with quiet sympathy. "With Yasmin Silvers."

"Ah." Lopez winked at Auden in a knowing way. His broad, good-natured face showed understanding and no hint of censure. "Well, I'm sure Saul has earned it. You know what they say, all work and no play . . ."

"It may be a business meeting."

"It may." Lopez smiled at Auden. "Then again, it may not. Your loyalty does you credit. Meanwhile, you are left here, to work and work and work. What time do you stop?"

"When I feel I'm not being productive anymore." Auden gestured to his desk, piled high with notes and folders and clipboards. He knew Nick Lopez's reputation, but it was flattering to have so important a man take a personal interest in what he was doing. "There's always plenty of work—especially now, when the support systems don't function."

"Of course. Work is important. But you are young, it ought not to be *all* work. You should have some social life."

"Is there any? I thought the city was at a standstill."

"In some ways. But life goes on, even now. As a matter of fact, this very evening—" Lopez paused. "Look, a couple of my friends are having a little party. I told them I couldn't make it, because I knew I would be coming here and I hoped to spend some time with the President. But now I can go. It's not far from the White House, across Lafayette Park and a few blocks north. The streets are dangerous, but I'll get a security escort. Why don't you take a break and come along with me?"

It was tempting. Auden was tired to the point where he wasn't sure he was getting anything useful done. On the other hand . . . "Senator Lopez, thank you for the invitation. But I don't think I should. I don't know your friends. They don't know me."

"It's quite informal, and there will be a fair number of people there. I suspect you will know some of them already." Lopez moved his chair closer. "I've been close to Jeremy and Raoul for years, you don't need an invitation if you arrive with me. And they are nice people. I'm sure you would like them."

"I wish I could. But I have a lot of work to do." Auden stared at Lopez's big, brown hand, with a thick gold band on its index finger. It was a contrast to his own forearm, white and freckled and golden-haired and just a couple of inches away. He withdrew his arm a little, trying to make the movement look natural. "It's really nice of you to ask me."

"I think you would enjoy yourself." Nick Lopez pulled his hand away and smiled warmly at Auden. "Look, this is going to sound peculiar. But are you scared of me?"

"*Scared*? Well, no, not scared, I wouldn't say that." Auden did his best to smile back. "But you have a—well, let's say, a reputation."

"Auden, for Christ's sake." Nick Lopez laughed aloud. "I'm a *politician,* and this is Washington. The original city for, 'Unless you've got something horrible to say about him, I don't want to hear it.' Remember Harry Truman's advice? 'If you want a friend in Washington, get a dog.' Sure, people say things about me. They say things about your boss, too. One day they'll say things about you."

"But there was—well, that court case . . ." Auden couldn't bring himself to be more specific.

"Raymond Silvers, and his attempt to kill me? That's a perfect example of what I mean. If you want to know what *really* happened, you should read the actual court hearings. You'll see that I didn't do a thing except reject his unwanted advances. But the media all hate me, I'm much too patriotic for them. They distort everything. I can't let their rumors and lies control my life. Or yours." He moved his hand again, this time placing it lightly onto Auden's forearm. Auden felt the goose bumps rise, as unwanted and as uncontrollable as a blush.

"Look," Lopez went on, "I'll make you a promise. You arrive at the party with me, but after that you're on your own. You talk with anyone you want to. You do whatever you want to. You leave anytime you want to. What do you say?"

"It sounds very interesting. I've hardly left my desk for two weeks. And I haven't been out to a party in months. My clothes—"

"—are fine, just the way they are. I told you, this is informal. One question, though. Do you have anybody at the moment?"

"You mean, anybody, like—"

"Yes, that is exactly what I mean. Look, Auden, I'm not being nosy, but I know one thing for sure. When I show up at the party with somebody looking like you, and people realize that the two of us aren't an item, that's the first question *I'm* going to be asked. So I'm asking you ahead of time. Do you have someone?"

"Not right now, Senator. Last year."

"Not 'Senator,' please. Call me Nick, or Nicky—you'll have to call me that at the party; everyone else does. And last year was last year, it doesn't count. We all have pasts. *Now the New Year, reviving old desires . . . Ah, my beloved, fill the cup that clears, today of past regrets and future fears . . .*" He took Auden's hand and squeezed it. "Now, I'm really in your power. You have a secret of mine that all Washington would love to know, something you must *never* reveal. Nick Lopez, quoting old poetry—and not even good old American poetry. It would ruin my reputation. Let's go."

And, as Auden rolled down his shirtsleeves and picked up his jacket, Lopez added softly and in a different voice, "There's one other thing I have to say, Auden. You can make what you like of this, forget it or ignore it or use it any way you choose. But so far as I am concerned, I'm really thrilled that you don't have anybody now."

14

When would the orbiters leave the space station to make their reentry?

Where would they land?

Who would be on each one?

Zoe Nash had taken total responsibility for those three decisions. "I'll tell you, when, and where, and who."

Zoe was confident, if not casual, and for that Celine was profoundly grateful. Thinking about the situation as she made her way through the silent interior of ISS-2, she knew she would have agonized endlessly and never been able to come up with answers. She was a natural procrastinator, able to see a hundred roads to failure.

How much preparation was enough? To Celine, two days was a ridiculously short time. On the other hand, you could check instruments and programs forever and still miss something. How did you divide the group in two? It was absolutely necessary, but how did you decide the mix of skills to place on each orbiter? The whole point of the Mars expedition crew was that it worked best as a single integrated unit.

Fortunately, Celine had a practical task to occupy her mind. She had been told to search the derelict for a dozen of a particular type of bonding clamp, needed in the orbiters, and she had located a whole cabinet of them in the central supply room of ISS-2. Now she was heading back through the desolate corridors. The previous two days had not hardened her to the sight of the frozen corpses, but she knew where they were and she had learned not to look at them.

At the open airlock she paused. In front of her, framed against the backdrop of a sunlit Earth, hung the *Schiaparelli*. It had been home for so long, the very idea of leaving it was frightening. To leave it in one of *those*—she glanced to her right, at the tiny, vulnerable orbiters—was doubly daunting. The interiors, even with the padded seats pulled out, were impossibly small. They were definitely one-person ships.

If everything went well, *Lewis* and *Clark*—Reza Armani's off-the-cuff names for the twin orbiters had stuck—would return to a torn and battered planet, whose peculiar cloud patterns and high dust clouds were evidence of the physical trauma that the world had suffered. What would the crew find when they landed? The radio signals remained sparse and weak, with some countries and continents totally silent. The *Schiaparelli* had sent calls for help and information on all frequencies. It had received not a word or a beep in reply.

Celine floated her way across to *Clark,* the nearer orbiter. She confirmed that the clamps were the right size and style to attach the hammocks to the walls, and performed the simple installation. The hammocks were tough, made of Mars tent materials that by good fortune had neither been landed on Mars nor discarded before the return trip. Without seats, hammocks would be the crew's only cushion against the high accelerations of reentry.

Celine tested that the bonds would hold for body loads up to thirty gees. Beyond that, humans would not survive even if the clamps could. She moved across to *Lewis* and performed the same task of installation. Then she headed to the home ship—home, at least, for another few hours—and passed through the *Schiaparelli*'s airlock. She removed her suit, rubbed her itching eyes, and floated on to the main cabin.

The other crew members were already there. Zoe gave Celine an inquiring glance, and she nodded.

"I found them. They fit."

"Good. Jenny?"

Jenny Kopal was crouched over a diagnostic pad. She shrugged. "I can only debug to a point using simulated inputs. According to every test routine that I have, the chips we put into the orbiters from this ship will perform identically to the dead ones they replaced. I loaded them all from the general program library for single-stage orbiters. But you know what they say. No matter how much testing you do, every program always has one bug left in it."

"Let's hope it's a bug we don't encounter before we're down on Earth." Zoe leaned back. "Alta?"

"I don't know." Alta paused and thought for thirty seconds. "I guess the orbiters are as ready as they'll ever be. I'm still worried about center-of-mass changes because of the unusual loading. But I think any one of us could fly one."

"Coming from a pessimist like you, I take that as a rave report. All right." Zoe leaned back. "It's showtime again, folks. And here is the plan. *Lewis* will perform reentry first. As you know, it can only hold three people. Those three are going to be Zoe Nash, Ludwig Holter, and Alta McIntosh-Mohammad. I will pilot *Lewis*. Then, unless someone wants to stay up here and wait for the next shuttle up from Earth"—Zoe smiled at her joke, but no one else did—"*Clark* will take Reza Armani, Jenny Kopal, Celine Tanaka, and Wilmer Oldfield. Reza will pilot *Clark*.

"*Lewis* will send telemetry back here all the time during reentry, except when it goes through the period of radio blackout. I believe the increased mass load on the second reentry will be more than compensated for by the opportunity to fine-tune *Clark*'s control parameters using the data from *Lewis*. Any questions so far?"

There was silence. It was obvious to Celine, as it must be to all of the others, that Zoe had included factors other than mass balance in deciding the complement of the two crews. She had placed the people pairs, Jenny/Reza, Alta/Ludwig, and Celine/Wilmer, on the same orbiter as each other. To some, that might suggest sentiment on Zoe's part. To a worrywart like Celine, it said that the reentry dangers were more than Zoe was willing to admit. She was offering them a chance to die as the couples that they had become.

"Now there is the question of *where*," Zoe went on. "Where should we aim to land? I think we can make one decision very easily: we avoid the Southern Hemisphere. We've picked up hardly a radio signal from there. Also, if we are off in our final along-track position, the Southern Hemisphere offers a higher chance of landing in water. The orbiters are not designed for an ocean splashdown, and even if they were I don't feel like a thousand-mile swim.

"The majority of the radio signals we have received come from North America, with considerably more from the northern states than the southern, and more from the east than the west. So north is good, and east is good. We are in a low inclination orbit, so a very high latitude touchdown is not possible. I think we can reach forty degrees north, and I propose that we try to do so. I will aim to make *Lewis*'s landing close to the fortieth parallel, near the eastern seaboard but at least a hundred miles from the Atlantic Ocean. Normally the orbiters can land on a dime, but we need a margin of error. I will not try to specify a final landing location now, because we have not been able to obtain a clear picture of surface conditions. We'll see what we have available when we get there. An airport would be nice, but any decent highway will do at a pinch. Naturally, once *Lewis* is down we'll send a message telling *Clark* what to aim for or what to avoid. We've been over all this before, in smaller groups. But does anybody have a question or a comment?"

She waited a few moments, and went on: "Then the only remaining question is, when?

"We will do one final start-to-finish checkout of everything, which ought to take no more than a few hours. After that, *Lewis* will take the next available reentry window. The main requirements are that we have a daytime landing—it's currently night in North America—and that *Lewis* has line-of-sight communications with those of you who are still here on the *Schiaparelli*. That means there has to be some orbit matching, but Jenny already did those calculations. Once *Lewis* is down, we can decide the schedule for *Clark* based on our experience. Any other questions?"

"I have been thinking."

To Celine's surprise, the speaker was Wilmer. He almost never contributed to group meetings. Quite often, he didn't seem to be listening. But he was. He would go away, brood over what he had heard, and return to offer crucial suggestions or devastating criticisms.

Celine decided that Wilmer understood, better than she had, the nature of this particular meeting. There would be no chance for later discussions. This was *it*, the final meeting of the Mars expedition until they were all once more on Earth.

"All right, Wilmer," Zoe said. "What's your worry?"

He put his hand up to scratch the top of his bald head—a habit that looked ludicrous and that Celine had not been able to change. It gave him a permanent and ugly red patch. "This is a suggestion, not a worry. You speak of a line-of-sight requirement for communications, and I assume that you mean radio signals. But I think we should also track the descent of the *Lewis* visually, using the biggest scope on the *Schiaparelli*."

"What would be the point of that?"

"Suppose that you encounter trouble during that period of reentry when ionization around the orbiter prevents the transmission of radio signals. Visual observation might then offer the only evidence of the nature of the difficulty."

"We don't anticipate trouble." Zoe glanced around the rest of the group, who were showing uneasiness in various ways at the implications of Wilmer's suggestion. "I guess we all like to think positive. But Wilmer is right. If anything were to go wrong with *Lewis,* the rest of you will need to learn all you can from our difficulties before *Clark* makes its own return from orbit. Celine, please make sure that the big scope is set up for continuous visual coverage of the reentry of *Lewis.*

"Anything else? No?" Zoe went on casually, as though orbital reentry to a radically changed Earth in an untested ship was the most routine operation imaginable. "Let's get to it, then. I'm fond of the *Schiaparelli,* and it's been good to us. But I'm a little bit itchy to get home."

"Day" and "night" on the *Schiaparelli* violated human nature and common sense. The Mars ship was locked into the same orbit as ISS-2, and every ninety minutes brought a new dawn and a new sunset. It took five of those "days," almost eight hours, before the motion of Earth and ship were synchronized, and Zoe was able to say from the controls of *Lewis,* "We have thrust. See you all down there."

Celine and the other three were in the control room of the *Schiaparelli,* where they could receive radio inputs from *Lewis* and visual images from the biggest of the onboard scopes. She looked at Jenny, Reza, and Wilmer and felt a strange uneasiness. Zoe, Ludwig, and Alta had not always been in the same cabin with her on the *Schiaparelli;* for much of the time on the return journey, they had all hidden themselves away from each other. But in a sense the other six had been "there," all the time. They had formed a unit, working together in the greatest feat of human exploration ever undertaken.

Now they were split, and even when they came together again on Earth it would not be the same. Something had been lost in that moment of *Lewis*'s departure. Celine hated the feeling of loneliness.

At the moment the orbiter was still close to them, and they did not need a scope to see the blue-white flare of its nuclear rocket. But *Lewis* dropped away steadily, losing altitude and velocity, and as the minutes passed the ship as seen without the scope dwindled to a fiery spark. It was beginning the long arc down to the atmosphere of the Earth.

"Everything is nominal." Zoe's voice was clear over the telemetry. "The control routines are behaving exactly as we hoped and expected. You will lose radio contact with us in eight minutes."

Even when ionization induced a temporary radio silence, the image of the orbiter would still be picked up by the big onboard telescope and displayed on the control-room screen. Celine looked, and saw that *Lewis* had already switched off its engine and turned for the nose-first reentry. The image of the orbiter was tiny but quite clear. She even imagined she could make out the dots of people's heads in the cabin's transparent viewport.

She glanced at the display showing elapsed time. Only nine minutes since first thrust. It felt much longer.

"Looking good." Zoe sounded a fraction fainter, but maybe that was Celine's imagination. "We are losing altitude as planned and are already experiencing atmospheric drag. We project loss of radio contact in five minutes and seventeen seconds, eight seconds ahead of schedule. Report back receipt of this signal."

Celine did so, automatically. The Earth below was invisible. It was still night there, though in another nine minutes Celine would look down onto a sunlit United States. *Lewis* was heading for a single-step reentry. There would be no "bounce" aerobraking as they had used it on Mars, skimming into the upper atmosphere and out again several times, like a pebble skipped across the surface of a lake and shedding velocity on each transit. The Earth orbiters and landers all accomplished reentry in a single pass. Aerodynamic and thermal forces were much greater that way, but the ships were designed to take it.

"The hull indicates an increase over predicted temperature," Zoe said. Her voice was overlaid with the faintest hiss and crackle. "Parameters are still within the predicted range. Ionization is beginning, somewhat ahead of schedule. We expect radio blackout in two minutes and eleven seconds, seventeen seconds ahead of schedule. Report back receipt of this signal."

Celine glanced at the other three in the control room. Jenny was serious, following the flight parameters coming over the telemetry and nodding approval. Reza was smiling, moving his hands as though he were flying the *Lewis* himself. Wilmer alone seemed worried, his hand to his chin and his heavy brow furrowed.

"Hull temperature is rising more rapidly." The distortion in Zoe's voice was greater. "It is a good deal more than predicted. I have to lessen the angle of attack and I project a change in down-range landing distance. I am taking manual control of orbiter attitude. We expect radio blackout in fifty seconds."

More than a minute ahead of schedule. Much too soon.

"Refer to visuals," Jenny said softly. Celine looked at the display from the big scope and saw on it a bright arrow trail. The *Lewis* was the silver tip at the head of the arrow.

Celine gave one rapid glance at the unmagnified display. The tiny mote of the *Lewis,* a hundred and more miles beneath the *Schiaparelli,* was not visible. She said urgently, "*Lewis,* we are losing radio contact. Report if you are hearing us."

The radio signal telemetry sounded in her ears as a loud hiss of static, within which every trace of Zoe's voice had been lost. The control board provided the real-time power spectrum of the telemetry, and it was pure white noise.

"They are entering the period of maximum drag and maximum ionization," Celine said—an unnecessary comment for the others in the control room, who knew it as well as she did, but needed for a full record of events. "This has occurred sixty-six seconds ahead of prediction. Radio contact has been lost."

The display from the big scope also showed the nominal flight trajectory for the *Lewis* as it had been calculated ahead of time. The two curves, computed orange and observed yellow, were diverging. Celine could see the separation increasing as she watched. The real ship was falling far behind its simulated twin.

"The atmospheric drag force is way high," Wilmer said suddenly. "The reentry angle must be too steep. It's as though they made an attitude correction the wrong way."

It was useless to ask how he knew—he had his own inexplicable way of making estimates. It was also pointless. The big scope was still providing its display. As Wilmer was speaking, the silver arrow tip brightened.

"Black body equivalent temperature of *Lewis*'s hull, forty-two hundred degrees," Jenny said. She was reading the output of the *Schiaparelli*'s bolometer. "That exceeds predicted maximum by six hundred degrees."

Still well within tolerances. The exotic materials of the orbiter's hull were rated up to fifty-four hundred degrees. But a normal reentry never came close to that. And Celine did not need the bolometric output to tell her that the temperature of *Lewis*'s hull was still increasing. The silver arrowhead had become a blaze of blue. Telemetry was a roar of static in her ears.

"Go *up*," Reza said urgently. He was working imaginary controls, pulling back on them. "Forget the one-shot reentry. Go higher, take another shot later."

Radio silence was two-way. There was no chance that Zoe Nash could hear him. Frictional heating surrounded the racing orbiter with a blaze of ionized gases.

"Black body equivalent temperature of *Lewis*'s hull, six thousand degrees." Jenny's voice was a dead whisper. Then, with urgency, "Cool *down*. You can't take that for long."

She was right. As she spoke, the blazing arrow tip vanished. It was replaced by a puff of white, round and delicate as a cotton ball.

Celine did not cry out. She leaned forward and covered her face with her hands. That innocuous cottony cloud was an incandescent rage of flaming gas. In its heart were Zoe Nash, Ludwig Holter, and Alta McIntosh-Mohammad, reduced to their component atoms in *Lewis*'s fiery explosion.

They would be carried away by the pendent winds, blown and dispersed by the restless violence of the atmosphere. If the three crew reached a single final landing place, no one would ever know it.

The control room was silent except for Reza's harsh breathing. Celine rocked backward and forward, unable to weep or to make any sound. All she could think was that Zoe, supercapable and superconfident Zoe, had been wrong.

Zoe would not be down on Earth in two days. Zoe would not be there ever.

15

The snow had ended. The wind was dropping away to nothing, and with the loss of cloud cover the night had become bitterly and unnaturally cold.

The ancient frigate chugged south at a leisurely eight knots, while at the bow Saul Steinmetz stood hatted, gloved, and swaddled in winter clothes. His brain was buzzing after a two-hour whirlwind of snap executive judgments that everyone else in government seemed too scared to make. One side effect of Supernova Alpha was Saul's own apparent apotheosis. No one questioned his authority to do anything.

The buck stops here. Good old Harry Truman, he said it better than anybody. But it would be nice to think you were making *right* decisions.

Saul was alone, but not, he was sure, unobserved. Even if the frigate crew could conquer their natural curiosity at having the President on board, his security staff were still on duty.

One week ago, heavy rains had pushed the river far above flood stage. The level was lower now, but when the snow melted the waters would rise again, farther than ever. The only evidence for wild conditions upstream lay in the large amount of carried sediment. At night, the heavy suspension of reddish mud did not show. The water lay thick and black as oil, parting smoothly before the old warship's advance.

Saul stared downstream. A light was blinking there, alien in its slow staccato. A warning? No, a message, that was much more reasonable. A message intended for this ship?

Peering at the point of light and wondering about its meaning, Saul allowed his mind to wander away to more personal questions. Was he going to learn something, as he believed, or was he running away? A thousand things needed doing back in his White House second-floor office. Auden Travis was the most diplomatic of aides, but his face had made his views clear when Saul said where he was going. There had been some kind of fight between Auden and Yasmin Silvers. Maybe tonight Saul would learn the cause.

And what was it between Saul and Tricia? Why had she called, out of the blue, after a two-year silence?

It was certainly not for lunch and a casual how-are-you. Tricia's whole history showed that she did nothing casually.

She had been born Patricia Stennis, poor in Toledo. At age eighteen she had gone to work for the country's biggest software company, where the next year at a Detroit trade show she had caught the eye of the aging majority shareholder. Six months later they married and she moved to California. She became Patricia Stennis Leighton, and soon after that, Patsy Leighton. She had been totally devoted and loyal to her husband for four years—until, suddenly and surprisingly, they had divorced.

One year after that Patsy was in Houston, the wife of an oil baron whose ranch sprawled across three hundred square miles and embodied an excess of all forms of bad taste. Trish Beacon, as she was now, enjoyed—or endured, though she would never admit it—two and a half years of Lone Star lifestyle, until finally she and Bobby Beacon divorced.

The next fall Trish married into some of the oldest money in the country. She moved readily, maybe even eagerly, from west Texas to Delaware. Again, she was unswervingly loyal to and admiring of her husband. Saul first met her at a reception in Wilmington when she was two years into her third marriage. She was now Tricia Chartrain. He found her breathtakingly attractive. She seemed to take little notice of him, then or at other dinners and social functions where their paths crossed. Always, she talked admiringly of her husband, Willis Chartrain.

A year later, she called Saul at his Atlanta office. She and dear Willis had divorced—she would prefer not to talk about it. She was in town for a few days, and without an escort for a dinner party. She remembered that Saul's headquarters were in Atlanta. Would he, as a great favor, consider being her dinner companion?

Would he? He had ended a long go-nowhere affair two months earlier, soon after the primaries made it clear that he had a good shot at the party nomination. But Saul was Saul. He set the machinery to work, and had a detailed report on Tricia in less than a week. Patricia Stennis/Patsy Leighton/Trish Beacon/Tricia Chartrain had played around some in Toledo and elsewhere when she was very young, but in her marriages she had been either faithful to her husband or infinitely discreet. An association with Tricia was unlikely to ruin Saul on the campaign trail.

In fact, the report came too late. Saul and Tricia had become lovers on the night of the dinner party. They remained that way, passionate and committed and inseparable, for the next six months. She had a way of devoting herself, totally and unreservedly, to Saul and his interests. It was intoxicating, something he had never known before. He knew that he would give her anything, or give up anything for her.

Anything, until the day his political advisers came to meet him on the campaign trail in Oregon. Tricia was away, spending a day or two with old friends from the Patsy Leighton software days in San Francisco. The message delivered to Saul was quite clear. They had the poll results and the analysis. Married to Tricia, Saul would lose his bid to be President.

He refused to believe it. He argued, he pleaded. She's beautiful, she's wealthy, she's kind and generous, she has an unblemished past.

"Yes, yes. We're not arguing with any of that. She may be a saint for all we know. But it's not relevant. Gotta be hard-nosed about this, Saul. Look at the data, look at the numbers. You marry her, you're dead in the water. She's been around the block too often, that last marriage was one too many."

Saul looked at the numbers. They were a disaster.

"Has anybody else seen these?"

"Only Crossley and Himmelfarb, the Palo Alto pollsters who did the analysis. They have instructions to keep everything confidential."

"God, I should hope so. Look, suppose I don't get married. What are the chances of making it to the White House as a bachelor?"

"We tested that, too." Out came more charts and displays. "It looks good. Seventy-nine percent, with a standard deviation of less than three points."

"Did the same people run this poll and analysis?"

"Negative. We used Quip Research out of Denver. We wanted an independent check on what Crossley and Himmelfarb came up with. So no one knows the whole story but us. Their results are consistent, though. Run without her, Saul, and you'll win."

"What about reelection, if Tricia and I marry once I'm in office?"

The looks they offered ranged from incredulous to uncomprehending. Reelection? Reelection was something you worried about in another four years. Four years in political forecasting was infinity, far over the horizon. Between now and then, the world could end.

That day, however, Saul faced a simple choice. He could have the White House in November; or he could have Tricia. At a ninety-seven percent confidence level, he could not have both.

"All right. Damnation." Saul looked at his watch. "I'll explain things to Tricia. Tonight."

He had explained. Silver-tongued Saul Steinmetz, who could make any human being understand him and what he was doing, if only he had a chance to sit down and talk to the person one-on-one, had explained.

And Tricia?

Saul stared out across the quiet waters and wished that he had brought a cigar with him. They were on the controlled substance list, as well as on his doctor's personal list of forbiddens for Saul, but Forrest Singer was not here. Nor, unfortunately, were any cigars.

The frigate had passed Alexandria twenty minutes ago, visible as a scattering of faint lights on the starboard bow. At their modest speed, Indian Head lay some minutes ahead. Maybe more than that. Saul had the feeling that their speed was less. He walked to the rail and peered over. Ripples were spreading in almost a circular pattern. The frigate was barely moving.

"Sir?" The musical voice came as a surprise from behind him. He turned to face a uniformed woman whose features were half-hidden behind goggles and a warm face mask.

"Yes, Lieutenant. What is it? Why are we stopping?"

"We have received a Morse code report of earlier activity downriver, sir. A dozen civilian vessels—fishing boats, we believe—crossed from the eastern to the western bank about two hours ago. The river appears quiet now, but the captain ordered a reduction of speed until we can be sure."

"Very good." Saul recognized the implied question. Was the action ahead related to the President's trip to the Indian Head naval facility? "Tell the captain that I have no idea what is going on downriver. If it involves the federal government in some way, I have not been briefed on the activity."

"Yes, sir."

"The captain should use his judgment, and resume speed as soon as he feels comfortable in doing so."

"Yes, sir."

The warmly clad figure saluted, turned, and marched away. Half a minute later Saul felt the throb of diesels through the plates of the deck. The pattern of ripples changed at the frigate's sides.

Morse code. That was the blinking light he had noticed earlier. How long since he had even heard the word? There must have been a frantic study of ancient manuals in the past couple of weeks. In an age of instant electronics, Morse code and semaphore were archaisms.

Were archaisms. Not anymore. Until the chips were back in production, Morse and semaphore were state-of-the-art technology.

Saul, looking higher, saw in the dark sky to the south another point of light. This one was of a fixed intensity, but moving steadily in the sky. It was a spacecraft, high enough to catch a sun that the ground had lost half an hour since. From the size and direction of movement, he was witnessing a transit of one of the two international space stations, once the home of hundreds of crew and scientists; now, a great floating sarcophagus.

The Sino Consortium had planned to launch a giant station, all their own, in mid April. It was their gesture of superiority, their finger raised to the United States: *You had your day, we are the top dogs now!*

Saul, chilled through his multiple layers of clothes, turned and headed aft. Today the Sino Consortium, if the reports reaching Saul were accurate, would have trouble launching a marble into space. So, unfortunately, would the United States.

The Indian Head facility was in mothballs, and had been for a quarter of a century. Only strenuous local politics had allowed its continued existence. According to the report pulled out for Saul before he left, the pre-supernova staffing of Indian Head had been at a caretaker level of twenty.

So why were a hundred people and more crowding the jetty as he came ashore?

Saul knew the answer when he saw the crowded ships at

neighboring berths and the insignia on some of the waiting group. He counted six full captains. Word of his trip had spread. Navy forces along the whole stretch of the Potomac from here to Washington had been placed on full alert.

He swore to himself. He had seen it again and again in the past two years. Nothing he had been able to say or do would stop it.

You asked an off-the-cuff question during a briefing, maybe about government personnel grades today compared with twenty years ago. Sometimes you were just making conversation. Your casual inquiry was noted and passed on. As it went down the line, it developed momentum. Soon it was a "presidential directive."

One week later, a massive report appeared on your desk. It was a comprehensive review of hiring and promotion policies throughout the whole of the federal government. It was stuffed with historical facts and tables and complicated charts, and it represented hundreds or thousands of hours of intense effort. Half a dozen staff members nervously awaited your request for a briefing.

And you? You didn't remember asking the question.

Yellow electric bulbs had been strung on wooden posts along the quay to provide an improvised lighting system. Saul walked the line of waiting personnel, acknowledging their salutes. He always felt a little bogus in the presence of the military. Because he had seen no service himself, he had been advised early in his political career to adopt a strongly pro-military attitude. He had done so, urging better appreciation for the peacetime role of the services. He really believed in that, but maybe he had overdone it. At any rate, he now seemed to be considered "one of them" by every serviceman and -woman.

Yasmin Silvers was standing in the group at the end of the receiving line. The weak yellow glow of the lights showed a strange look on her face. Bewilderment?

That would be reasonable. Saul felt sure that for the past few hours everyone had been asking her, directly or indirectly, the reason for the President's sudden decision to visit Indian Head.

Next to Yasmin a grizzled veteran stood at rigid attention. In spite of the cold he was in full uniform and wearing no overcoat.

"Welcome to Indian Head, Mr. President." The salute was slow and a little arthritic. "I am Captain Kennecott, OIC."

"At ease, Captain." Saul decided to put Kennecott out of his misery—and move the old man inside before they had a case of hypothermia on their hands. He put Kennecott's age in the early eighties. The commodore must be a reemployed annuitant, protected in his position by the Gray Rights laws. But no laws protected the old from pneumonia. "I would like you to provide me a full inspection of the base tomorrow morning, Captain. For tonight, though, I must meet privately with Ms. Silvers, and I plan no other functions. Everyone can be dismissed—and let's all get inside before we freeze."

"Yes, sir." Kennecott led Saul up a steep flagstone path cleared of snow, and went into the back of an old building of red brick. As they entered the ambient temperature rose fifty degrees. "So far as sleeping accommodations are concerned, and meals . . ." Kennecott turned to stare uncertainly at the six security staff who dogged Saul's footsteps.

"Whatever the kitchen happens to have available. I will need a room for private discussion with Ms. Silvers while I eat, but *what* I eat is of no importance. As for sleeping, do you still have visitors' quarters on base?"

"Yes, sir." Captain Kennecott blinked watery blue eyes at Saul. "Here in the Officers' Club. But, Mr. President, the rooms here in the Mix House are old and primitive and unused for many years. The BEQ's, Bachelor Enlisted Quarters, are even worse. They have never been updated for an integrated service. There was no budget for it."

"Do you have running water?"

"Yes, sir. The base has its own generators and storage tanks."

"Then we are better off than most people in this country." Saul looked around. He knew where Captain Kennecott was going: to an invitation to stay at his own house, which Saul did not want at all. "I'll stay here in the Officers' Club. Do you have a room right here where I can hold private meetings?"

"Yes, sir. And the kitchen is already open." Kennecott led them through the building and up one floor, to a blue-walled room holding a long oak table and twenty chairs. "If this would do?" He ran a gnarled hand lovingly along the smooth, still-polished surface. "This was our conference room, Mr. President, back in the days when this base still had a major mission as a naval propellant test center."

"This will do beautifully. Thank you, Captain." Old sailors didn't die. They went down with their bases.

"Thank you, sir. May I say what an honor it is to have you here? In one hundred and twenty-eight years since this facility was established, this is only the second visit from a sitting President."

As Captain Kennecott left, Yasmin Silvers nodded to Saul. "You really made his day."

"I hope so."

"Would you consider making mine?" Her voice changed. "By telling me what is going on?"

No "sir," no "Mr. President." Saul heard bottled-up bewilderment and unhappiness coming out at him. And he didn't know why.

"You mean, why did I decide to visit Indian Head?"

"I don't mean that at all. I mean, why did you arrange for me to go down to the Q-5 Syncope Facility, and not tell me that something peculiar was going on there? I gather all sorts of things happened downriver tonight. If I hadn't been stuck here because of the weather, I'd have landed in the middle of it."

"You think I set you up? That I knew what was going on there, but I sent you without telling you?"

"Didn't you? Yes, I do think that. I feel like an experimental animal."

"Christ, Yasmin. What kind of sadist do you take me for?" It was a reaction not to her anger, but to her lack of trust. That hurt. "You have a good brain. Use it, and *think*. Did I arrange for your brother to stick a knife into that twisted bastard rapist Lopez? Did I arrange for your brother to be iced down in Q-5, just so I could send you there? For your information, I didn't know that *anything* was happening downriver tonight. And I still have no idea what's going on there."

When Saul was angry he became cold and remote, not hot and loud. He had not raised his voice. That was just as well, because his final words came at the same time as the perfunctory knock on the door and the arrival of their food.

Did it really take nine people to serve bean soup followed by broiled fresh fish with potatoes and carrots? It did if you happened to be the President, and all the cooks on the base wanted to be able to tell their friends that they had served you dinner.

He and Yasmin waited in awkward silence as the plates and serving dishes were set out, along with glasses and a bottle of white wine that he had not asked for. She had an appalled and stricken stare on her face. She knew she had gone way over the mark for a presidential aide. And she had been wrong in her accusations. He knew it, too, but for the moment he could say nothing without making things worse.

The head of the group of waiters at last stepped back and cocked his head at Saul. "Mr. President?"

Saul nodded. "That's wonderful. Thank you."

You were polite to and praised strangers, but you told a staff member whom you really liked to use her brain and think.

"I'm sorry, Yasmin," he said as soon as the servers had left the room. "*Really* sorry for what I said. It's no excuse, but all the frustrations of the day came out at you." He waved to the food. "Help yourself. Eat."

"I can't." She swallowed. "Not yet. You—"

He waited, pouring and drinking wine that he did not want.

"You didn't know?" she said at last.

"I didn't know. I don't know now."

"Then why *did* you come here?"

Saul poured wine for both of them and served soup into Yasmin's bowl. He coaxed her to eat.

If the staff wanted to see something, they ought to have stayed for this. President turns headwaiter and wet nurse.

When she took a first spoonful he said, "I came here for two reasons, one professional and one very personal. You may find the first hard to understand, but I have more trouble with the second. To begin with, from February 9 until this evening I had not been out of the White House for more than a few minutes at a time."

"But that's because everyone comes to see you, to save your time. And you were receiving plenty of reports. I know, because Auden Travis and I brought them to you."

"You certainly did." Saul gave up on the wine, too sweet for his taste. Yasmin was drinking it much too fast. "Which reminds me. I'm not trying to change the subject, but what happened between the two of you just before you left?"

"Oh." Yasmin pushed out her bottom lip. "We had a bit of a fight."

"I could guess that. About?"

"Well, it began when he learned of your authorization for me to travel to the syncope facility. I wouldn't—couldn't—tell him why I was going. I said it was no business of his. So he started making guesses. I didn't respond, and he became upset because he thought you were sending me on some special secret mission. I told him that wasn't true. He didn't believe me. He accused me of having an unfair advantage dealing with you because I'm a woman. I told him it wasn't my choice, Nature did that."

"That's all you said to him?"

"Well, no. I kind of told him—"

"Kind of? I'd rather hear it exactly."

"Yes, but I wouldn't rather say it." When Saul remained silent, she went on, "All right. I told him that he'd fuck you himself if he had half a chance. I knew the cussing would annoy him as much as the thought—especially since it's true. He got madder than ever."

Saul shook his head in disbelief. "What did you expect? That after he heard that he would back down and apologize?"

"I wasn't thinking. Especially after he told me that I now occupied the most senior position I would ever have in my whole life, because I'd used up all the black-Hispanic-woman cards."

"And you of course, to avoid further argument, agreed."

"No, sir." Yasmin emptied half a glass of wine in one gulp and poured herself more. "I told him that I would go a damn sight farther than he ever would, and I didn't see why I couldn't be President someday." Her nostrils flared, and emotion thickened the air between them like hot, strong syrup. "I'm going to be the first female President, I told him, the way Saul Steinmetz is the first Jewish President. And to get there I'm going to jiggle and wiggle my sexy black-Hispanic-woman's ass any way I have to, with anybody I feel like. A damn sight more men will chase me, I said, than will ever go after you, Auden Travis. You should have seen his face when I told him that. He'd have murdered me on the spot if he could." She looked up at Saul, who was sitting with head bowed. "I'm sorry, sir. I'm not suggesting that I really do—well, you know. I was just mad at him. But you did ask for it exactly."

"I did, didn't I?"

"What happens now, sir?"

"Now I'm thinking that alcohol is not a traditional Jewish vice, but maybe I ought to give the wine another try." Saul raised his head, and their eyes locked. "Actually, I'm thinking that in a couple of days, you and Auden Travis will have to work together again—or one of you will be leaving. Maybe both of you. Do you want that?"

"No, sir." Her voice was a whisper. "I don't. I really don't."

"I thought not."

"I love my job with you."

"So there will have to be apologies, won't there? On both sides."

"Yes, sir." Her face was pale. "There will be apologies."

"Very good." Saul stabbed savagely at a piece of fish with his fork. "I know this was hard on you, Yasmin; but it was necessary. There's nothing wrong with ambition, but I insist on civility between members of my personal staff. Otherwise working together is impossible. Understand?"

"Yes, sir."

"All right. End of that subject. Let's return to our previous topic." From the miserable expression on her face, he was not sure that she remembered what it had been. He prompted: "I've been confined to the White House. I receive a ton of reports every day. And everything that I hear or see has been filtered."

That got through. She sat upright in her chair. "Not by me, sir."

"By you, and by everybody else. This isn't just Saul Steinmetz complaining. The same thing happens to every President. People tell a chief executive what they think he wants to hear. Rosy economic reports, high popularity figures, promising international changes, you name it. There's a competition to be the first with good news. Anyone who tells bad news tends to get weeded out—even if all the real news is bad."

"I don't hide bad news from you, sir."

"You try not to. And I love you for it." Saul wondered about that choice of verb, but Yasmin perked up visibly. Anyway, it was too late to change what he had said, and he went on, "I need inputs that tell it straight. Before the gamma pulse, I thought I had a way through the shield of people around me. My office was wired for direct data feeds. I could switch from space cameras to farm country to undersea to almost every state and city in the world. When I lost that service I felt I'd been blinded. Until it comes back there's only one answer: I have to get outside the White House and see for myself. Inspecting places like this is important. And I need help—I can't be everywhere. I'll give you just one example. The Q-5 is listed as a 'small' facility for extended syncope, but over eleven thousand prisoners are there—including murderers, human monsters, and a number of the country's most dangerous convicted terrorists. I have seen not one word about the condition of Q-5 in any report. When you go there to find your brother, I want you to keep your eyes open and give me a briefing when you get back to Washington. Something is happening at Q-5, but I don't trust my military advisers to understand what. They see everything through their own filters."

"I'll do my best. It will be difficult with Raymond to worry about, but I'll try to be objective."

Saul nodded and became quiet. He remained that way for a long time, slowly eating. So long that at last Yasmin, restored by wine, time, and silence to some of her natural sassiness, felt curious enough to prompt him.

"Sir?"

Saul looked up at her. She smiled, a warm but tentative smile.

"You said you had another reason for coming here to see me, sir. A personal reason. If you would like to tell me about that, I'd very much like to listen."

16

You heard talk of electrical power returning to the whole city, but so far there was no sign of it. The candles, flickering low, turned the long basement room to a maze of shadows. Auden Travis didn't see where Nick Lopez came from, but suddenly the Senator was smiling at his side.

"No rush, Auden, but it's thinning out." Lopez gestured to the door, where half a dozen men were putting on their coats. "Jeremy and Raoul would never dream of saying anything—we could stay here 'til dawn if we wanted to. But it's close to two o'clock."

"It can't be that late." Auden looked at his wrist, where of course there was no working watch. "It feels about ten o'clock."

"Believe me, it's not." Lopez took Travis's elbow. "They have to get up in the morning for work—and so do you."

"I suppose so." Auden moved toward the door at Lopez's gentle urging, but before he arrived there he turned his head for a final look down the room.

"Enjoy it?" Lopez asked quietly.

"I had a wonderful time, Senator."

"Nick."

"Nick." Travis took a deep breath. "I know this will sound corny, but I haven't enjoyed an evening as much as this in my entire life. It makes me feel almost guilty, having such a great time when the city and the world is such a mess."

"It is a mess, but not because of anything we did. I'm glad you liked it. I hope you'll come again."

"I'd love to. If I get invited."

"Oh, come on, don't be silly. Couldn't you see you were the hit of the evening?"

"I thought it was my imagination. Everyone was so *friendly* to me."

"And why shouldn't they be? You are gorgeous. And you deserve a few hours of pleasure. You work much too hard, you know. I hope Saul appreciates you."

"Oh, he does." But Travis couldn't erase the memory of the President running off after that whore, Yasmin Silvers. He wanted to pour out the truth to Lopez, but he couldn't do that. "The President entrusts me with a great deal of information," he said at last. *Except why he sent her to the syncope facility, then went running off after her. Though the last part isn't hard to guess.*

"He trusts you because you can be trusted," Lopez said. "I trust you already, and I don't know you well."

They retrieved their coats in silence and went to thank Raoul and Jeremy in the kitchen, who both gave Auden a hug and said, "Be sure to come again."

"He will," Lopez said. "I'll talk him into it. And now let's see what the weather is doing out there."

They left the apartment and started up the steps from the basement to the ground level. At the top the Senator patted the pockets of his overcoat.

"Uh-oh. My hat. I put it on the entrance table when I came in. Wait here, I won't be a second. Maybe you can take a look and see if it stopped snowing."

When he returned Auden was standing at the top with the outside door cracked open an inch. He had his eyes closed, but he turned when he heard Lopez's footsteps.

"It's not nice at all out there, sir. Freezing cold and deep snow."

"For God's sake, Auden, are you trying to make me angry? I'm not *sir,* I'm *Nick*. I'm your friend, not your superior officer."

"I'm sorry. Nick. It's hard to get used to it. You've been Senator Lopez in my mind for so long."

"Like some crumbling relic?"

"I didn't mean that at all. Nick."

"I believe you. Just what *is* it doing outside?" Lopez opened the door wide, and a blast of air and flurry of snowflakes blew in. "Jeez. Not nice doesn't begin to describe it. It's hell out there. Dangerous, too, without our security escort."

"Do you have far to go?"

"Me?" Nick Lopez stared at Auden. "I don't have to go anywhere. I live here. I have a big apartment—on the second floor, fortunately, since we don't have elevators now. But it's you I'm thinking about."

"You don't have to worry. It's only a few blocks."

"It's a good half mile. A five-minute taxi ride to the White House—except that now there are no cabs anymore. Auden, you can't possibly walk in this weather, in the middle of the night."

"I'll be safe enough."

"Don't bet on it. It's a zoo out there. But even if you don't get mugged, you'll freeze to death. And it's so unnecessary. You can stay at my place."

"I need to be at my job in the morning."

"And so do I. But you told me yourself, the President has gone off someplace downriver. He won't be at the White House in the morning. There's not a reason in the world why you have to be there before, say, nine o'clock."

"I don't know."

"Well, I do." Lopez closed the door firmly. "I'd be pleased and honored if you accept my hospitality for the night. And I'll be mortified if you refuse."

Auden hesitated. He had heard Nick Lopez's explanation, that everyone in Washington had a bad reputation and that he was no exception. Auden knew this to be at least partially true—he had heard scurrilous stories about almost everybody, from the President to eighty-seven-year-old Lucas Munce.

But inside every story there was likely to be a kernel of truth. Auden had heard wildly conflicting reports about Senator Nick Lopez. He was the finest man in Washington. He was a slave to his own sexual urges. He was a loyal friend who offered his friendship for life. He took young men, made them crazy about him, and dropped them without a second thought.

Auden should not stay overnight in Nick's apartment. Not because there was the stigma of illegality to the relationship—the brave gay men who stormed the barricades fifty years ago had forced those changes. But legality was insufficient to remove all stigma. Not every part of America was urban and cosmopolitan. Plenty of small-minded and small-town religious bigots would express open outrage if they learned that an aide close to the President was not heterosexual. One published word, and both Auden and the President could suffer. That was why since joining the White House staff Auden had been celibate for so long.

But tonight it was more than so long. It was too long. Auden felt wonderful, relaxed and giddy and amorous all at the same time. *Your loyalty does you credit,* Nick had said. *Meanwhile, you are left here, to work and work and work. What time do you stop?*

It seemed like he never stopped. But if Senator Lopez—Nick—felt free to take things easy for a few hours, why should Auden be any different?

"Well?" Nick Lopez was smiling, patiently waiting. "I'm telling you, I'll be heartbroken if you say no."

"If you put it that way . . ."

"I certainly do." Lopez put his arm around Auden's shoulder and steered him toward the staircase. "We'll go upstairs, have a drink and talk. We need to get to know each other—you were so popular tonight, I couldn't get near you. And there's one other thing."

"What's that, Nick?" Travis shivered slightly at the pressure of Lopez's arm, but he did not draw away.

"It's what we were talking about this afternoon, before we came here. My 'reputation,' as you put it."

"Oh, that." Auden laughed. He was no longer nervous. "I'm not worried about that anymore, now that I've seen how you are with your friends. I'm not worried about anything."

"Good. But I want to say one thing more. I value our friendship highly, for what it is now and what I hope it will become. So you have my promise: nothing will happen tonight that you don't absolutely want to happen."

"I know that, Nick. You don't have to make me any promises. I'm an adult." Auden nestled a little closer. He wasn't merely a career, he was a man, too, with his own needs. "I think I knew how things would turn out with us even before we set out for the party."

17

Art woke rested and curiously at peace. He had slept through the whole night, rare for him in the past few years. It took a few moments to realize that he had been awakened by the disappearance of the warm body next to his.

It was already full day. He turned his head, opened his eyes, and stared blearily at the dark shape outlined against the window.

"You're a blanket hog, d'you know that?" Dana sounded as lively as he felt comatose. "I had to fight for my share half a dozen times."

"Sorry." Art's throat and mouth felt dry, and his voice was gravelly.

"I bet. But there are worse bedtime sins."

"Like what?"

"We'll talk about it some other time. You can stay put for a while if you want, I'm going to boil water."

"What's it doing outside?"

"The snow has tapered off, but it's deep on the ground. It looks cold—colder than it should be this late in the year. I thought the supernova was supposed to make the world hotter?"

"On average. But mainly it screws up the weather." Art sat up, and felt the well-being that comes with a good night's sleep. "Instead of west–east patterns the winds seem to be running north–south."

"Straight from the North Pole." Dana was fully dressed. "I'll see you downstairs. We won't let the weather stop us."

As she went out Art pushed back the bedclothes and stood up. His knee gave hardly a twinge when he put his weight on it.

There was the real answer to arthritis: find a beautiful woman and use her as your warming pad.

He and Dana hadn't said a word since last night about Oliver Guest, but her comment as she left confirmed his own thoughts. They were going to take the risk. They would try to reach the Facility for Extended Syncope and wake up a multiple murderer—who also happened to be a telomod expert.

When and how would they go, and what would they do if they got there? Those were separate questions, to be answered later.

Seth Parsigian was already working the little stove when Art arrived downstairs. He must have been down to the basement and recharged it from the propane tanks. He was astonishingly grubby, but very alert. Maybe Dana was right, the man never slept. Today, though, Seth seemed preoccupied. He nodded to Art and said gruffly, "*Buenos días, hombre*. We got problems. We need ideas."

"How to find Oliver Guest?" Art accepted coffee from Dana and brought the cup to his face so that the steam could warm his nose. The room, like the whole building, was icy cold.

"Not how to find him." Seth was already dressed in outdoor clothes. "I know where Guest was iced down, it was in the syncope facility south of Washington at Maryland Point. Forty to fifty miles from here. Unless somebody moved him, and I don't see why anyone would, he's there still. Trouble is, we got no way to reach him. Roads are deep snow. Even our tractor wouldn't make it."

So much for Art's idea that he had the tractor well hidden. And notice how it had become "our" tractor. Dana, squatting on her heels next to Art, shook her head. "Even if the tractor would go through the snow, it wouldn't make sense to try. It's nearly April, the weather has to warm up soon. We can sit here and wait for a few days, then we can travel easily."

"We might, except for one thing." Seth gestured at one of the room's electrical outlets. "No power, no water, no services of any kind."

"We don't need them. We have food and warmth and shelter right here. We can manage."

"I'm not worryin' about *us,* sweetie. We're snug. I'm worried about good old Ollie. If we got no services here, I'll bet some old-style folding money they got none down at Maryland Point. What happens to somebody in judicial sleep when the power goes off? I assume they just snooze on for a while. But if the intravenous feeds quit, and the drugs and nutrients don't go in, what happens?"

"I don't know."

"Nor do I. Maybe the sleepers all starve an' die. Maybe they wake up and head for the hills. Neither one's any good for us. If Ollie turns to spoiled beef we're out of luck. And if he's awake and out of there before we're in, you can bet your ass and hat we'll never find him."

"Seth's right." Art warmed his hands at the little stove. "We can't afford to wait, Dana. We have too much at stake. Oliver Guest is our only shot at continued treatment."

"So we're all agreed." Seth stood up. "We gotta go, and soon. But how?"

"If we can't go by road," Dana said slowly, "what else is there? The monorail? I know the service is dead, but the tracks may be clear."

"Even if they are," Art said, "they won't help much. They run southeast from here, straight into the middle of Washington. We have to reach a lot farther south."

"On the river," said Seth thoughtfully. "Maryland Point is on the Potomac. How far are we from the river? If only we had a map of the area."

"I have maps."

"You do?" Seth Parsigian raised his eyebrows at Art. "You *really* planned ahead. You got precognition?"

"No. But I've got friends who must have." Art didn't try to explain. He said, "Wait a minute," and headed back upstairs. When he returned holding Ed O'Donnell's old maps, Seth and Dana were arguing, crouched together across the portable stove.

"South," Dana said. "No more than five miles."

"I don't think so. Five miles may be right, but you go west." Seth glanced at the three maps that Art held out. "The question is, what direction leads you fastest to the Potomac? If we can reach it, we may be able to run along it all the way to the syncope facility."

"If we had a boat."

"We get to the river, you let me worry about that. I'm a top scavenger." Seth opened one of the maps. "This should tell us. Except it looks like it came out of the Ark."

"The land/river boundary hasn't changed in fifty years." Dana leaned over so that she and Seth could study the map together. She touched one location with her finger. "Here we are, west of the freeway. And there's the river."

"Then we're both right." Seth was measuring using his index

finger as a rule. "The Potomac is just about as far away to the south as it is to the west. Say, five or six miles."

"That's beeline distance." Dana ran her finger straight across the map. "We'd never make it cross-country. It's more by road. But there are no roads to the west. We have a good road south, the one we are on. We can follow Seven Locks just about all the way to the river."

"If it weren't for the snow, we could." Seth sat back on his haunches. "You saw what it was like yesterday. If anything, the going will be worse today. If nobody took a mind to stop us—and I'm not comfortable with that assumption—you're talkin' about a full day's trek. And that's just to get us to the river. We have to go a lot farther. All right, folks, who has a better idea?"

He didn't speak like a man expecting an answer. But he offered no resistance when Art said, "Let me see," and took the map from his hands.

"You think you got better eyes than us?" Seth said, when Art followed an invisible line with his finger. "You see a road where we don't?"

"I think so. A sort of road." Art wasn't one to play word games, but he needed to be sure. He traced Seven Locks Road with his finger. It ran south in almost a straight line and ended just short of the river. He examined it in more detail, and shook his head.

"We already looked at that, Art," Dana said. "The snow is the problem."

"Not for us, it won't be." Art was sure. "The way we go won't be easy, but we'll have no trouble with snow."

Seth showed his teeth, though it was hard to call it a smile. "You plannin' to fly, baby?"

"No. There's more routes in the world than you'll find on a map like this. We'll use the storm drains. And though a road can go up and down, water only runs downhill. That's why you have to look at the contour lines."

"The *sewers,*" Seth said. "You want to run through the sewers and be knee-deep in shit? Do you know what you're suggesting?"

"Sewers and storm drainage systems aren't the same thing at all. They use the same underground paths a lot of the time, but you keep them apart when you can. As for knowing about them, I'd say I do. It's one way I make my living."

"Eh?" Dana stared. "Have you been lying to me? You told me you were a network and feedback analyst."

"I am. What do you think a storm drainage system is? It's

nothing but a big, complicated flow network. It happens to work with water, not electricity, but the basic principles are the same. You have line-carrying capacities, and variable loads, and peak load shunting. If you want to you can even make switches and amplifiers, through a thing called the Coanga Effect. But I won't get into that." Art spoke to Dana. "I admit I may have misled you a bit. I work with both electrical and water networks—and others, too, like oil and gas pipelines. But don't you think 'telecommunications network specialist' has a nicer ring to it than 'water and sewage network specialist'?"

"You just didn't want to tell me you worked in the sewers." Dana smiled at Art. "But is it safe to go into the storm drains now, after the supernova? How can you be sure that everything is still working? I mean, the whole power system is down, and I'd think the storm drains would be dependent on it."

"Not in this universe. You won't find electricity used, except here and there for maintenance. Think of it, Dana. In normal times, when is the electrical power in an area most likely to fail?"

"When you have high winds and a bad storm."

"Right. The last thing you want is a storm drain system most likely to fail when you need it most. The engineers don't assume electrical power is available when they design flood control and storm drainage networks. They assume the opposite—that no one will have power when the storms and floods are at their worst. Everything is controlled by the water loads themselves, through volumes and pressures and feedback to spillways and control gates."

"You're dead serious, aren't you?" Seth had become very still. "You think we can do it this way."

"I know we can. But if you have a better idea, I'll take it. I don't want to be Harry Lime any more than you do."

Art didn't expect the others to catch the reference, but Dana smiled and said, "Great movie. Maybe we'll go see it when this is all over. I'm persuaded. Now tell us the snags."

"The main thing that worries me is finding a good entry point to the storm-drain system. We're not water, we need a hole big enough for us to get through. There has to be one within half a mile at the most, for service access, but it might be hidden by snow. I'll go out now and search."

"Us, too?" Dana asked.

"Waste of time. You wouldn't know where to look. You stay here and get things together. Once we're in the storm drains, the underground part shouldn't be hard. There are walkways—narrow and low, but big enough for a person. All we do is follow the direction of flow, and that takes us to a river discharge point."

"After you find the entry point, how soon can we leave?" Seth stood up.

"At once. Snow and cold weather help, because we'll find very low runoff levels. But we'd better not be down there when the thaw starts."

"Not a chance." Seth touched the stove, snarled, and pulled his finger away. "Gotta cool this sucker off in the snow. Don't worry none about the thaw. Before that happens we'll be there and thaw old Ollie. He'll tell us what to do about the telomods, and we'll be back in business."

Not a word about whether or not old Ollie would choose to cooperate, Art thought as he muffled himself up to go outside. Would they be able to find the man, even if they reached the syncope facility? How do you find one convicted criminal among umpteen thousand others? What did Guest look like, even before he went into judicial sleep?

Art didn't recall the media pictures. A murderer could look like anyone.

Even Seth Parsigian.

They faced tough decisions before they left the Treasure Inn. There would be no tractor, no motorbike. Everything had to be carried on foot for an undefined distance.

Even the little stove was too much of a luxury. So was alcohol—a food of sorts, but not a nutritious one. Blankets and pillows were not heavy, but they were bulky.

The final list almost defined itself. Clothes, as many as you could stand to wear or to carry in a single bag. One thick blanket each. Food, but only in its most compact form: dried rice, ham, bread, cheese, and dried beans. Weapons, just in case.

At the last moment Art added a compass, candles, and the maps to his own load. He was sure to need light at some point, and the maps could fold to fit easily into his pocket along with his knife. As he packed away the first one, he noticed Seth Parsigian holding the map that showed on it the marked location of Art's house in Catoctin Mountain Park. Seth had handed it casually to Art, but the look on his face was more calculating than casual.

Dana and Seth had their own small group of "luxury" items. In her case it was soap, a hairbrush, and the long wrench she had used to break into the Institute. Seth had his hunting knife, pliers, and a flashlight that produced electricity not from batteries but by turning a hand crank to drive a generator.

A child's toy last Christmas—but not today. Seth used the flashlight to guide their way down the ladder and into the storm drain. Art looked carefully around. He saw debris left by recent high waters, but the level had receded a long way and the walkways were dry.

"This is better than I expected. It shouldn't be too difficult, all we need to do is follow the incline. Flat and down are all right, but we avoid any upward slopes."

Seth nodded and led the way. The storm drain tunnel was clammy and icy cold, but since they were all wearing extra clothes that was not a problem. After the first hundred yards Art dropped a few steps behind the other two. His knee was feeling pretty good, but he didn't know how far he might have to walk on it. He would prefer an even, steady pace, and no wasted steps. Whoever was in front had to make occasional side trips, when neither the compass nor the direction of water flow made the choice of branch clear.

Seth didn't seem to mind being asked to lead. The storm-drain tunnels added a strange booming echo off walls and ceiling, and after half a mile he began to sing as he walked. It was a dirge about two people called Saunders and Margaret, and the verse went on and on.

"That's *Clerk Saunders* he's singing." Dana had dropped back to walk just in front of Art. The path was not wide enough for two, and she had to turn her head to talk to him. The tunnel was not totally dark even without the flashlight, since every thirty yards or so the narrow grille of a storm drain, blocked by snow, admitted a diffuse, pearly light.

"It's a Scots/English border ballad," she went on. "All death and misery. First time I ever heard it with a West Virginia accent. I've never known Seth to sing before, either. He must be feeling good."

"Look where you're going," Art said gruffly, "or you'll be in the water." He was ashamed to say what he was actually thinking. The world had gone to hell, but he was feeling good. Better than when he left Catoctin Mountain Park.

"I'll give you a thought that should make us all cheer." Dana ignored Art's warning and again turned back to face him. "There are two and a half million lawyers in this country. What do you think they're doing now?"

"Trying to survive, like everyone else." Art wasn't sure she wanted an actual answer from him.

"Sure, but doing what? Nobody will be getting divorced, or arguing over a will, or ready to pay a lobbyist. Where my sister lives the economy has gone mostly to barter—food for clothes, fuel for the use of an old car. Lawyers don't actually *do* anything, so they have nothing to barter."

"You don't like lawyers?"

"I hate the sons of bitches." Dana sounded remarkably cheerful. "One of them sued on behalf of my sister, and she won. And you know what? His fee took every cent of the whole settlement."

"You've never dated a lawyer, then? I'd think they'd be buzzing around you, like flies round—well, like—bees."

"That's not what you were going to say, is it?" The path had widened, and she dropped back to Art's side. "Just as well you didn't stay with your first thought, or it's you who'd be in that water."

"I spend a lot of my time with men."

"Oh, yes? What's that mean? That you think it gives you an excuse for crude, sexist remarks?"

"No." Art wondered how he had got into this. He said doggedly, "I was just trying to point out that someone as attractive as you must get offers to take you out all the time, and a lot of those men would probably be lawyers. They're keen on trophy dates and trophy wives, women they can show off in public."

"I have dated lawyers," Dana said airily. "Three of them. They're the ones I hate the most. The bastards." She eased her way around a tall concrete pillar that narrowed the walkway, ducked to allow for the lower ceiling, and waited until Art had done the same. "That's not what I wanted to talk about, though."

"You could have fooled me. You were the one started on lawyers."

"I know. I was just feeling uppity. Must be the ambience. If I could carry a tune, I'd be singing, too. But I wanted to ask if you signed some sort of release document before you started the telomod treatment."

"I certainly did. A release from everything, so far as I could tell. I could be killed, ground up, and sold as cat food and the Institute wouldn't be held responsible."

"The same as mine. But do you remember any particular side effects of the treatment that they warned about?"

"They had a long list of possibles. Plain and fancy cancers, in addition to the one that brought me to the program. Nausea, bleeding, fits, fainting, headaches, seizures, liver failure, kidney problems." Art shrugged. "You name it. The list went on and on. I never had any of them."

"Do you remember anything—" Dana halted on the walkway, so that Art had to stop, too. "Look, Art, don't laugh at me, even if this sounds totally crazy. But did anyone or anything ever mention a side effect that could make you feel totally wonderful?"

"I don't remember one." Art gestured ahead, to where Seth was walking on steadily, farther and farther in front of them. He took her hand and pulled her forward with him. "We were told that if things went well we might have a normal life expectancy, even one beyond the normal. If we were lucky, we might see some rejuvenation effects, too."

"That's my point! I'm not just feeling better, I'm feeling *great*, the way I haven't felt for thirty years. I'm like a kid. I wake up, and the whole day spreads out before me. Even in the middle of this disaster, I look forward to things. And you, Art. You look ten years younger than the first time I met you. You're acting it, too. Don't you *feel* younger?"

"I guess I do." It wasn't the time to say that he had been feeling horny a lot, particularly around Dana. "I'm in better shape than I thought I'd be, three days ago. When I left Catoctin Mountain I expected that the drive down to the Institute on the tractor would just about kill me, and it didn't. Yesterday I felt fine. And last night with you was great, the best night I've had in years—I mean, the best night's sleep."

"I assumed you meant that." She gave a coarse, low-pitched laugh that echoed off the tunnel roof and walls. "Don't you think there's a faint chance I would have noticed, if you'd meant anything else? You don't have to tell me you slept well. I would have liked to talk last night, but you told me we ought to go to sleep. Then you went out like a light."

"You're worried about feeling well, are you? You shouldn't be." Art finally released Dana's hand and waved to an invisible Seth. The walkway was straight and they had allowed themselves to fall far behind. Now from in front of them a flashlight had turned in their direction. "I can't think of any bad side effect that makes a person feel good. I don't think there's any such thing."

"I hope you're right. But what do we know?" Dana walked faster. "We have to find Oliver Guest and learn exactly what's going on with us. I hope he can tell us more than the doctors at the Institute. I could never get much out of them."

"Medical caution." Art increased his pace to match hers. "Unless you want to call it medical cowardice. Suppose they predicted our condition, and things turned out some other way? Then they couldn't act like gods anymore."

"Sounds like you feel for doctors the way I feel about lawyers."

"Could be. One of them damn near killed me. That toe-tapping double-talking buckle-shoed charlatan." Art walked faster yet. One nice thing about feeling fitter, you had the energy for righteous indignation. "He was an arrogant little shit. If I hadn't ignored him and gone for a second opinion right away while he was still blathering on about allergies, I wouldn't be talking with you today."

"I sympathize with that feeling. But what can you do? The faith healers and karmic gurus are even worse."

They were almost up to Seth, who turned off his flashlight. Art could see him outlined against a lighter patch of wall. The tunnel made a right angle turn, and a brighter light came from there. He reached in his pocket for his compass. The water flow was southwest.

"Been enjoying yourselves, you two?" Seth sounded cynically amused. "Me, too. So are we ready for stage two? This might be a bit tricky."

The black water flowed on through a dark opening, but the walkway terminated at a wider platform. On the right, away from the water, a rusty iron ladder stood bolted to the wall. It led up to a square vertical metal grating through which weak daylight filtered. A thin layer of snow had found its way through to the platform beneath.

Seth went to the foot of the ladder and stared up. "If that sucker has a lock on the outside, we're in trouble."

"It shouldn't have. Service staff need to be able to get in and out of any access point." Art moved past Seth and climbed three rungs of the ladder. He held on with his left hand and reached up to the grating with his right. "The real question is, has it been used recently? There's a layer of snow behind the cover. That won't help."

He gripped the grating and pushed one-handed, as hard as he could.

"Is it moving?" Seth asked from below.

"Not an inch. I think it's frozen. It's hinged on the upper side. Dana, lend me your wrench, would you?"

He took the long tool and thrust it as hard as he could. The result was a loud clang and a shower of snow in his eyes. Art tried again. Snow again fell, more than the first time.

"I think it moved a bit." Seth was peering up from the foot of the ladder. "Come down, and let's try something different."

He took the wrench from Art, climbed the ladder, and halted on the second rung.

"The two of you hold me at the legs and waist. This needs a two-handed swing."

Dana gripped Seth's waist. Art reached higher, to support his lower back.

"Hold tight and try to catch me if I fall off. I'm not gonna hold anythin' back." Seth, turning sideways, gave an explosive grunt and rammed the wrench against the bottom of the grating.

"Any good?" Art again had a face full of snow.

"Nah. Nothing. Move, you mother, *move*." The wrench thrust out, again and again, while Seth grunted and cursed. At the fifth effort he moved higher on the ladder and said, "Watch out below. I'm dropping the wrench."

Art and Dana stepped quickly out of the way. A moment later came Seth's gasp of triumph. "Yeah, baby. Here we go."

He was pushing the grating, turning it upward on its hinges and climbing higher on the ladder. Finally he could scramble out through the square opening. He peered down at them.

"Come join me. Let's see if we know where we are and where we go from here."

Holding the heavy wrench in one hand, Art climbed awkwardly after Dana. Outside, he peered at the world through half-closed eyes. Daylight was blindingly bright after the gloom of the storm drains. He did not know how long they had been underground, but judging from the position of the sun in the cloudy sky it was early afternoon. The snow had tailed away to nothing.

Art surveyed the cold, still, and silent landscape. He stood at the foot of a bank covered with shrubs and small trees. Directly in front, in what he judged was roughly south, he saw a gleam of dull gray. Beyond that lay taller trees and, farther off, another and larger body of water.

"Well?" Dana said. She and Seth were staring expectantly at

Art. "This is your stamping ground, not ours. What do you make of it, stout Cortez? Where are we?"

Art was pulling out a map with fingers that still trembled from the effort to open the storm-drain cover.

"I'm pretty sure we are right here." He unfolded the map and placed his finger at a point on the bottom left quadrant. "Near a place called Cabin John. The water you see right in front of us is the C&O Canal—the Chesapeake and Ohio. We're at a spillway into it. You can't see the towpath on the other side because of the snow, but it runs all the way down into Georgetown. We couldn't use the canal, though, even if we had a boat, because it has locks all the way down, and you can't operate them without power. Beyond the evergreens is the Potomac River. Downstream is to the left. There are rapids, but the bad ones are upriver toward Great Falls."

"Boats?" Seth asked.

"I don't know if we'll find any close to here. There's a big boathouse downstream, on this side of the river. But it's about three miles away. And they rent boats that you row, not boats with motors."

"Renting ain't what we got in mind today. We'll borrow. But, boy, you weren't kidding. You really know this area."

"I guess I do." As Art replied he was taken by a memory, thirty and more years old, of a warm afternoon when he and Mary had walked the towpath together, gathering wild hollyhocks and sweet-smelling phlox from close to the water's edge. Two small boys were ahead of them, uncomfortably close to the quiet canal. Mary, worried not at all about Art teetering on the steep bank and in need of a steadying hand, had rushed off after the children. The summer memory was so piercing and so bittersweet that his eyes rejected today's snow and its leaden reflection in the canal.

"Art?" Dana tugged at his sleeve. More sensitive than Seth, she had caught something new in his expression. "Do you need to rest?"

"No." Art took a deep breath. No summer flowery perfume now, but the clean, cool smell of pine. "I'm doing all right. Where do we go from here?"

"We need a boat," Seth said. "Any sort of boat to carry us downriver. If we can get as far as Washington, I'll find us a power craft."

"How?"

"Don't know yet. We eat a bit, then we head for the houses

close to the river. There's a good chance somebody with riverfront property has some sort of canoe or rowboat." Seth stared up at the sky. "I figure we got four hours, maybe five, to sunset. Unless you want to sleep in the storm drains, by then we need to be afloat and cruisin' downriver to Maryland Point."

18

From the secret diary of Oliver Guest.

The lead prosecutor told the jury at my trial that I was "a sick parasite, preying on society."

Parasite on society; *this, mind you, from a lawyer.*

It was, furthermore, inaccurate. Biology admits three forms of interdependence in living organisms. First there is symbiosis *or* mutualism, *in which each of the participants benefits from and may indeed be dependent for survival upon the presence of the other. The mitochondria that serve as energy centers in each of our cells are a good example. We need each other. Then there is* commensalism, *where two organisms coexist but provide neither harm nor obvious benefit. Into this category I would place many of the protozoa in our alimentary canals. And finally there is true* parasitism, *where one organism does nothing but damage to the other. The* Ichneumonidae, *those wasps that both fascinated and repulsed Charles Darwin and led him toward atheism, are a fine example. The wasps lay their eggs in the living but paralyzed bodies of caterpillars and cicadas. It is difficult to discern any possible benefits for the reluctant hosts.*

The prosecutor's accusation was also unfair. I am not, and was not, a parasite, even stretching the meaning to accommodate popular usage.

I do not particularly blame the man. It is one of the unfortunate aspects of the legal profession that excess carries no penalty. There is never, for a lawyer, such a thing as too much. *Consider the oxymoron, a "legal brief." The prosecutor must have known that the evidence against me was overwhelming, regardless of questions of character. Had he made a speech testifying to my unhappy childhood, noble nature, and kindness to animals, it would not have affected the verdict. He could have served as a de facto defense attorney, and made no difference to the outcome.*

Actually, I might have preferred his worst accusations to the efforts of the defense counsel appointed by the state. She, with the best will in the world, decided that I had no chance if my plea for clemency depended on the physical evidence alone. Instead, she would prove that I was an asset to society rather than a parasite. Because of the value of my work, I ought not to be placed into long-term judicial sleep. She referred to my groundbreaking researches on telomod therapy, which she said was "even now being applied to a group of human experimental subjects." The jury stared at me. "Human experimental subjects" has a certain ring to it. Their eyes said, "Next stop, the gas chambers."

She then told them I was a world's leading authority on cloning, a subject that happens to be regarded by the general public with strong suspicion. Finally she emphasized what a genius I was, and showed how my career had been marked since early childhood by an outstanding brilliance.

You could see the wheels working inside jury heads.

Question: "Who do you want out on the streets even less than an insane mass murderer of teenagers?"

Answer: "An outstandingly brilliant and cunning insane mass murderer of teenagers."

I knew at that point what my defense attorney apparently did not: my fate, in spite of or because of her best efforts, was sealed.

19

The lesson had been driven home every day for a thousand days, from pre-mission selection to Earth orbit departure: the first Mars expedition faces more unknowns than anyone can guess. There will be injuries, there may be fatalities. No matter what happens you must regroup and assess your remaining resources; and you must continue.

Continue until you reach Mars; continue to descend to and explore Mars; continue until you return to Earth from Mars.

Celine raised her head and stared around the control room of the *Schiaparelli*. They had held together and worked together. They had overcome every obstacle. They had come so close to success, so agonizingly close; and they had failed.

The other three were ignoring each other, locked into private worlds of grief or guilt. Reza Armani had moved to one of the control chairs. He was working through the command telemetry as it had been received from *Lewis* until the final seconds of radio silence. With its help he was reconstructing every action that Zoe Nash had made, mimicking her exact sequence of movements at the ship's controls. He was muttering to himself, and his features twitched constantly. When the *Lewis* became a cloud of hot gas he appeared to lose touch with reality.

Wilmer Oldfield was also staring blank-eyed at nothing and apparently doing nothing. He had vanished inside his head, to a place beyond Celine's access or imagining. That didn't worry her. Wilmer did that all the time.

She turned to Jenny Kopal. She could understand what Jenny was doing, and sympathize with it. Somehow, the transfer of chips and library programs from the *Schiaparelli* to the *Lewis* had been botched. Since that responsibility was Jenny's, she felt she had killed Zoe, Ludwig, and Alta as directly as if she had driven knives into their hearts. She was poring, white-faced, over displays and transfer protocols.

And Celine's own failure? She knew it now, when it was too late. Zoe had made the decision to return to Earth two days after their arrival at ISS-2. She did so before they knew the extent of the work before them, before the orbiters were fully inspected, before Zoe or anyone else had a rational basis for setting a schedule.

Celine had been deeply worried by the impulsiveness of Zoe's action. But what had she done? Had she pointed out her reservations, knowing that her warning would be listened to and taken seriously—that this Cassandra was never ignored?

No. She had done nothing, overwhelmed by Zoe's personality and confidence and strength of purpose. Or—place the blame where it belonged—overwhelmed by Celine's own desperate longing to be home again on Earth.

She glanced around the cabin again, and found everyone's eyes on her.

What now?

"We saw what happened to the *Lewis*." Celine found herself speaking, in a voice surprisingly level and controlled. "We probably all have our own ideas as to what caused the disaster. At some point we will have to decide what to do about our own return to Earth. But not yet. Right now it is time for a group discussion."

That's right. Speak of the fate of the Lewis, *rather than of Zoe, Ludwig, and Alta. Keep the discussion as impersonal and unemotional as possible. Don't allow anyone to indulge in breast-beating.*

But at the same time a voice inside her was asking other questions: *Why am I doing this? Isn't this a job for someone like Zoe, a natural leader? Why me?*

And an answering voice: *Their deaths have changed all of us. Jenny is more human, Wilmer is more alert, and Reza is closer to the borderline between normal and psychotic.*

The other three didn't seem to find Celine's assumption of leadership as odd as she did. Jenny was rubbing her eyes, as though she had been secretly weeping, but she said quietly, "I think it is obvious what happened. I downloaded software modules for orbiter control from the program library onto spare chips available on the *Schiaparelli*. I installed those chips in the *Lewis*, replacing dead elements there. I believed that I had done everything correctly. But when Zoe tried to change the orbiter's pitch, the software module gave a command that drove the correction the wrong way. The orbiter was entering the atmosphere more steeply after the correction, instead of less steeply. Drag forces and frictional heating on the *Lewis* increased, rather than decreasing, until temperatures went past hull material limits. If only I had been more careful, and checked—"

"We don't know that's what happened." Celine cut Jenny off smoothly but firmly. "Did you find a software error that could produce an effect like that?"

"No. But I'm still looking. It's the only thing that could possibly—"

"Not proven. We need to hear from everyone before we attempt an analysis." Celine turned away from Jenny. "Reza?"

"Well, we may never know exactly what sequence of actions Zoe took." Reza's voice was higher than usual, but he picked up before Jenny could speak again. "There was no telemetry for the crucial period, because of ionization radio blackout. But the controls of the orbiters are quite a bit different from the controls of the *Schiaparelli* or of the Mars landers."

Speech seemed to have stabilized him, because his voice was more normal when he went on, "I know that, because I've had more practice sessions than anyone except Zoe herself. It would be easy, in the heat of the moment, to invert a control command and increase the angle of attack rather than decreasing it."

"If Zoe had done something like that she would have realized it in a split second," Jenny said. "She would have made the correction. She didn't." Her voice wobbled and rose in pitch. "I tell you, Reza, it's in the software routines."

"We'll discuss software and other possible causes later," Celine said curtly. "I don't want to talk about it now. Wilmer?"

She turned to him, without much hope of hearing anything useful. It wasn't clear that he had even been listening. While Jenny and Reza were talking he had made a peculiar little drawing, and now he was scribbling numbers.

"Oh, it wasn't the software." Wilmer grinned like an idiot. "At least, it was, but not at all in the sense that Jenny means." And then, while Celine glared, he went on, "Do you remember when we first noticed Supernova Alpha, you asked me what else it might do to the solar system? And I said, pretty much nothing, apart from melting ice for a while on the moons of the outer planets."

"I remember." With anyone but Wilmer, you would bat them over the head if they chose such an awful time to wander way off the subject. With Wilmer you waited. His digressions always came back to the point.

"Well, I was wrong," he said. "Stupidly wrong. Wrong in a way that anyone with a year or two of elementary physics could point out." He turned the sheet, so that they could see his drawing. It was of three concentric circles, with arrows pointing out from the second one toward the outermost. "We all know the pressure/volume/temperature relation for an ideal gas, Pv = RT. A planetary atmosphere satisfies that, almost perfectly. Increase the temperature and leave the pressure the same, and the volume increases linearly. Here's Earth's surface." He pointed to the inner circle. "Above it lies the atmosphere. Pump in heat, an incredible amount of it, from Supernova Alpha. For a couple of months it's like having two suns in the sky. The temperature of the surface rises. The atmosphere expands. Where does it go? The only place it can go." He pointed at the arrows between the second and third circle. "Upward. The whole atmosphere swells."

Wilmer released the sheet of paper with the diagram, and it hovered before him in the free-fall environment of the *Schiaparelli*'s cabin. "That's a general comment, but it's easy to catalog specific effects. First, there will be only a small change at ground level. The atmosphere has expanded, but its total mass remains constant. The surface will experience the same atmospheric pressure, because the whole column of air above it exerts the same downward force.

"But now think about conditions higher up. The atmosphere still becomes thinner with height, but it does so more slowly than it used to. So if you go high enough, the air is *more* dense than it was at that same height before Supernova Alpha. The drag force and frictional heating on a spacecraft will increase—and they have an *exponential* dependence on air density.

"The routines that we put into *Lewis* came from the general software library applicable to our class of orbiters. They provide an explicit calculation for drag force as a function of height, in terms of spacecraft angle of attack, mass, shape, and velocity—and air density. But it's the air density at a given height *as it was before Supernova Alpha*—not as it is now—that's in the equations. An acceptable angle of attack for a ship fifty miles up, moving through the atmosphere as it was two months ago, would be an absolute disaster today. No orbiter could stand the increased drag and heating. We saw what it did to the *Lewis.*"

Wilmer had credibility and authority on all matters scientific. He also spoke as though what he said was no more than common sense, and quite undeniable. Celine reminded herself that it was the unquestioned acceptance of authority—Zoe's authority, as head of the expedition—which had led her to remain silent before. She could not afford to do it again.

"You may be right, Wilmer. But you may be wrong." And when he stared at her in surprise—this wasn't the old Celine—she went on, "Jenny may be right, there was an error in the way the software was transferred, so Zoe's action drove the controls the wrong way. Or Reza could be right, it was pilot error on Zoe's part that destroyed the *Lewis.* The trouble is, we have no way of knowing which idea is correct. Even if you are right, there's nothing we can do to prove it."

"Oh, but there is." One nice thing about Wilmer, he was too intellectually secure to become upset when he was questioned. He rubbed at the top of his head and went on, "We lost radio telemetry for the critical period, but we have a complete visual record from the *Schiaparelli*'s big scope. That provides our observables. We can compute trajectories using a variety of different assumptions—that the angle of attack was adjusted the wrong way, or that it was reduced but the drag was already too high for that to help, or any other idea that anyone has. The right model is the one which minimizes residuals between computer and observed values. We can even use the difference between computed and observed data to calculate a density function for today's atmosphere, one that best matches a computed orbit to the observations. I'm sure Jenny can handle that."

"Jenny?" Celine looked uncertainly to Jenny Kopal.

"Easily." Jenny nodded. She seemed like a woman reprieved from a death sentence. "It's a nonlinear least squares fitting problem, but we have all the routines."

"So let's do it." Celine was about to add, *Soon, so we can get out of here and down to Earth.* But she was learning. "Take as much time as you need. You tell me when you're done. Then we'll discuss what comes next."

You could force patience on yourself and everyone else, but no one said you had to like it.

Celine watched Jenny working for a few minutes, with Wilmer

sitting by to assist if and when needed. Then she left the control cabin and wandered away to the *Schiaparelli*'s observation chamber. She had another mystery to ponder.

Zoe had been the leader of the Mars expedition. Ludwig Holter had been second in command. No backup to those two had ever been mentioned. Oversight, or deliberate act by the selection committee?

Now Zoe and Ludwig were dead. And Celine, without making any conscious decision, seemed to have taken over the direction of the surviving group. Did she want to do that? Or, inverting the question, did she have any choice?

Celine stared out at Earth, its surface again shrouded in night. The radio silence continued, broken only by weak and sporadic signals that addressed purely local problems of food, water, and power supply. The old Earth had been a celestial beacon, a roar of radio and television signals easily picked up when the *Schiaparelli* was orbiting Mars. That had gone. The firefly glow of light from the big cities was no longer visible. In its place she saw the ruddy sparks of bush fires across much of sub-Saharan Africa.

The planet to which she so much wanted to return was nothing like the world that they had left. If they survived to land on it, they would find a tougher, wilder place.

First, though, they had to live through the descent. Who would make the crucial decisions in the hours ahead? Put like that, the question of leadership became clear. She did not trust Wilmer or Jenny to direct the group. She wasn't sure she trusted Reza to do much at all, he was showing increasing signs of strangeness. And there was no one else.

Celine left the observation chamber and headed for the control room where the others were working. True, she did not wholly trust herself. But maybe Zoe Nash, for all her apparent confidence and certainty, had felt the same way.

Uneasy lies the head.

The important question wasn't whether or not you thought you were the right one to lead. It was whether others believed you were.

What am I? What is my function?

Celine, squeezed into the improvised hammock between Wilmer and Jenny and facing away from the front of the orbiter, felt a new wave of uncertainty rising within her. Reza sat behind them at the controls. Celine didn't like that, but she had no choice.

He was by far the best pilot. She could see his distorted image in the shiny rear panel, singing to himself. Unless she told him to abort in the next sixty seconds, the *Clark* would leave the safe haven of ISS-2 and begin reentry.

She had performed none of the data analysis and modeling that proved Wilmer's assertion was correct. That work had been done by Jenny and by Wilmer himself. It showed that the crew of the *Lewis* had died not because of pilot ineptitude or software transfer error, but because the equations embedded in the control programs no longer modeled correctly the atmosphere of today's Earth.

She had not changed the software, to incorporate the parameters of the new atmosphere determined by the data analysis. That had been Jenny's work.

Nor would she fly the *Clark* back home. That responsibility lay with Reza, now well into manic mood.

What, then, did she do?

She worried, when apparently no one else did. The others were completely confident that the problem that killed Zoe and the rest of the *Lewis* crew had been solved. As Reza cheerfully said, "Everything else was on the button, exactly the way it should have been. We've cleared up the only problem." Yet it was his partner, Jenny, who in another context had assured the group that test a program as you liked, it always had one bug left. And she and Reza apparently didn't realize that "program" was a general term, applying just as well to a return from orbit as to a computer subroutine.

Celine wondered how much longer she would have delayed the attempt to return to Earth, without Reza's remark the previous day: "The log shows this orbiter's past due for maintenance. There's a steady deterioration in condition, even when it's not being used."

Reza's reflection was staring at her. Apparently the sixty-second grace period had expired. It was now, or abort to a later time. Celine nodded. "Do it."

The thrust of the engines in front of her was silent and easy, apparently too gentle to affect their situation. It was surprising to watch the *Schiaparelli* and ISS-2 sail away ahead, continuing in their shared orbit. The orbiter had taken the first step, braking its motion enough to allow the trajectory of *Clark* to intersect the upper atmosphere.

Now it was simply waiting. But not for long. In less than

fifteen minutes they would know if the drag calculation had been the only problem affecting the *Lewis.*

No one was wearing a suit. Celine had wanted that as a precaution against the failure of cabin integrity and loss of air. Two minutes of direct experiment ruled it out. Even without suits they could barely squeeze into the *Clark*'s limited cabin space. With suits, forget it. The pilot might fly home, but no one else would fit in with him.

"Everything is nominal," Reza announced. "The control routines are doing exactly what we hoped. We are losing altitude as planned and are already experiencing some atmospheric drag."

He seemed without a care in the world, but his words made Celine think of Zoe. She had said almost exactly the same thing, shortly before the *Lewis* disintegrated to its individual atoms.

"Do the drag forces seem to be following the new model?" Celine was being pushed back into the hammock, harder and sooner than she expected. She had to ask if things were all right, even though there was nothing she could do if she didn't like Reza's answer.

"The new model works fine," Reza replied. His attitude didn't tell her anything. He sounded ready to fly a ship through the gates of hell. "We're coming down by the book. Trust crazy Reza. I think I could squeeze us a degree or two farther north if you want. It may be clearer there."

"What's the cloud situation?"

It was another problem, predictable but irritating. Normally the weather reports for a returning orbiter were provided by ground control, with access to metsat and to ground radar data. The *Clark* was forced to fly without any such aids. Reza was the only person on board who could see anything outside the ship.

"Continuous cloud cover below, cumulonimbus by the look of them. But we're a long way from touchdown. Drag is higher, skin temperature going up fast. Sit tight."

There was no choice. Celine didn't need to be told about the drag forces, she was pressing harder and harder into the hammock. Wilmer, to her right, was rolling in on her a little. The hammock support was not quite centered—her own fault, that had been her job. But he was quite a load, especially under what already felt like two gees and more.

"Hull temperature close to three thousand. We're pushing three gees and projecting more than five." Reza forced the words from compressed vocal cords. The ship's deceleration was still increasing. "If there's going to be unpleasantness, it will be right about here."

Unpleasantness. A pilot's gift for understatement. Their bodies had spent most of the past year in free fall, and the year before that in a Mars gravity only forty percent of Earth's. Five gees was intolerable. Celine had trouble breathing, and she could hear beside her Jenny Kopal's painful grunts. Wilmer was a silent lump at her side. How much more? And how much longer? Only the thermal skin of the orbiter's cabin wall protected them from the white-hot inferno beyond.

"Hull temperature thirty-three hundred." Reza's reporting of the instrument readings was barely intelligible. "Five and a half gees. Angle of attack holding steady. Rate of descent constant. Hang in there. I think we're through maximum drag."

It didn't feel that way to Celine. But then the force pressing her into the hammock became perhaps a tiny bit less. Breathing was agony, but a reduced agony.

"Hull temperature thirty-two hundred. Deceleration under four gees and falling. Rate of descent steady." Reza tried to shout in triumph, and managed a wheezy croak. "We're through the worst. We made it, guys. We've got lift. We're home."

Home? Not quite. But the *Clark* was no longer skimming like a flung stone across the skies of Earth. Celine could tell that they were flying, descending fast but buoyed upward by aerodynamic lift from the air. She struggled upright and turned in the hammock to face Reza.

"Where are we? Do you have any idea of our position and ground speed?"

"Don't know yet." He turned to grin at her. "The micropositioning circuit says thirty-eight north and eighty-two west, but I don't know how much we can trust it. Depends if the GPS satellites are alive. I'd like visuals, but it's nothing but clouds below. We're forty-one kilometers up, descent rate eighty meters a second, airspeed eleven hundred, heading nearly due east."

Celine wanted to see for herself. So apparently did Jenny. As the deceleration dropped they started to crawl to the top of the hammock. At the same moment they realized that it was not feasible. They would change the mass balance of the little ship, but worse than that they would crowd Reza's access to the controls. The overloaded orbiter was too small to permit passenger movement.

Celine strained upward for one moment above the edge of the hammock before she slid back to her old position. She glimpsed white clouds below and ahead, their rolling heads bright in western sunlight.

"I guess we can forget about ground assistance and ground information." Reza was focused on the cloudscape ahead of the *Clark*. "The only way we'll learn conditions below is to look at them."

He wasn't asking Celine, he was telling her. Did she want to second-guess him? She peered again over the edge of the hammock.

Reza had increased the angle of descent. The ship was swooping fast toward the cloud tops. "Seven thousand meters. Let's hope the altimeter works with the changed atmosphere." As he spoke the ship dropped into the clouds.

Ahead of the orbiter sat unchanging gray vapor. The ride became uncannily smooth. The ship might have been hanging motionless, except for the altimeter. Celine could see it in the diffuse light that permeated the cabin. Its display was flickering rapidly downward: six thousand—five thousand—four thousand.

At thirty-eight hundred meters, when she was beginning to panic, the orbiter vibrated heavily and a moment later was racing across the broken floor of the cloud layer.

Reza could see what lay below, but she could not. His low whistle did nothing to reassure her.

"What is it?"

"Snow. On the ground, everywhere. If it's deep we'll have problems landing. The orbiters aren't designed for that."

"*Snow*. I thought we were at latitude thirty-eight degrees?"

"That's what the instruments say."

"But that puts us nearly as far south as Richmond, and it's almost April. There shouldn't be snow."

"Hey. I didn't order it. I'm just telling you what we've got down there. And I don't like the idea of trying to land in it."

"Do you see cleared areas?"

"There was one patch of blacktop back there, looked like it could be a cleared runway. It's behind us now. And there's a big body of water ahead. It could be the James River or part of the Chesapeake Bay. Either way, it doesn't help—we can't land on water. We'd better take another look at what I saw, find out if we can land there."

The *Clark* banked steeply. Celine didn't need to be told that they were losing altitude fast. When the engines were off, the orbiters had the glide ratio of a brick. Reza was conserving power for the final approach and landing, assuming he would find a place where that landing was possible. The orbiter circled, losing more height.

"It's not a commercial airport." Reza giggled. "Not a military base, either. Not a highway. And not very big. But it's all we've got. Hold tight. I'll have to use the engines full throttle and bank at the same time to drop us in there."

Celine slid back down the hammock, to settle between Wilmer and Jenny. You dreamed for a whole year of the triumphant return to Earth. Although you never discussed it or admitted that you ever had such thoughts, you rehearsed mentally the words to be spoken as you emerged from the lander. Those dreams and words did not cover the case where you swooped to a blighted Earth across a snow-covered landscape, in a crippled and jury-rigged orbiter.

"We're very close," Reza said happily. "Ten seconds to touchdown. But we're moving too fast, and the strip we're landing on is shorter than I thought. Even with maximum retro-thrust we're going to overshoot the far end. Be prepared for something rough."

After that warning, the first contact of the orbiter with the ground seemed soft as a kiss. Celine heard the hiss of landing wheels and felt a tremor as they raced along the surface. The retro-thrusters howled, and once more she was pushed deep into the hammock.

"This is it," Reza said, and the orbiter shuddered and reared up onto its head. Celine felt one crushing moment of force. Then she was lying on her back, staring up at the cabin's rear wall. Wilmer was lying half on top of her, muttering and wriggling.

"Reza?" she asked.

"I'll live. I said you could trust me. How is it back there?"

"All right," Jenny said, and Wilmer added, "Me, too, but the side wall has bent in. I can't move until Celine does."

"Don't try." From the sounds, Reza was releasing himself from his harness. "Sit tight and I'll try to open the hatch. It's going to be tricky. We're in the middle of a snowdrift."

Sitting tight was easy. Unable to move, Celine could do nothing but wait and listen to Reza's gasps and grunts of effort.

"Good thing it slides," he said after half a minute. "We'd never have opened it outward against packed snow. And the drift is almost to the top of the door. Another half meter and we'd have to tunnel free. But I can get to you now."

He kicked at the banked snow, enlarging the hole, and used the space he had made to crawl upward and free the hammock clamps on one side. Celine, Jenny, and Wilmer rolled together to finish in a heap near Reza's feet.

"Anyone have some first words for our return to Earth?" he said. "The ones I'd been working on don't seem to apply anymore."

"We made it," Jenny said shakily. "In that last few minutes, I felt sure we wouldn't." She reached out and put her arms around his neck. "I've always laughed at you when you told me what a great pilot you were. But you are."

"You'd better believe it." Reza went on kicking at the snow, making a hole big enough to crawl through to the ground outside. "Celine, you first. You're the head of the Mars expedition now."

His words brought back to Celine the memory of the crew members who were not with them. The sheer exhilaration of being alive faded. She eased her way feetfirst into the hole that Reza had made, and the mound of snow crumbled and sank beneath her weight as she slid to the ground.

She stood up, waited for the other three to join her, then said, "We, the surviving members of the first human expedition to Mars, honor the memory of Ludwig Holter, Alta McIntosh-Mohammad, and Zoe Nash. Without the lessons learned from their sacrifice, our own return to Earth would have been impossible."

Jenny gasped, and all four bowed their heads. They stood shaky-legged and silent for half a minute in the long-awaited air and gravity of Earth. At last Celine looked up and made her first inspection of their surroundings.

She stood at the end of a long stretch of tarmac about fifteen meters wide and three hundred meters long. By her side the orbiter was nose-down and buried deep in a bank of snow that had damped the force of its collison. The ship was ruined and might never fly again, but crazy Reza could take pride in his piloting. Even orbiter specialists expected a runway twice as long and wide as this one.

Beyond the runway, hugging the ground and partly dug into it, Celine counted half a dozen wooden buildings. Gray smoke rose from the chimneys of three of them, and the snow had melted from their roofs. Around the runway, trees clad in the foliage of late spring stood bowed down by snow. More deep snow covered the bushes and ground between them. In the distance, white hills stretched to the horizon. The orbiter had landed in the deepest part of a valley. The air that filled Celine's nostrils was rich with strange but familiar smells, of smoke and pine needles and resin. She stretched her arms wide, luxuriating in wide spaces and open sky. The air was colder than she had expected.

"And you told me," Jenny said, "that the temperature on Earth is *higher* because of supernova heating?" It was less a question than a skeptical jibe intended for Reza, but Wilmer answered.

"Globally, and overall. But the effects you're most likely to notice are the fluctuations from normal weather. Like now. Much more chilly than usual for this time of year. Somewhere else, maybe down at the South Pole, it's one big heat wave."

"Then take me to the South Pole," said Jenny. Her teeth were starting to chatter. Celine suspected most of that was nervous reaction. On the other hand, Jenny was thin and lightly built, and she had removed her jacket on entering the *Clark* to provide a little more padding to the hammock.

"We have to get inside," Celine said. She gestured toward the buildings. "Inside there. They must have heat."

"And a place to rest." Jenny took a trial step, then another. "If we can walk that far. Ooh, Earth gravity. My legs feel like spaghetti."

Reza took her arm to help her. "Come on. Walk. We have to."

"Maybe not." Wilmer pointed along the valley, to a building shaped like an A-frame barn. The front had opened to reveal three odd-looking machines. They were painted dark red and had balloon tires, and a handful of people stood clustered around each one.

"We don't need to walk," Celine said. "They've noticed our arrival. We can relax. Thank God, we made it. We're home from Mars."

20

Saul was explaining to Yasmin the history of his relationship with Tricia. The facts were easy, though he didn't quite understand why he was offering them; and Yasmin did not ask.

Did not ask that question, at least; she asked a hundred others. Did Tricia know of his political aspirations when they first met? Had he been in a relationship of his own at the time? How old was Tricia? Was he upset by her multiple marriages and divorces? Did he know her previous husbands personally? Her present husband? Did he know her family? Had she met his mother and his sister? Did she know how much he was worth? Did she, in fact, even realize that he was rich?

As soon as they finished eating they moved into the next room, a small lounge with two old armchairs in front of a fireplace and a fake log fire. The room was heated by hot-water radiators that creaked and cracked as they expanded and contracted, so that Saul constantly glanced into the corners to see what else was going on in the room. He had come to the story of that final evening, when he had told Tricia that all thoughts of marriage must be postponed until after the election. At a critical moment, just as he was trying to recall his own exact words, the overhead lights flickered and dimmed to an orange glow.

He looked at Yasmin questioningly and she shook her head. "Nothing to do with me. It's midnight, and they've gone to low power to conserve energy. I suspect someone is trying to tell us it's bedtime. Go on."

The mood had changed as the hour advanced. Saul felt instinctively the shift in power dynamics. It was no longer a meeting of President and aide, but part of some undefined and evolving relationship. Differences of age and status were less relevant. Late at night, all cats are gray. And Yasmin's eyes were tiger eyes, glinting a yellow reflection in the half-light. She had drawn her legs up beneath her on the armchair and was leaning forward, crouched and ready to spring. He thought she looked too beautiful to be true; but that was not why he had come to Indian Head.

"I told Tricia this didn't change the way I felt about her," he said. "And we didn't have to wait forever. We just had to avoid being seen together until after the election."

"Did she make a scene?"

"Not a bit. We were in a San Francisco restaurant, the Catch of the Bay. Tricia listened to me very quietly when I told her. Then she said she had to use the rest room. She left the table. And she never came back."

"A shitty way to act, don't you think?"

"I guess so." Saul was convinced that Yasmin was talking about his action, not Tricia's.

"Did you call her?"

"Of course I did. I was off on the campaign trail the next morning, but I called her as soon as I could. All I got that night was her message service."

"Did you try to see her?" She rose from her chair in one fluid movement and came to perch on the broad arm of his.

"Not at once. I was all over the country, they had my every minute programmed. It was three weeks before Tricia and I were even in the same town. Then she wouldn't see me. Four weeks later, when I was up in Vermont, I received a media report that she had married Joseph Goldsmith." He wondered if the bitterness showed in his voice. "My staff briefed me about him. Someone who was everything I wasn't, first families of Virginia, horses and hunting and estates and a pedigree back to the mid-1600s."

"Was she seeing Goldsmith at the same time as she was seeing you?"

Saul stared. "I don't think so."

"Don't look amazed. It happens all the time where I come from. Go with one, keep another in cold storage just in case."

"I don't believe Tricia would do a thing like that."

"That's your option. But what's your theory? You must have one."

"I think she married on the rebound."

"A woman scorned? But she wasn't scorned, was she? She had

been asked to wait a while, that's all." Yasmin was staring sightlessly at nothing, her tawny eyes wide. "Something doesn't smell right. I need time to think about this."

"I've thought about it endlessly."

"Maybe. But you haven't thought as a woman."

"Meaning what?"

"Meaning you're like a lot of men, charitable when it comes to women's motives. Are you *sure* you told Tricia that you would marry her after the election?"

"Absolutely. I mean, I'm sure I said it, I couldn't have been clearer. But she hardly seemed to be listening. She seemed preoccupied, even before we began to talk."

"Did she have a key to where you were staying?"

"Yes. We were staying together."

"You were lucky. If you dropped me the way you dropped her, I'd have been over that same night and fixed you for life."

Saul winced. She was leaning over him, and she made a vicious snipping motion toward his genitals with her fingers.

He put his hands protectively in his lap. "You would never do anything like I did to Tricia, would you? You'd never treat a man so badly."

"I feel sure I wouldn't."

He sprang the trap. "Not even if you could be President if you dumped him? And if you had no chance if you stayed with him."

"Jesus. I should have seen that coming." Yasmin stood up. She had removed her shoes, and she began to prowl silently up and down in front of the dark fireplace. "Nolo contendere, isn't that what crooked politicians usually plead? You're right. For a chance—for half a chance—I'd do the exact same thing you did. Though you say you didn't really dump her, and she ought to have known that. But if she *thought* you had, I'm still surprised she didn't come along one dark night and castrate you."

Saul thought, *Maybe she did. I've been no use since.* He said, "So she was angry and disappointed and bitter, and she ran off and married someone else. I decided that for myself, long ago. What I don't understand is why she would call me, out of the blue, and say she wants to see me again."

"God, men can be so naive." Yasmin approached Saul's chair and hovered over him. "Isn't it obvious? She's divorced again, and she's hunting."

"Tricia isn't divorced. At least, she wasn't a couple of months ago. Since the supernova I don't think anybody could get a divorce no matter how much they wanted one."

"So I'm wrong. Did you agree to see her?"

"I'm having dinner with her tomorrow."

"Without her husband?"

"I suppose so."

Yasmin stared at him steadily, until he went on, "I mean, I feel sure her husband won't be there."

"And you still claim that she's happily married?" Yasmin spun away and went back to the fireplace. She rested her forehead on the cold stone mantelpiece. "You should ask Tricia what she wants from you. Don't ask me, because if I say something all you'll do is defend her. Why did you really come here?"

"I told you. I wanted to talk to you, to make sure that you were all right."

"Nonsense. You could have done that with a call. If I could contact the White House from here, I'm sure you could have reached me from there. You know why you came. It had nothing to do with my welfare."

Saul could hear the pain in her voice. He knew he was causing it, but he didn't know how. He stood up and went to stand behind her. When she did not move, he took her by the shoulders and gently turned her toward him.

"I didn't just call you, Yasmin. I came to see you. Why did I come? You say I don't listen, but I'm listening now."

He put a hand behind her head and pulled it forward to rest on his shoulder. For a moment she stood rigid, then he felt her relax.

"You came because you're scared of *her*." Her voice was muffled against his chest. "I don't know what that woman does to men, but it's quite a trick. Look at her track record. What Tricia Goldsmith wants, she gets. She didn't snag you the first time around, but only because you had one thing in your life, at that particular time, that you put above her." Yasmin straightened up and stared at Saul fiercely. "But damn it, I *still* don't understand. In fact, the more I think about this, the less I understand it."

"About Tricia and me?"

"About Tricia. Let's forget you just for the moment and concentrate on her." Yasmin stepped back. "I'm going to try to *be* Tricia. Tell me if this sounds right—and don't go out of your way to defend everything she has ever done. All right, here goes. I was born poor and a nobody. But ever since I became a teenager, I've been climbing steadily up the ladder of fame and fortune. True?"

"I suppose so. Of course—"

"I've reached the point where I have plenty of money. I've picked my husbands very well, so I'm also sitting well up on the social scale. You don't get much higher than the Chartrains. And now I've got Saul Steinmetz curled around my little finger. No, don't start denying it."

Saul had been ready to speak, but he managed to hold back.

"And now Saul is running for President. I'll be First Lady! There's only one condition: I have to wait a few months, until after the election, before we can be married. But that's no big deal. We'll still be having sex, though we'll have to do it more discreetly. And when he sees how sweet and reasonable and understanding I'm being about this, he'll love me more than ever. So I've got it made, if only I'm a little bit patient. And what do I do?"

"If Tricia—"

"I screw up and throw away my chances completely—at least for the time being—by marrying another man. He's rich, but so is Saul. He's part of the old monied set, but I've been there, done that. I've never been First Lady, though. And that's something I would really love. So what happened, to make me mess up so completely?"

"I don't know."

"Neither do I. But it makes absolutely no sense, psychologically. Do you mind if I, Yasmin, try to find out what really happened?"

"I wish you could."

"Can I say this is for the White House?"

"N-yes, all right. Look, if Tricia did decide she had made a mistake when she ran away, why did she wait two years before she contacted me?"

"I don't know, but I'll make a guess. It's the Virginia property laws. There's more than one way to screw a husband."

"You hate her, but you never even met her." And when Yasmin did not respond, "Look, I don't want to go on talking about Tricia all night, and what you're saying doesn't make sense. Even if I were scared of Tricia—I'm not, I'm going to dinner with her tomorrow—how would my coming here to see you change anything?"

"You don't want to talk about Tricia anymore? All right, let's talk about *you*. You're not scared of her in the usual way. You're scared in a different way, because you know quite well, even if you won't admit it, that one crook of her finger at you and you'd hop into bed with her again."

"I don't think that would work."

"Why?"

"There are . . . reasons."

"Well, I'm damn sure it would." Yasmin stepped back again, so that they were at arm's length. "How much honesty can you stand? You already told me tonight that you might have to fire me. Well, I'm going to give you a good reason to."

"You haven't said or done anything offensive."

"Just give me a minute. I know you weren't born rich, but you weren't born dirt-poor, either, the way I was—the way Tricia Goldsmith was, from what you've told me. She's come up a long way, but she'll remember. She learned to read men as self-protection. When you're poor they all assume you're available. Ever since I was a teenager I've watched men look at me, and I've heard them talk. They say, I'd like to help you with your career. But their eyes say, I'd like to fuck you."

"You think that's why I came to see you?"

"I asked you, how much honesty can you stand? I wish that *had* been why you came, it's so much better than the alternative. Sometimes in your office I wanted to grab you, but I didn't dare. When you said you were coming here I thought things might be different. There, now I've shocked you. Didn't you feel anything between us before this?"

Saul reached out and ran his finger along the smooth line of her jaw. "I felt it, of course I did. But there are things about me that you don't know."

"Like what?" She shivered. "Jesus, you'd better stop touching me. You're giving me chills and I won't be able to think. Things about you that I don't know? Well, I know you've not been able to get it up since you became President."

Saul froze, his finger still on her chin. "Where did you learn that?"

"From your doctor. No, Dr. Singer didn't tell me. But he's been in a terrible state since the gamma pulse wiped out the recording equipment. If he ever knew how to write anything but prescriptions, he's forgotten. He can be a pompous ass but he's conscientious, and he wants to keep full records of his meetings with you 'for posterity.' He used to dictate from his rough notes into his computer until it died. I told him I'd try to help. I said I'd take his recent scribbles and write them out properly and put them in order. He jumped at the offer. So I know that you've been impotent for over two years—since Tricia, in fact. No coincidence."

"You read *all* his notes?"

"Everything in the notebooks."

"About the tests he did? About my sex life?"

"Yes, I read all that." She laughed harshly at Saul's expression. "Oh, come on, I found that reassuring. Most women would. We're not looking for sexual freaks. And you have regular nighttime erections."

"When I'm sleeping."

"Yes, but it shows that everything's in working order. The problems aren't physical, as Dr. Singer pointed out. He mentioned three women in his notes."

"They were a long time ago, over a year. I thought you were only using his notes for the period since the recording chips stopped working."

"I started there, then I went all the way back to the first days of your presidency. It wasn't just nosiness. I was *interested* in you, you must have known that." She arched her neck, leaning into his hand on her cheek. "Telling you what the problem is won't do it. I'll have to show you. Let's start with those women. The ones it didn't work with. Would they be Leona Culbertson, Ruth Marshak, and Helen Lohmann?"

Saul withdrew his hand and stepped back a pace. "Now don't pretend you found *that* in Forrest Singer's notebooks. Even when I thought the records were all confidential, I never mentioned their last names."

"No. I did my homework. I checked your appointments calendar. There were plenty of lunch and dinner parties to choose from, and a guest list for each. But there weren't many showing one unpaired and unmarried female of suitable age and status, with the right first name."

"It's one of the hazards of being single, especially in Washington. People are always trying to play matchmaker."

"Of course they are. The trouble is, when other people try to fix you up they don't know your needs and tastes. And you went along with it. You gave Leona and Ruth and Helen a good old presidential try. But it didn't work."

"No, it didn't." *So that's what three miserable nights of flaccid flesh add up to: a good old presidential try.*

Yasmin moved into close contact again, her breasts against Saul's chest. "And you don't know why it didn't work. But I do."

"Then you're ahead of me."

"Because I have information you don't."

"About them?"

"About them and about you. Once I had their names I found out all I could about them. They were American thoroughbreds, every one, hostess guaranteed. We would never offer some half-caste mongrel like Yasmin to the President, would we? Our own reputation is on the line. We look for private schooling, family money, fifth- or sixth-generation American—not, God forbid, *Native* Americans, because they don't count. We can't actually go in and examine hymens and test for virginity, but these days a divorcée is quite acceptable. Youth and nice eyes and skin and figure are less important, but we do insist on one thing: for President Steinmetz, they must be *ladies*. How am I doing?"

"I don't think I want to hear any more."

"Of course you don't. Your mother tells you to meet 'nice girls'—I've heard her phone calls, the poor old dear. But she's your mother, she doesn't realize that it isn't the nice girls who excite you. I've watched you and I've listened to you for over a year. I know which women you respond to. The ones who turn you on aren't the ladies. They're the sluts, the tramps, the sexual daredevils, the women who will try anything—ones who'll give you as good as they get, and more. Did you tie up Leona and Ruth and Helen? Did they give you oral sex? Did you go down on them? When you left them, did you have teeth marks on your neck and claw marks down your back?"

"If you know them, then you know I didn't." But Saul was feeling a rising excitement, at odds with his calm words.

"So what did they do, lie back and think about the Pledge of Allegiance instead of the Washington Monument? No, you can't do that!" Saul had begun to rub her breast and erect nipple. She pushed his hand away, but their lower bodies remained in contact. "I said I'd have to show you, so I'm doing it. I was sure I knew what would get you going. I was right, wasn't I? You're not impotent, far from it. You pointed out that I never met Tricia. I didn't need to meet her. She fought her way up from nowhere, and all that experience showed up in bed. Her husbands had never known anything like it. Right? You must know."

"I don't want to talk about it."

"You don't have to. You gave me my answer. Now I'll give

you yours. Once you knew you were going to have dinner with Tricia, you arranged to come here and have dinner with me first. See, I probably look nothing like her, but I had the right feel to me. I was like your double-protection insurance policy. You know we could easily go for each other—we're already doing it. So if you can't perform with me, chances are you won't be able to make it with her, either. You'll be safe. But if it's a roaring success with me, the way you think it might be, then we'll fuck all night until you're so tired you couldn't get a hard-on tomorrow to save your life."

"That wouldn't work."

"Of course it wouldn't. I know men. Sexually, yesterday is like last year. But that's what you had in the back of your mind when you came here. And that's what's *really* making me mad, and it's the reason we're not going to do anything tonight."

"I could make love to you right now, right here."

"I know you could. Do you think I can't feel what's happening down there? But you're not going to. I'm not a trial run for a session with Tricia Goldsmith. My pussy isn't a magic charm that you can wear around your dick to protect you from her." Yasmin put a hand over her mouth. "Oh, my God, I shouldn't have said that. Now you'll *have* to fire me."

"You said you *hoped* we would make love."

Yasmin pushed him away. "I didn't say make love. I said fuck. Anyway, that was before I understood why you came here. If I left it to my feelings, we'd be rolling on the floor this minute. I'm not pretending I wouldn't enjoy it, either, or that I'm not attracted to you. And I love working with you at the White House, and for all the right reasons—nothing to do with sex. I have tons to learn, and you teach me so much."

"Learn about politics? I'm not sure I'd call that the right reasons."

"A better reason than most. I'm not saying we won't be lovers in the future, either. I think we will. But that has to be for the right reasons, too. And we should have privacy, and plenty of time. I bet there isn't even a lock on that door."

"I never looked. So what happens now?" Saul's excitement was waning as he accepted the idea that tonight Yasmin would not be persuaded. Again, there had been a subtle shift in the relationship. In this area, Yasmin was asserting her rights.

"We go to bed—separately," she said. "And tomorrow I head south to the syncope facility."

"Not alone, you don't." In another domain, his own authority came into play. "Something is happening downriver. You'll have a military escort."

"Fine. I have an escort. You do your inspection of this base. Then you return to Washington and have dinner with Tricia. If it helps when you're with her, think of what you'll be giving up with me if you fall into her clutches again. I don't mind being used in *that* way. And here's a taste of what you'd be missing."

She put one arm around his neck and gave him a long, searching kiss, while her other hand worked its way slowly down his belly. He reached around her upper thighs to pull her closer. She shuddered, took a step backward, and said, "Don't get me going again. I'm the one who has to say no, and that's not fair."

"Not fair? You started it." But Saul released her. "Do you want to leave here before I do?"

"You mean, to protect my good name?" Yasmin smoothed her dress and checked its fastenings. "I think it's too late for that. We've been alone for hours."

She opened the door and looked out into the hallway. "So much for reputations. Nobody. I suppose even a security man can tell when he's not wanted."

She walked a couple of steps ahead of Saul, then turned her head. Already she was looking more perky. "One thing you might want to fix, just in case you meet somebody on the way to the rooms."

"My hair?" Saul reached up to smooth his graying locks.

"Your zipper." Yasmin kept on walking. "You know, I don't think your mother would approve of me. I'm not a nice girl."

21

Pride goeth before a fall.

That, and a hundred other admonitions not to get too cocky.

Art lay on his back, shielded his eyes from the morning sun with his hands, and made another attempt to find a comfortable position.

The planks beneath him were of wet unseasoned timber, flat to the eye but not to the back. He had just spent six hours proving that. For the previous four hours he had been working a paddle, when any chance to lie down and rest seemed like a prospect of bliss.

Be careful what you wish for; you might get it. You didn't often experience such immediate verification.

After they came out of the storm drain Art had thought that the biggest problem in reaching the syncope facility was solved—and he was not the only one. Seth, too confident too soon, had predicted that he would locate a boat with no trouble.

Four hours of floundering in deep snow by the riverside taught them otherwise. They traveled less than two miles. At last they found not a powerboat, able to carry them quickly and comfortably downstream; nor a sailboat, where the wind could help. Their big find was a battered and unwieldy scow, half-rotted in its timbers and with mildewed cushions on its single seat. A pair of cracked paddles floated in the three inches of scum that had to be tipped from its flat bottom.

Spend the night moving downstream, or remain huddled on the snowy riverbank? That choice was easy. You pursue progress, even if you suspect that it is an illusion.

Art had gladly taken his turn paddling in the freezing hours before midnight, when hard physical effort was the best way to stay warm. He had labored again in the predawn gloom, when a great rush of wind raised whitecaps on the shallow river and drove the boat fast downstream.

The weather front passed through in less than an hour. When it left, the temperature was fifty degrees higher. Extra clothes had to be discarded, left in a heap in the bottom of the boat for use as makeshift bedding.

Now it was Art's turn to take it easy, drifting in and out of uneasy half sleep while Dana and Seth paddled the hulk downstream. Even with the steady push from the current, the boat was achieving no more than a couple of miles an hour. At this rate it would take days to reach the Q-5 Syncope Facility. By the time they got there, Oliver Guest's body in its cubicle could be thawed and rotten.

Why bother? Why keep going?

For the same reason that Seaman Edgar Evans, who pulled a sled the day he died, had kept going: you paddled because if you wanted to live you had no choice.

The change in the weather was bizarre. Twelve hours earlier Art had been chilled through every layer of clothing. This morning he was down to pants and a short-sleeved shirt, and still he sweltered under blue skies and rising sun.

The quiet splash of wavelets against the side of the boat was broken by a roar of engines. He opened his eyes and lifted his head. Off to the right, silver in the sunlight, two aircraft were lifting across the Potomac River.

"From National Airport," Dana said. She had noticed Art's movement. "Pity we can't get our hands on one of those. We could be where we want in fifteen minutes."

Art nodded, following the aircraft as they headed southeast. They were propeller planes, of a style not seen for forty years.

"Cessnas." Seth was tracking them, too. "Good to know something's flying again. But they're too rich for our blood. No good even if we could steal one. We don't want people to notice where we're goin'."

"We sure need something new." Art gave up the attempt to rest and sat up. So much for yesterday's feel-good moments. The long day and sleepless night made every bone in his body ache. "We'll take days to get there in this tub—if it stays afloat that long."

"We'll get there. But that's more our style than the Cessnas." Seth pointed to the riverbank on their left. Art, squinting that way with tired eyes, heard a throb of engines and saw a dark hulk moving into view around a snow-covered spit of land.

He shielded his eyes against the bright glare of sun and snow. "It's a Chesapeake fishing boat. Coming round Hains Point from Maine Avenue, heading down the Potomac to the bay. Their electronic gear won't be working, but they never rely on that anyway unless there's bad weather. For them it's business as usual."

"Or better than usual." Seth nodded to Dana and they began to paddle toward the other ship. "They can name their own price for their catch and cargo. Though I'll bet my ass and hat they're not takin' credit cards. What do you think they'd ask to pick us up and drop us off at Maryland Point?"

"I don't know what they'd ask," Dana said. "But it's too much. Didn't you just say we don't want people to know where we're going?"

"No need to tell 'em that. We get dropped off somewhere else. What's the nearest town to the syncope facility?"

"Riverside. But then we'd lose this boat." Art realized that he had changed his mind. Five minutes ago he hadn't a good word for the wreck he was sitting in. "We may need it when we leave the facility."

"So we'll keep it." Seth stopped paddling and stood up. The fishing boat was less than a hundred yards away, but it was moving at a respectable speed. Very soon it would be past them and beyond contact. The scow rocked as Seth shouted and waved.

The other boat didn't seem to change course, but someone on board must have already been watching them. The engines could no longer be heard and the ship was slowing.

"You in trouble?" A woman in black trousers and a dark gray T-shirt came to the low rail and called across to them. Her hair was tied back with a bright red head scarf. The boat was about ten meters long, black hulled with a green trim. The awning that sheltered the bridge was a matching dark green. On bow and stern, in white stenciled letters, were the words *Cypress Queen*.

"Not the usual sort of trouble." Seth sat down again, and he and Dana paddled closer. "But we need to be thirty miles downriver today, an' the way we're goin' we won't get there 'til half past Sunday."

"I'm not surprised, in that thing." The two boats were close enough for her to see the condition of the scow. "You'd be better off rowing a coffin. I won't ask why you're in such a hurry. But I'll tell you this: if you're asking for a ride, it'll cost you."

She turned. A gray-haired man in shirtsleeves had appeared from below. He must have noticed that the engine was throttled back and the *Cypress Queen* was no longer moving. "It's all right, Dad," she said. "You eat your breakfast while it's hot. We might be doing a little extra business."

"Hmph." He nodded and vanished below. Art felt his stomach rumble at the mention of food. He was as hungry as he was tired.

"How about a tow instead of a ride?" Seth asked.

"Can do that if you'd rather. But that'll cost you, too, just as much."

"How much?"

"How you gonna pay? Forget credit, and forget paper money. They're using them again in Washington, but out on the bay they're not worth squat." The woman was in her mid-forties, with a tanned skin showing the lines and wrinkles of too many hours of sun and salt water. She was close enough to peer down into the flat bottom of the scow, which was a jumble of their discarded clothes and blankets and carrying bags. "You don't seem overloaded with worldly goods, if you don't mind my saying."

Seth turned to Art. "What we got? I hate to give food an' weapons."

"Clothes, or blankets?" said Dana. "But we don't know what the weather will do next. Tomorrow could be as cold as yesterday."

"Two minutes more and we're off," the woman called down. "With or without you. We got work to do. We don't got all day."

"Oh, hell." Dana stood up. "I hate to do this, but I guess I have to." She had stripped down to her blouse for the hot job of rowing, and now she lifted it at the front and reached down inside her pants. She stood for a few moments, pushing her right hand deeper. After a few seconds she wriggled and crouched over farther.

"We don't take payment in bumps and grinds," the woman said. "Though I know Dad will hate it when he finds out what he's missing."

"These?" Dana at last had her hand free and she raised it. She was holding two coins between finger and thumb. "They're gold—solid gold."

"How do I know that?" But the woman sounded interested. "Gold is good, but can you prove it?"

"They're half-ounce twenty-two carat special issue, Canadian mint. They were a Silver Jubilee item, Queen's head on one side and a flower design on the other. I've had them in my family for nearly fifty years. You can take a close look at them when we're on board. We'll give them to you when you drop us off."

"I thought you didn't want to come aboard. Nature boy there"—the woman pointed at Seth—"said you wanted a tow."

"Don't listen to him. We want the boat towed, but these coins are worth a lot. We're entitled to more."

"Like what?"

"You mentioned a hot breakfast. And I'd love a place to pee where I don't have to stick my backside out over the river and wonder if I'm going to fall in."

The woman laughed. "Men lucked out on their plumbin'. But don't you just hate dealin' with females? They always negotiate for extras. All right, you can come aboard and we'll run a line to your boat. You're lucky, I'd never do this if we was headin' upriver. And don't blame me if she runs under when we start movin'. She ain't built for speed."

"Well, she's certainly not built for comfort." Dana went first. She put her coins away in her pocket, made a bundle of her extra clothes, and stepped across from the scow. A short ladder attached to the side of the *Cypress Queen* took her onto its deck. Art followed, almost missing his step. From fatigue or hunger, he felt dizzy. The smells of cooking made him salivate as soon as he set foot on the dark planking.

Seth waited, attaching the rope that the woman threw to him to a heavy metal ring bolted to the front of the scow. Then he came aboard in a single rubbery vault over the rail.

"Where you from?" The woman was already back at the wheel, powering up the engines. The *Cypress Queen* began to glide forward across the still surface of the river.

"Buckhannon." Seth made sure the scow was being towed smoothly behind. "You?"

"Clarksburg. Thought I recognized West Virginia in your voice."

"Same here. I'm long time gone, though."

"Me, too. I'm Eastern Shore now, got my mother looking after my kids 'cross the bay in Pocomoke City. Wouldn't want them around here, even if things was normal. You still got plenty of West Virginia in your voice. Lucky for you, or I'd probably have said no."

"Pretty bad reason to let somebody aboard your ship, the way he talks."

"Ain't that the truth? Never said I was smart, did I?" The woman nodded toward the hatch. "Go ahead, tell Dad you got breakfast comin' you."

Three steps led down to a cramped but tidy cabin. The old man nodded when Dana delivered his daughter's message. He gestured to bowls and plates on a rack by one of the long narrow windows and to a big iron pot standing in a hollow at one end of the table. Then he stood up and left without a word.

The woman appeared a minute later. "Dad said he'd rather spell me for a while at the wheel. He's none too sociable mornings. We got nothing fancy here, fish chowder, corn bread, coffee. We never expected visitors, see, but there's plenty. Dad likes to feel he can eat anytime he wants."

Art took the filled bowl that Dana passed to him. The chowder didn't bear looking at too closely. It included fish heads and fish livers and fish tongues and other less recognizable bits and pieces, thickened with sun-dried tomatoes and corn and seasoned with pepper. It was hot and rich and, like the bitter coffee sweetened in the pot with molasses, totally delicious.

The first bowl brought Art back to life. He nodded at the offer of a refill, set it in front of him, and kept eating. Across the table, Seth and the woman were talking. Their accents had thickened, and they spoke about unknown people and strange places. It occurred to Art that they were, in some perverse sense, flirting. This was another side of Seth, mixed in with the ruthlessness and cunning and animal vigor.

Nobody was as simple as he seemed—as maybe she wanted to seem. Dana, next to Art, had finished eating and was lolling toward him, her eyes closed and her head resting on his shoulder and left upper arm. Was she sleeping, or just pretending to? He stared at the spoon he was holding. It still dipped into the bowl and carried chowder to his mouth, but the operation seemed less and less under his control. He was vaguely aware of the old man sticking his head into the cabin and saying something to his daughter. If the man was here, and she was here, then who was steering the *Cypress Queen*?

Not Art's department, he decided. It was one thing in the world that he didn't have to worry about. He leaned his head to the left, to rest it for a moment on Dana's.

And suddenly he was asleep, as fast and deep as if the chowder in his belly had been seasoned with opium rather than pepper.

22

Art was awakened far too soon, by Seth shaking his shoulders. He opened his eyes and found Dana beside him rubbing her eyes and scowling. Neither the woman nor her father was in the cabin. The little room was stiflingly hot.

"We gotta make a decision," Seth said as soon as he was sure the other two were awake enough to listen. "Maryland Point is a mile ahead, on the port bow."

"Didn't we say we'd have them drop us off farther on, at Riverside?" Art drank from his mug of coffee, which now that it was cold tasted sickeningly sweet. "That's a couple of miles farther downriver than Maryland Point."

"It is. But I've been on deck with Janis, watchin' the shore. It must be thawin' like a son of a bitch, though you'd never know it lookin' at the snow. It's deep as ever, big drifts all over the place."

"The roads?" Dana asked.

"That's what I'm worried about. We might get off at Riverside and not make it to the Q-5 Syncope Facility."

"But if we can't get there, we can't get away from there, either."

"That's different. We don't hafta."

"Seth's right, Dana." Art turned to her. "If we find Oliver Guest and wake him up and have to wait a day or two before we leave, that's one thing. If we don't get there in time and he dies, that's another. We have to be dropped off at Maryland Point—as close to the Q-5 facility as we can get."

"But then the people here will know," Dana protested. "Even if they don't know who we're interested in, they'll realize what we're up to."

"That's all right. They won't talk. Not if we give them a gentle hint that we know what *they* are up to. Right, Seth?"

"That's my thinkin'."

"What they are up to?" Dana looked from Art to Seth and back. "I thought this was a fishing boat."

"It is," Art said. "But that's not all it is. They bring fish caught in the Chesapeake Bay up the Potomac to Washington. And they bring an unlicensed cargo of a controlled substance from the other side of the bay to the same market. Janis and her father are tobacco runners."

"Are you sure?" Dana raised her head and sniffed. "I don't smell it."

"You wouldn't," Seth said. "They have to be careful. She gave the game away a bit when she said they'd never have taken us if they'd been headin' upriver. That's when they have their cargo aboard. Now they're runnin' back relaxed and empty."

"With no smell," Art added. "It would be fatal for the *Cypress Queen*'s owners if the ship reeked of tobacco. They must have an airtight hold somewhere—maybe under the space that carries the fish. That would be good smell insulation."

"And I'll bet one other thing," Seth said. "Ol' Dad isn't just a runner—he's a user. A chewer, I'd guess, when he's belowdecks. He was all set for a quiet wad after breakfast when we rolled in. No wonder he left us an' went topside. Up there he's probably a smoker, too."

He raised his eyebrows at the other two. "Well? Are we all agreed?"

"Maryland Point," Dana said. "As close to the facility as they can get us."

Art nodded.

"Good enough." Seth headed for the cabin steps. "I'll tell Janis. Though I'll be surprised if she hasn't guessed. We're about as obvious as they are."

At the top he turned. "If you gotta perform any last personal rites before we leave, do it now. Five minutes, we'll be gone."

The Q-5 Facility for Extended Syncope was visible from the river. Bare, ugly, and ominous, it formed a gray cube jutting up from the level ground. A tall wire fence, apparently continuous, ran around it forty yards from the windowless walls.

Art walked toward it for a closer look. He felt enormously

better after the food and rest, but his stomach was quivering with tension. They were going to learn in the next few minutes if all their efforts had been a waste of time.

He bent to examine the snow-covered base. "This is normally electrified, but not at the moment. We might be able to get through with Seth's pliers. That will be a tough job. I say we go around and look for a gate."

"Right. Has to be." Seth led the way, trudging through the deep virgin snow in sunlight hot enough to trickle sweat into their eyes. "Chances are, the official way in's on the opposite side, 'cause that's where the road runs." He halted suddenly. "Or mebbe not. Take a look."

He had come to a place where the fence turned through a right angle. Along the new side the snow had been flattened to make a path three feet wide. The snow base showed footprints, so many and overlapping that they could not be counted. They ran in both directions, and a heavy object had been dragged one way to smooth and partially erase them.

"That settles one thing," Dana said softly. "We're not the only ones with the idea. What sort of people were sentenced to this facility?"

"Murderers, mostly." Seth was bending low, examining the footprints. "Rapists, sadists, torturers. Terrorists. Enemies of the state, whatever that means. Hey, I see different sizes here. Men and women both, by the look of it. Question isn't, who'd they put here? It's who'd try to bring somebody out at a time like this? Most people have trouble fending for themselves."

"Anyone afraid that the Q-5 judicial sleep maintenance system has broken down, like everything else. Anyone with a relative or friend they're desperate to save." Art was moving on ahead of Seth. He didn't have time for philosophical questions, only for whether Oliver Guest was alive or dead. Did that make him worse than Seth, more obsessive about his personal future?

"There's a gate ahead," Dana said. "A big one. And it looks open." She was hurrying along behind Art. She caught his arm, slowing him down. "Art, be careful. We have no idea who has been here. They may be here still."

"She's right." Seth was coming up behind. "Somethin' weird about this. There's a regular driveway from the main road to the gate. You can follow its line from the shrubs on each side of it. The snow on the drive hasn't been disturbed, all it shows is birds' feet and animal tracks. Then there's the cleared path we came in on, runnin' along the fence and back toward the river. Why didn't they use the real road?"

"Whoever came here, it wasn't an official maintenance group." Art had reached the gate, twelve feet across and nine feet high. The trampled path through the snow turned in, leading toward the double doors of the facility itself. "See, they hacked right through the locks. That takes a heavy bolt-cutter and plenty of strength. I don't think I could do it."

"You'd be surprised. You could if you had to." Seth moved to Art's side. "I agree with Dana, we gotta be careful an' ready for anything. But there's no way we stop. Let's go."

They were approaching the building from the north. As they moved from bright sunlight into its squat shadow, the drop in temperature hit Art hard. He saw Dana shiver. Physical, or psychological? Within that two-hundred-foot faceless cube, more than eleven thousand living humans had been placed in judicial sleep.

And what lay there now? Eleven thousand prisoners, or eleven thousand corpses?

"Main door locks are broken, too." Art found himself speaking in a whisper. "More proof we're not seeing official action."

"But the doors are closed." Seth's voice was as soft as Art's. "If the lights don't work inside—I'll take bets on that—it's a good sign. They already left, whoever they were. What's wrong?"

The last words were to Dana, who had stopped and placed her hand on her throat.

"The smell." She stepped back a pace. "Don't you smell it, too?"

Art didn't. That was no surprise. He was a family joke for his inability to identify—or even to detect—odors. ("The milk is a bit spoiled, you think? Give it to Uncle Arthur; he'll never know the difference.")

But Seth was nodding. "I do now, after you point it out."

"What is it?" Art asked.

"Same as in the city, only not so strong." Seth pulled the double doors open wide and grunted in disgust. "Except now it is."

Dana gagged and put her hand to her mouth. Even Art couldn't miss it. A ripe, sweet smell of rotting flesh surged out from the opened door and hit him in the face like a hand from the grave.

"Put somethin' round your nose." Seth was tying a scarf around his head. "We have to find out. Is it all of 'em dead or just some?"

Dana shook her head and stepped back again. "I can't. I'm sorry, but I just can't."

"You stay here." Art squeezed her hand. "Watch the doors. Shout if anyone comes."

He tied a cloth around his own face, though he was not sure he would need it. He and Seth went forward. Shouts from Dana would do no good, because if they were caught inside there was no other door. It was just a way to make her feel better.

He was more than pleased when a few seconds later she caught up with him.

"You're a gutsy lady," he said. "Will you be all right?"

She nodded. She was veiled up to her eyes. Even he could smell her. "Drenched my head scarf in the only perfume I have." Her speech was muffled. "I was saving it for some big seduction scene, but I guess I've blown that chance."

"Perfume's wasted on me. I can't smell worth a damn, you know that." He nodded forward, to where Seth had taken out his flashlight and was shining it around. "Save it for him."

Her eyes rolled. "Don't make me laugh, or I'll have to breathe."

Cheerful small talk. The surest sign that you were edgy.

The inside of the syncope facility matched the outside: gray, drab, and utilitarian. One long corridor led to the left, a matching one to the right. From each, all the way to the back of the building, side aisles ran off at sixteen-foot intervals. They held the body drawers, two feet by two feet by eight, packed side by side and one on top of the other like a library stack of stored humans.

The elevators for higher floors were on either side of the main doors. They were not working now, but iron stairs for use in emergencies stood next to them, rising up and up in dizzying turns until they vanished in the upper gloom. Seth's flashlight was not strong enough to carry its beam the full twenty floors to the dark ceiling.

"We still got the same problems." Seth stopped cranking the light. They stood together in the faint light coming in through the open double doors and waited for their eyes to adjust. "We didn't solve 'em comin' here, and I don't see we're nearer to solvin' 'em now. How do we find Oliver Guest? How can we be sure we got the right man? I'm not even askin' how we revive him when we find him."

"There has to be a filing system." It seemed gruesome to apply that term to stored people, but Art couldn't think of a better one. "And I bet it's simple, because the only people you can get to work in a place like this have to be morons."

"Or necrophiliacs," added Seth. "I doubt if most of them are any too bright, though."

They walked slowly to the first tier of body drawers and picked the third one from the bottom. Its aluminum end contained a grille for the circulation of air and was held shut by a cheap catch at the top. Seth shone his flashlight on the square panel.

"Not wasting the public's money on extras, are we?" he said. "Here's one question answered. This is an ID plate. 1–0128–394, that has to be a prisoner number. And Desmond Lota must be his name. And here's a date, 27/04/11. That has to be when he gets out. He's a JS short-timer, can't have been in for much. A year from now he'll be up and moving."

He placed his light flat on the grille and bent beside it. He shook his head. "Can't see a thing. Oh, well."

He reached up and turned the catch. The end panel dropped vertically until the drawer was fully open. Seth leaned forward, but at once jerked back and took two steps away. "Shit." He was coughing and choking behind his scarf. "It's putrid. I think I'm gonna puke."

"Let me." Art grabbed the light, worked the crank, and stepped to peer into the open drawer. The judicial sleep criminals were stored feetfirst and he was staring at the top of Desmond Lota's head, hairless and purple-blotched in the pale beam of the flashlight.

The drawers sat on lubricated runners that must have been designed for ease of maintenance and were useful now. An easy pull brought the drawer out until Art could see the whole body. It lay naked, with IVs and sprays still in position. Desmond Lota's skin sagged on his arms and legs, but bulged tight on his grossly swollen belly. The pneumatic system that rotated the criminals to prevent sores was still functioning at some level, because as the drawer reached the end of its travel the body was rolled through thirty degrees on its air pad. That led to a loud belch of escaping gases and a smell that made even Art blench and step back.

"This one won't be coming out—not next year or in a hundred years." Art pushed the drawer hard and closed the end panel as soon as he could work the catch.

"Do you think they're all like that?" Dana stood half a dozen steps away and had avoided the worst of the stench. Seth was apparently still speechless, hands covering his nose and mouth.

"I might, except for one thing." Art was walking along the aisle, shining the light on each end panel's ID plate. "The people who were here before us took something or somebody away with them. We saw the marks in the snow. I can't see anybody stealing a rotting corpse."

"Why would some people have survived, when others died?"

"I can only guess. But the nutrients and somnol and ion balancers probably go to the IVs in each drawer through a gravity-assist delivery. Without a working heating system, you'll also find temperature differences from top to bottom of the building. If that's the case, different levels would be treated differently when the chips died in the monitoring system."

"Higher levels would do better than ground-floor ones?"

"Or worse."

"Let's go find out." Seth had recovered enough to grab his flashlight back from Art. "If Oliver Guest is dead meat, the sooner we're out of here the better."

"One other thing." Art followed as Seth headed for the metal staircase. "Do you remember how long his sentence was?"

"Hell, I don't know. A gazillion years. He didn't just kill a whole bunch, he picked teenagers. Pretty ones. He'd be iced down to the max. Why you want to know?"

"We might get lucky. I noticed every ID in the first aisle had a wake-up time in the next year or two. It would make sense to stow short-timers on the lowest level, and a five-hundred-year sentence up where you don't need to check it so often. And the longer terms use different drugs to maintain judicial sleep."

They were climbing the open lattice of the metal staircase as they spoke. Art, last behind Dana, found it hard work. Seth was well ahead but paused at the fifth level, not to let the others catch up but to inspect one of the aisles and its body drawers.

"Fourteen years to go on this one. Comin' along." He was shining the flashlight on a plate. "Like to take a look?"

Art nodded. The rest for his lungs was welcome. He started to open the drawer, and at once knew he did not need to go any farther.

Seth was backing away. "Don't tell me, I can smell it. Another maggoty one. Let's go."

This time they plodded up another eighty feet before Seth halted and shone his flashlight along an aisle. "We got problems. No ID plates."

"Then we must have gone too far." Dana was a full level

below, on one of the staircase landings. "They wouldn't use the highest levels until the facility was filled all the way up. Shine the light back here, let me take a look." And, a moment later, "This shows a 2735 revival date. Fat chance he's got. He's going to die."

"But is he alive now?" asked Art. He hurried to join her. He felt sure that Dana was not going to risk opening the drawer.

He was right. "You tell me," she said, and stood warily by as he opened the catch. "I don't smell anything bad."

"Because he's not dead!" Art watched the slow rise and fall of a naked chest, then looked down the long aisle as Seth approached to give them more light. "The trickle supply system must still be working. What now?"

"Put him back. Tough for him, but we're not here on a prisoner humanitarian release program. He'll have to take his chances."

"I didn't mean that." Art closed the drawer and tagged the latch. "My question was, how do we find Oliver Guest? He should be somewhere on this level with the other maximum sentences."

"Unless he's already been taken," Seth said.

"Why would anyone except us do that?" But Art was following the beam of Seth's flashlight, and now he saw it, too. A drawer, all the way along, was open and empty.

"We knew somebody was here before us," Dana said. "We shouldn't be surprised."

"And they weren't after Guest. That's good news." Seth had moved along to examine the ID on the other drawer. "The name's sort of familiar but I can't place it. Who the devil is Pearl Lazenby?"

"I don't know. Whoever she is, she should have been iced down for a long time." Art pointed to the date. "2670. Somebody didn't want her around for a while. She's out of here way ahead of time."

"She was the leader of that big religious group," Dana said. "The Legion of Argos. Her people didn't use her real name much, that's why you didn't recognize it. They called her 'The Eye of God' and they said she could foresee the future."

"That woman!" Seth closed the drawer. "Then she oughta be in here forever. Her group killed a ton of people. It wasn't a religion, it was a cult."

"Your cult, my religion. The Legion of Argos certainly got one thing right. They prophesied a coming disaster." Art unwrapped the cloth from his face. "I think we can manage without these—even you, Dana. But our problem isn't solved. How do we find Oliver Guest?"

"The hard way. We look at every drawer." Seth started walking. "Come on."

Art did the arithmetic as he followed. Eleven thousand prisoners in judicial sleep at this facility. Twelve levels occupied. They might have to examine close to a thousand IDs if the prisoners were spread evenly.

But what better way to spend your time? Art walked behind the other two in silence, up and down each aisle, checking to make sure nothing was missed.

Five aisles covered, out of a total of ten. They crossed to the other side. A sixth, and Art began to wonder what they would do next. Without Oliver Guest the last hope of telomod therapy was gone.

"Jackpot," Seth said. He was leading, and he spoke so softly and casually that Art, ten yards behind, had no strong reaction. It was Dana's gasp and cry of excitement that brought him hurrying to join them.

"How about that." Seth was cranking furiously, and his light pointed straight at the ID plate.

Art read the inscription. *12–0456–97. Dr. Oliver Samuel Guest. 2621.* Below it were handwritten words. *You are a monster. May all your dreams be nightmares, your final hours agony, and may you rot in hell forever.*

"Not too popular with somebody," Seth said. "And now the real question. Dana, want to do the honors?"

The body drawer was six feet off the ground. Dana stood on tiptoe, opened the front panel, and peered in. "He's alive!"

"And we have to make sure he stays that way. Seth and I will have to loan him clothes, otherwise he'll freeze." Art stared around in the gloom. "There must be special equipment to lower the drawer to the ground. But I don't see it, and chances are it's not working."

"We'll have to do it ourselves." Seth began to reach up, then paused. "I was gonna say, we bring the drawer out all the way an' lower it between us. But that's too risky. Suppose the drawer weighs five hundred pounds? We'd drop it an' kill him."

"Dana will have to stand on our backs and unplug him. Then—if the publicity about somnol and judicial sleep isn't one big pack of lies—he ought to wake up without any action on our part. And then we can roll him off and lift him down."

"Yeah. And then it gets *really* interesting." Seth leaned over, placing the top of his head against the bank of closed drawers. "I'm ready. Your move, Dr. Frankenstein. Wake the monster."

Dana hesitated. "Do I just unhook everything?"

"We don't know. I guess so. He shouldn't need any life-support system once he's awake." Art was also bent and waiting. "Use your good judgment."

"Right." She placed one foot into Seth's cupped hands and scrambled onto their backs. "Though I'm not sure 'good judgment' applies at all if you wake up a man who killed eighteen people."

Dana inspected Oliver Guest with the aid of Seth's little flashlight. His nude body was festooned with monitor cables and sensors and tubes, but after the horror of Desmond Lota's bloated corpse he looked reassuringly normal. He might have been simply sleeping. True, his skull was hairless, and his skin cool to her touch, but the muscles beneath had atrophied little during his five-year coma. The electronic stimulator apparently worked as advertised.

The spray delivery system worked through skin osmosis, and those attachments were easily removed. So were the twin tubes at the corner of Guest's closed mouth and the sensor at his left eyeball. The harness that held and rotated Guest's body ought to be easy, too; she could just undo the straps. The urethral catheter would be straightforward, and the anal peristaltic activator was already uncoupled from the body. Guest was lucky. Had the gamma pulse arrived during the once-a-month period when that device was in the rectum and operating, he would now undoubtedly be dead.

The six IVs were another matter. They entered veins at both elbows, at the hips, above the navel, and on one side of the neck. The skin around the six slender tubes was red and slightly puffy. She wasn't sure how to remove them to do the least damage.

One of the two backs she was standing on moved a little under her foot. "How's it goin' up there?" Seth said from his head-down position below her. "You makin' progress?"

"I'm going as fast as I can. I don't want to kill him."

"That's all very well." It was Art, wheezy and muffled. "But you're damn near killing us. You should have taken your boots off."

"A bit late to tell me. Hang in there." Dana made her decision. She had hesitated because she wasn't sure what to do. Waiting added no information. She unstrapped the harness and opened it, then pulled out the urethral catheter. It seemed to come out forever, but maybe that was normal for a man. Oliver Guest would probably scream the next time he had to pee. From everything she had heard, he deserved that and worse.

The IVs gave the most cause for concern. She tugged delicately at the one in his left elbow vein, and it didn't move.

No time for niceties. She yanked harder until it came free.

Blood? She bent low. A few drops but nothing to worry about. They would wipe him later, once he was off the drawer.

She removed the other IVs, wincing a bit when the tube in his navel came out snaking and bloodied for a foot and a half. Where had it been connected, and what did it deliver or remove?

Oliver Guest should be able to tell her, he was a doctor. But first he had to survive and waken from the coma. Was there any change in the infinitesimal rise and fall of the chest? She couldn't see one, though in principle the process of awakening had already begun.

Dana eased the body to the edge of the drawer until she was afraid to bring it farther. She looked down. "He's in position. Hold tight, I'm coming off. Be ready to catch him—he might slip."

She shouldn't have said that. Art and Seth straightened at once and reached up to steady Guest's body and make sure it didn't fall. Dana's feet slid off their backs. She tried to protect the flashlight, dropped it, and landed on the metal floor on her tailbone with a jolt that rattled her teeth.

"Shit!" She rubbed at her backside. "What did you do that for?"

They ignored her complaints. "Never mind your ass," Seth said. "Get that flashlight goin', an' stand in between us an' shine it up. I got the shoulders, Art got the legs, but we can't see what we're doin'. If we have problems, grab his middle an' steady him as we bring him down."

It was easy to give orders, but if Dana worked the flashlight crank she had no hands free. Something had to give.

"Take a good look where you want your holds to be. And then be ready to bring him down in the dark."

Dana worked the light to its brightest beam, keeping it going until Art and Seth were sure of their holds. She looked where her own grip on the body should be, stuck the flashlight quickly into her pocket, and reached up fast as the light faded.

Even with three people it was an effort. Oliver Guest was a big man, and Dana felt as if at least half his weight fell on her. She braced herself, tightened her jaw, and lowered him as slowly and carefully as she could to the floor.

"He's down." Art's voice came out of the darkness, beside her on the floor. "But where the devil is the flashlight? I can't find it."

"It's in my pocket. Wait a second."

By the time Dana had the beam working again, Seth had already removed his jacket and was opening his shoulder bag. "You wearing two pairs of pants?" he said to Art.

"Yes."

"I'm not, and I got no spares. You'll have to come through with that. I'm givin' up my jacket an' a shirt. We have to keep him warm, and he has to be able to travel. How about shoes?"

"I've got these boots, the ones I'm wearing now, and a pair of regular shoes in my bag."

"Can he have your shoes?"

Art bent to examine Oliver Guest's feet. "They'll never fit him—his feet are too big. But he can have the boots. They were borrowed and they're like boats on me."

"An' I have socks, plenty of 'em. Hey, that's good." Art had pulled a candle from his bag, lit it, and placed it on the floor. "Now we can manage without the flashlight," Seth went on. "Can you get these onto him?"

He handed a pair of underpants to Dana. She moved to the bony feet and slipped the clothing over, pushing it carefully up the long legs. The calves and thighs were as hairless as the head, some side effect of the somnol or maybe of the long sleep itself. She felt awkward tucking in sex organs so she could pull the underpants up to his waist. His genitals were those of an adult male, but pink and hairless as a baby's. His belly, unless it was her imagination, had warmed a few degrees since she had pulled out the IV.

Art and Seth had been busy on the upper body. Oliver Guest was now dressed in a shirt, sweater, and a jacket a size too small. Art was working the hands with their long, thick fingers into a pair of black gloves. They moved him to the tiers of body drawers and propped him up there before tackling pants, socks, and shoes.

"Ain't he a beauty?" Seth said. "How'd you like to find this under your bed one dark night?"

Oliver Guest's eyes were slitted open and the skin around them had an odd yellowish tinge. That, together with the bald bulging skull and the complete lack of eyebrows, suggested some evil idol from an ancient temple, brooding in the yellow glow of a worshiper's single candle.

"Come on, Doctor G.," Seth said. "Can you hear me yet? Guess not, but we hafta do this. You'll lose too much heat without it."

He was holding a green cloth cap with earflaps. He placed it on Guest's head and pulled carefully down until it was only an inch above the narrow eyes. Seth lifted an eyelid and peered at the pupil behind. "Gettin' a reflex reaction to light. He's comin' along."

The other two were busy at the lower end. Working together they eased Art's spare pair of trousers onto Guest's legs and up to his middle.

"Too short," Art said. "He's at least three inches taller than me. But it won't matter once we get socks and boots on. They'll come more than high enough to cover him."

"Quick as you can," said Seth. "Then we done our best. The rest is up to him."

"I think he's still feeling the cold," Dana said. "I'm noticing a shiver in his foot as I pull on a sock. Do we have any way to warm him?"

"Not 'til we can get him outside, and he needs to be conscious for that." But Seth took his own blanket from his pack and began wrapping it tight around Guest's body. "Can you do the same with yours? He's a weight. We'll have one hell of a time gettin' him down them stairs 'less he can walk."

Working together, they swaddled Guest from chin to feet. As they placed him back in position against the bank of drawers, the mouth opened and they heard a faint exhalation.

"What did he say?" Dana was behind the awakening man, making sure that his head did not bang against the metal of the drawers.

"Nothing." Art peered at the eyes, open wider now but with eyelids that fluttered randomly and erratically. "I think he was just groaning."

"That's one thing you never hear when they talk about judicial sleep," Seth said. "They tell you it's not painful when a person goes under, it feels the same as nodding off for a nap. But what about waking up? That might hurt like a son of a bitch."

"I looked into it four years ago," Art said. They had done everything for Oliver Guest that he could think of, now it was wait and see. "I was down to eighty-seven pounds and my future seemed nonexistent—this was before I found out about the telomod program. I thought maybe if I was iced down for fifty years, by that time there'd be a cure. You know what they told me?"

"Let me guess." Dana leaned against the racks of body drawers, placed her palms together, and took on the earnest expression of a funeral home director. " 'Although we understand the reason for your request, Mr. Ferrand, you must realize that the extended syncope facilities are built and maintained using public funds. We cannot allow unsuitable and unqualified individuals to be placed there. Have you considered private alternatives?' "

"You ran into the same jackass as I did!"

"It looks like it. Aaron Petzel?" When Art nodded, she went on, "I got so mad with him, but it wasn't worth it. *The expense of spirit in a waste of shame*. He was such a sniveling bureaucrat, he acted like somnol wasn't a restricted drug and private groups were allowed to possess it. I told him that taxes from me, and people like me, built and ran every one of those syncope facilities, and paid his fucking salary as well."

"What did he say?"

"He told me not to use such language in his office. I never went back."

"I did—twice. The next time I said to him, 'Let's get this straight, Mr. Petzel. The only people who can be placed in an extended syncope facility are people who've done something terrible. Is that right?' And he said, 'That is correct, Mr. Ferrand. The extended syncope facilities are part of the criminal justice system of a civilized society.' When I went there again, I said, 'Mr. Petzel, I owe you an apology. Now I understand the way that the system has to work. I'd have to kill somebody or do something really bad to get into an extended syncope facility.' And he said, 'That is correct, Mr. Ferrand.' 'Good,' I said. 'That's what I'm going to do. And you, Mr. Petzel, are going to help me. You'd better keep your eyes open from now on, night and day, because I'm coming after you. I will kidnap you, hide you away where no one can possibly hear you scream, and kill you. You will die very slowly and painfully, and I will record every step of the process. Then I will give myself up. That ought to be enough to get me a long sentence in an extended syncope facility, wouldn't you say?' "

"Nice." Seth nodded his approval. "You didn't do it, though. Pity, because I'd like—"

"He's awake," Dana interrupted. "I don't think he can move yet, but look at him. He's listening."

"That's the way it's supposed to be," Art said. "There's no pain when you wake up, but sensory systems respond before motor systems. He can probably hear us, but he can't answer any questions."

"How long?" Dana asked. She had her head cocked to one side. "How long before he can stand up and walk?"

"Half an hour, maybe three-quarters."

She stood up. "That's too long. We're in trouble."

"We got half the day still," Seth said. "An' the weather's improvin'. We're in good shape."

She held up her hand. "Shh. And listen."

Now Art could hear it, too; a growl of large vehicles driven in low gear, more than one and steadily becoming louder.

Seth was already by the staircase, peering downward. "Comin' here," he said. "Not that there was ever much doubt, this place is in the asshole of the state with nothin' here but the syncope facility."

He returned to the group, rapidly but silently. "There could be a whole bunch of 'em. They're sure to have lights. If it's Pearl Lazenby's buddies, they got guns as well. The front door's the only way out, an' they're comin' in that way so we can't use it, even if we could get down there. The front door's busted, too, so anybody will know somebody's here or been here. We can't stick big boy back in his drawer an' say we're tourists, 'cause he's wakin' up."

He glanced from Art to Dana. In the candlelight his eyes were like a snake's, lively, flickering, and lighter than usual in their color. "We're in trouble, amigos, like Dana says. Question is, what are we gonna do? We've come too far to give up now."

23

Celine had been awake for more than twenty-four hours, and the week before that had been one long effort. Fatigue and the familiar-yet-strange air and gravity of Earth gave to everything a dreamlike halo. She stared at the red utility vehicles in the opened A-frame barn. She could hear running engines and see spouting black smoke behind the rear balloon tires.

Two of the trucks moved out of the building and came rolling toward them. One woman and one man sat in the front seat of each, apparently identical people dressed in identical tunics. They halted ten yards in front of Reza and Jenny, blocking progress toward the barn. One of the men descended.

Celine froze, and her dream mood vanished. The man in front of her was holding a light submachine gun, which he swung easily in an arc to cover the whole of her group. The woman in the other truck had a second weapon, raised and ready.

Celine became unnaturally alert. Who greeted strangers—unarmed strangers, who had made an obvious emergency landing—in such a fashion?

"You probably think that guns don't work no more," the man said in a Texas twang. "Well, folks, that sure don't apply to this one. You wouldn't like it one little bit if I have to demonstrate. In one minute, you're going to tell me why you came here. First, though, I want you to explain how you could fly that danged thing." He pointed his gun toward the *Clark* orbiter. "It's recent make, an' it sure has to be full of chips."

"It *is* full of chips." Celine disliked everything about the man. Belts of ammunition hung over his shoulders and around his chest. Two handguns sat in holsters at his waist. His smile was fixed, without a trace of humor, and he had the cold, unblinking gaze of Celine's own abusive father.

"As you can see," she went on, "we couldn't fly the orbiter too well even with working chips. We were lucky to be able to make a landing at all. We need help."

The man nodded slowly. His brow furrowed, as though he understood—or listened to—only a few of her words. "Now, lady, was your ship stored underground? So that the gamma pulse didn't ruin it?"

"No. The chips in that orbiter were a long way from Earth when the pulse hit." Celine gestured, to include Wilmer, Jenny, and Reza. She spoke slowly and carefully, seeing his finger tight on the trigger. "We were in deep space, returning to Earth from Mars. We landed at this location because we had no choice. We had to adapt an orbiter using our own equipment and programs, and this was the only landing site that we could reach." She hesitated before the next words. "We are the only surviving members of the first Mars expedition."

It was a bad moment. Nowhere near as awful as watching Zoe and the others immolated on their attempt at reentry, but piercing and heartbreaking in its own way. Talking about the expedition made the contrast more striking. A couple of weeks ago they had done it all, they had won it all. The crew was returning intact and healthy, coming home to certain honor and glory and acclamation.

Now they stood, the lonely four who had lived, cold and exhausted in this snow-covered valley, facing a hostile man who showed no shred of interest or excitement at meeting the first people ever to walk the surface of the red planet. So far as he was concerned, they were just intruders. At her words he had raised his gun and was pointing it at her chest.

"You are defilers of Heaven." He was broad-chested and tall, topping even Wilmer by a few centimeters. The left side of his chest and the cuffs of his long-sleeved gray tunic bore an unfamiliar emblem, a bird's scarlet talons enclosing a green globe. "If your fate lay in my hands, it would lead you straight to hell. Into the vehicles. And giddyup!"

Celine was afraid, for Wilmer and Reza more than for her and Jenny. They were all used to taking orders—but not from strangers. Jenny would be cautious. Unless Celine acted at once, though, either Reza or Wilmer was likely to balk. Given Reza's unpredictable mood for the past few days, he might do absolutely anything.

"Come on," she said, and moved quickly forward to climb

the step into the backseat of one of the trucks. She sensed rather than heard the stir of rebellion on her right, and patted the seat. "That includes you, Wilmer. This is no time for heroics."

Her companions hesitated, looking from the man to the woman with the gun in the other truck. To her relief they moved forward without arguing. Wilmer settled himself on one side of Celine, placing his little backpack on the seat next to him. The man with the gun took the seat on the other side. "Smart move, lady," he said gruffly. "If you got troubles, you sure brung 'em on yourselves. Didn't you know your actions defiled God's domain? As for your arrival here, that was foreordained."

Reza and Jenny had gone to sit in the other vehicle. Celine decided that they would have to fend for themselves—perhaps not too difficult, since no one but the man with the machine gun had so far said a word. She turned to face him, and found that his gun was still pointing at her chest.

"You must know who we are," she said. "I'm sure that for months before Supernova Alpha, the media were full of news about the Mars expedition. I'm Celine Tanaka, and I was in charge of instrumentation. But who are you, and what is this group? Why do you say that our arrival was foreordained?"

Knowledge is power. When you can't do anything else, try to collect information.

He scowled. "Call me Eli, an' a devoted servant of the Legion of Argos. That will be enough. As for news of you and your flight, I didn't hear nothing. The media, as you call them, are pure corruption." His voice changed to a programmed chant. " 'Attend not to their mindless babble of invented trivia, nor to the self-aggrandizing trumpeting of their own importance. They are the instruments of Satan. Reject them, and dismiss their posturing.' We done that, even at the height of their power. Then God's strike came, and they were smashed. That is a blessing."

"So, Eli," asked Wilmer, "if you didn't get news from the media, how do you know anything about the Mars expedition?" He was leaning across Celine, and she knew that look. It was blind obstinacy combined with a lack of concern for consequences. Wilmer was as tired as she was, and at the end of his patience. If he started needling Eli it could be fatal.

"Wilmer Oldfield, shut up," she said, and gave him a sharp elbow in the ribs. Before he could do more than grunt in surprise, she turned to the other man. "Forgive his lack of control—or my lack of control over him. I'm afraid that our party lacks the strong discipline of the Legion of Argos since the death of our original leader. I now serve as leader, but I am new to the task. I request that you ignore all communications from this group that do not come to you directly from me."

She was taking a chance—among other things, on what Reza and Jenny might be saying in the other car. But Wilmer had understood the message of the elbow. He remained silent. And organizations generally approved of what they practiced. Eli was nodding with what might be approval.

"Without discipline," he said seriously, "there can be nothing."

He made no attempt to answer Wilmer's question of how the Legion of Argos knew about the Mars expedition. Celine wondered if she could find a more tactful way to phrase the same inquiry, but the two cars were already moving into the A-frame barn. The wooden door swung closed, and Eli indicated with his gun that they should step down from the truck.

Celine descended with difficulty. Their original mission plan had called for them to be coddled and resting after the return to Earth, sitting in a quarantined facility while their bodies made a first readjustment to higher gravity and physicians tested them inside and out for evidence of un-Earthly organisms. Instead, after days of tension and sleeplessness they were forced to remain alert for new danger.

She stepped close to Jenny, waiting by the other vehicle, and said softly, "Anything I should know about while you were driving in?"

Jenny shook her head. "I think they must have taken vows of silence. Nobody spoke, so we didn't."

"Good. Take my lead, and tell Reza to do the same. Treat me as an absolute boss. Don't say anything unless I ask you to. I'll explain when we have privacy."

"I'll tell Reza, and hope. But he's still acting weird. That guy giving you trouble, is he? Bet he's not one of their top people. Pushy type." But Jenny was turning away as she muttered the last words, so that the approaching Eli did not hear her.

Maybe he wouldn't have noticed anyway. Celine saw that he was talking and listening on a black handset. At least some radio communication was still working—or more likely working again. The world was fighting back. Supernova Alpha was not going to wipe out civilization.

"Right," Eli was saying deferentially. "Very good. I sure understand that." Then, in quite different tones to Celine and the others, "As I said, your arrival was foreordained. Our leader, newly returned to us, confirms it. She says that she will meet with you and she will speak to you in person. It is a great honor."

Celine saw Reza's expression. Angry now, he seemed ready to say, *Damn right it's an honor. She'll have the honor of meeting the members of the first Mars expedition.* Jenny gave him a warning nudge.

"Meet here?" Celine asked, before Reza had a chance to speak.

Eli shook his head. "Six kilometers from here."

"Which is where?"

He stared at her. "You don't know where you are?" His smile for a moment seemed as though it might reflect an actual feeling of pleasure. "Oh, I like that. We got us one prize example of arrogance and folly. You fly across space, millions an' millions of miles to no place, intruding upon the very domain of God. You come on back. An' you tell me you don't know where you are when you git here. Do I have it right?"

"We don't know where we are. I am not from this part of the country, and the last step of the return to Earth was not as we had planned it. We landed somewhere in the northeastern United States, that I am sure, but I could not tell you where within a hundred kilometers. Where are we? And where will we be going?"

Eli turned to wood again. "I don't believe I oughta answer that question, 'cept to say you'll travel to the headquarters of the Legion. If the leader permits, you may ask questions. If she chooses, she may decide to answer."

"How should I address her? Doesn't she have a name, other than just being your leader?"

"If the leader permits, you may ask her name."

And if she chooses, she may decide to tell me. We already went through that one. Celine was fishing again—and getting nowhere. If she couldn't do better than this, she ought to hand over to one of the others.

"We are ready to go," she said. Delay would do nothing but make them more tired, and she was beginning to feel giddy and nauseated. They were long overdue for food and sleep. The members of the Mars expedition had been chosen for cast-iron stomachs and physical stamina, but there were limits. "We all need rest."

"After you meet with our leader."

"When will that be?"

"Right soon. We're heading there at once."

Celine expected to be told to return to the vehicles. Instead, Eli motioned them forward. At the rear of the barn a wooden trapdoor had been lifted. An iron ladder descended from it. Wilmer followed a woman with a shotgun, climbing down backward but turning his head to see where he was going. Reza and Jenny went after him.

Celine stood on the brink, staring down. The ladder was not a long one, it had nine or ten steps and ended in a narrow space lit by hanging lanterns. The walls and floor, all that she could see of them, were dark-stained wooden boards. Celine smelled creosote, turpentine, and moldering earth.

"Don't just stand there, lady." Eli spoke from close behind her. "Git on down."

Had it all been a lie? Eli had made his own feelings clear. He would kill them gladly. And the space below more resembled a grave than a meeting place with the Legion's leader. For all Celine knew, the command had been "Get rid of them—at once."

With the gun at her back, Celine had no choice.

She took a deep breath and climbed down the ladder.

24

Celine found herself not in a room but a tunnel, running away in front of her in a long arc until it curved out of sight to the left. The roof, like the walls and floor, was timber, heavily braced every twenty yards. Lanterns, located at the braces, did not use the oil that their appearance suggested. Their light came from electricity, carried by power lines looped to brackets on the walls.

Celine turned to Eli, who had arrived at the foot of the ladder. "I said that we need rest, but maybe I didn't put it strongly enough. I don't think you realize what my crew has been through. For the past six years, we have never lived in a gravitational field as strong as that of Earth for more than a few minutes at a time. Our bodies are exhausted. It is impossible for us to walk six kilometers—or even one kilometer—before we have had food and sleep."

"Did I say you'd have to do that?" Eli gestured ahead. "The leader knew, just like she knew about the supernova without bein' told. She said you'd be tired. You don't have to walk six kilometers, not even one. Think you can manage fifty yards?"

"Yes."

"That's all I'm asking. After that it's comfort city. See 'em yet?"

Celine saw them. Steel rails three feet apart, with wooden sleepers between, began at a buffer in the middle of the tunnel. Two cars, five feet wide and ten feet long, sat on the rails.

"Runs straight to headquarters," Eli said. "Electric power, or hand-pumping if you want or need it. We'll use the 'lectric today. The leader told me to get you to her in good condition. It's better than defilers deserve, but it's orders." He motioned to Reza and Jenny, who were already standing by the cars. "On board."

The cars were open, their bodies formed from a single piece of molded graphite composite. The seats seemed at first of the same material, but they were soft to the touch and gave luxuriously under Celine's weight. She settled back with a sigh. Five minutes of this much comfort, and it would be hard to remain awake. The only car controls that she could see were two foot pedals in front of Eli. She looked around. Wilmer and Celine sat right behind Eli, with Reza and Jenny behind them. Two uniformed women at the back rode shotgun—literally. Their weapons were old-fashioned, but armed and ready.

Eli pressed the right pedal and the car moved forward with a steady surge of acceleration. When the speed leveled off they were probably moving at no more than twenty miles an hour, but the low roof and uncertain light made it seem to Celine that the dark board walls flashed past at monstrous speed. The tunnel had become almost straight, descending steadily. She tried to estimate the gradient. Even if it were as little as one in fifty, six kilometers of this would plunge them a thousand feet underground—more than enough to shield completely from the gamma pulse. With the rest of Earth devastated, the technology of this mole group might have come through unscathed.

Reza leaned over Celine's shoulder. "I don't understand what's going on here," he said loudly. "There's no way that all this could have been built *after* Supernova Alpha hit. This place must be ten years old at least."

Maybe Jenny hadn't delivered Celine's order to remain silent, or maybe Reza in his present strange state had misunderstood. It made no difference, because Eli was turning eagerly in his seat to face them.

"Old? It sure is! We've been buildin' here for twenty year an' more. We knew it was comin'!"

"You knew about the supernova?" Wilmer asked. "You predicted it. How?"

"Why, it was prophesied. In the leader's writings, long before she was a martyr to the cause. She knew. She said the supernova would come, and we would go from strength to strength. We have, and we will." Eli's face was alive with rare excitement. *" 'You must continue the labor, as we have labored together for fifteen years. In this dark hour, take comfort. Do not fear for me, nor grieve at my leaving. Labor on. Very soon, within this mortal lifetime, I will return to you.' "*

Celine hoped that the others would know enough to keep

quiet. Reza and Wilmer, unknowing, had found the button that worked for Eli and the Legion of Argos: evangelical zeal.

" 'Before the second prophecies of the Eye of God, there will be certain proof that my resurrection is imminent.' " The voices of the two women added to Eli's, in a slow, chanted litany that echoed along the dark tunnel. *" 'There will be portents. When these signs appear, prepare for my return: Another sun will rise in the southern sky, turning night into day. Winter will become summer. Heat will draw from the seas the poison fogs of contagion, dropping their pestilence on the land. Fire and floods will sweep away nations and powers and principalities. Hot winds will scourge the face of Earth, scattering it like dust across the whole world. Lightning from afar will shatter the false temples of Mammon and destroy the fools who seek to defile the face of Heaven. In that same hour, as the trappings of false governance are broken, you will come to me. I will rise again, as our star rises. The Eye of God will prophesy, and the holy work of cleansing our nation and our world will begin. This time there will be no turning back, no quarter given.' "*

The car was slowing. Celine had felt her ears pop twice, more evidence that they were riding deeper and deeper below ground. The seat was as comfortable as ever, but any fear of nodding off was long gone. *The Eye of God.* The group had been known as the Legion of Argos long before its charismatic leader rose to notoriety. The *Schiaparelli* had already boosted away from Earth orbit by the time of the trial, but beamed radio reports provided coverage. The "Eye of God"—Celine would surely remember the woman's name if she were less tired—had demanded absolute obedience from disciples and followers. As evidence of commitment to the causes of the Legion, she had directed a group of recruits to kill the four judges who had ruled against her in a property dispute. They had done that—and much more.

Celine felt her stomach tighten. Eli must be a minor player in the organization. But he, or one of the armed women sitting at the rear of the car, could have been in that group of blood-besotted recruits. And the Mars crew were defilers of Heaven. Better hope that obedience to the orders of the leader remained absolute. The Eye of God wanted the crew to arrive in good condition.

The holy work of cleansing. As the car stopped and Celine descended, she stared again at the emblem on Eli's tunic. The scarlet talon grasping the blue-green globe of Earth. It made sense now, but only as a symbol of insanity.

How many people were in the Legion of Argos? Was the

group big enough to be a national threat? One thing was sure, Eli was not about to tell her.

They were descending again, this time in a regular elevator. Celine could not be sure that it needed microchips for its operation, although almost every device made in the past thirty years had chips in it somewhere. Suppose they were a thousand feet down. Then the natural shielding of Earth's crust should damp below danger level any electromagnetic pulse from Supernova Alpha.

Wilmer would be able to tell her in a moment at what depth that was true, but now the elevator door had opened. Eli was urging them forward, remaining inside himself.

No guns, no threats? It seemed that way. Celine walked from the elevator into a pleasantly furnished executive office. Half a dozen padded chairs were grouped around a glass-topped coffee table. On the table sat a painted samovar and a tray of cups. At the other side of the room a longer table formed a T-shape with a big desk at one end of it. The oddity was that Celine could see no telcoms, no displays, and no terminals.

And no guards. Only one other person was present, sitting in a chair by the coffee table. She smiled warmly and beckoned the new arrivals to come forward and join her.

"I know you are terribly tired," she said. "It won't make you feel any better, but let me tell you that at the moment I myself am hardly able to stay awake. I wanted to spend just a few minutes with you, before we all collapse into bed. Please sit down."

She was a big woman, full-figured, probably close to six feet when she was standing up. Her hair was long and auburn, piled up onto the top of her head, and she had a pale, unblemished complexion and clear skin. Her eyes were bright gray, with a touch of golden brown at the center of the irises. At the moment the skin beneath them was dark-smudged with weariness. Her age might be anything from forty upward. The voice was warm and musical, with careful diction and soft vowels. Celine tried to analyze the accent, and decided that the speaker was native-born American, probably from somewhere like Tennessee. Her manner was utterly unlike Eli's wooden personality.

"I was told that you were with the Mars expedition." The woman made a quick survey of the four arrivals, and by some instinct spoke directly to Celine. "I find that totally fascinating. I have just awakened from judicial sleep. But before I was placed there, six years ago, I recall that there were to be seven crew members. Did the plans for the expedition change?"

She showed no hint of shame at admitting to a crime bad enough to justify her commitment to a syncope facility.

"There were seven of us." Celine sat down, and Reza, Wilmer, and Jenny followed her lead. "All the way to Mars, and on Mars. We had a problem on our final descent to Earth, because all the people on the space stations are dead and the ground support network is not working. The rest of our crew died attempting atmospheric reentry."

"That is truly terrible." The woman had turned her head, and Celine could see two angry red stigmata on her pale neck. "You have my sympathy. But we do not know the ways of God. Comfort yourselves, if you can, with the thought that no one dies without a purpose."

"It's hard to think that way at the moment."

"Impossible, I should think. But give yourselves time. And if there is anything that I can do to ease your grief, please let me know." The woman leaned forward and extended her hand. "I am Pearl Lazenby. Welcome to the Legion of Argos."

Pearl Lazenby. Celine knew she would have recalled the name once she was less exhausted. More difficult was the match of the apparently charming woman in front of them with the reputation of the Eye of God. That analysis would have to be postponed until she could think more clearly.

"I'm Celine Tanaka." She gestured to the others in turn. "Reza Armani, Jenny Kopal, Wilmer Oldfield. I'm sorry if this sounds rude, but the man who brought us here—Eli—was not pleasant at all when he heard we were the Mars crew. He accused us of defiling Heaven."

Pearl Lazenby had been repeating their names under her breath. Now she nodded. "I'm afraid that he was right. All space beyond Earth is God's domain." Her smile took the edge off her remark. "But I'm sure you did not initiate the Mars program, or sell it to a credulous world, or provide any part of its funding. You are merely the brave souls who believed the publicity and volunteered to fly the ship. Eli is wrong if he criticized you. You are to be pitied, not censured, and forgiven rather than punished. Behave acceptably, and you will be treated well here. I guarantee it."

Wilmer leaned forward. "Eli said that you knew about Supernova Alpha before it happened. That you've been preparing for its effects for twenty years. Is that true?"

Pearl Lazenby was filling a cup from the tall painted samovar. At Wilmer's question she passed the tea to Celine and leaned back.

"That is a very complex question. If I say I knew in 2006 that a specific star would turn supernova in the year 2026, that would not be correct. However, I was certain that some great catastrophe would take place over the whole world in that particular year—this year—and I saw many of the consequences."

"You mean you *foresaw* consequences."

"No, Dr.—Oldfield, was it? I said that your question was complex, and it is." Pearl Lazenby sat, a little painted cup steady in her hand. She became perfectly still. Her eyes widened, although she was looking at no one. "When I was eighteen years old—nearly twenty-eight years ago, I was hardly more than a child—I began to *see*. I witnessed events that had never happened. It might be broad daylight, and I would watch a fire at midnight, a woman with smoldering clothes carrying two infants from a burning building. It might be evening, and I would witness a redheaded man's fevered death by the light of dawn. I dared not drive, because when I *saw* I could observe nothing else around me.

"You might think that my visions would have drawn wide attention, but they did not. The year that my seeing began was 1998. The world then was full of millennial prophets and vast prophecies, and what I saw was nothing compared with other warnings: Judgment Day, and World's End, and Armageddon, and Ragnarok. I saw only smaller events, taking place at a time that at first I could only dimly suggest.

"As the months and years passed, that changed. The millennium came and went, and the universe did not seem to notice. Prophecy went out of fashion. But what I saw became more vivid and more precisely placed in time. I could mark on a calendar what I saw, and when that day or week arrived the media would report it. Little by little, I realized that my gift had been given to me for a reason. At first I had no idea what, only that some great task lay ahead.

"And then, twenty years ago, my fate was revealed. One night I could not sleep. I did not understand why, until in the hours before dawn I saw a thousand disasters. I saw floods sweep away cities and dams and levees. I saw fire run unchecked across a thousand miles of parched forest, jumping rivers and gorges, and man-made firebreaks. I saw dust storms swirling and smothering over a whole continent. I saw icebergs in tropical seas, and great whales basking in summer heat. All these things would happen at once, as the world tottered under a gigantic blow from Heaven. The damage would be made worse by a false faith in new technology, new technology that seemed like magic.

"And the Word came to me. What I *saw* would happen not then, nor in a week or a month or a year, but in twenty years. The machines of that time, the near-intelligent machines of which their creators were so proud, would fail. And even that was not the worst news. Unless humanity learned a lesson, and cooperated over the whole world, a still greater disaster would come. I could see no details, but all would die. Humankind had only one hope, one way of averting that new catastrophe. The City of God must be created here on Earth. It was my role to lead that building. Humanity must be purged of evil, if necessary by force. It was my role to lead that purging. Humanity must be cleansed of sin, even if it meant scraping to the bone. It was my role to be the Eye of God, to prophesy and define what must be done. Then it would be my task to lead the carrying out of that cleansing. I could not rely on new technology, but *old* technology would provide me with my tools.

"I did not like the burden laid upon me. I fought against it, prayed that the cup might pass. I tried to reject it and to deny it. I hated many of the things that I knew I would be required to do. But, finally, I accepted my destiny." Pearl Lazenby turned to Wilmer and offered the cup that she was holding. "Would you like tea?"

He shook his head, and leaned toward her. "You saw disaster in this year, 2026. And you saw a possible later disaster. When? What did you see around 2076?"

"Fifty years from now?" A frown wrinkled the skin of her high forehead. "I saw nothing. Should I have?"

"Yes. In that year, or within five years of it, a second great disaster will arrive."

"What kind of disaster? Can you describe it?"

"Yes." Wilmer's face took on the blank look of Pearl Lazenby's, five minutes earlier. "Let me put it in terms easy to understand. There will be fire in the sky, as a deluge of high-energy particles hits our upper atmosphere. We will see auroras bright as no one has ever seen them. Worse trouble follows. For a short time the atmosphere will become opaque to visible wavelength radiation—darkness at noon. When sunlight returns, Earth will be unprotected. The ozone layer will have been lost. Ultraviolet radiation will hit Earth more fiercely than we have ever known. And while this goes on, the global temperature will rise. The thermal shock to the planet will be ten times that of the past two months. Civilization, even if it has been rebuilt from today, will crumble and collapse."

"You *see* it." Pearl Lazenby was sitting bolt upright, absorbed in Wilmer's words. "That's it, isn't it? You *see* these events."

"You could say that I see them, yes."

"But where does your vision come from?"

"From the equations governing stellar energy release, clear to those who can read them. It is in the formulas for element nucleosynthesis, in the equations for radiative transfer, and in the quantum laws that govern the interaction of the electromagnetic field with atoms and electrons. It was foreordained by the occurrence of the supernova itself. And beyond 2076, far beyond it, I see a faint shadow of something even more ominous."

"Can others see these things?"

"Some. But if I am honest, I have to say, not many. It requires a lot of training."

Pearl Lazenby subsided slowly in her chair. "It is like my own gift. It must be grown from its first seed. Native ability is nothing without long, hard work. Could you teach me to see as you do?"

"I think not."

She nodded. "Any more than I have been able to teach others. I accept that. It was clearly foreordained that you come here. You will tell me more of your visions. But not today. You are, I know, exhausted, and so am I. My people will show you to your accommodations." She did not seem to move, but three armed women appeared at the door of the room.

Celine took the hint and stood up. The others of the Mars group, more slowly, followed her example.

Pearl Lazenby rose, too, a little unsteadily. She patted Wilmer's arm. "We have much to learn from each other. Good night."

She waved to the uniformed guards, who escorted Celine and the others away.

Following Celine's lead, Wilmer, Reza, and Jenny said nothing until they had been taken along another underground corridor and shown two small rooms, each containing two cot beds. The armed women motioned Reza and Wilmer to place their small backpacks in one room, Jenny and Celine to use the other.

"What about food?" Celine asked. "It is many hours since we ate."

One of the women shook her head. "There will be no food

tonight." She had the same wooden manner as Eli, and she spoke as though she grudged every word. "Mealtimes are fixed. At seven in the morning, at midday, and at six at night. Anyone who does not eat at those times does not eat."

"I don't believe it. Food must be available for people who have been working late or working at night."

"There will be no food tonight."

"Then tomorrow I will report your action to Pearl Lazenby herself. She said that we would be treated well here. She does not expect us to be starved."

Mention of the leader's name had an immediate effect. The other two women turned to the one who had spoken and Celine could see fear and worry on all three faces. After a few seconds the first woman nodded.

"You will have food. But you must eat here, nowhere else." She nodded to one of her companions, who hurried out. "Tonight you may not leave these rooms."

"Believe me, we don't propose to go anywhere. We are hungry and exhausted. Something to eat, then we'll collapse into bed."

"We will be on guard outside, to make sure that no one tries to leave. Your food will be brought in." The woman looked all around the room as though searching for some invisible escape route, nodded, and motioned to the other woman. They left in silence.

Celine looked at Jenny. "Are we going to let them dictate who sleeps where?"

Jenny shook her head. "I don't see why. It's our business, not theirs."

She moved her pack to the bedroom with Reza. Celine brought Wilmer's things in with her. Then she sat down on the bed and stared at him thoughtfully.

"You know, sometimes I wonder about you. All that stuff about visions and foreordained disaster."

"I told the exact truth," Wilmer said placidly. "When a supernova occurs, the initial burst of radiation must be accompanied by particle emission. Those ions travel more slowly, at a small fraction of light speed. *Foreordained* describes very well the nature of physical laws, and the inevitable future arrival of a particle storm from Supernova Alpha. Thousands of scientists on Earth could have told Pearl Lazenby that. And if she'd asked me, I could have suggested a possible way of avoiding the disaster. But she didn't. I guess scientists don't have much clout in this place."

"But what about *her* visions? That's all mystical gobbledygook."

"*We* think so. But she believes what she sees, and so do her followers. That gives her visions a reality that we have to accept, even when they sound vague enough to apply to a lot of natural disasters." Wilmer motioned toward the door. "Those guns are real. The willingness of her followers to do anything that Pearl Lazenby commands is real. Based on the evidence, I can make a case that she has a better handle on reality than the rest of the world. After all, she was the one who predicted and prepared for disaster. We had no idea it was coming."

"I agree with Wilmer." Reza had been standing in the doorway, a rapt expression on his face. He came forward. "She *knew,* many years ago. No one else did. There are more ways to truth than science admits. I think that Pearl Lazenby is an amazing woman."

"Or at least a lucky one," Jenny said. She came across and sat on the bed next to Celine. Her eyes were red from fatigue and loss of sleep. "Don't glare at me like that, Reza, pure luck would do it. Pearl Lazenby decided, for whatever reason, that she disliked smart machines that made use of microchips. So she predicted that they would fail, and after that she and her followers avoided them. Did you notice the railcar we rode here on, and those guns and bullets? They were *old*. No chips in them."

"Maybe. But they are more useful than anything that *does* use chips." Reza seemed ready for more argument. "So who was the smart one, tell me that. Pearl Lazenby, or the rest of us? Hate the Legion of Argos as much as you like, you can't deny that her prophecies came true."

"By dumb luck." Jenny stared up at Reza, who shook his head. Celine sensed a new tension between them. "Pearl Lazenby and her followers are one-eyed prophets," Jenny went on, "in the country of the blind. She knows she has a temporary advantage, and she intends to do something with it. My question is, what? How many followers does she have? A thousand, or a million? Where are they? And what are they going to do?"

"She made her intention clear enough." Celine was watching the other three closely. "You heard her, humanity has to be cleansed of sin, even if it means 'scraping to the bone.' I don't know what that means, but I don't like the sound of it. We have to find out what they propose to do—and we have to find a way to warn other people, so the Legion of Argos can be stopped."

"I do not think that they can be stopped." Reza stared at Celine defiantly. "Not by anyone or anything. The Eye of God has seen the future."

"Stopping them certainly won't be easy." Celine changed her mind about what she was going to say next, as the door opened and two women entered carrying trays of food. She took the offered bowl of thick lentil soup, and went on, "We don't have enough information. We don't know what's been happening in the world since the supernova. We don't even know where we are, within a couple of hundred kilometers. One thing's for sure. In the next few days we must all become the most loyal, devoted, and dedicated members that the Legion of Argos has ever had. And I suspect that Wilmer will be our star performer."

25

The thaw at the Maryland Point Syncope Facility was not a local event. It extended from the hidden Virginia valley, where the *Clark* orbiter had made its emergency landing, all the way north across the Appalachians to the Pennsylvania/New York border.

The Indian Head naval base lay well within that region. Saul had gone to bed—alone, and far later than he cared to recall—in a starless night of crackling frost and sudden wind. He awoke to clear, bright morning and the steady trickle of snowmelt from a slate roof. He frowned up at the yellowed ceiling, and realized that he had been roused by a brisk rat-a-tat-tat on the thick oak of the bedroom door.

A head peeked discreetly into the room. "Good morning, Mr. President." A huge tray loaded with covered dishes went onto the cherrywood table by the door. The head—it was attached to a young woman in an old but well-laundered white uniform—nodded. She withdrew before Saul had time to notice her rank, or wonder what the woman would have done if she had walked in on a naked President. The stock diplomatic answer—"Sorry, madam"—wouldn't work in this case.

He walked over to the window. It faced west, across the three-mile-wide Potomac. In all that broad expanse he could count just seven vessels. Four were Navy ships, moving away from Indian Head. Saul guessed that they were part of last night's flurry of activity when word spread along the river of his trip by water to Indian Head. Only one ship now lay at the jetty where he had landed. It was smaller than the frigate that had brought him, and it had the lines of a small tugboat.

The other three were fishing boats, all heading downstream to the bay. The river was a flat calm, and the lines of their wakes lay ruler-straight on the surface.

Good. If Yasmin had any trouble traveling to the Q-5 facility by road, she would certainly be able to get there by water. Which led to one other thought. He walked back to the bed, picked up the unit on the bedside table, and stared at it dubiously. It lacked control panel, display, antenna, and keypad. As he held the truncated black cone to his ear, a voice said, "Yes, Mr. President?"

"What year was this telephonic unit made?"

"I don't know, sir."

Ask a stupid question. Saul suppressed the urge to inquire if the man at the other end had been sitting up all night, awaiting a possible presidential call. The odd thing was the chatter of children's voices in the background.

"One of my aides, Ms. Yasmin Silvers, will be visiting the Q-5 Syncope Facility today. In view of last night's activity downriver, I would like her to have a military escort."

"Very good, sir. It will be arranged."

Which ought to be enough—except for a possible excess of zeal. "Not a big escort, please. No more than a dozen."

A moment's hesitation, enough to make Saul think his added command was justified. "Yes, sir. Sir, I have two hundred and seventy-three messages for you here, forwarded from Washington."

"Hold them for me." *A quiet morning, by presidential standards.* "It is not necessary for me to meet with Ms. Silvers before she leaves. And if convenient to Captain Kennecott, I will be ready for a review of the base in thirty minutes."

"Do you wish to speak with him, sir? He is right here."

And probably has been, poor devil, since before dawn. "Yes, put him on, if you please. Captain Kennecott? Good morning to you. Yes, it looks as though we have a much better day for a tour than yesterday. No, as a matter of fact I haven't tried it yet. But I'm sure the food will be fine."

Saul hung up, reflecting that in many ways it was better to be asked about a meal before you tasted it. A relay of cooks had probably been working on *that* since before dawn, too.

They had taken no chances. A dozen different dishes sat on the tray. Saul drank hot tea with lemon, ate a piece of brown bread onto which he slathered several ounces of grape jelly, and resisted the urge to explore a large, light blue egg.

Salmonella tested? Not in this universe. The standard household test kit undoubtedly contained at least one chip.

Captain Kennecott was waiting in full dress uniform. He was not alone. Saul accepted a bouquet of thornless red roses from a shy three-year-old toddler whose finger went up her nose as soon as she had delivered her gift.

He smiled and thanked her with grave politeness. *I am President of* all *the people.* You had to work on that at first, but after two years it became automatic. It was even true. She would remember this seventy years from now.

"Is there anything you would particularly like to see?"

Captain Kennecott's question was a natural one, but Saul couldn't answer it. He had come here on inexplicable impulse. Impulse would have to guide him still.

"I would like to see the weapons storage."

"We had anticipated that." Kennecott turned and nodded to a woman in civilian dress, who left at once. Saul noticed the captain's left hand, its skin smoother and whiter than the right. It was a grown prosthesis, a combination of Voorhees-McCall nerve cell regeneration with tissue engineering. The technique was still experimental, no more than five years old. But Kennecott was well over seventy. In which war had he lost it?

The captain had seen his look, and flexed his hand. "Good as new, sir. Feels like a natural arm. I suppose in a way it is. My own DNA, even if I didn't grow it myself. No chips in it—thank God."

Saul changed his mind about the captain. Last night he had noticed the big Adam's apple, tired eyes, and deep-lined cheeks. Kennecott had seemed old and frail, a man out to pasture. Today he was someone who noticed everything, alert and in command, a man who had adapted rapidly to deal with the unexpected factor of a presidential arrival.

Saul tried a guess based on age and casualty rates. "Vietnam?"

Kennecott laughed. "No, sir. I was there, all right, Navy aviator, but I came through without a scratch. Then I was fool enough to do this to myself on a peacetime run. Flying an F-24 modification in '05."

"You weren't invalided out?"

"They tried. I pulled every string in the Disabilities Act."

They had been walking as they talked, down the slight slope that led away from the Officers' Mess and the river beyond. The group of well-groomed children had disappeared. The military escort remained a careful ten paces to the rear. The air was so warm and the sun so bright that Saul imagined he could see the snow on either side of the path melting away before his eyes.

Kennecott made a right before they reached the building labeled prominently as Bachelor Enlisted Quarters, and led them on through an open gate. Saul read the sign on the high wire fence: AUTHORIZED PERSONNEL ONLY BEYOND THIS POINT. NO FOREIGN. The flower beds and neat shrubs emerging from the snow on either side of the gate seemed incongruously at odds with the brusque sign. The brick building beyond was square, huge, and windowless.

The civilian to whom Kennecott had signaled earlier was waiting at the open double doors. Saul had his first chance for a good look at her. Thin, late forties, maybe five-three, she stood between white-painted shell cases taller than she was. Blond, straight hair. Probably in first-rate physical condition except for the fair skin whose rugged look suggested too much direct sunlight. Why didn't she replace it with a cultivated mask of her own face, cheap and easy to grow?

"Mr. President," Kennecott said. "This is Dr. Madeleine Liebchen. She is the person best qualified to answer any technical questions you may have."

Liebchen. Little love. Saul did the translation instinctively as he shook her hand. *I think not.* Eyes of a wonderful sapphire blue gazed coldly into his.

That look of unconcealed contempt gave Saul another reason why Captain Kennecott was likely to accompany them everywhere. *I am President of* all *the people*—if they will allow it. Many people disliked politicians. A rather smaller number hated them. A few went past that, and tried to kill them. Saul possessed various built-in protections, painfully installed after nomination night. His blood seethed with morphing antibodies, supposedly able to handle any natural or manufactured virus or bacterium (including the interlocking plasmid composite that got President Johannsen, in '18; it was the top-secret pictures of Johannsen's corpse, bloated so that the nose was no more than a dimple in the swollen head and the testicles were the size of grapefruit, that had persuaded Saul to take the treatment).

The implant in the roof of his mouth offered different protection. It would supposedly detect a million different poisons alone or in lethal combination, and trigger an involuntary regurgitation reflex. Except that the damned thing surely wouldn't work at all now, since all the chips had gone belly-up.

Saul took a second look at the scowling Dr. Liebchen. No virus, and perhaps no poisons, but that still left bullets, bombs, teeth, wild animals, knives, nooses, and nuclear weapons.

Dr. Liebchen was probably just a woman who regarded politics and politicians as beneath her. That did not make her dangerous. Kennecott must know her well. He did not judge her a threat. But how well had Johannsen's sister known Eileen Wilmore Bretherton, when she brought her to that fatal dinner?

Unlike one of his less illustrious predecessors, Saul could chew gum and walk (oral history suggested a more basic body function) at the same time. He could in fact do much more. While his internal thoughts reviewed the fate and frailties of past Presidents, he offered polite conversation to Kennecott and Liebchen. And at the same time he examined a variety of proximity fuses, artillery and artillery shells, rockets and rocket launchers, mines, torpedoes, and depth charges, all massed in tight phalanxes along the building's concrete floor.

After ten minutes he halted. The entourage came to a stop with him. "Captain. Dr. Liebchen. When I asked to see the weapons stored here, I meant active, usable weapons. This seems more like a museum." He gestured around him. "I know the Indian Head facility contained modern weapons, but everything here is very old. Those torpedoes . . ."

Dr. Liebchen said in a brittle voice, "Every one of the weapons you are looking at is in perfect working order. If you would care for a demonstration—"

"Allow me, Madeleine. I know you never take credit." Captain Kennecott stepped in front of her. "Mr. President, when this base was hit by the gamma pulse we lost all external communications. For the first seventy-two hours I did not know if we were dealing with a natural phenomenon or the first stage of an external attack. It seemed safer to assume the latter. Dr. Liebchen's discovery that many of our weapons were useless seemed to reinforce the notion of a coming assault by external agencies. Without direct orders, Dr. Liebchen embarked at once on an all-out night-and-day effort to divide the weapons stored here into two classes: working and nonworking. At first it seemed that the division was chronological. Old weapons worked, newer ones did not. As the effort proceeded, Dr. Liebchen determined that the problem was in fact electronic in nature. A wide class of electronic devices no longer functioned at all. New weapons are more dependent on such devices. The age correlation was an effect, not a cause." Kennecott swept his arm around to cover the whole building. "Everything here may look old—and be old—but it works. If Indian Head were called upon for combat support, today, thanks to Dr. Liebchen's tireless efforts we would be able to provide it."

"My congratulations to everyone here." Saul turned back to Madeleine Liebchen. "Particularly to you, Doctor. And the other weapons, the new ones that don't work?"

"They are separately warehoused, pending a decision as to their disposal." The bright blue eyes were no longer cold. They were sparkling. Saul was not naive enough to take credit. It wasn't his praise, or anything else he had done. It was pure passion for her work. Madeleine Liebchen had done a superior job, and took pleasure in that.

She went on, "The nature of the malfunctions soon made it clear that the problem lay in the microchips. They cannot be repaired. They must be replaced. I could do that work, in many cases—if there were a source of replacements. But recent contact with other defense facilities suggests no such possibility in the immediate future."

"Have you been able to do an assessment of your overall war-fighting support potential, compared with that before the gamma pulse?" Saul had picked up a good deal of military jargon from General Grace Mackay.

"It is between seventy and one hundred and forty percent." Dr. Liebchen answered without hesitation.

"One hundred and forty! You mean you might be *more* able to provide support now?"

"No. I mean that the answer to your question depends upon the nature of the assumed threat. The seventy percent number measures our support capability compared with its level before the gamma pulse, against an adversary whose fighting potential is *unaffected by the pulse*. That is not at all a reasonable scenario. Therefore, I estimated the effects of the pulse in diminishing adversarial war-fighting capability. To do so, I made use of previous estimates of the technological basis for foreign weapons. It turns out that our most likely and formidable potential foes—the Golden Ring compact—rely on chip-based weaponry even more than we do. We are, in that sense, better off—one hundred and forty percent better off—than before. Is that clear?"

"Perfectly clear." Saul wanted to add, *Dr. Liebchen, I think you are absolutely wonderful. How about a job in Washington?*

He had enough sense not to say any of that (although the offer of a Washington position would indeed come, via Grace Mackay). What was Madeleine Liebchen doing here, in the middle of nowhere? Maybe she was a wind-and-water fanatic, as her ruined complexion suggested. Saul, whose idea of wide-open spaces was the atrium of a big hotel, was not going to find out. He went on, "I am terrifically impressed by the speed with which you have reacted to a unique problem."

"Thank you, Mr. President," Captain Kennecott said gruffly. "We just think of it as standard operations, Navy style. I'm sure other naval facilities have done no less. Shall we continue the tour of inspection?"

"Certainly." Saul had learned something enormously important in the tour of Indian Head. He couldn't yet say quite what it was. Everything had to ferment for an hour or a day in the murky wort of his subconscious, then he would know.

They moved on, wandering through the married housing with its children's playground, past the deserted gymnasium, into the dusty library. Lots of old books there, and in the aisles between the stacks the forlorn and useless terminals. Beside the buildings, heaps of snow had a shrunken, defeated look. Clouds of gnats burst from the shade of towering magnolias, heading for sweaty faces and every square inch of exposed skin. The tall privet hedge on the road to the dead weapons warehouse, confused by weather that made no sense, had blossomed in a wild, perfumed, over-the-top-boys-it's-now-or-never riot of white.

Saul was having the same spring-is-busting-out feelings. Indian Head had been a stimulant and a restorative—even the cathartic session with Yasmin felt full of future promise. He looked fondly on everything, including Dr. Liebchen, and did not mind when she frowned back at him.

At the entrance to another anonymous warehouse, he paused. Magnolias and munitions were all very well, but it was reality time. Washington waited.

"Captain Kennecott, this has been so interesting, I've lost track of everything. What time is it?"

"Ten minutes before noon, Mr. President." The captain apparently had access to the Great Chronometer of the Universe, or at least a wholly nondigital watch.

"So late? I had no idea. I'm afraid I must be leaving. I must be back at the White House this afternoon."

He had expected at least a token expression of regret. Kennecott said only, "Yes, Mr. President," but Saul was trained in nuances. He heard unexpected satisfaction in the captain's voice, and he caught the rapid eye contact with Dr. Liebchen.

It could be simple relief at getting rid of him, but Saul didn't believe it. The pair of them were up to something. He would have suspected a formal salute and maybe the presentation of a memento of Indian Head, except that it was such a mismatch with his mental picture of Madeleine Liebchen. She would recoil at the notion of lapel pins and ceremonial farewells.

He was right, and he was wrong.

Saul and his band of followers and security staff walked back toward the river. The memento was waiting behind Mix House. A gigantic gray machine stood on a level concrete pad forty yards from the water, its forty-foot rotors drooping.

"All yours," Captain Kennecott said. "Of course, you might say that as Commander in Chief it was yours already. And it is rather old. But we can guarantee this machine is perfectly airworthy. We'd be honored if you would take it for your use in Washington, maybe station it at Andrews AFB along with Air Force One."

"What model is this?" Saul didn't want to mention that he couldn't identify most modern fighters, still less an ancient helicopter.

"A Sikorsky CH-53A—a Sea Stallion. It went out of use more than thirty years ago, but I'll still take it over most modern choppers." Kennecott patted the side of the monster affectionately. "Carries eight tons, travels five hundred miles at up to a hundred and seventy knots. You and your whole party can be landing on the White House lawn in twenty minutes."

Twenty minutes. No leisurely return trip, then, but Saul didn't regret that. He shook hands all around and his thanks to Captain Kennecott were totally sincere. From the moment when he saw the Sea Stallion, he had known what needed to be done when he arrived back at the White House.

As Saul climbed into the helicopter's great hollow interior, big enough to take a fair-sized truck, another thought hit him.

Washington waited. Tricia also waited. In six hours, he would be face-to-face with her for the first time in over two years.

26

From the secret diary of Oliver Guest.

Never match wits with a Jesuit. *I don't claim that was my waking thought, because in those first few minutes I either had no thoughts at all or I did not later remember them. Returning from the dead is nothing if not confusing.*

But I did think about Father Carmelo Diaz and the deal that we had made. Then not long afterward I realized that my eyes were open. I could see a light. I also realized that someone was speaking, although not to me; and I found that I could not move a muscle, not even an eye muscle. This was terribly frustrating. I saw only what was right in front of me, and that badly out of focus.

Wherever I was, and whenever I was, I knew two things with certainty: I was alive; and I was not undergoing a standard revivification.

Not, at least, revivification as it had been known at the time of my descent into abyssal sleep in the year 2021. For of course, I assumed on waking that I had been in abyssal sleep. Only later did I learn otherwise. So my mind said, this is 2621. I have served my sentence, and I have survived.

Consciousness was not continuous. Clouds of darkness billowed in and out. In random snapshots, by a weak and flickering light, I saw people.

First it was a stocky, strongly built man with ill-cut short hair and a two-week stubble of black beard. He was dressed in grubby black pants and jacket, and he was wrapping a blanket around me.

A total collapse of civilization, with this as a specimen of degraded humanity? Possible, but not plausible. What he said was nothing out of the ordinary ("He's a weight. We'll have one hell of a time gettin' him down them stairs 'less he can walk.") but the accent was pure West Virginia. I couldn't believe that the dialect would have survived unchanged over six centuries. Could he be a criminal, sentenced like me in 2021 and only recently revived?

Someone else was behind me, moving my head. A woman's voice sounded close to my ear; low, pleasant, New England. I made a huge but unsuccessful attempt to turn and look in that direction. Another man moved across my field of vision. He was older than the first by fifteen to twenty years, but just as badly dressed. As he peered intently into my eyes, he said, "There's no pain when you wake up, but sensory systems respond before motor systems."

Local accent, Baltimore–Washington corridor, for a guess. I didn't think he was talking to me. I was just a piece of near-dead meat, and his words were addressed to his companions. He was right about the lack of motor control, wrong about the pain. I was on fire from head to toes, and I couldn't even moan.

I suffered another welcome voyage to nowhere, short or long. When I came back there was less burning in my veins, and a new urgency in West Virginia's voice. "We're in trouble, amigos, like Dana says. Question is, what we gonna do? We've come too far to give up now."

Even crumbs are welcome when you are starving. Dana. I had a name.

Baltimore answered, "Only one thing for it. He has to go back in the drawer for a while, and we have to split up."

"Why, Art?" It was the woman. "Why not all go to the ground floor together, and try to talk our way out of it? We can say we came to look for a friend who'd been put here. We found the gate open—which is true—and we found him dead. Whoever they are, they'd have no reason to think we were lying."

"No good," West Virginia said. "We might be able to

talk our way clear. But what if Joyboy here gets so he can move while we're doin' it, an' starts rattlin' his cage? We'd be in deep shit. An' no matter what happened they'd have old Ollie instead of us."

"But what else can we do, Seth?"

"Art's right. We split up. Here's my suggestion. You an' Art go do your song an' dance for whoever's down there. Before that, you stick me an' Dr. G. back in his body drawer, both of us together. I'll take responsibility for keepin' him quiet—one way or another." His voice took on a sly and mocking tone. " 'Less you want to switch, sweetheart, an' you cuddle up with Doctor Demento. You ever get cozy with a homicidal maniac?"

I knew two more things with reasonable certainty. One: I could not be six hundred years in the future. All the speech patterns were too little changed. Two: West Virginia Seth was not my first choice as a dinner companion. I would find a way to get rid of him.

Not today, though. I needed a lot of information about my present surroundings before I made any moves. I also had as little control over my own body as a dead pig. The three of them grabbed me. There was a good deal more talk among them, that I was too sick or bewildered to follow. My carcass, attired from the feel of it in the same ragtag assortment of clothing as my captors/saviors, was rolled unceremoniously into a deep drawer. One of the people—presumably Seth—squeezed in next to me. The drawer silently closed.

I lay in darkness for an indefinite period. I think I may have been unconscious again, for after a faint and distant sound of voices and the soft breathing of my companion, I heard nothing at all. My first intimation of returning body control was the sound of a groan—my own.

A hand covered my mouth. At the same time I felt a stab of pain in my chest.

"Feel that?" Seth whispered in the darkness. "I hope you can—for your sake. You want to live, you lie still an' do what I say. One false move, one squeak, the knife goes through your heart. You hear me?"

I did not point out to him that his own rules presented me with an insoluble problem. If I replied or did not reply, I would be stabbed. Nor, despite increasing evi-

dence of returning muscular control, was it at all clear to me that I could *answer. What I could and did do was gasp.*

The knife pricked harder. "You are awake. Say something—softly."

"Muscles." My throat was full of phlegm, but I hoped he could understand my gargle. "Cramps. Bad."

"All right. I'll try to help you through. Keep as quiet as you can, an' let me know if I hafta muffle you."

I did not ask how. I lay, cold but sweating, as cramps attacked every muscle of my body in turn. After the first two I didn't need to say a word. West Virginia Seth felt what was coming and covered my mouth with his scarf until the spasm was over.

After a while, between bouts, I said, "What year is it?"

He didn't run me through the heart. He said, "What?"

"What year is this?"

"2026. Are you Dr. Oliver Guest?"

"Yes."

"The telomere treatment pioneer?"

"Yes."

Another surprise. A more natural next question would have been, "The serial child murderer?" Like me, West Virginia Seth had his own unusual priorities.

That was the end of the conversation for a while. I pursued my own thoughts and I assume that he followed his. Before the cramps had run their course, thirst took over as a worse torment. I tried to sit up. He restrained me with a rough hand on my chest and a terse "Quit that."

"I don't care what you do to me," I said. "I have to drink, or die."

"You might do both. You oughta be used to dying." But he wriggled around in some way I could not see, and the body drawer moved out on its runners. "Been a while since I heard anythin'. Let's see if Art an' Dana handled 'em."

I could walk, but barely. The hardest part was the descent from the body drawer. After that I had a strong arm and the stair rail to help me. As we approached the ground floor the unmistakable stench of decomposing hu-

man flesh assailed my nostrils. Previous experience, both professional and personal, allowed me to ignore it.

I stumbled at last through the big double doors, released my hold on West Virginia Seth, and fell on my face. If he spoke while I licked and crunched and swallowed mouthfuls of blessed snow, I have no idea what he said.

Finally he reached down and lifted me bodily. He was strong, far stronger than he looked. "I don't know if you're overdoin' it there, Doc," he said, "but I can't afford you to get sick. We got enough worries as it is. Come on."

He helped me walk around to the back of the building and seated me on a concrete block free of snow. He sat down beside me, the knife again prominently displayed. I had a first clear impression of the outside world.

A great square building of gray concrete stood at my back. In front of me, trees with the foliage of late spring stood with their trunks deep in snow. The breeze on my forehead felt summertime hot. Beyond them, a great river or bay sat lazy in the sunlight. I saw waterfowl, thousands after thousands of them, floating placid on the calm surface.

"Might be our dinner there," said West Virginia Seth. "How you feelin'?"

"I was sentenced to judicial sleep for six hundred years," I said slowly. "That meant until 2621, and I'd have been dead long before that. I thought I had a deal. I was supposed to be put in abyssal sleep instead."

"Lucky for you that you weren't. Otherwise you'd now be real dead dead."

"What happened?"

"To your deal? Damned if I know. But other stuff happened, a whole shit-pot full." He went quiet.

"Are you going to tell me?" I said after a while. I was still scooping up snow, quietly, and transferring it to my burning mouth.

"I'm going to trade with you. You tell me what I need to know, I tell you stuff." He still held the knife, but now he was using it to shave thin slices from a piece of cooked ham. "Before we start, just so you don't get a wrong notion in your noggin, I'll tell you the deal. I know what's been goin' on in the world for the past six years. You have no idea. You're also in bad shape physically. For all we

know, the next few days you fall down in a fit or burn up in a fever. S'pose you need help an' I'm not here to give it. What you gonna do? Go to some house an' ask? I don't think so. They find out who you are, Dr. Oliver Guest the famous child murderer, they run screamin' or they turn you in. I won't do that. You may not believe it, but you need me as much as I need you."

I realized there was important information in that statement, though I was not yet in a position to assess fully its significance.

"I didn't know that you did need me," I said.

"I do. We do. But don't kid yourself. If I have to, I'll gut an' flay you."

Anyone from my former life could have told Seth that it was not wise to make jokes at my expense. I am a person who takes himself seriously. However, I did not judge that he was joking. My uncouth West Virginia companion was deadly serious.

Caveat, Doctor. I would be very careful.

"You first," he said. "Talk. Tell me all about telomod therapy."

"All? The subject has evolved over many years of research."

"Gimme the highlights, then. We got lots of time, and I'm in no hurry. Talk."

"Where should I begin?"

"Assume I don't know a thing." He presented me with a handful of greasy ham shavings and a piece of dry bread. "I was a businessman, not a scientist."

This was a businessman, this crude and dangerous ruffian? No. He was a businessman. And now?

In a world apparently gone mad, a little more insanity made no difference.

"Almost every cell in your body has forty-six long strands of DNA called chromosomes," I said. "Do you understand so far?"

A nod. "Keep goin'. If I want backup explanation I'll tell you."

"When a body cell divides, the double helix of the DNA unwinds. One spiral goes in one direction, the other in the opposite direction. When the process is finished, in place of the original double spiral we have two identical *double spirals. The cell can now divide to give two daughter cells."*

I paused. Something odd was happening to my body. Tingling had begun in my extremities, suggesting that the process of awakening still had a long way to go. And, more disturbing, there was tightness in my chest. It would be an awful irony to waken from half a decade of judicial sleep only in order to have a heart attack and die.

Seth said, "Get on with it, Doc. We don't have all day."

So much for sympathy and tender loving care. I forced myself to take a deeper breath.

"The cellular division process is neat, efficient, and I would say beautiful. But there is a complication. During the copying, the very end of a chromosome is not duplicated. So with each cell division, the chromosomes gradually shorten. That should mean gradual loss of genetic material, but one thing saves us: the actual ends of each chromosome do not contain genetic material. Instead, they have a repeating pattern of molecules called a telomere. *The telomeres contain no part of the genetic code. They are there only to protect the true genetic material. On each cell division, the telomeres shorten. When they are reduced to a certain point, the cell can no longer divide."*

I looked at West Virginia Seth, who hardly seemed to be listening. "Do you already know some of this?"

"Know all of it." He grinned at me again. "No offense, Doc, but I have to check you out. You been asleep for six years. For the past two weeks, your life-support system's been a piece of junk. How'm I to know if your brain's what it used to be, 'cept by askin' you things I already know?"

He was right. It was the age-old conundrum: How do I know that the 'me' who wakes after a night's sleep is the same 'me' who went to bed? I don't. I merely employ it as a working assumption, for lack of anything better. But after a sleep of six years?

I thought of my treasures, locked away in their hidden store. They might not have survived for six hundred years, but six years was a near certainty. I felt my breath quicken. In one way at least, the essential I *remained unchanged.*

Seth had been studying my face closely. Too closely. I reminded myself that crudeness and barbaric behavior do not necessarily imply lack of intelligence.

He waved the knife at me. "If you're all done dreaming, get on with it."

The incongruity of it. A lecture on the basics of telomod therapy, facing a snowy landscape under a sky of pale blue, in a changed world about which I knew little or nothing. Seth might be lying about the last point, but his appearance and my own premature resurrection inclined me to believe him.

"Since the telomeres shorten on cell division," I said, "that should be the end of the story. It isn't. There is an enzyme called telomerase *that rebuilds telomeres. In humans, telomerase is found mainly in two types of cells. The first kind is the germ cells, so every fertilized egg begins its division with full-length telomeres. The second kind is cancer cells. Almost all cancer cells contain telomerase. That's how they can reproduce indefinitely, until they overwhelm and kill the host."*

Again I was forced to pause. My breathing was easier, but now I had no feeling in my hands—no body sense that they were even there. My arms seemed to end at the wrists.

Seth was glaring at me again. It was pointless to tell him of my woes. I forced myself to continue.

"Telomod therapy for cancer, which is what you had"—I was guessing, but he did not contradict me—"is a delicate balance. First, a patient is treated with a telomerase inhibitor. The cancer cells continue to reproduce rapidly, but their telomeres shorten with each division. When the telomeres are gone, the cells die. The cancer dies. The patient, assuming that the telomerase inhibitor was suitably applied, does not die."

"Not quite." Seth stared out across the peaceful river. "He gets real damn close."

I could have made a grab for the knife, sitting on the concrete block. I had more sense than to try. Thus far the information transfer had been almost all one way.

"The treatment is unpleasant," I said, "but consider the alternative. And there are possible compensations beyond the obvious benison of a cancer cure. If a patient were

simply treated with telomerase inhibitor, death would soon follow. Every telomere in every cell would shorten, until the cells reached the Hayflick limit and could no longer give viable daughter cells. You would age rapidly, you would die."

"That's what the Institute told us. Telomeres shorten, I'm a goner. But there's a way out, right?"

"At least in principle. Assuming that the delicate point is reached where the cancer is dead and the patient is not, a telomerase stimulator is administered. The body's cells have their telomeres restored to their original, juvenile length. Naturally, nothing can be done to restore dead cells; but the patient is in a very real sense rejuvenated. Of course, you now face the possibility of new cancer. Telomod therapy must juggle telomerase inhibition and stimulation, in a manner different for each patient. It is not clear what the life expectancy of a patient given such treatment might be." I stared at Seth. "At least, we did not know at the time of my descent into judicial sleep."

"We still don't. An' it's worse than that."

"You knew all this?"

"Yeah. Pretty much. I told you, I had to check you out. But now there's stuff I don't know, an' I'm hopin' you do. You feelin' okay?"

I was feeling, if not okay, a good deal better. I had hands again, and my chest no longer hurt.

"Paradoxically," I said, "I am feeling sleepy. Apparently five years and more are not enough."

"You can follow all right, if I talk?"

"I think so. Nudge me if I drop off."

"Trust me. You won't."

He told me little about the general events of the past six years, and rather a lot about Supernova Alpha. I assume that any reader will already know what he said, and I will not record it here. (Yes, of course I assume there will be readers. Did any diarist, no matter how the material was hidden or encoded, *not* assume that the entries would someday be read? A secret diary can be many things, but unless it is destroyed there is one thing it can never be, and that is secret. You still do not agree, although your unseen presence at my shoulder provides the ultimate proof that I am right? Then ask yourself why Samuel Pepys wrote all *sexually explicit material of his diaries in Latin, rather than in English.)*

I was shocked by what he told me. I was also relieved. My implant, with an operating lifetime designed to allow authority to track me to and beyond my final release, surely depended on working microchips. And amid global turmoil and deaths numbered in the millions or billions, my own little misdemeanors would never be noticed.

I was free, as never before. Or I would be, provided that I practiced suitable restraint and patience.

"Let me summarize," I said, when Seth reached a suitable breakpoint in his narrative. No matter how long he spoke, we both realized that he could never tell me everything that had happened. For one thing, he had limited information sources. "You had been monitoring your own status with the help of a full genome sequencer. Now the sequencers are useless. You want an alternative technology that will allow you to continue to monitor your condition, and provide telomerase inhibitor or stimulator as needed."

"You got it. Question is, can you do it?"

"I would logically say yes, wouldn't I, regardless of truth? But I will do more than say, I will tell you how. Let me begin with a question. What do you know of the history of sequencing the human genome?"

"I know it was done over twenty years ago."

"Correct. But what you may not know is how major an effort it required at that time. The tools were restriction enzymes, chemical tests, chromosome sequence matching, partial data bases, and a limited knowledge of molecular biology; crude and primitive by today's standards, but all that were available. Hundreds of groups worked together to produce the sequencing of the three billion nucleotide bases in the human genome. It took over twenty years of steady work. At the end of that time one—one!—individual genome had been mapped."

"You tryin' to discourage me and get yourself in real trouble?"

"Not at all. I am pointing out that modern sequencers, all dry and all digital, represent a marvel of twenty more years of progress in both medicine and technology. A genome, any genome, can be totally mapped in a few hours by a modern sequencer. Unfortunately, all such devices

became brain dead the moment that the gamma pulse from Supernova Alpha created its EMP. I feel sure that when you discovered this, you were in despair."

"For ten minutes." He sounded like a man who was not exaggerating. "I been through despair before, an' I didn't like it."

"So let me offer you reason for optimism," I said. "You and your friends were given sequencers because it is much cheaper and easier to offer a standard mass-produced instrument than it is to produce a made-to-order device. But of course, you had no call for the full power of a genome sequencer. All you wished to know was the condition and length of the telomeres, those tiny fragments at the very ends of each chromosome. You didn't care what bases were in them, only their length. A full sequencer is huge overkill for such a task. I can show you how to accomplish the same result with the aid of five standard wet chemistry procedures, tests which can be applied to anyone after fifteen minutes of instruction. I will do this, provided that you are able to offer me a suitable quid pro quo."

He nodded. It was clear that despite his deliberate pose of the barbarian at the gates, he had understood every word that I said. I wondered again about his background. There was more here than the good ol' boy pose. In the hours that we had been talking, the sun had moved around so that it was directly in our faces. In its afternoon light his eyes seemed wolf eyes, more yellow than brown. I was exhausted. But an absolute need to match him drove me to alertness.

"Here's the deal, Doc," he said confidentially. "You show me an' Art an' Dana—yeah, I know, but I might need 'em later. This ain't a game to play solo. Anyway, you show us what we need, how to keep the treatments goin', how to know they're working. An' after that you're a free agent. We won't tell anybody you're out. We won't ever look for you."

"Unless something goes wrong, and you need me again."

"Well, yeah." He grinned. "I won't say no to that. We all do what we hafta do."

"About your two companions. Are you suggesting

that they have already agreed to the terms that you propose?"

"No. And I'm not sure they would. They're different from me—from you, too, Doc. But you don't need worry about them. I'll handle 'em if I have to, once you and me have an understandin'."

He held out a dirty, broken-nailed hand. "I'm Seth Parsigian. Do we have a deal?"

After a moment I took his hand and shook it. "We have a deal."

I trusted Seth—trusted him to pursue his own interests, to the exclusion of everything else. I knew exactly what he was like.

And I knew one more thing, with certainty. When the right time came, when I was no longer dependent on his assistance and his special knowledge, I would send Seth Parsigian beyond this vale of joy and tears. I would kill him. We would see, paraphrasing his earlier crude parlance, who was eviscerated and lacked an epidermis.

I stood up, stretched my tired limbs, and looked around at the scattered clouds of the late afternoon sky. I hurt in half a dozen places where IVs and catheters had been removed. My muscles were weak. However, all those effects of my long coma were minor and predictable. They should soon vanish.

It was good to be alive, awake, and on the way back to normal.

27

At one o'clock exactly Saul stepped onto the south lawn of the White House.

The flight from Indian Head aboard the Sea Stallion had been breathtakingly fast. A formation of bright blue Air Force jets—old F-16s, Saul thought, though he was not sure—had accompanied them for the last few miles along the Potomac, before dipping wings in unison salute and peeling off to the west.

Dinner with Tricia was not until six. No one should be waiting to see him, since he was not expected back until late afternoon. He had five free hours, time he had gained by rapid travel from Indian Head.

Saul headed straight indoors, reflecting how age changed a man. He remembered an afternoon, forty-five years ago, when the electronic teaching system had failed and he and half a dozen other kids were released early. They stood in a ring and speculated how they would use the time. The afternoon stood open, an endless stretch in which they could do anything they liked.

But when I became a man, I put away childish things. The Christian Bible, surely. *Time is money.* Who was that? Harder, but probably Ben Franklin. Saul paused in the outer room, where Auden Travis was giving instructions to three messengers from the Hill.

"Good afternoon, Auden. Would you locate General Mackay, and ask her to come to my office as soon as possible?"

"Very good, sir. I had no idea that you would be here so soon. Secretary Munce was in the building, most anxious to talk to you."

"Did he specify a subject?"

"No, sir."

"If he's still here, tell him to join me and General Mackay. What I have to say is relevant to him, too."

"Yes, sir."

"Are you feeling all right, Auden?" Travis seemed different.

"Perfectly fine, Mr. President."

"Good. Tell General Mackay to come right on in when she gets here. No need to announce her arrival." Saul continued to his office. If Auden Travis was different, it seemed a change for the better. He was handling the messengers more easily, emphasizing what he wanted but doing it with a joke. Maybe Saul ought to leave the White House more often.

The list of calls on his desk was the same as at Indian Head, with additions and an ordering of priorities. Auden Travis had appended his own notes to some of them:

> *Sino Consortium, economic collapse reported. Famine, epidemic disease, civil war. SecState seeking policy position. Aid question.*
>
> *Bad news Hawaii—tsunami, 70-foot crest. Call Sen Kidjel.*
>
> *Undefined emergency Florida, SecInt in transit w. Air Force assistance.*
>
> *Fraser River, Columbia River, Red River, unprecedented flood stage. VP plus governors in best position to handle.*
>
> *VP: 3 calls from him, no need call back—says best he remain on West Coast pro tem. Reports recovery there slow, but definite.*
>
> *AgSec says Midwest food shipments resumed, reserves ample, but winter wheat crop total loss. Emergency farm assistance needed Wyoming, Colorado, New Mexico.*
>
> *Sen Lopez and Cong Mander request meeting ASAP.*
>
> *EuroPres requests summit soonest. SecState stalling.*
>
> *GPS back in business.*
>
> *Air Force report orbiter burn-up in atmosphere. Believes it was failed return of Mars expedition.*
>
> *Gen Mackay has report on telecommunications activity.*
>
> *New maps in office show estimated country conditions, weather patterns.*

Travis's staccato style displayed his new confidence. Saul turned to the wall map. It had been drawn on an old flatbed plotter, but the colors and legend were bright and clear.

Blue: infrastructure hurt, but recovering. Green: badly hurt, but recovery likely. Yellow: almost destroyed, no sign yet of recovery. Orange: known total destruction of infrastructure. Red: condition unknown, but destruction presumed total.

You could go around the world, country by country, and note the color code. Brazil was orange. The whole of North America showed blue or green. Central America was mostly orange, as were the Federation of Indian States and the Sino Consortium. Northwest Europe showed blue. Fourteen of the west Asian states were green. Micronesia was red, along with Patagonia and Australia.

Or if you wished, you could stand back and examine not individual states but broad swaths of color. Then the global picture jumped out at you. The world changed from blues and greens in the north to lurid orange and red in the far south. Supernova Alpha had injected its slow heat poison into Earth's lower hemisphere, and human civilization south of the equator had writhed and died.

There were two exceptions to the general rule. All the Golden Ring countries had been dependent on the microchip technologies. Too dependent. Gold was now orange.

And Africa was a special tragedy. After centuries of failure, technology had taken hold across the continent. The old scourges had seemed defeated. Malaria, malnutrition, river blindness, sleeping sickness, leishmaniasis, yaws, bilharzia, and rift valley fever were everywhere in retreat under the benign rule of the Pan-African Federation.

And now? Now red blanketed the continent from the Mediterranean to the Cape of Good Hope. *Ex Africa semper aliquid novi*—always something new out of Africa. Except that in Africa itself, nothing new seemed possible. The timeless troubles had won again.

Saul turned to the display of weather vectors. They showed an unusual amount of hemispheric mixing, north and south, but conventional circulation patterns were also appearing. Maybe there would be a fall harvest after all. Earth was shrugging off the effects of Supernova Alpha and fighting back.

The steady click of heels sounded behind him. General Grace Mackay marched in and stood at attention. Saul nodded in greeting.

"Sit down, General. And answer a scientific question for me, if you would be so kind."

"If I can, sir." She sat down, but seemed just as much at attention.

"All the extra heat pumped in by Supernova Alpha must be melting a hell of a lot of ice. How much will the sea level be raised when we're all done?"

"I can't tell you that, sir, but half the world's oceanographers must be working on the question. I'm sure that the Deputy Science Adviser could give you an estimate."

"And I'm sure that anything Dr. Vronsky has to say will be scientifically accurate—and unintelligible. Would you ask him, and give me a translation?"

"I'll certainly try, sir." Her confusion showed on her face. "Was that why you wished to speak to me?"

"No. I just thought of that when I was looking at weather patterns. I've had something different on my mind for the past few hours. General, tell me about interservice rivalries."

"It is discouraged and completely prohibited, sir, according to the interservice agreements of '14." The smoothness and speed of her answer suggested that the question was no surprise at all.

Saul offered his sunniest smile. "I know that, General. Murder and theft are prohibited, too, under much older statutes. They seem to thrive still."

"Yes, sir."

"However, I didn't ask you here to debate regulations. As you know, today I was at the Indian Head naval base. I saw a wide variety of naval weapons, old but in good working order. I also saw cargo planes, battle helicopters, grenades, rifles, and artillery that didn't belong in naval operations. I wouldn't have been surprised to see orbiters and heavy ground tanks."

"Yes, sir."

"And on the flight back, I was accompanied by a squadron of Air Force fighters. Did you give orders for that to happen?"

"No, sir, I did not."

Saul dropped into his chair, leaned back, and adopted a more casual tone. "So here's my question, Grace. What has your own attitude been for the past two months toward interservice rivalry?"

The steel went out of her backbone, and she, too, leaned back. "I have actively encouraged it, sir. I take full responsibility for my action."

"I'm sure you do. What I want to understand is the logic behind it."

"Failing the presence of an external enemy, sir, nothing so provokes a military individual to maximum effort as the chance to advance his or her own service."

"Army has to beat Navy?"

"Exactly. Sir, if you feel that my actions are contrary to your objectives, then I will be happy—"

"Don't say it, Grace. Don't even think it. Your job and mine are the same: we have to pull this country back together as fast as we can. If the services work best to get back in business when they compete, that's just great. Go on with what you've been doing. But now I have another question for you." Saul paused, his attention drawn to the tall, craggy man who had appeared and stood motionless at the door. "Come in, Mr. Secretary. I've got something that should involve you as much as it does General Mackay."

Lucas Munce was Secretary for the Aging. At eighty-seven he was exactly what Saul wanted to be at that age (not very likely, Saul admitted, unless he could somehow add six inches to his height and turn a rich chocolate brown). Munce made a stately entrance, inclined his shaved dome to the President and to General Mackay, and moved to the indicated seat.

Saul waited until he was comfortably settled, then went on: "In the past two weeks I have received reports of the crippling effects of Supernova Alpha on this country's military strength. To put it in simplest terms, most of our high-tech weapons have become pieces of junk. The only exceptions are the submarine command and anything in deep mountain storage. It seemed that three months ago we were secure. Suddenly we have become vulnerable.

"At Indian Head I learned that I was asking the wrong question. Military strength means nothing in absolute terms. If I have a spear, and you have nothing, I have military superiority. I want to know the supernova's effects on other nations. Are we *relatively* stronger or weaker than we were before? That is the issue I would like you, General, to address."

"I will take it as my top priority."

"Call Captain Kennecott at Indian Head. Request the services of a civilian scientist, Dr. Madeleine Liebchen, to help with the work."

"Yes, sir. May I tell Captain Kennecott that this is a presidential order?"

"That will be fine. But let me warn you, Dr. Liebchen hates Washington."

"I was once in the same position myself, sir, and I can appreciate it. I will find a way to handle things."

Saul turned to Lucas Munce. "Which brings me to my next point, and I'm very glad you're here to respond to it. My experience at Indian Head suggests that although our military forces love new weapons, they hate to throw anything away. Around the country we have big stockpiles of equipment thirty years old and more. It doesn't depend on microchips—but it does depend on people who know how to operate it. I want you to seek out men and women with experience of turn-of-the-century military equipment. Most of them will probably be retired. I would like them brought out of retirement for as long as the present emergency lasts. Do you think that is possible?"

"Mr. President, it's more than possible. It is a wonderful opportunity. Many retirees will jump at the chance. The most difficult part of my job is to make older people feel needed."

"I'd like you and General Mackay to work together on this."

"Yes, sir." Munce said nothing more. He sat quietly, his long-fingered hands interlocked.

"But you wanted to see me about something else," Saul prompted.

"I did." Lucas Munce looked pointedly at Grace Mackay. "This is a personal matter, and one of some delicacy."

She stood up at once. "Anything else for me, sir?"

"I'd like an estimate of the military strength of other nations in three days."

"I'll have you preliminary numbers, sir, within twenty-four hours."

As she nodded and left, Saul wondered what Munce was going to tell him. He knew for a fact that the Secretary of Defense and the Secretary for the Aging had a high regard for each other. What could Munce have to say that he would not say in front of Grace Mackay? Was he going to announce his retirement? Was he sick? He certainly didn't look it, but he was eighty-seven years old.

Lucas Munce waited until the door had closed, then said at once, "Let me immediately come to the point, sir. I am being *recruited.*"

Saul hid his sigh of relief. Who wouldn't want Lucas Munce to work for them? The man was honest, intelligent, had enormous presence, and worked harder than most people half his age. He was also a man who had lived long enough to be aware of his own worth. The puzzle was that Saul had always thought him beyond financial temptation.

"Government can't compete with industry when it comes to money, Lucas. You know that."

"I have little interest in money." Munce smiled. "At my age, Mr. President, the attainable modes of enjoyment are restricted. In saying that I was recruited, perhaps I chose the wrong way to put it. I was approached last week by Athene Willis. It seems that she is a great-niece of mine, though I hardly know her. But I checked, and she is indeed Eileen's kin; so I agreed to meet her. As it turned out, being a relative was just a convenience to attain my ear. The significant fact is that she is close to the Congressional Senior Caucus. In a most delicate and subtle way, she suggested that great changes were on the way for this country. She informed me that those changes would be brought about by Congress; that they could offer wonderful opportunities to me, personally; but that those opportunities would never materialize so long as my loyalties remained with President Saul Steinmetz."

"She came right out with all that? Lucas, it sounds neither delicate nor subtle."

"It didn't begin that way, Mr. President. The first time through, I made it clear that I had no idea what she was talking about." Munce's voice changed, becoming thinner and creaky. "I'm just an old man, you see, who can't follow anything that's not shoved right up my big old nostrils."

"You didn't mention that you lecture at Wharton on econometric theory?"

"I fancy that somehow slipped my memory, Mr. President. Anyway, when young Athene realized how decrepit I was, she began to work at it harder. I still didn't catch on, and she finally let slip a reference to one group: the office of the House Minority Leader. She caught her breath when she realized what she'd done; but of course it was all right, because I did not react to it."

"House Minority Leader. Sarah Mander. Not the most obvious person to recruit Lucas Munce."

"My impression exactly. So far as Ms. Mander is concerned, I am just another jungle bunny."

"Don't feel too bad. To her, I'm an upstart kike who bought his way into the White House. But Sarah is smart in some ways. She knows that if she could get you, you would deliver a huge constituency. How many people in the country are over sixty-five?"

"Before the supernova, there were fifty-seven million. That is close to twenty percent of the population. Today, I'm not sure. Disasters hit hardest on the very young and the very old. One might argue that the old, who are aware of the extent of the problem as the young are not, are likely to be claiming their Final Rights. On the other hand, suicide generally diminishes in times of war, which the present situation may well approximate. I am still seeking accurate figures."

"Suppose you say no to your recruiters?"

"I intend to. You mean, will I be safe?" Munce paused, and rubbed at his gray-stubbled cranium. "I think so. They gain little by taking me out. I'm expendable, since you would appoint another Secretary for the Aging. My question is, are you safe? They can't make big changes unless the President goes along."

"I already had that thought myself. I think that I'm completely safe, but I need to talk to the Vice President."

"Brewster Callaghan?" For the first time, Munce seemed surprised.

"That's right. He is my personal shield."

"But isn't the Vice President on the West Coast?"

"He is indeed. Better that he be there." It was a rare moment of satisfaction for Saul. Lucas Munce usually knew and understood everything; now here was something that had escaped the most senior Senior Citizen. "Do you remember the Watergate hearings, and the resignation of President Richard Nixon, back in the 1970s?"

"Remember it?" If Lucas Munce was perplexed by the change of subject, it didn't show. "Mr. President, I don't just *remember* that event. I was *there*. At the time of the Watergate hearings in 1973 I was in Washington, working as an aide to Senator Howard Baker."

"So you also remember the Vice President of the time."

"Indeed I do. It was Spiro Agnew. As I recall, we had some considerable contempt for the man and never referred to him by his name. We used an anagram."

"An *anagram* of Spiro Agnew?" It was Saul's turn to be surprised.

"I'm afraid so." Munce shrugged. "The follies of irreverent youth. However, I suspect that I digress."

"Not so far as I'm concerned, you don't. My God, Lucas, I

hope that someday soon you write your memoirs. What did you call him?"

"Mr. President, I invoke the Fifth Amendment. I leave the working out of the anagram to your own ingenuity, and admit only that the result is vulgar and involves adding a body part. But I do not see the relevance of either Richard Nixon or Spiro Agnew to today's situation."

"Richard Nixon was protected from impeachment, so long as Spiro Agnew was Vice President and would assume the presidency in Nixon's place. Half of Washington knew that Agnew was a crook, and a boneheaded one at that. They had to get rid of Agnew before they could really go after Nixon."

"Which they did." Munce nodded. "I played some small role in that myself. Agnew resigned rather than face legal action for the bribes that he had taken."

"And after that Congress could go after Nixon. Now you see the similarity."

"I do. Sarah Mander and her cronies may dislike you, but they positively hate the policies and priorities of Brewster Callaghan. As long as he is Vice President, you are safe."

"Which is why I think I need to add to his security detail. Keep stringing your grand-niece along, would you?"

"I will indeed. Sometimes one feels it necessary to apologize for blood relations." Munce rose to his feet and inclined his head in a formal bow. Even in that position he looked down at Saul. "Thank you for your time, Mr. President."

"Thank you for vital information." Saul glanced back at his desk. Already the intercom was buzzing. "Excuse me."

He touched the switch as Lucas Munce made a leisurely exit. "Yes?"

"General Mackay is here, sir."

"Auden, she just left."

"Yes, sir. But she is back. She says she has the information that you requested."

On relative military strength? That was impossible in the few minutes she had been gone.

"Have her come in." And, as she entered, "Yes, General? Sit down."

"Thank you, sir. You didn't specify a level of urgency for your question about global sea-level changes. But I went and asked Dr. Vronsky, and he gave me a worst-case answer immediately."

"He had studied it already?"

"No. He worked it out while I watched."

"And I thought I'd asked a hard question. What's the answer?"

"The rise could be substantial, as much as twenty-five feet. On the other hand, it probably won't be anything like that much."

"That's so vague, it's useless."

"I know. Vronsky promised a better number in a few hours, after he's had a chance to talk to the specialists. He says this is not his field."

"Then how was he able to come up with an answer at all?"

"From first principles." She held out a sheet of paper, with half a dozen lines of scribbled numbers. "Here's Dr. Vronsky's arithmetic. Assume that Supernova Alpha shines as brightly in Earth's skies as the sun, for a period of two months. The amount of heat per unit area pumped into the Earth by the sun is a well-known number, it's called the solar constant. The Earth presents one whole face to the supernova. Assume that all the extra heat goes into melting the Antarctic ice cap—a worst case, because melting of floating ice won't affect sea level. The total volume of ice melted comes out to about two point seven million cubic kilometers. Spreading that over the world's oceans, Dr. Vronsky calculates a possible rise in sea level of about twenty-five feet. Sir?"

She had heard Saul's muttered curse.

"It's all right, General. I was hoping for a much smaller number. Twenty-five feet sounds pretty damn bad."

"I'm afraid it is, sir. Dr. Vronsky says that a twenty-five-foot rise would have a huge effect on all the flora and fauna of the world's coastal zones. The shorelines would also become unrecognizable, and we'd lose the use of many major ports. On the other hand, he emphasizes that he made gross worst-case assumptions. There are more clouds now, so there will be more reflected energy. Much of the heat hitting the Earth, from both the sun and Supernova Alpha, will go right back into space. His best guess is that the actual sea-level rise will be no more than a foot or two."

"I like that a whole lot better."

"Yes, sir. We can live with it."

"We'll have to—even if it turns out to be twenty-five feet. Thank you, General."

"I'll get back to you when he has a tighter estimate." She stood up, and paused. Saul did not look like a man encouraging her to leave.

"I'm afraid I have still another question for you." He waved a hand. "Sit down, General, if you would. This is an awkward one."

"Sir?"

"Has anyone in the past couple of weeks approached you and suggested that in the future you might do better with a job other than the one you have?"

"Ah." The ramrod spine bowed a little, and she leaned against the back of the chair. "So you know. I wasn't going to bother you, because it sounded like nonsense. But I did have that strange conversation at Admiral Watanabe's memorial service, ten days ago."

"Strange, how?"

"General Beneker came up to me. We did Turnabout control work together, back in '07, and we were both friends of Watanabe. We chatted for a few minutes, then Beneker said, 'Times of crisis are times of opportunity for military people. I think it will be the same this time. There will be some real plums to be had when it's over.'

"I agreed with him, because he's right. There will be a lot of positions to fill. Then he said, 'But not if you stay where you are now, Grace. You'd have to move. If you have any interest, I can introduce you to the right people.'

"I just nodded. I mean, I'm Secretary of Defense. It's a tough job, but no one could possibly offer me anything I want more."

"I'm glad to hear that. Were any other names mentioned?"

"No. About fifteen minutes after he talked to me he was nose-to-nose with Congressman Otamo. But that could have been coincidence."

"Or maybe not. Let me know, would you, if there's any follow-up? Or if you hear of something similar with anyone else."

"You think there's a problem here, sir?"

"I don't know. But I do know I can't ignore it."

After she left Saul wondered if he should have told her about Lucas Munce. Probably not. It wasn't a problem you could solve by sharing, he'd have to sort it out himself. He stared at a presidential portrait on the wall. Harry Truman hadn't said it quite right. "The buck stops here." He ought to have said, "*All* the bucks stop here."

How long would the sea-level rise take to happen? Maybe by the time it did, Saul would no longer be President.

As he picked up the telcom unit to begin working the list of urgent calls (*most* urgent calls—everyone claimed urgency) Saul's eye went once more to the framed portrait of Benjamin Disraeli.

That man had seen his own share of disasters. His career had been long and hard and often discouraging. He was sixty-three years old when he became Prime Minister of England, and his first term had been for only a few months. But he offered perhaps the most comforting thought that anyone in his or Saul's position could be given: "Politics abides, but what politicians can accomplish is always necessarily ephemeral."

Saul loved being President. You did what you could; but no matter how much you loved it, when you left office you might well thank God that the job could not last forever.

28

Art began to regret their decision the moment Seth climbed into the body drawer alongside Oliver Guest.

"All right," Seth whispered. "Close it."

Art hesitated, then leaned down toward him. "Don't get any cute ideas, Seth. You'd never have made it this far without Dana and me."

"I know that, for Christ's sake. You think I'm gonna head for the hills with Ollie here?"

"I'd look for you forever if you tried it."

"I know that. I don't want you chasin' my ass. 'Til we get our treatment goin', we're in this together. Come on, close the damn drawer!"

Art, finally ready to slide the drawer shut, paused again. "Where will we meet?"

"Jeez. We never talked about that. Gotta be someplace we're sure of. We might have to hole up for a while."

"The Treasure Inn?" Dana suggested.

"Nah. Not safe enough. Better be your cabin, Art, up on Catoctin Mountain."

"You don't know where it is."

"I do. I looked at the maps when we were back at the Treasure Inn gettin' ready to play sewer-men."

"But—" Art began.

"I can find the place. Trust me."

"Hurry up," Dana said urgently. "I can hear them moving around down below."

The drawer slid closed, while Art stood and worried. It was too late to change, and there was no other choice. Art in the drawer with Oliver Guest? He was older than Seth, and he lacked the killer spirit. Dana with Oliver Guest? Even worse. And the body drawer held only two, even with a squeeze. It had to be Seth and Oliver Guest. Maybe they were vicious enough to cancel each other out. But the thought of them at Art's cabin made him awfully uneasy.

"Come on." The candle was out, and Dana was whispering to him in the darkness. "We have to try and get all the way down before anyone knows we're in the building. We don't want them coming up here."

She took his hand and they tiptoed to the staircase and crept down from floor to floor. There was enough noise from below to cover any small creaking of the metal rails and grilles.

Art could see a dozen people now, each with an electric flashlight. He leaned close to Dana and whispered, "They're spreading out. If we can get all the way down and outside and they don't notice . . ."

They moved faster. The lights had dispersed and moved into the aisles. Art and Dana were at the bottom of the stairs and heading for the open double doors when a man's voice called loudly, "Over here. I think this is the one."

Half a dozen people popped into view from the other aisles. Most rushed right past Art and Dana, but an older man in a dark blue uniform took a second look and halted in front of them. He had a gun in a holster on his left hip, and he put his hand on it.

"You're not with us. This is a secured facility. What are you doing here?"

They had not rehearsed a story. Dana, faster than Art, said at once, "My uncle is in here. We thought that after the supernova things wouldn't be working. We came to see if he's all right."

"You broke in?" The officer gestured to them to walk with him.

"No. The doors were already open."

That happened to be true, but apparently it was not enough.

"What's your uncle's name?"

Dana hesitated, but Art jumped in. "Desmond Lota." He hoped he had remembered the name correctly. "He's my cousin. He ought to be over there."

He pointed back the way they had come. The other man nodded, but he motioned to them to keep walking with him. "We'll check in a minute." His nose wrinkled at the stink, stronger the farther they went inside the building. "I wouldn't get your hopes up."

The other people were standing in two small clusters halfway down one of the aisles. They took no notice at all of the new arrivals.

"Don't come any nearer," one man in the farther cluster said, but he was not addressing Art and Dana. He was talking to two women, the older one with her arm around the other's shoulder.

Another man was standing by an open body drawer. After a few more seconds he turned away and shook his head. "I'm sorry. This is the right one, Raymond Silvers. I am afraid he is dead."

"Oh, Raymond." The younger woman made a low, mewing sound. "I want to see him." She tried to pull free and walk forward. Two men stood in front of her, and the other woman held her more firmly.

"I don't think that's a good idea, miss," one of the men said politely. "It would be best if you get outside, into the fresh air. We'll take care of the formalities here."

The rest of the group turned. Art and Dana found themselves swept along, the uniformed officer still close at their side. When they were at the double doors, he halted.

"Do you know where your uncle is?" he asked Dana.

"I do," Art said. In daylight, he could see how pale Dana had become. Fatigue and the nauseating smell in the steadily warming building had brought her close to the edge. "Does she really have to go in? After what you found already?"

"I don't see why." The officer gestured to one of the other men. "Keep an eye on her, please. For the moment she's in your custody." He turned to Art. "What's your name?"

"Art Ferrand." The old principle: the fewer lies you told, the easier it was to keep track of them; and he had no idea what questions Dana might be asked.

"Lieutenant Commander Strasser." He did not offer Art his hand. "Come on. Let's take a look. Can you stand it?"

Art did not know what Lieutenant Commander Strasser was referring to, the smell or the prospect of identifying the body of a dead relative. He simply nodded, and they returned to the dark depths of the building.

"He ought to be on the third level up." Art did not want to say the name again, in case he had it wrong. He was walking slightly in front of Strasser, while the officer shone his flashlight on the serried banks of body drawers.

To change the subject, Art asked, "Was that her father back there?"

"Her brother, I gather." Strasser's manner became slightly less formal. "Horrible business, this whole thing. Maybe we ought to have worried about this place sooner, but with everything else going on it has low priority. And they are all criminals. Is this the one?"

In the beam of the flashlight, Art saw the name, Desmond Lota. "That's it."

"Can you stand to do this?"

"I'll be fine." Art already knew what was coming. It would actually be easier on him than on the other man. "Let's do it."

They slid the drawer open. The body of Desmond Lota, bloated and purple, lay before them. Strasser quickly pushed the drawer closed again.

"I'm sorry." He was breathing hard. "Sorry about your uncle."

"Cousin. Desmond was supposed to be awakened in another year." Art did his best to sound heartbroken. "It was never supposed to be a death sentence."

"Tough." Strasser breathed again, loudly, as though he had been trying not to. "But you break the law, you take your chances."

"I guess so." Art began to walk back toward the entrance, not waiting for Strasser's approval. The longer he and Dana were separated, the greater the danger that they would tell inconsistent versions of events.

Strasser didn't object. He seemed in just as much of a hurry, and his face was pale when they emerged from the building. The awful sight and stench had broken through his official attitude that squeamishness was for civilians. He even seemed to regard Art with a bit more respect.

Dana was waiting anxiously by the doors. Art shook his head. "I'm afraid that it's bad news."

She was much better at acting than he was. The change in her face from hope to grief was totally convincing. "Can I—"

"You don't want to see him, Dana."

Strasser nodded his agreement. "You really don't. He's . . . well, we'll take care of the suitable disposal of the body. I'm afraid that in the circumstances there can be no formal funeral ceremony at this time."

"We understand that. Thank you, Commander." Art was itching to get away, before more questions were asked about his fictitious cousin, Desmond Lota.

He nodded and started to back off, but Strasser held up a hand.

"Excuse me, but there is one other matter that must be resolved. This is a government detention facility, and someone has broken into it. Now, you say that it was this way when you arrived—"

"It was."

"But if that's the case, it leaves open the question, who did break in? And why?"

"I don't know," Dana said. "But when we arrived there were marks around the side of the building as though something heavy had been pulled along the ground there. And when we came inside there were wet footsteps on the metal staircase."

Art stared in disbelief. She was inviting them to explore the higher levels of the syncope facility, where otherwise they had no reason to go. Did she *want* Seth and Oliver Guest discovered? But she was staring at him in turn, expectantly, as though waiting for him to speak.

"They must have gone upstairs," he said at last. He had it now. Dana couldn't tell the Navy people about the empty body drawer of Pearl Lazenby, because there was supposedly no reason for Art and her to have gone up there. She wanted them to go up and "discover" it.

"I can help to check what's going on there," he went on. "The stink inside doesn't bother me all that much."

He had added the reference to the smell deliberately. Strasser nodded. He looked far from happy. He could order a subordinate to go with Art but apparently that was in conflict with his ideas of the proper duties of a leader. Finally he turned to the rest of the waiting group and said, "Any volunteers?"

The young civilian woman whose brother had been found dead stood alone, facing away from the building and apparently blind to everything. The others looked at each other. After a few moments two enlisted men, both approaching Art's age, stepped forward.

"Pratt and Jarnile. Very good." Strasser handed his flashlight to Art, the final statement that he himself would not be going. "Be as quick as you can."

No question about that in Art's mind; again, there was the problem of what Dana might be asked while he was gone. He walked back through the familiar double doors, half a step behind the two enlisted men. They ought to find the empty body drawer, but he must find a way to make them go straight to it. Leading from behind. It was a concept not totally alien to the military.

As the beam of his flashlight played on the steps of the staircase, he realized that there really were footsteps on the stairs—his, Dana's, and Seth's. He let Pratt and Jarnile discover the footmarks for themselves and lead the way. Only when they were coming to the twelfth floor did he push past them, flash his light in the right direction, and say, "Here. This way."

After that he could follow and watch and take no further action. Jarnile spotted the open drawer along the fifth aisle, and led the way excitedly to it. While Art stood and watched, Pratt read aloud the name of its former occupant. It was obvious it meant nothing to him or to Jarnile.

"Get the ID number, too," Jarnile said.

"I will. Do you think there might be others?"

"It would take ages to find out." Art shone his flashlight up and along, to emphasize the spaciousness of the interior. "Didn't your commander say to get back quick?"

"He did." Pratt stuffed pencil and paper back in his pocket. "Come on, Nat. Any more decisions, they better come from above."

Art trailed a step behind on the way down. His knee was sore again, and he didn't want to steal Pratt and Jarnile's moment of glory. As he emerged into sunlight he glanced at Dana. She winked. Everything's all right!

Pratt was telling the story. Open body drawer, ID number, original release date. Strasser was nodding approval in a formal way. When it came to the name, though, the civilian woman swung around suddenly.

"Who was that?"

Art realized that he had read things wrong. Somehow, she outranked all the Navy people. She had been crying, but in a pent-up, tightly controlled way that made her face puffy but left no tear marks on her cheeks. When she was not so upset, with those features, eyes, and skin she would be beautiful in a foreign and exotic way.

"She's a strong woman," Dana said softly at his side. "No whining and moaning, even though it's her own brother."

He nodded. "Gorgeous, too."

There was little chance that the comments would be heard. Pratt was again pronouncing the name on the body drawer, in a near shout as though volume added to clarity.

"Pearl Lazenby," the woman said, far more quietly but with great intensity. "I had no idea that she is in this syncope facility."

"Was," Pratt volunteered, while Commander Strasser glared at him. "She's gone. The drawer was empty when we got to it. Who is she?"

Strasser shot at him flames of coming retribution, but the woman answered as though indifferent to military protocol.

"Pearl Lazenby is the Divine Seer, the Eye of God. The head of the Legion of Argos. Now does she sound familiar?"

"Chief Loony in the Loony Legion," Jarnile exclaimed. "Lordy. You mean that somebody let her out?"

"I mean exactly that," the woman said. With the new information she was energized, freed for the moment from grief. "Not only that, I bet I know when it happened. Last night there was all that activity down this way on the river. Her followers came over the river and took her, dead or alive, conscious or unconscious. There's supposed to be more than a million of them, scattered through Virginia and West Virginia and North Carolina. She could be absolutely anywhere by now. We have to let people know about this. I have to call, then I must get back to Washington."

She turned to Art and Dana. "You must have been here first, after they escaped with her."

Art's faint hope that he and Dana would be overlooked in the new excitement and free to go their own way vanished. "I suppose we were."

"Then you must come with me. You may be able to add important details. I can't tell you how much trouble Pearl Lazenby might cause—especially now, after the supernova disaster."

It wasn't couched as an outright order, but it might as well have been. Art also realized that it was the fastest way to get the whole group away from the syncope facility. Seth might have Oliver Guest under total control, but they couldn't lie squeezed in a body drawer forever.

He walked along the path away from the building, aware that Dana was following. In the road stood two purring gray behemoths. It was hard to know what they had been originally—troop carriers, dump trucks, heavy weapons transporters—but now they were buses, with rows of open metal seats below a blue awning of canvas.

Art made sure that Dana was right behind, then chose a half seat at the rear hardly wide enough for two people.

She smiled as she squeezed in next to him. "So far, so good."

He couldn't answer, because the other woman had moved to stand next to where they were sitting.

"I really appreciate your cooperation," she said. "I only just learned of your own loss."

Art nodded, and felt totally bogus.

"My name is Yasmin Silvers." She paused expectantly and held out her hand.

"Dana Berlitz."

Art leaned across. "Art Ferrand."

"Were you going back to Washington anyway?"

"North of there," Dana said, and Art was glad she was not more specific.

"Well, then this trip won't be totally wasted for you. And you will be doing a valuable service."

"I don't know about that," Dana said, while Art wished she would just shut up so the woman would go away. "It's my impression that Washington wouldn't recognize a service if it fell on them. The sooner I'm out of there, the better."

"You've had bad experiences?"

"More like *no* experiences. Even before the supernova, I could never get anywhere with the government. What it's like today I can't even imagine. It's always an endless trail of forwarded messages and useless holograms. I can never tell if it's the people who are half-wits or the smart programs derived from them. We'll get there this time, and either have to talk to a machine or some dim gas cloud of a bureaucrat."

Art caught on to what Dana was doing. People who are in trouble rarely cause more trouble; they want to draw as little attention to themselves as possible, so they keep quiet and don't complain. Dana's aggrieved air was very persuasive.

The woman smiled for the first time. It lit up her face and made her even more attractive.

"I'm sorry you've had such rotten experiences in the past, and have such a low view of government services. But tomorrow, I really think you'll have the ear of someone who can get things done."

She walked away to a seat closer to the front of the converted bus.

"And you thought she was gorgeous *before* she smiled," Dana said. "Tomorrow, eh? I guess we're stuck with a night in Washington."

"And a bed," Art added. "I can feel my skeleton poking

through and touching the metal. A bed, a bed, my kingdom for a bed."

"Me, too. And a *shower,* even more than a bed. I wonder where Seth will sleep tonight?"

It was the wrong question. Art, just beginning to feel that he could relax, thought again of his cabin in Catoctin Mountain Park. Dana, sensing the change in his mood, said nothing more. The buses started moving and rumbled their way north, while the two sat in silence. Snow still lay on the fields and by the side of the road, but the air was warm as early summer. The solid partition across the bus's cargo compartment supported Art on his right, Dana's thigh was a comfortable presence on his left. Despite the discomfort of the seat he found himself drifting off.

It was a change in the note of the engine that brought him back to the present. The bus had stopped. It was deep dusk.

"Are we there?"

"No." Dana was leaning far out over the side. "We're nowhere. There's a kid standing by the side of the road. Maybe seven years old. He only has pants and a shirt—no shoes—and he's crying. We've picked him up."

"Good." They were moving again. Art was ready to settle into a dazed but hungry torpor when Dana suddenly asked, "What's the current world population?"

"Eh? The population. Today it has to be anybody's guess. Before Supernova Alpha I think it was about eight billion."

"Right." She leaned toward him and laid her head on his shoulder. After another minute she added, "You know, we get it all wrong. We say the supernova was a disaster."

"Are you suggesting it *wasn't*?" Art loved Dana's head on his shoulder and the soft hair against his cheek, but her comment made no sense at all.

"I'm telling you it wasn't. It wasn't *a* disaster, a single disaster. It was eight billion separate and individual disasters—to you and me and Yasmin Silvers who lost her brother, and Desmond Lota's family, even if they don't know he's dead, and that poor little boy we just picked up. They are all disasters. Every one of them was awful, and every one is important. But all we'll ever learn about in detail is maybe half a dozen."

"Mm." She was right, of course.

"But you don't feel like discussing it," she said, reading Art's mind. "That's all right. You don't have to. I'm just talking philosophy."

"Mm."

"Better that than politics, if I know you. Don't worry, I won't talk either one. Have your nap, sweetheart."

Art felt like saying he had been doing fine with the sleeping before he was interrupted. Instead he closed his eyes and decided that he was just like Joe's dogs. You could cuss and swear at any one of them as much as you liked, and all the dumb thing heard was its own name. The mutt sat there and thumped the ground with its tail every time it heard that one word.

What Dana had been saying for the past few minutes was already fading. The only thing Art had transferred to long-term memory was that she called him *sweetheart.*

29

Grace Mackay left Saul's office at close to two o'clock. He worked nonstop for the rest of the afternoon, devouring his backlog of calls and throwing off decisions with a speed and energy that had Auden Travis in a daze. Dozens of items were delegated to agency heads, with a brief scribbled note: *Handle as you consider appropriate, feedback to me only if problems.*

At five-thirty, Saul poured himself a stiff single malt on the rocks. He went on working. At five forty-five he refilled his glass with ice and whiskey.

At six precisely, Auden stuck his harried head inside the door.

"You told me not to tell you before six o'clock whether or not Mrs. Goldsmith had arrived. It is now six. Mrs. Goldsmith arrived at five-thirty. Major Gallini took her to the small west wing dining room, poured her a glass of white wine, and sought to engage her in conversation. She expressed a preference to be left alone, but asked him to leave the bottle."

Travis seemed tired, but he also had an air of excitement. Saul looked for, and did not find, any hint that the aide disapproved of what he must surely regard as a coming presidential tryst.

"Thank you, Auden. Would you please pass the word to Mrs. Goldsmith that I will join her in ten minutes."

"Certainly, sir."

Auden retreated. Saul swirled melting ice cubes in his tired drink and drained the remaining half inch of whiskey. He walked over to the portrait on the wall and spoke aloud to it.

"I'm nervous, you know."

"I realize that."

"What would you advise, Dizzie, speaking as an old friend?"

"Marry an older woman, as I did. Mary gave me both a fortune and unceasing devotion."

"Isn't it rather late for me to consider that solution?"

"I do not see why. In political terms, you are a young man."

"But this isn't politics. You were only in your early thirties when you married. I'm in my mid-fifties. Anyway, I wasn't asking for advice in the long term. I meant, what would you advise for *tonight.*"

The room remained silent. The hologram projection area sat empty, as it had been for two weeks.

Another casualty of Supernova Alpha; Saul had loaded into the Persona every recorded word spoken or written by Benjamin Disraeli. The Persona had a real-time bus to every relevant history site. Each incident of the Prime Minister's life, well known or newly discovered, was contained in the data base, and the Persona employed a state-of-the-art expert system. Two months ago, this dialogue would have been real rather than imagined. The Disraeli Persona would have offered useful advice. Now it was not clear that the Persona existed even in backup storage. Had any of it been placed in a medium unaffected by the electromagnetic pulse?

"I guess I'm on my own."

Saul walked through to the outer office. The two drinks had been strong ones, and he felt slightly off balance.

"Auden, I don't think I will be back in the office this evening."

"Very good, sir."

"I will not be leaving the White House. I will have no need of security, and short of another supernova or a major war I do not want to be interrupted."

"Yes, sir."

Still no hint of censure, but as Saul walked past, Travis added, "Sir?"

"Yes?"

"Since you will not be working here, I would like to go out for the evening. Friends of mine are holding a small party, and they have invited me."

"Go, Auden, go. Have some fun. Fill the cup that cheers. You know what they say, all work and no play . . ."

He walked on, wondering what had made Auden Travis jerk up in his chair at those final words. Did Auden have some assignation of his own? If he did, good luck to him. The man deserved a break.

The interior of the White House was unusually quiet. Saul's heart was thumping as he walked slowly to the west wing dining room. He wondered why he was having dinner with Tricia at all; it no longer seemed a good idea.

She was the only person in the room, seated at a long, low-backed green couch on the wall by the window. As he entered she came to her feet and turned toward him in a single graceful movement.

"Saul! It's wonderful to see you."

No hint in her manner of any breakup. No suggestion of a two-year separation. Tricia was elegant as ever, dressed in a knee-length dress of midnight blue that outlined her small, firm breasts and showed off one bare shoulder. The kiss on the cheek that she gave Saul was a model of proper formality. But before she moved away she kissed him again, a quick and searching contact of lips and tongue with quite a different message.

"Here," she went on calmly. She turned to the side table, picked up two glasses of white wine, and handed the fuller one to Saul. "I was drinking before you arrived. I don't want to get too far ahead—you know me, two glasses and I'm out of it."

Saul took a cautious sip. It tasted like a fine Puligny Montrachet, with none of the additives that Tricia on occasion indulged in. She didn't know he'd had two substantial scotches and was actually ahead of her.

Or did she? She might well have smelled whiskey on his breath. Tricia was alert in all her senses.

And she was as beautiful as ever.

"It's good to see you, too, Tricia. Where's Pomerance? He was supposed to be here."

"He was. I told Mungo that if he didn't mind I wanted to serve dinner for you myself. I've known him for ages, and like a dear he agreed."

Tricia's comment went beyond a simple statement of fact. Her acquaintance with the White House extended beyond Saul's tenure. He could certainly deal with Mungo Pomerance, the White House head of arrangements and master of the kitchen for fifteen years, but he would hesitate to attempt what Tricia had done, banishing the majestic and magisterial Pomerance from his own domain.

See, Tricia was saying. *I know how to handle the White House staff, and they like me. Wouldn't I make a wonderful First Lady?*

The truth was, she would. Tricia had all the charm and social graces that Saul felt he lacked. She was at ease with diplomats and ministers. At the same time, her early years had given her a rapport with service personnel from waitresses to window washers. She would make a marvelous First Lady for President Saul Steinmetz.

There was, of course, a minor problem. Tricia happened to be married to someone else.

"How's your husband?" Saul asked abruptly.

Tricia glanced at him over the top of her glass, her dark eyes catching color from her dress. "Joseph is fine."

It was a typical Tricia answer. She had never said one negative word to Saul about her former husbands, why would she be any different with her current one? But there was an obvious next question: Does Joseph Goldsmith know you are here tonight, dining alone with a former lover?

Saul did not ask. Tricia could reply, in all innocence, that she had no idea they would be dining alone. Hadn't Saul told her that he had business to conduct, and others would be present?

On the other hand, she knew his strong preference for one-on-one meetings.

She gestured to the table, where two places were set on the red cloth. "I don't want to rush you, but if I don't get some food soon, the wine will make me woozy."

Saul sat down. He had offered the dinner invitation, but Tricia was apparently in charge. She was over by the side table, adding dressing to the endive salad, tossing it, and transferring it into two bowls using a long silver fork and spoon. She lifted the lids of the serving dishes and rapidly served medallions of beef, green beans, roasted peppers, and potato croquettes. The portions were generous.

"Pour the wine, would you?"

Again there was an unstated message. *I know you like to handle the wine. I know you like your salad served at the same time as your entree. I know you like your plate well filled. I know you'd starve rather than eat a parsnip. I know your tastes, you see—*all *your tastes. Don't we make a wonderful couple?*

We do indeed. But we're not a couple anymore. Saul poured the wine, a Jordan Cabernet Sauvignon '05. Tricia possessed an uncanny ability to ferret out his likes and dislikes and remember them exactly. She would never wear yellow when they were together, or serve him cheese at less than room temperature, or pour wine into small glasses, or bring cooked cabbage or tomato juice within a mile of him.

"Here's to us." She slipped into her usual seat on his left, squeezed his hand for a moment, and raised her wineglass. "You'll have to say if this is all right. I opened it to let it breathe, but you know me and red wines. I never can tell."

Saul tasted the wine, aware as he did so that her fingers were gently rubbing his palm. "It's fine. In fact, better than fine. Splendid."

It was as if there had been no breakup between them, no election, no long separation, no supernova; the world not in chaos, whole continents not blighted, darkened Washington beyond the curtained window not torn by upheaval worse than the burning of the sixties or the Turnabout riots of '07.

Oh, call back yesterday, bid time return. The temptation was strong. For one evening at least, bring the past alive; eat, drink, talk, and laugh together, and see where the night leads.

But to do that, you must forget the suffering beyond the White House walls. While you are enjoying your meal, dining as well as if there has been no worldwide disaster, what are Americans across the country eating? Are they eating at all?

You are the President of all *the people.*

Saul ate and drank in silence. He was a man complex enough to enjoy thoroughly the food and wine, while at the same time aware of those less fortunate. After a few minutes he realized that Tricia was staring at him, waiting.

She smiled when she caught his eye. "Ignore me, sweetie. I know you have lots on your mind. I'm fine just sitting here. Unless you feel like talking about it?"

She leaned over and refilled his glass. He noticed that hers was almost untouched. Tricia had the same attitude as Henry Ford, who believed that a car could be any color so long as it was black. For Tricia, a wine could be any color provided it was white.

He had nothing to say; then suddenly, with Tricia's eyes fixed steadily on him, he desperately needed to spill out the thoughts that had been boiling in his mind for the past two weeks.

He pushed away his empty plate. "I was thinking this afternoon about the supernova. Trying to put it in some sort of perspective. I started to think about my father. I've told you about him before, haven't I?"

"Yes, but tell me again." She was half smiling, the tips of her teeth just showing. "This time it will be different."

Saul picked up his glass, peering into its ruddy crystal ball.

"Maybe it will. Maybe it will. I was born the year after men first landed on the moon. My father worked at Lewis Research Center, one of the facilities of the old NASA. Space exploration was his life. If my mother hadn't put her foot down, my name would be Saul Armstrong Aldrin Collins Steinmetz. He was sure that we would have a colony on Mars by the end of the last century, that by now we'd be settling the Jupiter system and beyond. He didn't realize—ever—that the space program had been born ahead of its time, as a political stunt.

"He died in 1999, when he was sixty-five. That was young to die, even then. What happened in the seventies, eighties, and nineties broke his heart. When I was twenty he was my age now, but he was a sad, disheartened old man. He would sit on the porch and reminisce about the sixties, what he called the 'Golden Age' of space exploration.

"He didn't live long enough to learn that the Golden Age was in the future, not the past. When people first went into space it was a balancing act where you might fall over anytime. Every component was stressed to the limit, just to get to orbit and back. The pioneers had all the courage in the world. What they didn't have were good computers, molecular machines, and designed construction materials.

"Worst of all, they didn't have the right energy sources. Nuclear power is the key to space, but it was ruled out for forty years by the 1963 Test Ban Treaty. Can you imagine riding a chemical explosion to orbit? That's what the designers were told to use, chemical reactions with one-millionth the energy of nuclear reactions. It's as though you called in the world's best bridge builders and said, we want you to build bridges across the San Francisco Gate, or Sydney Harbor, or the Verrazano Narrows. We'll give you money—though not quite as much as you need. And oh, yes, there's one other point. You've got to use wood as your building material. We know about iron and steel and aluminum, but for social reasons they are unacceptable.

"So the astronauts and cosmonauts were hurled into space using chemical rockets. There was no margin for error. And most of them lived, and a few of them died, and people like my father faded into despair. By the time the revised outer space treaty was signed in '05, it was too late for him."

He was lecturing, to Tricia who either knew it already or didn't need to. She didn't seem to mind. She was leaning forward, food and drink forgotten. It was one of her most endearing aspects. When she was your partner she focused her attention on you and you alone, as if there were no other people in the world.

Except that she wasn't *his* partner, not now and not for more than two years. She was married to Joseph Goldsmith. Saul ought to be asking what she was doing here tonight rather than dwelling on his own obsessions.

She was nodding at him eagerly. "Go on, Saul. I'm listening. If you are worried, I want to hear."

"I am worried, but more than that I'm thinking I'm a lucky man. I always told myself that I was so different from my father. Now I realize I'm just like him. He spent decades pining for the space program that seemed within reach when he was twenty-five years old. It didn't happen, not in his lifetime.

"When I was twenty-five, I had my own vision. The whole world was going to be one, tied together by electronic information transfers. I wondered when I would find time to sleep, because the financial deals I wanted to follow around the world were in every time zone. I knew the markets by heart, and all their hours of opening and closing: Auckland, Sydney, Tokyo, Seoul, Beijing, Jakarta, Rangoon, Bombay, Karachi, Tehran, Beirut, St. Petersburg, Cairo, Cape Town, Rome, Paris, London, Rio, Buenos Aires, Santiago, New York, Toronto, Chicago, Houston, Mexico City, San Francisco, Honolulu. I zigzagged north and south while moving west with the sun, hemstitching the world. I was sure what the future held, and it meant that I had to be everywhere."

Saul paused. "I'm sorry, Tricia, you know all this stuff. I'm babbling at you. It's the wine."

But it wasn't the wine. It was Tricia's eyes, intent on his, signaling that he was telling her the newest, most important, most fascinating information in the world.

"Go on, Saul."

"Well, I'll keep it short. My future didn't happen, either. The Turnabout Riots happened instead. Fears of invasion of privacy, return to real currency, the mektek factory revolt, the jobs-for-humans movement, refusal to accept electronic data. This country led the retreat. I felt twenty years ago as my father must have felt fifty years ago. My future was destroyed. I went into politics to try to save it.

"I failed here at home. But other nations and strategic alliances moved ahead while we seemed to be stuck, going nowhere.

"Now I imagine what would have happened to this country if

I had succeeded. We would have been twenty more years down the road to a total electronic culture. Supernova Alpha would have done to us what it did to the Golden Rim and the Sino Consortium, every element of the economy ruined.

"I totally believe what I'm going to say now, although I can never suggest it in public: the Turnabout Riots were the best thing that ever happened to this country. We could be infinitely worse off. And we would have been—if my future had happened."

Saul studied his glass. He didn't remember drinking from it, but again it was empty. Three-fourths of the bottle of Cabernet Sauvignon was gone. He wondered if he was boring Tricia, despite her apparent rapt attention. He was certainly talking too much. More than he had ever intended to. He turned to her.

She read it as an invitation to speak, but her response surprised him. "Do you think there is any way that the supernova could make someone go insane?"

"Not that I can imagine. Who's the person?"

"Joseph. My husband."

"I know who your husband is." It occurred to Saul that in fact he knew little about her husband beyond his name, and that he disliked the man for the good and at the moment sufficient reason that Joseph Goldsmith had Tricia, and Saul did not. Of course, she must have somehow agreed to the arrangement, but that was not the point. The point was that Tricia was really *his,* not Goldsmith's.

He had the sense not to mention this. Instead he said, "How old is he?"

"He's fifty-six."

"Joseph Goldsmith is fifty-six? But that's my age!"

She laughed at him, the throaty chuckle that he liked so much. "I know. I'm told that more than one person can have it. But you are in much better shape than he is."

"He's too old for you. Why do you think he might be going mad?"

"He won't leave the house. He won't even come out of the basement. He says there are rays from the supernova that will sterilize him."

"That's news to me. My scientific advisers have said a lot of things about the supernova, but not that."

"Joseph doesn't take any notice of scientists. He's quite well off, you know."

It was like saying that Hitler was not altogether a nice chap, but Saul just nodded.

"He's planning to have deeper and deeper levels dug," Tricia went on. "Under the house, so we can go down there and save ourselves from the rays. There's no way he could be right, is there?"

"He sounds insane."

"I think he is. He wants me to stay down there with him. But I won't." Tricia popped to her feet, went across to the side table, and poured the remainder of the bottle of white wine into her glass. She drank it in two gulps, returned, and leaned over to run her wet tongue over Saul's ear. "Hearing you say that is a big load off my mind."

Hearing that your husband is crazy is a load off your mind? Saul didn't say that. He could feel the mood swing. Tricia's face was different now. In the old days, the looseness of mouth and flushed cheeks signaled sexual urgency. She sat down, and her stockinged foot touched his ankle and wriggled up his calf.

How could she move so quickly from worry to open lust? In the same way that he had moved in that direction himself, from the moment when she spoke of her husband as though of some stranger. Tricia always claimed that she just read Saul's moods and responded to them. A chameleon, he thought. And then, a sign of how far from sober he was, *La Dame aux Chameleons.*

"Back in a moment." Tricia was on her feet again. She slipped out of the room, touching the light switch as she went to leave Saul in semidarkness.

He stood up, too, and went to stand in front of the couch by the window. Outside, the city was brighter. General use of electricity was heavily restricted, but power was creeping back into the grid. Two weeks ago it had been riots and fires and murder in the streets. He had feared the collapse of society and a countrywide descent to barbarism. It turned out that most people, no matter what they might have said before Supernova Alpha, wanted their central government. To restore it, and keep it, they were performing miracles of improvisation.

An old cargo plane lifting off from National Airport reminded Saul of his flight back from Indian Head. That led his thoughts to Yasmin. By now she must have been to Maryland Point and the Q-5 Syncope Facility. She would be rejoicing, or she would be in mourning.

Yasmin was deeply suspicious of Tricia, without ever meeting her. *She's divorced again, and she's hunting.* Yasmin sounded confident, a woman assessing another woman's motives. But Yasmin admitted that she didn't understand at all why Tricia had walked out of Saul's life two and a half years ago. And Yasmin was not unbiased. Saul played a role in her own ambitions.

He heard a rustle of fabric behind him, and turned not knowing what to expect. In the old days Tricia had been a constant sexual surprise, coming to him as anything from demure virgin to nude porn star.

She was still wearing the dress of midnight blue, but she was now barefoot. She came into his arms and nestled her face against his neck.

"You're still thinking, aren't you? Saul, you shouldn't. This is the time in the evening when your brain ought to be turned off."

She snuggled close. He leaned over and smelled her skin, perfumed now with the added musk of sexual desire. He reached down to the hem of her dress and ran his hand up inside the front of it. As he expected, she was bare; and she was ready.

So was he, reassuringly erect and firm. Yasmin's warning from the previous night was faint and far-off. But it was enough to make Saul murmur, as he nuzzled Tricia's bare shoulder, "You feel so good. Why did you ever leave me?"

She was breathing hard through her mouth. She pulled away to look into his eyes. "I thought you didn't want me. It broke my heart. I couldn't bear it and I ran away."

It didn't make sense—he had told her that he did want her, very much. But in Saul's present condition, perfect logic was not important. He put his arm around her and tried to ease her down onto the couch.

To his surprise, she resisted. "No, Saul. Not now."

It could be part of a game, although it didn't sound like one. He tried again. She pulled away and stood head lowered, her arms by her sides.

"I'm sorry." Saul reached out and stroked her bare shoulder. "I thought you were ready."

Thought. He had been absolutely sure. But Tricia was shaking her head and backing away.

"It's not that, Saul. This is all my fault, I should never have started. I'm still a married woman. But seeing you, and kissing you, and you touching me, it made me so excited. I felt as though we had never been away from each other. But now—I can't."

She was leaning over, picking up her shoes. She hurried to the door, paused on the threshold, and turned her dark head. "Oh, Saul." Her voice trembled. "I've missed you so much. You have no idea. I wish we could, but I just can't. Not while I'm still married. Please forgive me, and let me go."

She vanished into the darkened room beyond the door. Saul took two steps after her, and stopped. What would he do if he caught up with her? It wasn't a sex game, she wasn't being coy. He couldn't—and wouldn't—drag her back against her will.

Saul wandered through into the bathroom off the dining room. Tricia's stockings and panties formed a crumpled ball in front of the sink. He reached down, picked them up, and stood with them in his hand. They provided more proof that Tricia had been very ready for lovemaking before she abruptly changed her mind. He thrust the stockings and flimsy damp panties into his pocket and stared at his own reflection in the long bathroom mirror.

He thought he looked normal enough. No visible evidence of the overwhelming sexual excitement that he had felt three minutes ago, or the awful sense of letdown he was feeling now. Tricia was probably feeling even worse.

But . . .

His instincts told him that something else was going on, something that he did not understand. He could not get to it without more information—and not in his present fuddled condition.

I'm still *a married woman.* And again. *Not while I'm* still *married.* Was she saying that she and Joseph Goldsmith were in the process of splitting up? She certainly had grounds, if Goldsmith had become a raving lunatic. But if she was in the process of getting a divorce, why hadn't she said so outright?

Saul wandered slowly back toward his bedroom through a silent White House. He could see the irony, even if he could not appreciate it. He had been without sex for a long time, more than two years. There had been opportunities, with willing partners, but he had been unable to perform.

Now in the last two evenings he had been ready, eager, and able. In both cases, after a roaring start, the woman had balked and left him frustrated.

Saul took off his clothes and went naked to bed. Two successive blue-ball nights. He had known nothing like it in the four decades since he was an eager teenager.

There was only one consolation. Even if the statistic formed some kind of melancholy presidential record, it was not likely to find its way into the histories of the Steinmetz White House.

30

Celine awoke to music, faint, far-off, and very familiar. That driving bass and those dissonant brass chords had given her energy on a thousand mornings. It was the anthem for their expedition: *Mars,* from Gustav Holst's suite *The Planets.* The team had chosen it together after final selection. She listened to its urgent pulse for twenty seconds before she recalled where she was.

Earth. At last. But a changed Earth. Zoe, Alta, and Ludwig, companions for more than five years, dead. A difficult landing, followed by a bizarre encounter. The past twenty-four hours had been one prolonged nightmare.

She listened, grieving for lost friends, until the final chords. Music for the Mars expedition. So why was it playing *here,* deep underground in the lair of the Legion of Argos? Pearl Lazenby disapproved of all space travel.

Celine opened her eyes. If the music had given her strength on a thousand mornings, it must do so one more time. She sat up. Before going to bed she and Wilmer had pushed their cots together. Then she had fallen asleep so quickly that it made no difference. She glanced across at him in the faint light coming in from under the door.

He was sound asleep on his back, his mouth open. She looked at him fondly. It took more than music to budge Wilmer. He woke in the morning only for food. In the first few weeks of their relationship it had also been for sex—Celine was a morning person—but he had complained so abominably about being wakened and about his need for calories that she soon gave up the effort. Anyway, fifteen minutes from the start she would be on her own in bed.

Wilmer's idea of afterplay in the morning was a stack of blueberry pancakes and a quart of milk.

She slipped out of bed and went to peek into the other room. Jenny was asleep. Reza was over in a corner, eyes closed and meditating in the lotus posture. There was no point in talking to either one.

Celine put her shoes on—she was otherwise fully dressed—and went across to the door. Rather to her surprise, it was unlocked. As she opened it she saw why. There was no place for a lock, but with her first step outside a gray-clad figure rose like a ghost from the floor.

"You are awake." No greeting, no cheery good morning. It was a male, younger than any she had seen so far. In the dim light and with his oversized uniform he looked about fourteen. He held his semiautomatic rifle as though it made him more nervous than it was likely to make anyone else.

"I am awake," Celine said. "My companions are still asleep. What time is it?"

For a second, she wondered if even that information was restricted. But at last the youth said, "It is almost seven o'clock."

"Then it is time for breakfast. We had no real dinner last night. How do we get food?"

That seemed to baffle him. He rubbed his chin, which was sprouting faint downy signs of a beard, and hesitated.

"I will have to get someone to bring you food."

"And I need to use the bathroom."

He turned his face away and looked very uncomfortable. "I will get someone to deal with—that problem. I was placed here only to make sure that no one came out through this door."

"But I just *did* come out through it."

The attempt at a lighter tone was a waste of time. He stared at her and said again, "I will have to get someone else. Do not go anywhere. I will bring someone who can answer your questions."

He marched away along the corridor. Celine called after him, "Why are they playing that music?"

He turned his head. "In honor of the surviving members of the returned Mars expedition." He did not stop, and Celine's call, "But that's *us,*" received no response.

She went back inside and poked Wilmer hard in the ribs. He grunted and burrowed under the blankets. "What do you make of that, cobber?" The heap of bedclothes did not move. "Everyone here agrees that we defiled Heaven by going into space. Pearl Lazenby told us so herself. Now they're playing music to celebrate our safe return. Are we heroes or villains?"

Jenny appeared in the doorway, rubbing her eyes. "We're villains," she said. "You don't guard heroes to keep them from wandering around."

"You tried it?"

"In the middle of the night. The guard was asleep on the floor. I'm afraid I trod on him. I guess I'm lucky he didn't shoot me."

"No. He'd have to get somebody else to shoot you. But if we're villains, why were they playing the *Mars* music in our honor?"

"I heard that. I thought I must be dreaming. If they're playing anything, though, it's on orders from Pearl Lazenby. They don't blink in this place without her approval."

Celine sat on her cot. "If that music was played in all the corridors and tunnels, a lot of her followers will be wondering why."

"As we are." Jenny sat down next to Celine. "She must have a plan. She wants to use us in some way."

"Which would mean she intends to keep us, and not let us go."

"I hope you're wrong." Jenny rubbed at her thigh muscles. "We're weaker than anyone here, and I don't think I could walk a kilometer in this gravity. But I want out. If Pearl Lazenby is running a puppet show, I won't—"

She broke off, because a woman in her early thirties was coming in through the door. She had a round face, straight black hair cut short, and a kindly expression. She was dressed in a plain gray blouse and pants. Incongruously, she had an automatic pistol stuck in her waistband. A ruddy-faced older man weighing at least three hundred pounds waddled in behind her. Like Eli, his chest and cuffs bore an emblem of scarlet claws. His was more elaborate, a triplet of talons surrounding and clutching the central blue-green globe. On his belt he wore a holster containing a revolver, so ancient that Celine had never seen one like it except in museums.

"Good morning." The man's wheezy tone, unlike Eli's the night before, was polite and deferential. "My name is Samuel. I understand that you would like the use of a bathroom, and then breakfast."

"We would."

"Then you women will go along with Naomi to the bathroom facilities. She will then escort you to breakfast. She is suffering a penance of silence, so please do not try to talk to her." He waved a plump hand, and the woman nodded at Celine and Jenny.

"You will meet your menfolk later." Samuel's voice became hushed and positively oily. "I noticed someone in meditation in the other room. I assume that he is the one with the powers of prophecy, of special interest to the Eye of God. Naturally, I will respect or even anticipate his wishes in every way possible."

"Actually, no. That's not him." Celine didn't like being demoted to a second-class citizen, even politely. "The man you saw is Reza. The man you *want* is Wilmer. That one." She pointed to the untidy heap in the bedclothes as she and Jenny followed Naomi toward the door. "You'll have to wake him up. Good luck with that. He's not at his best in the morning."

Facilities at the Legion of Argos headquarters looked crude, but they worked fine. Celine had forgotten how good a torrent of hot water could feel, beating down on your head and shoulders under a full Earth gravity. She stayed and wallowed for ten minutes, and came out to find that her clothes had disappeared. They had been replaced with new underwear, shirt, and pants, all white and all just a fraction too big. Her shoes were where she had left them. Jenny was waiting, dressed in an identical outfit. With the silent Naomi leading the way they moved side by side down a long narrow hall to an automated cafeteria, where trays of food were dispensed from a moving belt.

"Notice something?" While Naomi was picking up her tray, Celine had her first chance for a private word with Jenny. Just because Naomi did not speak did not mean she did not listen—and report.

"If you're worried about what was in your pockets," Jenny said. "Don't. I grabbed everything before they took our clothes. They say they're just cleaning them."

"Not that. I mean the people we've seen. No blacks, no Hispanics, no Orientals. I think the Legion of Argos is a whites-only group. You, Wilmer, and Reza certainly qualify. I'm borderline, but Pearl Lazenby's attitude last night suggests I'm acceptable."

Naomi was approaching. Celine and Jenny settled down to a silent meal.

Celine had plenty to think about. More and more, she felt certain that the members of the Legion of Argos from the top down were mental cases. Prophecies, penances, holy cleansings, arbitrary murders to settle grievances, ethnic entry requirements, guns everywhere, regimented behavior, visitors who were effectively prisoners—all the signs of a paramilitary religious cult. And added to that, Eli's exultant "there will be no turning back, no quarter given." The cult was approaching a point of no return. The right word from Pearl Lazenby, and the members would move to violent action.

The Mars expedition had to get out of this underground labyrinth, as fast as possible. And they had to make sure that other people were warned.

Was she overreacting, worrying too much? If so, she could see no penalty to that. What she could see were practical problems.

First, where were they? It would do no good to escape to the surface and find you were lost in a wilderness. None of them was in any condition to trek miles over rough terrain. Reza had brought them down, to his best guess, somewhere north of Richmond, Virginia. The big question was their longitude. Were they east or west of the Shenandoah Mountains?

Second, where would they go if they did escape? Her instinctive answer was Washington. There the Mars expedition was sure to be taken seriously. Anything they said would be given plenty of attention—unless the country had totally disintegrated under the impact of Supernova Alpha, in which case nothing they said or did would make much difference.

Celine felt a tap on her arm. It was Naomi, pointing to the old-fashioned watch on her wrist and then to Celine's plate. A question. Had she finished eating?

She nodded. "I'm all done. But I thought that our male companions were going to join us for breakfast."

Naomi shrugged. It occurred to Celine that the assignment of a mute guide might be quite deliberate. Maybe her mining for information the previous night had not been so subtle as she imagined.

"Our unctuous friend only told us we'd meet them 'later,' " Jenny volunteered. "He was careful not to say when."

"Which could mean anything from a minute to a year from now." Celine turned to Naomi. "Unless you are to take us somewhere else, I would like to see more of the Legion of Argos headquarters. It seems fascinating. We arrived last night, very tired, and we were able to take in very little."

It was worth a try, but Naomi shook her head. She tapped her watch, stood up, and beckoned them to follow. As they replaced their trays before leaving the dining room, Jenny whispered to Celine, "I was no help, was I. You want to get a good look at this place."

"Sure. If we're to find a way out . . ."

Naomi was with them again, urging them on, and for the moment Celine could say no more. The Legion member walked between her and Jenny, down another long corridor. There seemed an endless number of them, poorly lit and branching off at regular intervals.

Suddenly they were in a hurry. Naomi marched faster on a twisting, turning path. It was not the sort of tour that Celine had in mind, and she itched for a map of the whole place. Pearl Lazenby and her disciples surely had them. If they had been digging for twenty years, as Eli said, the whole countryside must be honeycombed. The corridor they were in now looked like an old working mine, drilled through grayish white rock and shored up in places with iron beams. As it narrowed they had to walk in single file, Celine in front and Naomi in the rear.

The tunnel took a final turn and Celine emerged into an open chamber, hundreds of feet across and with a knobby ceiling of whitish pink far above. The floor was white, uneven, and gritty beneath her feet. The illumination came from standing light fixtures, scattered here and there. She realized that they had entered a natural limestone cavern. A broad platform stood at the far end, with scores of rows of seats facing it.

Naomi walked past Celine and led the way forward along a central cleared aisle. The platform held a long wooden table and five chairs. Naomi indicated to Celine and Jenny that they were to ascend the dais and take the seats at each end. When they were in position she went to sit in the back row of facing seats.

Jenny looked along the table at Celine. "What now?"

She spoke softly, but the stone-walled chamber caught her voice, carrying it to the farthest corners and bringing her words echoing back.

Celine did not dare to answer that if Reza, their best geologist, could get a look at a cavern like this he might be able to make a good guess at their location. It was no longer the danger of Naomi alone overhearing what they said. The room was filling with gray-uniformed people, walking in through half a dozen entrances and quietly taking their seats. Every person in the front rows wore the scarlet talon on cuffs and breast. One woman set up a camera in the central aisle, sighting it on the platform. When she seemed happy with the setting she turned and extended one arm upward. The audience rose and stood waiting.

To stand or not to stand? Celine knew that Jenny's eye was on her. She decided to remain seated and argue with anyone who didn't seem to like it. To make sure that she would not be influenced by possible gestures from the audience, she leaned back and studied the cavern ceiling.

It had been modified from its natural form. Broken stubs of stalactites, painstakingly trimmed, stood out from the surface. Looking closely, Celine could see that the ceiling was not the uniform color of its first impression. Thousands of little scarlet talons had been painted on the original white limestone, blending from a distance to create the illusion of a continuous surface of light pink.

She glanced out at the audience. They were ignoring her, looking past the platform at something behind Celine and Jenny. She heard footsteps, and resisted the urge to turn until a hand touched her shoulder. Then she looked up and saw Wilmer settling into the next seat. Like her, he was outfitted in a clean white uniform. Next to him, in the middle, was Pearl Lazenby, and beyond her Reza was sitting down by Jenny.

Pearl Lazenby wore a long white sleeveless dress, dotted with the scarlet talons and blue-green globes. She gestured to her followers, and they settled into their seats. She remained standing.

"I know that many of you are becoming impatient." She began without preamble, in an easy, conversational tone. "How long, you ask, before our role in the holy cleansing, so long awaited, can begin? When I returned among you, the Eye of God promised another portent. Until that time, we could not act. The Eye of God told you that we would receive a message directly from Heaven, brought to us by a human messenger. Most of you probably assumed that I would be the messenger. That is not the case."

With the filled seats damping the echo, the chamber formed a natural auditorium. Pearl Lazenby's voice carried easily, without amplification, to every part.

"Eight years ago, the governments of this world conspired to create an abomination. Not content to contaminate God's realm close to Earth with human presence, they decided to invade another sphere. The nations would cooperate in building a ship to carry humans to the planet Mars, where another part of God's creation would be despoiled.

"And so the Mars expedition was born. Conceived in folly, executed in sacrilege, doomed to failure. Before the expedition was over, even as the Eye of God had prophesied, the hand of the Almighty smote the impious nations. They writhe as I speak in chaos and confusion. The time of the Legion of Argos is close to hand. Yet the Eye of God knew, and foretold, that a final message must be delivered before we can rise in wrath and righteous action."

Yesterday, Pearl Lazenby had seemed to Celine like a sincere but misguided woman, no different from any of the millions of professed psychics, clairvoyants, and seers scattered around the world. Certainly, she did not seem the person to create and lead a million-strong movement of religious extremists. But yesterday, as Pearl Lazenby had told them, was an unusual day for her as well as them. She was recently returned from judicial sleep, and she had been exhausted.

Today Celine could hear the difference. She would even say that she could *feel* it. There was no scientific explanation for the gift that some humans have, to take and hold and move a crowd. But the gift was real. Pearl Lazenby had that power, more than anyone Celine had ever met. It was an electric force, beyond words, reaching out to envelop her audience.

And the underlying message was very disturbing: anything connected with the Mars expedition is evil. The nations that conceived the expedition are already shattered. Now the four survivors of the expedition are sitting at the table with Pearl Lazenby.

Were they going to be offered in some barbaric ritual sacrifice? The audience remained silent, but Celine could see violence and vengeance on their faces.

"The promised messengers have arrived." Pearl Lazenby opened her arms wide, palms down, to take in the others at the table. "They are here with me. These are the four surviving members of the Mars expedition: Celine Tanaka, Wilmer Oldfield, Reza Armani, and Jenny Kopal. But"—she spoke over a rising mutter from the audience—"do not make the mistake of judging them guilty, as the people who promoted and funded the Mars expedition are guilty. These four are brave and innocent victims, dupes of their secret masters. They took great risks, and they have endured great hardships. Their companions and closest friends died.

"But they have survived, to bring their message direct from Heaven. This is the sign, the message we have awaited. You have been patient, and now our time is close, our tide approaches the flood. Within one week I promise action. Already, the word has gone forth to prepare and to congregate here. The message from

Heaven tells that the great space stations, those sacrilegious insults circling and observing for so long above our heads, have been destroyed. The people who operated them are all dead, and we are at last free from intrusive eyes. We pray for their poor damned souls, even as we bless the hand of God that destroyed them. And we welcome into our midst these four messengers from the realm of Heaven. It was surely foreordained that their return to Earth would bring them directly here, to the sanctuary of the Legion of Argos. Nothing would give me more pleasure than to see them unite with our cause. I ask you to express your gratitude and pay tribute to the surviving members of the Mars expedition."

Every person in the chamber rose to applaud. They stood clapping for many seconds, while Celine sat and stared straight ahead. During the long months of the Mars return she had sometimes imagined a scene where she and her companions were safe home on Earth, basking in a standing ovation. She would never have believed that it might take place on a wounded planet, in a natural cavern far underground, with an applauding audience of religious and racist maniacs.

Wilmer reached out and tapped her shoulder. He had risen to his feet, and Pearl Lazenby was motioning to Celine to do the same. Jenny was standing, and so was Reza.

Well, what the hell. It was quite clear that Pearl Lazenby was using their arrival for her own purposes, but adulation beat lynching any day of the week.

Celine stood up. As the noise in the chamber reached a new crescendo, she confirmed her resolve to get away from the Legion of Argos as soon as possible. If you had to go along with the madness for a while, it was a small price to pay for escape. Just so long as you didn't catch it yourself.

Celine raised her hand, smiled, and acknowledged the applause of the audience.

31

After the audience's long—and perhaps not entirely voluntary—applause for survivors of the Mars expedition, Pearl Lazenby turned to Celine.

"I'm afraid that I now have practical business to take care of. I have been away for a long time, and certain elements of the Legion of Argos require correction." That had an ominous ring to it, but she went on serenely, "I do not wish to bore you with trivia. So I have made other arrangements, which I hope you will find interesting."

It was a dismissal, polite but unequivocal. At Pearl Lazenby's signal, four men approached the platform. One was the wheezing Samuel, and the others bore the same triple-talon insignia of senior members of the Legion.

"Call me David," one of them said to Celine. He looked older than the others, with the tanned skin and steady crow's-footed eyes of a game hunter and marksman. "If you will now follow me . . ."

She had expected to be reunited with Wilmer and Reza. Instead she was apparently to be separated from Jenny.

After a moment of hesitation, Celine went with him. In the business of gathering information, four separate collectors were more efficient than a single group. There had been no opportunity to confer, but on a point so fundamental the other three were unlikely to disagree.

Unlike Naomi, her new guide was more than willing to talk. "Our leader is sure that you will share our goals," David said as soon as they were away from the others. He fixed Celine in the crosshairs of his gaze. "Of course, you must first be familiar with and understand us. We have one hour available to us. Is there anything particular that you would like to see?"

It was an educated upper-class voice, dispelling Celine's notion that although Pearl Lazenby might be an exceptional woman, her followers were deluded simpletons. David might have been chosen specifically to convert her, but she must be careful what she said. The gray eyes studying Celine were dangerously intelligent and thoughtful.

Tell the truth. "Pearl Lazenby is astonishing, but I know almost nothing about the rest of the organization. The Legion of Argos has the reputation of attracting extremists. I would like to be sure that your reputation is undeserved."

"To counter extreme evil, extreme actions may be necessary. But the best way to demonstrate what our society is like is not to talk, it is to show. As we walk together, I want you to ask yourself: Have you anywhere on Earth—or on Mars, for that matter—seen or heard of a group of people who work so peacefully and cheerfully toward a common goal? Why don't we take a look at one of our schools."

He smiled at Celine's expression. "Yes, we have children, so of course we must have schools. Old-fashioned, by today's standards. But I have yet to be persuaded that the new methods work better than the old."

They were walking side by side, steadily but not fast, along one of the many tunnels. He seemed aware of Celine's space-weakened muscles, and he allowed her to set the pace. She took her time and made careful note of their path.

"Does the Eye of God prescribe particular teaching methods of the schools?" she asked.

She was fishing for information, and innocently enough. But it brought a frown to his face. "I will forgive your remark," he said slowly, "since it is based on ignorance. But you are guilty of blasphemy."

While she halted and stared at him in surprise, he went on, "The title the 'Eye of God' may be applied only when referring to prophecies. In all other matters, she is to be known as the leader or our leader. A few old friends are permitted to call her Pearl or Pearl Lazenby."

The smile came back to his mouth, but Celine was watching his eyes. They were cold and clear, without a trace of humor or compromise.

She thought, *My God, he's crazy. And he looks and sounds so normal.*

She said, "I'm sorry. I did not know the custom."

"Very well." He began to walk. "As I said, it is forgiven. Since it was your first offense, I will not report it."

Observe, don't speak. Celine followed him along the corridor. It continued for another fifty yards, then made a sudden turn and ended at three elevators. David led them through the open door of the one on the right. Next to the control buttons sat a dozen small icons. Her companion pressed the top button, next to the symbol of a book. As the door closed and the elevator began to ascend, Celine identified some of the other icons: a scythe, a gun, a cross, a skull, a ladder, and a hammer.

But what were the others? A lamp? A waterfall? A spoon? A bed?

As the seconds passed, Celine was able to confirm her impression of the previous evening. The headquarters of the Legion of Argos was buried deep underground. They were going up and up and up. She could hear the groan of the cable and the rattle of other elevators passing them. She was convinced after a while that she could feel the air pressure changing.

Finally, as the urge to ask where they were going became irresistible, the elevator slowed to a halt. The door creaked open. David urged her forward.

They were in a dim-lit room about fifteen feet square and seven feet high. The far wall was one great window. Two men were standing by the glass, looking through into another room at least three times the size.

David walked Celine forward as the two men turned. He whispered to her, "Observers," and to them, "This is Celine Tanaka, here to see the school."

The men wore the usual gray uniforms, but their insignia were different. The scarlet talon was present, but next to it was a lurid human eye. The men nodded to Celine. "Very good to meet you in person," the shorter one said. He spoke in the same hushed voice. "We saw you with the leader. As a matter of fact, you are on delayed relay right now. Come and watch, but speak softly."

He turned back to the window without offering an explanation of his words. Celine, moving to his side, found she was looking at a brightly lit room full of small children. From her position they were all in profile, while on her left and facing the youngsters stood a woman about forty-five years old. The desks were solid wood, handmade, and like everything else in the room a generation or more out-of-date. The learning equipment was noninteractive, obsolete long before Celine had begun her own formal education.

Behind the woman, and finally making sense of what the man had said, hung a big projection screen. Celine had a moment of shock when she saw her own picture displayed there. It was replaced a few seconds later by Wilmer's image. Pearl Lazenby's voice accompanied the pictures, saying: ". . . directly here, to the sanctuary of the Legion of Argos. Nothing would give me more pleasure than to see them unite with our cause. I ask you to express your gratitude and pay tribute to the surviving members of the Mars expedition."

As the scene expanded to include everyone on the platform, with Pearl Lazenby in the center chair, the sound of applause from the projector's sound system swelled. Celine saw the children in the room hesitate, then start to clap their hands at a signal from the teacher. She wondered. Why hadn't anyone turned to stare at her and the men with her? Then she realized that this dim-lit room made the window into a one-way mirror. The children could not see anything on her side of the glass.

That was equally true for the teacher. Did she know when someone was watching? She was saying, with what Celine heard as a note of slight nervousness, "Now, children. You have heard our leader tell us that these people came as messengers from Heaven. You remember the prophecy of the Eye of God. What does it say? 'When the word comes from Heaven . . .' "

After a moment of hesitation, the chorus of young voices picked up the prompt. " 'When the word comes from Heaven, the Hour of Judgment will be here. We will go forth as one, and we will save the world from sin . . .' "

They continued chanting their lesson, but Celine was no longer listening. She had noticed that the wall at the back of the room, behind the children, contained a window. It stood at an acute angle relative to her position, so she could see only a thin oblong of what lay beyond; but that oblong showed the dazzling white of undisturbed snow, with a twig of evergreen shrub angling across the top corner.

The school was not in the deep subterranean caverns of the Legion of Argos's headquarters. It was all the way up on the surface, where children in the break from lessons could go outside and play in the sun.

If these children played at all. There was no sense of joy in the schoolroom. Uniformed seven-year-olds had the grave faces of old men. The teacher was nervous. Her expression had the uncertain misery of Celine's mother when her father came home late. Would it be flowers and a kiss, or rage and a black eye?

"You stay out of this, young lady, or you'll get a damn sight more than you bargain for." Celine had flown a hundred million miles to escape that memory, and it was still here. She shivered and turned to the people standing next to her. Their faces were stern and unsympathetic. Observers. Two of them, for a single teacher. On the watch for any sign of deviation in what was being learned—and taught.

"Is she on some kind of probation?" she whispered to the man on her right.

He frowned, as though she had said something ridiculous, and shook his head.

Celine backed away from the window. It was not just David, it was all of them. The leaders of the Legion of Argos were out-of-this-world mad. Rigid in outlook, intolerant of minor differences. In other centuries they would have led the Inquisition, tortured the heretics, burned the witches.

And Pearl Lazenby, pleasant, sympathetic Pearl, was worst of all. She set the rules for everyone.

David was walking toward her. "Did you see what you want to see here? If you would like to speak with the children, they would consider it an honor. We would have to approach through a different route, of course, because the observation rooms do not have direct access to the school."

Celine breathed deep and distanced herself from her own emotions. "It would be interesting. But if we have only one hour I would rather see something else."

"What?"

What? "Can we look at—the kitchens?"

He stared at her. "You want to see the kitchens?"

"If that would be all right. If it's permitted."

Celine knew what she really wanted to see: whatever lay beyond that other window. But he must not suspect.

. . . our time is close, our tide approaching the flood. Within one week, I promise action.

To counter extreme evil, extreme actions may be necessary.

• • •

Pearl Lazenby was busy and could not be disturbed when they arrived back at the deep levels. Celine pleaded fatigue and was allowed to eat and return to their sleeping quarters. The young man assigned by David to take her there treated Celine with great respect, but his continued armed presence outside made her status clear.

She remained there alone for over an hour, until Jenny arrived. They sat side by side on two cots and spoke in whispers.

"Reza and Wilmer?"

Jenny shook her head. "Weren't with me. I never even saw them. I wish Reza were here, I'm worried about him. He's changed a lot since Zoe and the others died. Last night it was all Pearl Lazenby this and Pearl Lazenby that. Where did you go?"

Celine summarized her trip to the school and the kitchens, and her reaction.

Jenny nodded. "Same with me. Organized, and clean, and scary. This isn't their only facility—they're scattered across at least three states."

"The big question is still, how many? It's clear they intend to cause trouble."

Jenny put her head close to Celine's. "I think I know. I was shown a group training for military action. They only looked about twelve years old. I asked if everybody had training like this, and my guide said yes. I asked how many people reported to the next level up, and he said it was always ten people. I didn't dare to get too nosy, but as we were leaving I asked the number of levels between this group and the leader. He told me, six. That means they have more than a hundred thousand people, trained and under arms."

"We have to collect information—" Celine broke off as the outside door swung open.

Wilmer and Reza marched in. Without a word from either of them, Celine could see that they were in very different moods. Wilmer was cheerful and good-humored, what she called his after-lunch look. Reza's eyes were dark and distant.

"About time," Jenny said. "I waited in that lunch place for nearly an hour. Where were you?"

"Meeting with Pearl Lazenby." Wilmer sat on the cot next to Celine. It sagged under his weight. "For more than two hours. She wanted to know how I made my 'prophecies' about what will happen to the Earth fifty years from now."

"I hope you didn't tell her," Celine said.

"Of course I did. I explained about electron degeneracy and

heavy ion emission and gas cloud optical depth. I don't think she understood one word, but she seemed impressed by what I told her. She wants me to stay here. I would be her special adviser."

Wilmer's words confirmed all Celine's suspicions. She wanted to say, *That does it, we're getting out of here* now, *before she makes us all her converts.* But her built-in worry button had been pushed. Caution came with it. She could not forget how Zoe had rushed to action, and its terrible effects.

She forced herself to think. They were still weak after their long journey through space; snow on the surface would make travel hard, even if they could reach it. Celine had an idea that she was reluctant to discuss generally, because of Reza. All signs of the old mercurial Reza Armani had vanished. Now he spoke hardly a word. He seemed to be off in a different world.

So she said only, "We are very lucky to have found a place where we can eat and rest and get our strength back. We should make the most of it. And we need to compare notes."

Jenny picked up Celine's unspoken message. She stood up. "They'll be coming for us again in a couple of hours. We might as well take a rest." She took Reza's hand. "Come on. I want to hear what you've been up to."

He said nothing, but he did not resist as she led him through to the other bedroom. It was Wilmer, easygoing and unperceptive Wilmer, who after the two were gone frowned at Celine and said, "Is Reza all right?"

"Why shouldn't he be?"

"I don't know. Seems to be behaving a bit funny, that's all." He scratched his head. "Well, it's been a hard few days. He'll be all right once we're out of here. So what were the two of you up to this morning?"

Thank God for Jenny. Calm, logical, and understanding, she provided Celine's sanity check for the next forty-eight hours. They tried to stay together during the sightseeing sessions, as servants of the Legion of Argos took them through miles of underground tunnels to visit the dormitories, workshops, and depressingly well-stocked arsenals. Electric power came from two nuclear plants, meticulously maintained. Celine checked the radiation level outside a reactor pressure vessel and found it hardly above background. Better than USMA industrial standards.

The Legion of Argos members were doing more than *show,*

they were *showing off.* The mood was jubilation and anticipation. The followers of Pearl Lazenby were going to carry out, in just a few days, their great project—the "holy cleansing," promised for so many years. Celine and Jenny hid their own feelings, and did their best to express approval and admiration.

Back in their quarters they compared notes on what they had seen and talked again about getting away. At Celine's insistence they did so with a mixture of cryptic words and gestures, meaningless to anyone who might be listening. There were no signs of surveillance equipment, but with so paranoid a group the possibility could not be ignored.

Celine was pleased with everyone's improving physical condition, but not with much else. She had been able to think of only one method of escape. They needed a fallback plan. The other big question was timing. They would get only one shot, and they had better not botch it.

Jenny had another worry. Celine learned about it on the late morning of their third day underground. As the two of them were eating in the half-filled cafeteria, she said to Jenny, "Tonight."

It was a statement, not a question. Jenny took it for granted that Celine was now their leader and made the major decisions. This time, however, Jenny glanced carefully around them and replied, "I don't know."

"You don't feel we're ready?"

"I'm more than ready. It's Reza. You haven't seen much of him except at mealtimes and in the evenings. But I sleep with the man and we've talked a lot. Especially about Pearl Lazenby."

"Do you think she sees him as a possible convert?"

"I know she does—not just him, all of us. Doesn't Wilmer talk about Pearl Lazenby, too?"

"Of course he does. But you know Wilmer. When it comes to thinking bad of people, he's an innocent. He believes that Pearl Lazenby is wrong and a bit off the wall, but he doesn't see real danger in her. Reza has an unstable side, you know that better than I do. If they're trying to recruit him, and you think he might be vulnerable—"

"It's worse than that." Jenny paused, and took another careful look around her. Then she said, louder than was wise, "He's trying to recruit me!"

It ought to have been a surprise, but it wasn't. The nagging doubt had been with Celine since the first evening, when Reza stood in the doorway with that enraptured look in his eyes and assured them that Pearl Lazenby was an amazing woman.

"You've talked to him?" Celine said. "You pointed out the terrifying side of all this?" She waved her arm, indicating the dead-serious diners and the spotless room.

"I've tried. I can't get through to him. All he'll talk about is the Legion of Argos and Pearl Lazenby. When we first arrived here I didn't see how anyone could fall for the Eye-of-God guff. Now I get nothing else. I hoped at first that it was just one of his phases, so he'd come out of it and see through her. But he hasn't. He's getting worse. And to trust him with any escape plans at all . . ."

"We can't. Absolutely not." Celine stared down at her half-filled plate. She couldn't eat any more. She knew how Jenny must have agonized, keeping the problem to herself and hoping that Reza would come out of his strangeness. Finally, with a time set for attempted escape, she had been forced to speak. And she was ashamed.

Celine's own problem was different: How could she organize an escape for four people, when one of them might refuse to go—worse than that, might betray their plans for what he saw as their own good?

"Tonight," Jenny said suddenly. "You're right, it has to be as soon as possible. They are getting ready for action, they might decide to move us or split us up anytime. We dare not wait much longer."

It was going to be hard for Celine to explain that Reza simply could not be trusted. But Jenny was continuing, "Between eleven o'clock and midnight. You and Wilmer will have to take care of the guard, if there is one. You've got to do everything quietly. I'll keep Reza occupied."

She held up her hand as Celine began to speak. "You are usually the boss, but this is different. It's too important to run an added risk. Nothing bad will happen to me and Reza—they'll be glad we're loyal converts. I'll tell them that we had no idea what you and Wilmer were planning, you didn't take us into your confidence."

Celine opened her mouth, then closed it.

"Eleven o'clock," Jenny went on calmly. "Not before. And no more discussions about what you're going to do. That way, I won't be able to tell them—no matter what."

No matter what. Forcing information out of Jenny by torture?

Surely even Pearl Lazenby would not try that. But her fanatical followers . . . *Humanity must be cleansed of sin, even if it means scraping to the bone.*

"Jenny—"

"Are you going to have dessert?" Jenny turned toward the serving line, as though she wanted to see what might be available. "I don't usually; but today I think I will."

When there is nothing to be said, the best thing to say is nothing. Celine reached across the table and took Jenny's hands in hers. "Eleven o'clock. Not before."

The next problem was Wilmer. One reason Celine was so fond of him was his openness, which led to his inability to either hold grudges or keep secrets. Normally she liked that, but today she didn't dare to tell him anything. The four of them ate a late dinner in an atmosphere that Celine found totally artificial. She and Jenny prattled trivia, spouting any nonsense that came into their heads. Wilmer pretended to be listening and occasionally he nodded politely; Celine knew that he was busy inside his head.

And Reza took no notice of anyone. He was smiling and looking off into the distance. Something wonderful was happening there, and he was watching it.

They were back in their living quarters by nine-thirty. Pearl Lazenby, in spite of her welcoming words, had not taken away the guard. It was the same youngster as on the first night. He had learned from experience and had brought a sleeping bag.

Celine went inside and came back with a pillow. "Here. This ought to make you a bit more comfortable. Good night. We'll see you in the morning."

He smiled his thanks. She didn't like that. What she was doing was deceitful, to someone who was hardly more than a child. She tried to justify her action to herself with the thought that if the guard were sound asleep at midnight, she would not need to knock him unconscious. The other half of her brain, giving her an argument as usual, pointed out that the guard's punishment by his superiors would be much less if he *were* knocked unconscious.

As she went back inside, Jenny caught her eye and shook her head.

No good. Reza doesn't seem interested.

Making love would have been a preferred answer. Celine was not particularly inquisitive, but they had been together many months on the *Schiaparelli*. Living space there was very tight and privacy almost nonexistent. She knew that Reza tended to fall asleep quickly and deeply after he and Jenny had made love.

Celine went across to Wilmer and took him by the hand. To Jenny and Reza she said, "Good night. See you tomorrow."

As they moved into the bedroom she could sense Wilmer's surprise. They had given each other none of the usual signals during dinner, and they were a couple to whom foreplay was very important.

"Are you feeling all right?" he asked as soon as they were alone.

Celine peeped out of the almost-closed door, confirming that Jenny and Reza were following their example and heading through into their own bedroom.

She sat down on one of the cots. "I'm fine. But we have to talk."

He flopped down next to her, with a what-did-I-do-now look on his face.

"It's nothing you did or I did," Celine went on, "but in a couple of hours, the two of us have to escape to the surface and make a run for it. Shh!"

His sudden turn had made the cot creak and its head bang against the wall. "Jenny—"

"Whisper!"

"What about Jenny and Reza?" Wilmer didn't have a whisper, but he did lower his voice.

"They won't be going with us. Shut up now, and I'll explain."

He listened in silence for the next few minutes, interrupting only once to say, "Break it with what?"

"A piece from one of the cots, assuming we can get it off. That won't be easy, because we'll have to work quietly."

He nodded. As she continued with her explanation about the problem with Reza's conversion, and Jenny's solution to that, he moved over to the other cot and stooped beside it. Three minutes later he came back to sit beside her. He had a smug look on his face. In one hand he held the solid I-bar leg of the cot. His satisfaction disappeared when Celine said, "Wrap a piece of sheet around it. You may have to hit the guard on the head with it."

"But he's just a kid. He hasn't done anything to us."

"Then you'd better hope he's sound asleep when we leave. If not, we have to knock him out."

"Can't we just tie him up and gag him?"

"Not quietly. Suppose Reza hears and comes out to see what's happening? Be quiet now." Celine listened closely for a minute. "Good. Jenny did it after all."

"Did what?"

"Never mind. Lie there and rest. We'll need all our energy in another hour or two. Sleep if you can."

Advice easy to give and impossible to follow. Celine lay on the cot, rehearsed their coming actions, listened for the end of the rhythmic sounds from the next room, and watched the clock. It was quarter past eleven when she nudged Wilmer—he had fallen asleep almost at once—and sat up. She switched off the light in the room.

"Celine." Wilmer spoke softly, his head close to hers.

"What now?"

"We have to bop him. If we don't, they'll never forgive him for going to sleep."

"I know. I thought of that, too. Can you do it?"

"I hope so." He gripped the cloth-wrapped iron tightly as Celine tiptoed to the door and eased it open. The young guard was sound asleep just outside, his head on Celine's pillow. With his fair skin and unlined face he looked about ten years old. Wilmer raised the cudgel, and stood frozen. He shook his head.

Celine took the club from him. "It's worse for him if you don't," she said, and swung hard to the right side of the defenseless head. The young face went slack.

Celine looked down in horror. She forced herself to whisper, "Get a sheet. We don't know how long he'll be unconscious. We have to tie and gag him."

And hope to God I haven't killed him. While Wilmer was back in the bedroom she made a quick inspection. The head above the right ear was swollen. She could feel no depression beneath it. The skin was unbroken, and he seemed to be breathing normally. She eased him from the sleeping bag.

After he was bound and gagged she had to make another decision. Should they leave him outside, where anyone in the corridor could find him? Or drag him inside, where his absence from his post might be noticed?

Right decision or wrong decision, it was a leader's job to make it. With Wilmer's help she worked the bound youngster back into the sleeping bag, pulled it high on his face to hide the gag, and pushed him up against the closed door to their rooms. If anyone walked by, the lad was sleeping but everything was normal. If Reza opened the door, he would see that the rooms were still being guarded.

"Come on. Bring the club, but take the cloth off it." She was carrying their provisions, all the food that she and Jenny had been able to smuggle out of the cafeteria without anyone noticing. Wilmer had a blanket. It was pathetically little for an escape into the unknown.

"What about his gun?" Wilmer was bending over the guard's body.

"No. If we have to shoot, we've lost. We'll never get away if they're following us so close."

She started off through the dimly lit tunnels, torn between haste and caution. For once, the rigid rules of the Legion of Argos were an advantage. There were hours to work, hours to eat—and hours to sleep. The corridors were deserted.

The elevator took forever to arrive. When it finally came, the clanking of chains and groan of its cables seemed loud enough to alert anybody near. Celine hustled Wilmer aboard, hit the button beside the top icon of a book, and waited in agony until the door closed and the car began its slow ascent. The light was off and she did not know how to switch it on. They rose forever, in total darkness.

Her memory of the observation chamber beside the schoolroom was inadequate. She remembered only one entrance, that from the elevator. Was there another, that would lead through into the school?

The room was in darkness when they arrived. They waited, until at last Celine's eyes adjusted to the weak glimmer coming to her from the observation window of the schoolroom. Celine went to the glass and peered through. The light was pale moonlight, and it was streaming in at the outside window.

She turned to Wilmer, a ghostly silhouette outlined against the wall of glass. "Smash it. We don't have time to look for another way."

She did not see him nod, but she heard the words: "Cover your face."

He put his shoulders and all his weight into the swing. The sound of iron I-bar hitting thick glass was unbelievable. The secondary noises, as Wilmer trimmed the bottom edge of the hole so they could walk through, were not much better. And then suddenly the only sound she could hear was his heavy breathing.

"Come on. We'll try the door on the left, and if it's . . ."

It was unlocked. Before she had time to think, Celine was through and standing outside on flat concrete. It was the school's playground. In front of her stood a row of swings, a monkey puzzle, and a seesaw. The sight was so normal and yet so surprising that it made her breath catch in her throat.

She looked around. On their left was a line of rounded hills. To the right, a half-moon hung low in the sky. The face shone a curious orange-yellow—an effect of Supernova Alpha? A week ago they had been coasting far beyond it, approaching a crescent Luna that partnered a crescent Earth.

She sought familiar stars. Wilmer was ahead of her. "That's north," he said. He was pointing in front of them. "See, there's Cassiopeia, and there's Polaris. Which way do we go?"

He expected her to provide an answer. She didn't have one. In a sense, it didn't matter. They simply had to escape from the Legion of Argos. But the whole escape would be pointless if they did nothing with the information that they had gained.

Reza had been a damned good pilot, with a pilot's instinctive sense of place. He thought he had brought them down somewhere north of Richmond. If that were the case, the hills on the left would be part of the Shenandoahs. And Washington would lie ahead, to the northeast.

Then there was the moon. It was to the east of them, so it must be rising. That meant they would have light to see by—or to be seen. By dawn, they must be far enough away to go safely to ground.

"We go east," Celine said. "It will be flatter in that direction. We'll make faster progress."

"Right." Wilmer lifted the iron bar. "Do we still need this?"

"No. You can dump it."

Celine spoke without thinking, and she took for granted Wilmer's prompt release of their homemade club. But then, as she led the way east toward the strange orange moon and across a spongy damp meadow scattered with Queen Anne's lace and tall ferns, she thought very hard.

What has happened inside, to turn me into a woman who gives orders and expects to be obeyed without question?

How different are Celine Tanaka and Zoe Nash and Pearl Lazenby? Are we all sisters under the skin?

Maybe, as long as I have thoughts like this, I'll be all right.

32

Art and Dana were heading for Washington, after a night where a hot meal and a soft bed had been wonderful luxuries. Yasmin Silvers had tried for an aircraft from Indian Head, but all the planes were assigned to other missions. She had settled for a topless converted Jeep, with an engine so loud that Yasmin as driver had to turn and shout if Art and Dana were to hear a word.

It didn't matter to Art. He had always preferred driving to flying. The morning continued yesterday's heat wave, the snow was gone, and a breeze felt good on his face. The sun warmed the top of his head and threw golden highlights off Dana's hair. He had never seen it so light in color. His only problem was a terrible thirst.

They were approaching the city from the south, cruising along the elevated freeway. The AVC system that controlled vehicle speeds and separations was out of action, but the road held an amazing amount of traffic. Most of it was cars less than ten years old, presumably with fix-ups that bypassed fuel injectors, catalytic converters, and anything else that depended on chips. Tinkerers must be in huge demand. But Art also saw square-built Japanese imports from the eighties, a diesel Rabbit like the first car that he had ever owned, vintage Harleys, a finned American monstrosity older than he was, a dune buggy, a Knighton DB-4 in perfect condition, and dozens of VW bugs—the originals, not the late nineties reissue.

Happy days, when a car still made you a king. Art closed his eyes, snuggled down in the seat, and lost himself in memories.

That was when Dana reached out, touched his hand, and said, "Don't worry. Your friends will be fine."

She had noticed his silence, but misunderstood. At breakfast Art had confided his worry that Seth Parsigian and Oliver Guest were heading for his home in Catoctin Mountain Park, while he was forced to go to Washington. He had friends there.

But in the Jeep he had not been thinking about them at all. The sight of the cars from other generations had pushed him far into his own past. He had been reliving the September evening when a multivehicle pileup totaled their van and came so close to killing Mary.

Art had no intention of telling any of that to Dana, even though she would probably be sympathetic. And he didn't need to, because she assumed that his mind was on the situation up at Catoctin Mountain.

So what was he doing, head close to Dana's to overcome the engine noise, staring up into a smoky blue sky and explaining what had happened thirty years ago? He blurted out everything, all the details; more than he had ever told anyone before. That was before an AVC system existed, he explained, and the cause of the pileup was a doctor who had changed lanes sharply to avoid a truck entering the freeway. The domino effect went all the way to the fastest lane. Mary had been overtaking there when her van was sideswiped and pushed farther over. Another two feet and she would have hit a concrete overpass support, head-on, at sixty miles an hour.

She had been untouched. Later they had laughed about it together, agreeing that it was the close call of a lifetime. Who could have guessed, then, that she had only six years left?

As Art fell silent, Dana reached out and patted his arm. "I'm sorry. Sad memories. But I'm glad you told me."

"I shouldn't have."

"Of course you should," Dana said. "You needed to." She turned, presenting Art with a view of the back of her blond head.

He looked beyond her. As they came closer to the center of Washington, traffic slowed to a crawl. The roar of the Jeep's engine reduced to a threatening grumble and normal conversation became possible. Every traffic light was out, and the police at major intersections lacked experience. The Jeep had halted with a dozen cars in front of it, waiting for the hand signal to proceed. A boy about ten and a girl not much older were pushing a baby carriage along the median beside the line of stopped cars. A hand-lettered sign on the front of the carriage said FRESH FRUTES AND VEGATIBLES.

"One more casualty of Supernova Alpha," Dana said. "Without spell checkers, maybe we'll learn to spell again."

"We never did before we had them." Art leaned out of the Jeep as the carriage reached them. "What fruit do you have there?"

The grubby-faced boy held up a little basket. "Strawberries. That's all. Nothing else ripe yet."

"How much?"

The boy conferred with the girl, then asked, "How would you pay?"

"Dollar bills."

"All right. Twenty dollars."

Art exchanged looks with Dana—good news; currency was back in use again, at least in Washington—and said, "I bet there's not more than a pound in that basket. Talk about robbery!"

The girl scowled at him. "It's not. You're lucky to get these. It's supposed to be too early for strawberries, but most are already rotted. Take 'em or leave 'em."

Art handed over the money and gave the basket of strawberries to Dana. He peered into the baby carriage as it went by.

"Now that's interesting."

"What is?" Dana was turning over the fruit, looking for the ripest. She handed one forward to Yasmin, gave another to Art, put one in her own mouth, and said indistinctly around it, "These haven't been washed. They're not very big, either. What's interesting? They seemed like ordinary vegetables to me."

"They are. Radishes and lettuce and onions, early peas and beans. It's what's *missing* that's interesting."

"All right, Sherlock. I'll take the bait. What's missing?"

"No signs of the bigger-better-tastier-faster recoms. You'd expect the carriage to be full of gene-spliced forms. Not a one."

"So?"

"So we and our science created superior specialized food plants, precisely tuned to a particular ecological niche. Then the niche disappeared. The older, more primitive forms survived." Art accepted another unwashed strawberry and ate it cheerfully. "A man could become philosophical about that."

"A man better not, unless he wants a woman to ignore him." Dana sat up straighter and stared ahead. "*Now* what's going on?"

The Jeep had been on Maine Avenue, ready to follow the traffic north onto Fifteenth Street. There were signs of major clear-up efforts, but the streets still held scattered heaps of trash and rubble. Instead of steering a way around them, Yasmin made an unexpected right turn at a narrow ramp and rolled down below street level.

"Avoiding bottlenecks in the middle of town," she shouted back to them. She sounded pleased with herself over the engine's rattle. "We'll go the rest of the way underground. Save half an hour."

Art thought again how tough she must be, under the sexy and decorative exterior. She had to be thinking about and grieving for her brother, but she held it under tight control. He was admiring Yasmin for that when Dana glanced at him in the sudden gloom and said, "An underground road system in Washington? That's a new one on me."

"Me, too. And I thought I knew the city pretty well. If it's going to be like this all the way, I don't think we'll save much time."

The Jeep had stopped at the bottom of the ramp. The automatic gate designed to accept an ID card was not working. It stood wide open, but a man in Army uniform stood by the gate. He took the pass that Yasmin held out and examined it closely before he waved them on. A couple of hundred yards farther along, the whole process was repeated.

"The Pentagon?" Dana asked, after the third halt and inspection.

"But then we'd have to cross the river. Maybe Capitol Hill?"

Yasmin must have heard their questions, but she pointedly did not answer them. All she said was, "It's a lot quicker when the automatic ID checks are working."

She made a final left turn and the Jeep emerged into a vast parking garage. The floor was blacktop, the whitewashed ceiling lit by fluorescent bulbs and no more than seven feet high. Yasmin drove all the way to the far end. The spaces there were tiny, designed for electric urban runabouts. Each had a sign: RESERVED, SPECIAL STAFF. PARK IN DESIGNATED SPOTS ONLY. AS A COURTESY TO THE NEXT USER, MAKE SURE THAT YOUR VEHICLE IS PLUGGED IN FOR RECHARGE. *DO NOT OCCUPY MORE THAN ONE SPACE.*

Yasmin parked the Jeep neatly, but it was so wide it sprawled across two spaces. She shrugged. "So they'll probably sue me. Come on."

They climbed down. Art took three steps and paused, puzzled. After a moment he realized what the problem was. It was like the gene-spliced fruit and vegetables, something noticeable by its absence. His right knee was guaranteed to stiffen up after hours in one position. This morning he felt not a twinge. It must be the telomod treatment, it could be nothing else. The urgency hit him again. He and Dana needed to get out of here and learn what was happening with Seth and Oliver Guest. Without the genome scanners, everything going on inside their cells was guesswork.

He hurried after Yasmin and Dana, in through yet another checkpoint complete with armed guard. Then it was an elevator, rising steadily for four floors. And, at last, they were inside a structure designed for people rather than vehicles.

Yasmin picked up a telcom by the elevator door, made a connection, and said, "Yasmin. I'm back."

Art sensed an odd tension in her voice, but she went on, "How's his schedule? Yes, ten minutes should be enough."

She led them along a short corridor, saying good morning to the handful of people they passed. Clearly, she was a regular. And clearly, this was the house of someone very rich. Everything—pictures, carpets, drapes—was either an antique or a superb fake.

At the end of the corridor Yasmin paused. "I hope this goes all right, but it may not. A couple of days ago I had a horrible screaming fight with the man inside this room. We said some pretty awful things to each other. I want to patch things up, but if I can't, please remember that it's nothing to do with you."

They entered a smallish room, whose only occupant sat at a cluttered desk before a thick-paneled door of dark wood. He stood up as they came in, an unusually handsome young man whose face was a picture of uncertainty. He and Yasmin stared at each other for a few seconds.

"Want to go on working here?" she said at last.

He grimaced. "Is that what he said to you? It's exactly what he said to me."

"Me, too. What did you tell him?"

"I said, yes, I want to work here. More than anything I can think of."

Yasmin nodded. "That's pretty much what I said, too. He made me feel about two inches tall."

"I know. The worst thing is, he was absolutely right. Can we have lunch today?"

"I'd like that. We'll compare wounds." Yasmin turned to Art and Dana. "This is Auden Travis. Auden, this is Art Ferrand and Dana Berlitz. They were at the syncope facility, too."

Travis nodded, but he hardly glanced at the two visitors. He was looking appalled at Yasmin. "I heard," he said. "I should have mentioned it before, instead of talking about our jobs. I'm really sorry about Raymond. It must have been awful."

"It was. Worse than I thought. But it's over." Yasmin swallowed and looked toward the paneled door. "Anyone with him?"

"Not at the moment. They found another big store of RAM chips, way underground at Cheyenne Mountain. Giga capacity, not tera, so they're all pretty much out-of-date. But we had a few million flown in yesterday. A technician slapped a bunch of them together in parallel, and was in here earlier trying to get the holo projection unit up and running. He left about fifteen minutes ago. He said he'd be back soon. So it's a good time." He glanced back to Art and Dana. "They were checked?"

"Back at Indian Head. All we could with the deep scanners out of action. They're clean."

That meant little to Art, but Auden Travis nodded and said, "It's what we have to settle for at the moment. Go ahead."

Yasmin moved to the door, knocked, and opened it. She ushered Art and Dana in ahead of her.

Art found himself in a big, airy office with a high ceiling. That's all he had time for, because once his eyes reached the man standing by the window he could look at nothing else.

Saul Steinmetz. Not quite as tall as he seemed on media releases, thinner, and with the stoop of a scholar. As he turned, penetrating eyes of pale gray skipped rapidly from one person to the next.

"Very sorry to hear about your brother," he said to Yasmin. And, to Art and Dana, "And you lost a relative, too. Terrible business. I wish I could think of something better to say."

He did not go through the charade of pretending that they might not know who he was. And he obviously knew who they were and where they had been. Art immediately wondered what else Steinmetz might find out. That they were not related in any way to the dead Desmond Lota? That they had no valid personal reason for a visit to the Q-5 Syncope Facility? He glanced at Dana, and saw that she was having the same worries. Her eyes were wide, fixed on Saul Steinmetz.

Very deliberately, Art forced himself to turn his head and look over to the corner of the office. Something odd was there, something he had caught from the corner of his eye as they entered. It was a ghostly projection, an insubstantial hologram of a man with the wall showing through his head and body. The head and mouth and eyes moved in stop-action jerks, like an old-fashioned clockwork figure.

The tick-tock man, Art thought.

"That monstrosity is supposed to be Benjamin Disraeli," Steinmetz said. He had caught and followed Art's look, and he spoke in the friendly and informal tone that came across so well at public meetings and press conferences. "Not quite what he was before Supernova Alpha. But maybe none of us is. I'm promised something better before the day's out."

He gestured to an oval coffee table surrounded by chairs at the other side of the office. "The more I hear about Pearl Lazenby and the Eye of God and the Legion of Argos, the less I like the sound of them. Look at this."

He held out a black-and-white photograph. "Taken with a long focus camera from a high-flying military aircraft over North Carolina. See the lines of dots, like columns of ants? Those are people, coming out of one of the Legion of Argos strongholds. So far as we can tell, they're moving north. Did you know that her followers have been saying for years that she prophesied her own return from judicial sleep? She was sentenced to six hundred and fifty years. All logic said that she would die of natural causes, centuries before her time was served. But she was right, and logic was wrong."

He turned to Art and Dana as they all sat down. "Yasmin tells me that you were the first people to come across Pearl Lazenby's empty body drawer. I'd like you to tell me exactly what you saw in and around the syncope facility. What direction you approached from, what condition the ground was in, tell everything. Take as much time as you want, and try to forget that you are in the White House. Yasmin asked for only a few minutes, but you have as long as you want."

Steinmetz had noticed Art's and Dana's discomfort, and read it as nervousness in the presence of the President. But that idea wouldn't last. Art knew Steinmetz's reputation, as someone with an uncanny gift for reading people far below the level of words. Now he and Dana were proposing to lie to the man—and hope to get away with it. It would never work, not in this world. Those pale gray eyes were frighteningly luminous and knowing.

Dana was staring at him, expecting him to take the lead. Well, he would—in a direction she might not like at all.

"I'm going to do what you ask," Art said slowly. "Even though at first you may not think I am. And this will take a little while." He looked again at Dana, and was encouraged by her nod. She understood, and she approved. "My name really is Art Ferrand, and this is Dana Berlitz. But we are not related to each other. And we didn't have a relative at the Q-5 facility. We went there for a quite different reason."

Tell everything.

Art began to describe telomod therapy, and was surprised by Saul Steinmetz's quick, "I know about that. Experimental, right? Go on."

Art started over, this time with his call to Dana from Joe's house in Catoctin Mountain Park. Then it was the journey to the Treasure Inn, the ruined Institute, the decision to look for Oliver Guest ("Guest and telomeres? I thought he was the clone man." "Telomeres, too, Mr. President."), the trip through the echoing storm drains, and the scow and tobacco runners' boat down the Potomac, all the way to Maryland Point. The story sounded unreal, as much as the events themselves now *felt* unreal.

Steinmetz said hardly a word. A couple of times he nodded, and once when a buzzer sounded he told Yasmin, "Tell 'em not now, no matter who it is."

Art described the river landing at Maryland Point, the discovery of the trails from that side of the fenced facility around to the front, the broken gate. He told how they had found at first only corpses, but at the higher level at least some of the sleepers were alive.

He looked Saul Steinmetz straight in the eye. "We didn't try to save them. We kept moving."

The President nodded. "We're on to that. Don't worry. What next?"

It was the finding of Pearl Lazenby's body drawer, empty. Then the resuscitation of Oliver Guest, interrupted by noises from below.

"We didn't want to be discovered, doing what we were doing."

"Of course not." Steinmetz spoke as though that were obvious. "For one thing, it might have been Pearl Lazenby's followers again. Then you'd have been in real trouble."

"So we left Seth with Oliver Guest, back in the body drawer."

"You weren't worried about him? Left behind with Grisly Guest?"

"You don't know Seth. Anyway, that's the last that Dana and I saw of them. We came down, and we met Yasmin. And she brought us here."

"She did, indeed." Steinmetz stood up and walked across to the window. "You're telling me the truth. Why?"

Why? Art and Dana stared at each other. "We'd never have convinced you with a lie," she said at last.

"You might have, if you kept it simple and agreed to your story ahead of time. I'm pretty good, but I'm not infallible. Ask my mother, she'll tell you. But you told the truth. I'd like to know the reason."

"I didn't decide to tell the truth," Dana said. "But I'll tell you why I agreed with Art when I realized where he was going."

"That will do fine." Steinmetz came back, sat down, and speared her with that luminous gaze that made her feel pinned in her chair. "Why?"

"You said that telomod therapy is experimental, and you are quite right. Nobody knows the possible side effects, or what will happen to the patients in the long term. But the hell with the long term. Who cares about that if you're dead?"

" 'In the long run, we are all dead.' Not the words of our quantized friend over there"—Steinmetz glanced across at the spectral shade of Disraeli—"but of the economist, John Maynard Keynes. I agree with him completely. We have to worry about now, today, and worry about later if and when we have time."

"Well, without telomod therapy I would be dead today. So would Art, and so would Seth Parsigian. Every doctor I went to before I found the Institute for Probatory Therapies said the same thing: try to put your mind at ease and prepare for death. I wouldn't do it, and I won't do it. We may not seem to be dying to you, but we have no idea what might happen next. The Institute is gone, the genome-scanning equipment is useless, and our doctors are dead. The only person we know who has a prayer of telling us anything is Oliver Guest. But suppose we can't find him? Suppose he gets away from Seth, or kills him, and disappears?"

"Given his past history, that's not at all improbable. People have said many things about Dr. Oliver Guest, but no one ever said he was less than brilliant. Now I think I see it, but let me make sure. You are telling me all this, so that if you are unable to find Guest, the government might help you?"

"Yes." Dana glanced to Art for confirmation. "That's exactly it. We agreed to try to rendezvous with Seth north of here, and at the moment we don't even know a way to get there."

"We could certainly help with that." Steinmetz's voice was gentle and understanding. "But don't you see that what you are asking is both illegal and impossible? You want me to sanction the continued liberty of a convicted criminal. Not just a minor felon, one who did not deserve his sentence"—Steinmetz bound Yasmin to silence with a strange glance—"but one of the most demented and horrifying murderers in history. How am I supposed to justify that? What will my political enemies say when they find out?"

A gargling sound came from the corner. The hologram brightened, and the figure within it became opaque and three-dimensional. After a few seconds the image vanished with a loud sizzling noise.

Steinmetz scowled at the empty corner. "I take that as an appropriate opinion on the opposition. But now do you understand?"

Dana nodded slowly. She seemed crushed. It was because of the look on her face that Art blurted out, "If you help us to find Guest and you let us talk to him, we'll try to make sure he's captured."

He knew it was stupid as soon as he spoke. Steinmetz raised his eyebrows. "Let's see if I have this right. If we help you, you'll help us catch him; but you were the ones who let Guest out in the first place. If it weren't for you, there would be no problem. I assume you're familiar with the man who kills his parents and asks for special consideration from the court because he's an orphan?"

His words were harsh, but the humorous gleam in his eye took the edge off. Art decided that Saul Steinmetz was a very hard man to dislike—and more dangerous because of that.

"Put yourself in our position." Art had nothing to lose. He opened his shirt, raised his undershirt, and pulled the front of his pants lower. The clean-edged scar ran from the right side of his ribs down his bare belly to well past his navel. "I have half a dozen more like this, from operations before I found the telomod therapy. The treatment saved my life, but I don't know for how long. Without doctors who know what they're doing, I'm under a death sentence. Not just me—Dana, and Seth, and all the others in the program. We three just happened to be near Washington after the supernova zapped the microchips. Wouldn't you be ready to try just about anything if you were one of us?"

His shirt was still open. He began to move it across to the left. Steinmetz held up his hand.

"No need. One picture is worth a thousand words. I don't think two would be more persuasive." He turned to Yasmin, who was staring at him steadily. "I have to, don't I? I know it's different, but it's not different enough. And politics is the art of the impossible." He turned back to Art. "How long before your friends—no names now, even though we're not being recorded—how long before they're supposed to meet you up north?"

"It depends how long it takes them. They could be there now."

"They could. But you're not. Here's what I can do for you. Government vehicles come and go from Washington all the time. You work out with Auden what's going tomorrow morning, to where you need to be. I don't want to know the place. You then have four days. After that we are going to discover that Oliver Guest is missing from the Q-5 Syncope Facility, and I'm going to mount a full-scale manhunt for the famous murderer. If you turn him in before that, fine. But don't mention me or the White House, because nothing like this meeting ever happened."

He stood up. "One other thing. However this turns out, I want you back here to give me a personal report. Whatever you say won't go beyond this office. And now I must get on to other things. Do you realize that you've been here for over an hour?"

"We're sorry," Dana said.

"No, you're not." Steinmetz held out his hand. "Nor am I. Good luck."

She took it, but gripped it in both of hers. "Why are you doing this for us, sir?"

"I am the President of all the people. And if I were in your position, I suspect that I'd have done exactly what you did." Then he winked at Art and Dana, and the urge to smile back was irresistible. "And sometimes when you're President, you have to do something that nobody else in the whole damn country could get away with, just to prove you can." He shook Art's hand. "You go ahead, I need a private word with Yasmin on another matter."

When they were outside the door, Dana asked softly, "Did you vote for him?"

"No. I liked him, but he was running against the first woman candidate *ever*. Did you?"

"No." She laughed. "I thought he was too rich. You'd vote for him next time, though?"

"You better believe it. After today, if he asked me nice I'd marry him." Art realized, too late, that the man who had greeted them—Travis?—was still in the room. He had a puzzled expression on his handsome young face.

33

From the secret diary of Oliver Guest.

My relationship with Seth Parsigian has undergone a curious evolution over the past several days. It is, to invoke the vocabulary employed elsewhere in this diary, a form of restricted mutualism. We need each other. On the other hand, we both know that our value to the other will at some time cease. We are therefore wary, releasing just enough information to satisfy the other while retaining his dependency. It is bounded symbiosis.

Initially—I am making this diary entry a few days after the fact, for reasons that should quickly become obvious—initially, as I say, Seth's and my priorities coincided. We needed to remove ourselves far from the Q-5 Syncope Facility, and find a way to reach my home and laboratory. The tools to produce a simple monitoring device of Seth's telomeres lay there, together with certain things of mine that he did not need to know about.

In those first hours, I was perforce almost useless. Weak physically, I was also ignorant of the ways of the world following the supernova. I had to rely on Seth. I also had an opportunity to observe him.

There was plenty to respect about Seth Parsigian, if not to admire. My roundabout attempts to learn more about the two people with him at the syncope facility produced a genial smile. "No, Doc, you don't need to know about 'em. You picked up their first names, what more do you want? Anyway, you'll probably be meeting 'em in a few days. Gotta be patient."

Be patient. *Good advice; but for both of us, hard to follow. Our need to reach my home and lab as quickly as possible was a shared need. When he learned where I had lived before my capture and sentencing, he groaned and said, "Glen Echo. Jeez, that's almost back where we started. We'll have to go all the way upriver. An' we'll never make it the same way we came. How are you feelin'?"*

"With some effort, I can probably stand."

"I was afraid of that. We can forget walkin' the roads anytime soon. So it's gotta be the river." He stood up. "I'll be quick as I can, but I might be a while. I could say, stay here, but I guess you're not plannin' on goin' anyplace."

He left me sitting on the block behind the syncope facility. I do not mind admitting that at that moment I had my doubts. My sustaining thought was that he needed me even more than I needed him. Even so, I was at a low ebb when he finally returned. He must have been away at least six hours, and though the night air was mild I could not lie down and rest in snow. I sat with my head in my hands, close to exhaustion.

"All set," he said. His trousers were soaked halfway up the thighs. "Got us a boat, didn't even have to kill anybody."

Was he joking? I had seen the gun and knife hooked into his belt. I suspected that he meant me to notice them. With his assistance I stood up, held his arm for support, and shambled down a dirt trail leading to the wide Potomac.

I had my first direct proof of a changed world. The night river, once busy at all hours with commerce and pleasure craft, sat calm and empty. Not a light showed, on the water or on the far-off other bank.

The object he led me to did not deserve the name of boat. It was a filthy, broken-sided scow, its flat well littered with items of rubbish.

"This!" I hissed at him. "We'll never get to Glen Echo in this."

He grinned at me, teeth white in a nearly invisible

face. "No, we won't. This is what I came here in, but it won't take us back. I did my scouting in it, and it will take us to the real boat."

"Why didn't you bring the 'real boat' here?"

"You'll see. Let's get you aboard. Sorry, but you have to get your feet wet."

He helped me splash through a foot of water and hoisted me effortlessly over the side. More proof, if I needed it, of his physical strength. He settled me aft, went to the bow, and picked up a paddle. "We can talk now if you want," he said. "But we'll come to a place where we have to be real quiet. I'll let you know ahead of time. Sit back and relax."

I was too tired to talk, and too uncomfortable to sleep. We moved onto the dark water and slipped lazily downstream. The wrong direction for Glen Echo, but Seth seemed to know what he was doing.

After about an hour we passed a couple of moored sailboats. "Those," I said.

Seth shook his head. "Flat calm. We need engines."

Twenty minutes later we came to an inlet where recent high water must have created a strong whirlpool. The shallows were full of flotsam, everything from tree limbs and wooden crates and beams of timber, to a miscellany of shattered light boats and the wreckage of a light aircraft.

"Pity we don't have us one of them, in working condition." Seth grunted. He pointed to the plane. "We'd be at your place in half an hour. Course, we'd need parachutes, too—I reckon nobody's wavin' you in to land these days at local airfields. Now we've got to be pretty quiet. Nothing but whispers. We're nearly there."

He was appallingly cheerful. I wondered if I had cast my lot in with a madman.

In reality, I had not cast anything. I hadn't picked Seth. He, together with his two friends, had picked me. That pair was much on my mind. They knew that I was awake. Even were Seth to vanish into the great hereafter, I would know no peace so long as they knew what had happened, and were in a position to talk.

Be patient. *I had little choice.*

Seth stopped paddling. In silence, we drifted up to another boat. It was a squat oblong, painted some distaste-

ful color that looked in the dim light to be a drab olive-green. Two small outboard motors hung at the rear, propellers out of the water.

"Mil spec," Seth whispered. "Old, but these mothers were made to run forever. An' it has half a tankful."

"It's chained up."

"It sure is. Don't know how near the owner might be. That's why you gotta be real quiet now. When we go, we go fast—no stoppin' to pick up passengers. Climb in, I'll hold us steady."

Exhaustion made me clumsy. Seth had to be wincing as I stood up and toppled from the scow into his new find. The thump when I hit the bottom boards seemed to carry across the whole river. I crawled to the middle of the boat and lay there. Seth released his hold on the scow and came over the side as silently as a dark-clad ghost.

He lowered the outboard motors into position. The clicks as he primed them with fuel were audible to me, but I suspect that from the shore they sounded no louder than insect noises.

Seth slipped loose the chain securing the boat at its bow to a solid post on the shore, and lowered it link by link into the river. He came to my side and bent close.

"According to the control setting, the two motors are power-matched and synchronized." His whisper was barely audible, a mere breath of sound. "I can't tell if they are until I start them. Grab hold of something and hang on tight. I'm going to full power right away. Things might be messy at first."

I saw his teeth. The lunatic was grinning at me.

"That's if we're lucky," he went on. "If we're not, and the motors won't start, we'll be sittin' ducks for anybody who comes out to see what all the noise is. We can't have that. So if we don't have power inside half a minute, you and me have to get out of here. We'll go over the side. Don't worry none about drowning, 'cause I'll hold you up."

He moved forward to the little cabin and the controls, giving me no opportunity to ask, We go into the river, and then what?

I lay flat and clutched a center post around which a

thick rope was neatly coiled. It should have been around Seth's neck. I had been better off than this in judicial sleep. An electric motor hummed a few feet aft, followed by the racheting racket of a pair of starters. Our efforts could no longer be mistaken for insect noises. The insect to produce so loud a sound would be the size of a horse.

The starter motors clattered on and on. I was bracing myself for the plunge into cold river water when suddenly the gasoline engines fired in unison. The noise level went from frightening to monstrous as Seth—too soon, the engines were still cold—gave them full throttle.

The engines coughed, spit, backfired, and finally hit a rhythm. The boat surged forward on a curving course that would run us right into the riverbank. Seth turned us at the last moment, juggled the power of one engine, and headed for midriver.

He turned to grin at me.

"Synchronized, my ass." He had to shout to be heard above the engines. "But we're doing fine now. Once we're half a mile out, I'm going to take the power up all the way. Then we head upstream. And you can have a sleep"—on the bare boards of a pitching boat, surrounded by a din loud enough to burst eardrums—"and dream about home, sweet home."

Home, sweet home. Seth seemed oddly confident about what we would find there, and I suppose that was my fault.

In my eagerness to assure him that I would be able to provide equipment to monitor the condition of his and his companions' telomeres, I had omitted to discuss one crucial point. Not about the scientific techniques, which were every bit as simple as I had suggested. Given a few hours in my home lab, I could put together a sequence of observational methods and wet chemistry tests to replace the role of the defunct genome sequencers.

There was, however, a default assumption in all this; namely, that my home lab still existed.

The law admitted an odd ambivalence regarding the property rights of individuals sentenced to judicial sleep. On the one hand, I and others like me were alive. New evidence establishing our innocence might one day be dis-

covered, and we would then be resuscitated. It would thus be wrong to confiscate our possessions or to apply inheritance laws while we were still alive.

On the other hand, someone sentenced to centuries of judicial sleep, with overwhelming evidence of guilt, had a negligible chance of ever waking. We might, however, live for seventy or eighty years, until at last we died in our sleep of natural causes. What, during all that time, was to be done with our property?

The heirs, naturally, wanted everything to be theirs as soon as possible. No one is more rapacious, ruthless, and impatient than a loving family member.

The law, faced with a difficult decision, did what it often does. It looked backward for guidance, and invoked the ancient principle of usufruct. This permits an individual to enjoy the use of something without owning it, to the extent that such use does not destroy or reduce value. In other words, an heir could live in the house of a person sentenced to judicial sleep, and use that person's possessions, but could sell neither house nor anything in it as long as the person remained alive.

This took care of all cases but one: that of an individual with no known heirs.

My parents were dead. I had been an only child. Upon my arrest, anyone who might otherwise have claimed kinship rushed to distance themselves from me. After my descent into judicial sleep, my property—including house and laboratory—had come under the stewardship of the government.

The question was, what had they done with it? Left it empty? Rented it out? Made it into a local landmark, like Clara Barton's house a couple of miles away? The last idea was remarkably unlikely, but the subject was on my mind as we cruised steadily upriver.

Steadily. Seth, after the first dash away from possible pursuit, had cut back our speed. There were good reasons for this. First, someone who wishes to be inconspicuous does not roar along in the darkness at thirty knots. Second, when you can see almost nothing ahead of you, self-preservation recommends that you proceed slowly.

The boat did not have a cabin, but there was in the

bow a partial deck. It was big enough for a man to crawl under, and he would be hidden there from anything but a close inspection. When dawn approached, Seth suggested that it might be the best place for me. The place was filthy, but I was too tired to argue. I lay down on a heap of old tarpaulins and dirty sacks, thought longingly and lovingly about my darlings, and was asleep within seconds.

I awoke to the sounds of silence. The engines no longer roared, the slap of water on the bow had ended. The air was hot and humid, with an oppressive heavy feeling to it. I crawled out from under the deck overhang feeling worse than when I went to sleep.

Seth was stretched out by the controls, his head pillowed on his arms. I wondered how long he had been lying there. I had been asleep for a long time. The sun was high in the sky, the snow on the shore was melting away before my eyes. The boat sat close in, its bow wedged among a mass of overhanging bushes. The river was narrower and faster-flowing. We had come a long way upstream.

I sat down, leaned over the side, and scooped up handfuls of water to splash on my face. Assuming that Seth had told the truth about the date, this was my first wash in nearly five years. I had not intended to drink the river water—it was brown and muddy—but as soon as it touched my lips the urge became irresistible. I drank from my cupped hands. The water tasted wonderful.

It seemed to me that I had been remarkably quiet, but Seth apparently slept like a cat, one eye always open. I heard him grunt behind me, and I turned. He was lying in the same position with his head on his hands, but now he was staring at me.

"Do you know where you are?" he said.

"No."

"That's bad news. Maybe I screwed up." He moved to a sitting position and pointed along the river. "I don't know this part of town very well, but I know how many bridges there are across the Potomac. I counted them as we came, and according to me that next one—see the abutments—should be upstream of where we want to be. So I thought right about here would be Glen Echo."

"Maybe it is." I stood up. Now I felt hungry, but my

legs were far less shaky. "I've never seen things from the river side before. Once we're ashore and looking back this way I may be able to place us."

"Yeah. First things first, though."

He moved to my side and drank as I had drunk. Then he stood and casually urinated into the water. I reminded myself that the world had changed with Supernova Alpha. Anyone who hoped to survive would have to change with it. I followed his example.

The food that he produced from his waterproof bag looked much the worse for wear, old bread and cheese squashed together in a solid block. I ate my half without hesitation, and wished for more.

He hoisted the bag on his shoulder. "Ready?"

We had to move the boat, pulling on the branches of overhanging bushes until we reached a place where the bow could be run all the way in to a clear piece of riverbank.

Seth went first, scrambling up a few steps and turning to see if I needed help. I was pleased to find that I didn't. Once I had been unusually strong. With luck and exercise that strength would come back.

We headed away from the river through scrub and second-growth trees, and within fifty yards reached a wilderness of mud and gravel. It ran beside a broad empty trench with scattered puddles of water along the bottom. Seth looked at me expectantly.

"It's the C&O canal," I said. "Or it was. Something has happened to it."

"Supernova Alpha. The freak weather ripped all sorts of things to pieces. Do you know where you are?"

"This mess used to be the towpath. It runs all the way from Georgetown up to Cumberland and beyond, a couple of hundred miles. We could follow it either way, but I don't know which one will take us toward my house."

"Isn't there a way to find out?" He was on my territory now, and he knew it. I sensed his heightened awareness. "I don't like the smell of the weather. If there's something unpleasant on the way, I'd like to be inside."

"There are locks all the way along the canal," I said. If by "inside" he meant inside my old house, I wanted him as relaxed as possible. "We ought to have no problem. Each canal lock is marked with a number. All we have to do is

walk to the closest one, then we'll know where we are and how far we have to go. The lock nearest to my house is number seven."

"Right. Can you walk?"

The physical effects of judicial sleep on a resuscitated subject are small. It is ironic to reflect that my own efforts on clone stability, prior to my capture, had been in large part responsible for minimizing the deleterious effects of long-term syncope. Seldom does one derive such direct benefits from one's professional work. I felt that I could indeed walk, a considerable distance if necessary. However, I saw value in concealing this from Seth. A weary Seth Parsigian was preferable to a fully alert one.

"I'm better than last night," I replied. "But I tire very easily."

"Right. Stay here, then. I shouldn't be long." He set off to the left, along the muddy apology for a towpath.

I leaned against a mulberry tree already set with green fruit, and examined everything in sight. I had walked this towpath often, valuing its tranquil environment whenever my research called for protracted sessions of hard thought. It may seem strange that now I recognized nothing. Five years is surely a short time for an entity that has been in existence for more than two hundred years. However, we are talking of a surprisingly fragile physical structure. Twice before, to my knowledge, the canal towpath had been swept away and the canal partially destroyed by extreme weather. The Potomac River behind me was no more help. The pattern of islands was different from what I remembered.

The recent legacy of Supernova Alpha offered one advantage. My home lay on the side of the canal farther from the river. We would not need to use a lock bridge, because traversing the empty canal bed was a simple matter.

Seth was heading back toward me. I looked for signs of weariness in his gait, and saw none. He was impressively (and depressingly) tough and resilient.

He pointed downstream. "Other way. I walked to lock eight. How far between locks?"

"Variable. But lock seven is less than a mile from here." I felt, and tried to hide, my urgency. I was only a

few minutes from home. What would that home be like, after five years and more of government management?

We walked side by side along the muddy remains of the towpath. I began to share Seth's concern about the weather. It was warm and sunny, but I felt on my face a strange and gusty breeze. The air seemed heavier, dragging and retarding our footsteps. We crossed the canal at lock seven, made our way for a hundred yards along a major but empty parkway, and were at the edge of a residential territory.

Now I had a legitimate reason to hurry. We did not want to be seen. We kept an eye out for other people as we went up the hill, turned a corner, and were in my driveway.

I am, with certain exceptions, indifferent to possessions. But I cannot deny the excitement and pleasure that filled me when my house came into sight. Excitement, pleasure, and at the same time trepidation.

Long before I suffered discovery and arrest, I had taken steps to hide my treasures. I thought I had hidden them well.

The question was, had I hidden them well enough?

34

Auden Travis behaved as though requests to find space for strangers on government vehicles came every day.

"Cap what?" he said. He was bending over a thick folder, a compilation of computer listings, typewritten pages, and handwritten notes. "I can't find it."

"Catoctin Mountain Park." Art looked over Auden's shoulder. "It's north of here. I can show you on a map."

"That wouldn't help. All the transportation information is in terms of highway numbers. I need to know those. Unless he promised you a helicopter?"

The power of the presidency—and the temptation to lay false claim to it. "No. We have to ride on whatever's going. But the roads are easy once you get outside Washington. North on Interstate 270 as far as Frederick, then Route 15 north heading toward Harrisburg. We only need a ride as far as Thurmont. We can walk to Catoctin from there."

"Harrisburg is good. State capital, sure to be something going that way. Here, this ought to do it." Travis looked up at Art and grimaced. "Provided you don't mind riding in the back of a cement truck."

"It's better than the way I came down. When?"

"Tomorrow morning, nine o'clock. That's the best I can do."

"What will we do today?"

"Anything you like. I wouldn't recommend going too far because of the weather."

"It's marvelous outside."

"It won't be." Travis opened another folder and showed it to Art. "See the map? Hurricane Gertrude hit Cape Hatteras last night. The seventh hurricane since February 9, and it's not even the season. The forecasts say we'll get the tail of it later today—pretty bad wind and rain. If I were you I wouldn't go out at all."

"What about food?" Art was already hungry.

"You can eat in the cafeteria in the Old Executive Office Building. Get there through the underground passage. The food's not great, because it's from the national reserves. Tonight I'll find a place for you in the East Wing."

"We'll sleep in the White House?"

"That's right. For free." Travis smiled at Art. "I won't tell you how much some people have paid for the privilege." The multiline unit at his right hand began to buzz. "Anything else? Then check with me later for the room."

They were clearly dismissed. They wandered off into the White House interior, staring at everything. No one stopped them, no one took much notice. The only person who said anything was a short man in a check suit, who gasped, "Excuse me, I'm late" as he dashed past them.

"Oh, my fur and whiskers," Dana said. And when Art stared at her, "Don't mind me, I'm in a giddy mood. It looks like security checks apply only for entry and exit. The question is, if we go outside will we be able to get back in?"

They were on the second floor, and their wandering had brought them to a big window with dusty sunlight streaming through. Art walked to it and ran a finger down one of the panes. It left a streak.

"My dear, it's *so* hard to get good help these days. Even if you're President." Art was feeling giddy, too, if that was the word for it. He had slept wonderfully last night, he didn't have an ache or a pain anywhere in his body, and he would be in a real bed again tonight. He gestured outside. "Look at that. Auden Travis was right, and I was wrong."

They were facing south. On the right Art could see the east end of the Reflecting Pool, dazzling in the sun as its shallow waters broke into whitecaps. Straight ahead was the Monument, its solid bulk able to withstand the strongest wind. Far beyond, a dark line of clouds crept westward along the horizon. And much closer, within the White House grounds, trees bent and swirled and shivered.

It was pleasant to watch, and to know that you were snug inside; until Dana said softly, "I wonder where Seth is? I wonder where he and Dr. Grisly will spend tonight."

Art hoped for Seth's sake that it would be somewhere comfortable—and nowhere near Catoctin Mountain Park. His friends there were tough, and they were wily; but Ed O'Donnell and Joe Vanetti would be no match for Seth Parsigian and Oliver Guest.

He and Dana turned from the window view, with its first signs of approaching Hurricane Gertrude. The mood had changed. Dana's question had depressed both of them, and without speaking they headed down to the lower level. Art asked a guard how to reach the tunnel to the Old Executive Office Building. It must have been a standard question because the woman rattled off directions without thinking.

Though it was long past a normal lunchtime, the cafeteria was crowded. They walked by the long service counter, examining the choice of food.

"Auden Travis must be a lot pickier than I am," Dana said. "This all looks good except the pastry. But the *ambience*. I guess they don't want people staying too long when they have work to do."

The place was like a dungeon, plain gray walls and ceiling, dull black floor and tables, gunmetal chairs. They loaded their trays, paid—a surprise to Art; he had somehow imagined that a White House cafeteria would be free—and searched for an empty table.

There was none to be found. They were forced to sit with another couple: Scott and Jenna Fredden, according to the name tags on their government badges. The pair ate steadily and spoke not one word to Art and Dana or to each other. Art and Dana followed their example, until finally the two stood up—in unison—and left.

"Charming," Dana said when they had gone. "What do you think? Man and wife, or brother and sister?" She was not expecting an answer because she continued, "I'll tell you something odd. I've known you for three years. But until this morning, I never knew you had that scar on your belly."

"No reason why you should. I've got plenty more. You probably have some, too."

"Me? I'm a regular road map. But I don't think I'd inflict myself on the President of the United States. You've got nerve."

"He didn't seem to mind."

"It's his job to be diplomatic. Do you know what upset me most when I learned that I had cancer? I'll give you a hint, it wasn't the prospect of dying."

"If you're anything like me, I bet it was this." Art held up his fork. "See, I do this without thinking about it. My body is completely under my control. Talk, sing, dance. I could catch a ball or button a shirt. Then one day those things became irrelevant. I learned there was a whole lower level of activity going on inside me. Not only couldn't I control it, I didn't even *know* about it. I only found out what it was doing when it started to hurt."

"Exactly." Dana was staring at the fork, still upheld between Art's thumb and forefinger. "Until I got cancer I hardly knew that I had individual cells. Cells were weird little crawly things I'd studied in school, amoebas and junk like that. And chromosomes, I never gave them a thought. But all of a sudden, a test showed that there were these bits of *me,* and they copied themselves. My own cells were out of control, they were going to keep making copies until they killed me. The first time I saw a blowup picture of one of my own cancer cells, I wanted to scream, 'What are you doing, you stupid bastard? You're *me,* don't you know that? You're the same as I am, my own flesh. You shouldn't be trying to kill me.' "

Dana paused and looked around to see if anyone else was listening. They were. Three people at a nearby table got up and left. She took a deep breath. "Sorry. Do I sound crazy?"

"Not to me you don't." Art put down the fork. "I didn't have a big reaction when I received my diagnosis of cancer. My moment came later, when I was accepted into the telomod therapy program and told how it was supposed to work. I was pretty far gone, down to eighty-five pounds and in a whole lot of pain. So I didn't understand most of the details. But when they dripped the telomerase inhibitor into me through an IV, I knew the idea was to stop the cancer cells rebuilding the bits at the end of their chromosomes. I knew it was going to be hard on me, too. My own fast-dividing cells would be hit, and I was going to be red-raw ulcers all the way from my mouth to my ass. I didn't care. I lay on the Institute cot, and I watched that drip go in, and I said, 'Suck on that, you fuckers. You're not me anymore, you're traitors. Either you win, or I do; but it won't be both.' "

It was his turn to look around. The cafeteria was still fairly full, but nearby tables were conspicuously empty.

Dana picked up her tray. "Come on. I find this fascinating, and so do you. But Lazarus Club members are in the minority here. We should go."

"In a minute. Take my tray, would you." Art hurried back toward the cafeteria entrance. When he returned a couple of minutes later he was holding half a dozen wrapped packets. "Just sandwiches. But I thought if the weather gets too bad to go out, and this place closes . . ."

"Smart thinking." Dana stared at the packages. "You know what would go really well with them? Beer. I'm dying for a beer. You don't suppose—"

"Not a chance. You're in a government building."

"I know. But I'll bet the White House—"

"That might be different. You heard Saul Steinmetz. Rank has its privileges."

"Why don't we go back, find out from Auden Travis where we'll be sleeping—"

"And see what else we can get out of him? Great idea. You want to go right now?"

"If you're done interrupting my sentences." Dana helped herself to a big handful of napkins and handed them to Art to take along with the sandwiches. "On the way, let's see if we can reach the outside and get back in without going through a guard post. I'd like to take a firsthand look at the weather. People are saying that we're at the tail end of Supernova Alpha, that the worst is over. I'm not sure I believe it. Even if we are, a scorpion has its sting in its tail."

It was hardly necessary to go outside. Art and Dana stood under the shelter of an arched doorway on the west end of the White House. Even with partial shelter, the wind ripped at their clothes.

Two men in Air Force uniforms came out and stood next to them. Dana asked, "Do you know what time it is?"

The shorter officer turned to her. "Sixteen hundred hours, going on midnight. Four o'clock. Did you ever see it so dark so early?"

"I bet we'll get to Andrews just in time to be told all flights are grounded," the other man said.

"Better that than fly in this." The short officer turned up his collar. "Well, as my grandmother always said, worse things happen at sea. Come on, the longer we wait the wetter we'll get." He ducked his head and moved out to receive the full force of the wind. His companion gave a theatrical groan and followed.

Art grabbed Dana's arm as a stronger buffet threatened to knock her over. "It's ridiculous to think of going outside when the weather's like this. Let's find Auden Travis and see where we'll be sleeping."

"All right." Dana allowed herself to be steered back inside. "But don't forget beer. Unless he comes through with that, I'm ready to brave the storm."

35

Auden Travis did not lead them to beer or anything else. He could not, since he was not in his office. When they got there a note was pinned on the locked door: BACK AT SEVEN-THIRTY. BERLITZ/FERRAND: SECOND FLOOR, ROOMS 225–226.

"Which settles that," Dana said. "It's going to be a dry evening."

While they were on the way upstairs, thunder and lightning had started outside. The building had switched to an emergency lighting system, steady but dim.

"I suppose they have other things on their mind," she went on. "All right, let's see where they've put us. I've always wanted to sleep in the Lincoln Bedroom."

Room 225 turned out to be nondescript but adequate, with an adjoining door leading through to Room 226. It faced north across the city, currently the scene of a staggering lightning display. Art left Dana testing the springs of the double bed and went on through to the other room.

The difference was striking. Room 226 was four times the size, with ample room for its king-sized bed, sofa, end tables, armchairs, desk, and standing wardrobes. A kitchenette led off it, with refrigerator, oven, and breakfast table. On the table Art saw a basket, with a note from Yasmin Silvers: *He said the sight of your bare belly made his day. It made him think of the old pictures of Lyndon Johnson showing off the scar of his gallbladder operation.* Inside were crackers, bread, cheeses, an iron-hard salami, and butter. Some of them had come from an old government stockpile—the date on the cheese was 2020. But the bread was fresh, and next to it stood the main prize: two bottles of wine and a box of assorted fizzes. Yasmin had even included a corkscrew and glasses that looked like antique crystal.

Art wandered back to the other room, where Dana was emerging from the bathroom. "Loads of hot water," she said. "I'm going to shower forever. I was too tired last night and I didn't have time this morning. What's the other place like?"

"I suppose it will have to do. I've only got one complaint."

"What?"

"The red wine is all right, but the white wine is at room temperature. It ought to be chilled."

She was heading through the connecting door before he finished speaking. When he came to her she was cuddling the bottle of red wine to her chest.

"Next time I see President Steinmetz, I'm going to kiss him. How do you work this crazy corkscrew?"

"Pressure. The needle on the end is hollow. Stick it through the cork and pump. No, not like that. Let me."

While he opened the bottle, Dana examined the fizzes. "Elevs, holds, dorphs, and morphs. Good stuff. Didn't the President make a speech last year, deploring the use of fizzes?"

"I'm sure he did." Art was drawing the cork with care. "No problem for him—he's not a user."

"How do you know?"

"Too old." He handed Dana a half-filled glass. "Same as me. It's a generation thing. We did pot and booze the way new-century youth does snap and fizzes. Bring the basket and a knife."

Art picked up the bottle and his own glass and carried them through from the kitchenette. He settled onto the sofa, pulling an end table in front of them. Dana followed, but she made a quick detour to examine the bathroom.

"There's a *bathtub*," she said as she sat down next to him. "A huge one. You can wallow in it, probably even swim in it." She held out her glass for more wine. "Pour, and sit still. I want to look at something."

"You're supposed to savor it, not guzzle it." But Art sat obediently still as she came around the back of the couch and bent to examine the top of his head. "I don't know what you're looking for, but I won't be surprised if you find it. We've been living pretty dirty."

"Not head lice, if that's what you mean. But I found what I was looking for." She came around to the front again. "One more thing. Let me have another look at that scar, the one that pleased President Steinmetz so much."

Art had his mouth full of bread and salami. It was easier to obey than to argue. He opened his shirt and lifted his undershirt. Dana bent low and examined his chest and belly.

She nodded in satisfaction and sat down. "I thought so. I've noticed that you've been looking at my hair a lot. What do you think of it?"

"I love it. It's lighter. As though the sun is bleaching it."

"What sun? We've only had a few bright days in two months. Do you know what I thought, when you arrived through the snow at the Treasure Inn? I thought, he's been using protos on his hair. It's fuller and darker than it was before."

"I have *not.*" Art was indignant.

Dana laughed at his expression. "It's a generation thing. You think that using conditioning protozoans in your follicles is one step away from head lice. But then I asked myself, where could he have got them? The supply of follicle protozoans dried up when Supernova Alpha hit. I know, because I *did* use them after I started to gray. They only live forty-five days, then they have to be replaced. Without them, my hair should be growing out gray. I looked in the mirror this morning at Indian Head. Not a sign. My hair is growing in the color it was when I was twenty. And there's this."

She leaned forward and ran her finger along the line of Art's scar. He jerked forward. "That tickles!"

"I bet it wouldn't have two months ago. It was scar tissue, with no feeling in it. Did it used to be a sort of purple-red?"

"Of course it did. It still is." Art craned forward. It was impossible to get a head-on look at his own belly without a mirror.

"No, it isn't. It doesn't look like a normal scar anymore. I thought so in the President's office, but it wasn't the time to mention it. Take a peek at this." Dana put down her empty glass, stood up, and removed her jacket. She pulled her blouse clear of her pants and opened it at the front.

"Here." She squatted in front of Art and pointed to a vertical scar running from between her breasts to two inches above her navel. "Describe how that looks. Touch it, and tell me how it feels."

Her face was averted. Art ran his finger gingerly along the line of the scar. "It's soft. And it's about the same color pink as your lips."

"It didn't used to be. They carved a malignant tumor the size of a banana out of there, and because they wanted to be sure to get it all they didn't use microsurgery. The edges used to be rough. The color was an ugly purple. I hated to look at it. Now I don't mind at all. Feel your own scar. You can't see it properly, but put your hand on it. Isn't it the same as mine?"

Art closed his eyes and ran a finger along the familiar line. "It's softer than it used to be. But not as soft as yours."

"That's because I'm a woman, with a woman's skin. Take a look at this one. It used to be even worse."

Dana stood up. She slid the waistband of her pants down until it was at the level of her hips. The revealed scar ran horizontally, below her navel and across the full width of her belly.

"The Grand Canyon, I used to call it, rough and jagged and hard. Not anymore. Feel." She took Art's hand and ran it along the length of the scar. "New skin. The Institute doctors said to me, We'll give you a telomerase inhibitor. That will kill off your cancer cells because they can't reproduce when their telomeres become too short. Fine, I said. What happens after that? Well, we'll have to give you telomerase boosters, otherwise none of your cells will be able to divide and you'll develop progeria symptoms. All right, I said, and after *that*? What else will the stimulators do? Will they rejuvenate me just at the cell level? Or will there be effects on my whole system? Might I regress sexually to childhood? Might I get cancer again, all over me? Those were questions that nobody could answer. I remember Dr. Taunton telling me, 'We're not allowed to experiment anymore with animals; so I'm afraid that our experimental animals have to be humans.' That's you and me, and Seth, and Morgan Davis, and Lynn Seagrave, and all the rest of our therapy group. We are the test hamsters.

"Hey! Are you listening to me?"

Art was staring at the curve of Dana's belly. His fingers had run the length of the fading scar three times, stroking more than feeling. He blinked, and leaned back to look up at her.

"I don't believe this." Dana pulled her clothes into position. "Look at you down there. You're horny as hell."

She was right. Art couldn't deny the evidence. "I didn't mean—" he started.

"You are one sick guy, do you know that." Dana dropped onto the sofa next to him. "I sashay into your room at the Treasure

Inn, and all I have on is my shortest slip. I've always been told that I have sexy legs. So hint, hint. Result: nothing. Well, maybe you were exhausted from your journey. I come into your room the next night. We snuggle up together under the blankets. I curl up against you. Hint, hint—I mean, I'm *in bed* with you, what more could you ask? Result: you fall asleep. I wonder what's wrong, with me or with you. But today you get one finger on my *scars,* for Christ's sake, and it's *whoosh,* rocketship time."

Telling the truth had worked this morning. Maybe it would work again. "Dana, I've always thought you were terrific—looks and courage and personality. I knew you must have young studs after you all the time. You said, since you were twelve. And here's me, a lot older, hobbling around with a bum knee. I thought I didn't have a chance."

"I *hate* young studs. And you don't know how old you are. Neither do I. We might be on the brink of immortality, or we could have less than a year."

Art stood up. He took Dana by the hands and lifted her to her feet. "Come on. I may be an idiot, but I'm not that big an idiot. Tell me something four or five times, and I usually get it. You look gorgeous." He pulled her close and buried his face in her neck. "And you smell wonderful."

"I thought you were famous in your family for having no sense of smell? It's a good thing, too. I haven't had a shower in a week. Where are we going?"

"We're regressing to sexual childhood, and I'm halfway there. We're going to the bathroom. Then I'm going to fill that giant tub, and I'm going to put you in it. And I'm going to soap you all over."

"Ooh. That's more like it. What then?"

"I'm going to rinse you and dry you and powder you."

"And what happens after that?"

"Wait and see."

"Not even a hint? I'm a verbal person."

"No. Deeds, not words. It's a generation thing. Bring the wine."

Dana's naked body was not as Art had imagined. She was thinner and more muscular. Her skin was finer and smoother. As she said, the pattern of scars from neck to groin was more extensive than his own. The records of her past suffering were indented, exciting, soft to the touch.

While she sat at the dressing table and drank wine, she made him do everything: run hot water for many minutes into the eight-foot circular tub; find a monstrous plastic jug, ideal for rinsing; hunt for bath crystals and soap and shampoo and towels in the closet; and, at last, remove her clothes. She made no move to help.

When he lifted her to lower her into the water, she laughed at him. "You're crazy. Take your clothes off, too, or they'll get soaked."

He stripped, aware of her eyes. As he removed his pants he said, "Do you know what Lady Mary Wortley Montagu did when the poet Alexander Pope made a pass at her?"

"I don't, and I don't want to. But I know you. You're going to tell me anyway. What did she do, grab his canticles?"

"Much worse. She laughed at him. It's a man's worst fear."

"Nonsense. You mean it's *Art Ferrand's* worst fear. But it never happened to you, did it?"

"Not yet. Anytime now." He picked her up, stepped into the tub, and sat down into hot water that had been quite tolerable when he tested it with his hand. She laughed at once at the expression on his face.

"You big sissy. If I can stand it, you can."

"Easy for you to say." Art ran cold water and examined the block of soap. He didn't want the apocrine variety, with phages that began work on contact with human skin and removed all natural scents. He hated that loss of pheromones—one of the few things he could actually smell. "You're lucky," he went on. "Women don't feel heat so much. Your delicate bits are all internal."

"Sure, we're lucky—with ten times the chance of developing bladder infections. Men have better plumbing. No!" Art, after soaping her belly and pubic hair, was ready to move on to other matters. "That wasn't the deal. You promised me a rinsing and a drying."

"You don't need it."

"What I need and what I want are two different things. I didn't *need* anything after that first neck nuzzle. Didn't you ever hear of foreplay?"

"After my time. It's another generation thing."

"Then I guess I'll have to show you." Dana had been lying on her back, almost floating. She sat up and took the soap from Art. "Relax."

"If you do that, I won't." Art wriggled away across the tub.

Dana followed him, lathering him from chest to belly to genitals. "Go easy, or I won't last ten seconds."

"Oh, you big baby. You were the one who said he didn't need dorphs and holds. You'll be fine." She poured a jug of warm bathwater over his belly and erect penis. "There, that didn't hurt, did it? Lie back."

"I thought you wanted me to dry you."

"I changed my mind." She climbed carefully on top, and kissed his wet nipples. "You can dry me later. We have all night. It would be a shame to waste this."

Art gasped as she sank slowly onto him. Maybe it was the telomod therapy, maybe it was long abstinence, maybe it was Dana herself; but he couldn't remember such an intense physical response. Not ever. Not even—a quick stab to the heart, mingled pleasure and guilt and pain—with Mary.

The memory came and went in a moment, drowned out by warmth and urgency and lapping water. Art opened his eyes. Dana was straining upward above him, her hands on his shoulders and her face hidden. He could see the pulse beating in her neck. The past vanished. She caught him, swallowed him up, and held him in the present.

Art awoke in total darkness, unsure at first of place, and then of time. Afternoon gloom had moved smoothly into night. He and Dana had been too busy to notice. They had made love urgently, then slowly and lazily.

Now—say it was the rebuilt telomeres, you could blame them for anything—now he was interested in sex again. Hey ho, telomeres. A youthful desire, a mature appreciation. *If only youth knew, if only age could.*

And he was *hungry.* Cafeteria sandwiches and the unopened bottle of white wine beckoned from the kitchenette table.

How long had he been asleep? Dana was still sleeping. Naked and on top of the covers, she smelled of sex. *Reeked* of sex, wasn't that what people always said? So much for his family's theory of olfactory inadequacy. Or should he credit telomod therapy for that, too?

He eased his way to the side of the bed and crept through into the kitchen. Nine-thirty, according to the clock. Time for a little something. It was harder to take the cork out in the dark, but he managed it. The sandwiches were all the same, so it didn't matter which one he got. He took two, and carried them with a filled glass over to the window.

Hurricane Gertrude might be over the hill, but she refused to admit her age. Sheets of rain drenched the window. Between gusts, flickers of lightning on the horizon backlit the trees writhing in the storm.

Hey ho, the wind and the rain.

Art watched the storm, ate and drank. The level in the wine bottle sank steadily. He went back for another sandwich. He did not recognize his own deep melancholy until warm arms reached around him and he felt Dana's breasts against his back.

"It's all right." She moved to cradle his head against her chest.

"I'm sorry. I didn't mean to wake you."

"You didn't. But if you want to talk about Mary, it's all right. I know you've been thinking about her."

"How could you know that?"

"You said her name."

"Oh, no. I did? I'm sorry. I didn't mean to—I didn't know—"

"Not when we were making love. That would have been harder to take. But when you were nodding off afterward, you muttered, 'Oh, Mary.' "

"I didn't realize. I had no idea."

"Of course you didn't. Art, it's all right. Do you hear me? *It's all right.* I just wish you found it possible to talk about her. What she was like, how you met, how you lived. It would be good for you."

"Maybe. It's . . . hard."

"It sure is. I understand how hard. Perhaps sometime I'll find a way to tell you why I understand."

"You don't have to tell me, Dana. I know already." He felt her jerk away from him. "I've known for a while. It's your son."

"Who told you that?"

"You did. A mother has a grown-up son, but she never mentions his name. She never says what he's doing. She never wonders what happened to him after Supernova Alpha—not even to ask if he's alive."

"He's alive."

"That's good. If you would like to tell me—"

"No. Maybe sometime. Not tonight." She put her hand on his shoulder. "I'm no sweet young thing, Art, no matter what you may think. You've got damaged goods here. Will you come back to bed—please? And hold me."

"I'll do whatever you want me to do. I suppose there's no chance of more sex, is there? Don't get upset, that was supposed to be a *joke*."

"With men, sex is *never* a joke." He knew from her voice that she was smiling-sad. "Come and hold me, Art, tell me that I matter. And I'll do whatever you want me to do."

36

Strolling with Wilmer on the surface of Earth, beneath the light of a rising moon; during the long journey home Celine had dreamed of such an evening. There was no place in her imaginings for mud, exhaustion, and nervousness that drove her along as fast as the sticky ground would permit.

They trekked east from the Legion of Argos stronghold, relying on moonlight to guide them across a meadow and a small stream; on, through dense and clinging thickets over the brow of an endless hill; on and finally down, into the flat and swampy floodplain of a broader river.

As the first flush of pink separated eastern sky from dark horizon, Celine stopped and turned.

"It'll soon be light enough for them to see us. We have to make a choice. We can keep going and hope to find a main road or a house. Or we can look for a hiding place and wait until it's dark before we walk again."

Wilmer pointed ahead, to a scattering of dark patches in the grass across the river. "Cows. They must belong to somebody."

That was all she could expect from him: information, but not opinion. He was saying, without words, *You are the leader. You make the decision.*

Celine crouched down onto her haunches. Her thighs and calves ached. She could feel deep fatigue, physical and mental. If they found a road or a farmhouse within a mile, fine; if not, she would have to rest anyway. The riverbank, with its tall sedges and rushes and easy access to water, was a better choice than open fields.

"We'll stay here until it gets dark."

Wilmer nodded and walked forward to the river's edge. He took one step into the water, then moved sideways.

Celine saw what he was doing. No footmarks, no trail that could be followed. She stepped into the water and went after him.

"You've done this before."

"Nah."

"You grew up in the Outback."

"Yeah. But I never went outside the house if I didn't have to. Books were my thing. I read about all this stuff."

He was crabbing along the bank through shallow water. The place he chose was a dense clump of waist-high reeds, twenty feet across. Anyone lying in the middle of that would be invisible from every direction except straight above. If the Legion had helicopters, Celine and Wilmer were out of luck.

"Fill up on water before we go," she said. "Guzzle. It's our last chance before evening."

They drank from the river, eased ashore, and flattened a patch big enough for two people. Celine examined the ground before she lay down. Soft mud. Sharp-edged grasses and reeds. Low thorny plants, with spiky leaves and fruit like little green tomatoes. Tiny frogs, no bigger than a finger joint. Insects, buzzing and flying and crawling. Add to that the fear of discovery and capture and the promise of a hot and cloudless day. Rest would be difficult.

Wilmer stretched out full length and was asleep in less than a minute. Celine stared down at him. How could he do that? He must have no imagination, none at all.

She lay down beside him. She did not remember closing her eyes.

When she woke the light was different. She sat up, stiff in her neck and in the arm she had been lying on. The sun had moved across the sky, now it was hovering above the wooded hill to the west.

Wilmer was in the same position, but sometime during the day he had squirmed around. The top of his head wore a cap of dried mud, and brown streaks covered his cheeks. He looked like a figure from the past: primitive, relaxed, at ease with Nature.

Stone Age Wilmer. She let him sleep on, while she cautiously stood up and looked around them. If anyone had asked her to describe Earth in a single phrase, until today she would probably have said it was a water world. Now the right answer was obvious. Earth was a life world. It was fertile, fecund, rioting with runaway living things. Within forty yards of where they lay she could see scores of different kinds of plants and animals. They were competing, cooperating, reproducing, growing, dying, eating, and being eaten.

She sat, marveling at the mystery of her home planet, until the light faded and it was time to wake Wilmer.

When they set off again, Celine soon learned that she had made the wrong choice. A blacktop road ran parallel to the river, no more than half a mile from where they had lain. Their hideout was too far away to hear traffic, but as they walked toward the road they saw and heard battered trucks chugging along it.

Celine faced another decision. A motor vehicle could take them away, much faster than they could go on foot; but a car or truck could also be a Legion of Argos search party.

She turned to Wilmer. "Stay out of sight unless I tell you it's all right. If they get me, keep heading east. Try to get to Washington and warn people about what Pearl Lazenby is doing."

She walked out onto the road, turning when she got there to make sure that Wilmer was invisible in the shadows. The first car that came along was driven by a woman in her fifties. She gave one frightened look at the muddied scarecrow waving from the shoulder of the road, and speeded up.

Celine spent the next ten minutes rubbing mud off her face and clothes and doing what little she could with her tangled hair. Maybe it worked, or perhaps the driver of the little blue pickup was a brave woman.

She braked and leaned out of the open window. "In trouble?"

"Sort of. We were in an accident"—no point in making things complicated by talking about the Mars expedition or the Legion of Argos—"we need to get to a telcom."

"Lucky if you find one these days that works. But I can take you to a telcom nexus in Woodridge." The woman cocked her head at Celine. "You said *we*?"

"Two of us." Celine faced into the darkness at the side of the road and called, "Wilmer." She turned back to the woman. "He looks a mess, but he's all right."

The woman watched Wilmer shamble out of the darkness. "I'll take your word for it, ma'am. But if you need a ride again, I suggest you don't take turns standing in the road. And don't feel insulted, mister, but I'd rather you didn't trek that mud into the front here."

"No worries." Wilmer hoisted himself over the tailgate, while Celine climbed into the passenger seat.

"We really appreciate this. How far is Woodridge?"

"Eight or nine miles. Where you heading?"

"Washington."

"That's a hundred or more. No way you'll do it tonight. You'd best stay in Woodridge."

"Is it safe?"

That earned Celine a puzzled look from the driver. "I always thought so, though these days who knows? Five men shot in Charlottesville last week, but that was for riots and looting. Let's put it this way. I doubt you'll see anything in Woodridge as scary as your buddy in the back there."

"You weren't scared by him."

"You think so?" The driver reached down to her left and produced an old but well-polished gun. "I think maybe this helped."

She dropped them off in the middle of town. As Celine got out she said, "We really appreciate this."

The woman squinted up at her. "You're not on the run, are you? You don't seem the type."

"Not from the law. We're just looking for somewhere safe."

"Aren't we all?"

The telcom nexus doubled as a transport repair center.

"Lucky for you," said the man who ran it. He was outside, working on the engine of a big diesel runabout. When Celine rapped on the hood he emerged from under it with black oil smears on his hands, shirt, and forehead. "If it weren't for these fix-ups, I'd be long closed. The telcom system's unreliable. Hardly anybody tries to use it."

"We have to," Celine said firmly. "We have to reach the office of international space activities in Washington."

"Do you now." The mechanic wiped his hands on his pants. "You got money?"

"Not a penny."

"So how you propose to pay?"

While Celine was considering her answer, Wilmer said, "We'll tell you a story. It's worth more than the price of any telcom call."

The man looked Wilmer and Celine up and down. "You know, I might just be inclined to believe that. Let's go inside. Australian, aren't you? Then I reckon you won't say no to a beer while you're talking."

37

The storm moved quickly through the city. By seven in the morning, the only signs of its passage were ravaged trees and sheets of standing water on the Mall.

Sarah Mander sat at the highest level in the Capitol, stared vacantly toward the Monument, and sipped spiked ginseng. Last night's deluge had been replaced by a warm, gusting wind from the southwest. Shallow pools of water dwindled and dried as she watched. In the bright light of morning her face was pale and tired and revealed the faint lines of expert surgery.

"I am not," she said at last, "a morning person."

"Don't be upset if I say that's obvious." Nick Lopez was smiling, bright-eyed, and brimming over with energy. "I suggested that we meet here this early only because it's quiet. And I already checked this room for bugs. It's clean. Every bugging device I know about died when the chips did."

"What time did you get here?"

"Shortly before six. I was up at five."

Sarah Mander inhaled steam and blinked as the spiked augment hit her. "Five. In the *morning*. Are you always like this?" And even before his nod, "I hope to God I never wake up next to you. Not that there's much chance of that. I'm sure you're thinking the same thing."

"Sarah, my dear, I would never be so ungracious as to refuse *any* invitation from the House Minority Leader."

"Sure." Sarah placed the plastic cup on the windowsill. "Save the oil for your boyfriends, Nick, and let's get down to business. Why not give me your general impressions, and I'll do this when I disagree." She waved a languid hand. "I probably have enough strength for that. I'll talk more as I wake up. Ready when you are."

Lopez bounced to his feet and began to pace, his footsteps loud on the mosaic of marble tiles. "To say it in one sentence, we are recovering faster than anybody thought possible. All our submarine forces were untouched, and they have as much firepower as they ever had. We have a few working fighter planes—modern ones—in a couple of the western underground facilities. The fix-ups for older ones, fighters and bombers, go faster every day. The supply of chips from deep warehouses is bigger than expected—"

"*Old* chips."

"Sure. But they work, and the main differences are in memory. The toughest problem is making sure that the chips go where they're most needed."

"Do you think Steinmetz is doing a bad job on that?"

"No. His performance is first-rate. Meanwhile, the rest of the world is in deep shit. They're killing each other around the Golden Ring, and they're eating each other in South America. God only knows what survivors in Australia are doing. It doesn't really matter, because I don't think there are many of them. The case for a global Pax Americana grows stronger every day. All we need is for the President to lead it—"

"Which he will never do."

"—or get out of the way. I'm not sure you're right about Steinmetz. He's a bleeding heart, but he's also a pragmatist. And he's no fool. There may be ways to persuade him—or get others to."

"That I want to hear. What do you have?"

"Mixed news. First, I struck out completely with the Secretary of Defense. I don't know if General Beneker mishandled it at Admiral Watanabe's memorial service, but Grace Mackay blew him off. She seems rock-solid loyal to Saul Steinmetz."

"That's what I've heard. And I got nowhere with Lucas Munce. We can forget about the Secretary for the Aging."

"I thought you had his great-niece in your pocket."

"I did—I probably still do. But I've lost faith in her. Athene Willis told me the old man has lost it, that he's become senile and had no idea what she was talking about. I'm damn sure he knew *exactly* what she was getting at. I heard him testify to a House subcommittee a couple of weeks ago on the special problems that Supernova Alpha presents to the elderly. He spoke without notes, and he poured out facts and figures like a twenty-year-old. Highly impressive. *He* manipulated *her*."

"I thought you didn't like him."

"I don't. He's still a nigger. He just happens to be a *smart* nigger. The worst kind." She stared around her. "This place better not be bugged."

"It seems a little late to worry about that."

"Don't get me wrong, Nick. If we recruited Lucas Munce, I'd work with him as willingly and as cheerfully as I work with you."

"I'm sure you would. I'll take that remark in the honest spirit with which I assume it was intended. But it's no, so far as Lucas Munce is concerned."

"And it's no for Grace Mackay. Mixed news, you said. What's the good part?"

"I decided that since we were having no luck with intermediaries, I would become directly involved. I now have a pipeline right into the heart of the White House."

"Really? I don't suppose you'd be willing to tell me who and how?"

"Sarah, you know I would trust you with my life."

"Can it, Nick."

"All right. The person is Auden Travis, that delightful young man who serves as the President's secretary and close personal aide."

"Ah. I should have guessed. That's someone I could never have delivered—though I question whether your pipeline runs into his heart. Isn't he loyal to Steinmetz? Everything I've heard about him suggests that."

"He is. Auden is principled and honorable, and he sees his duty to the President as a sacred trust. But lovers have a special relationship. I serve on the Senate Select Committee on Intelligence. In any investigation, pillow talk is assumed—no matter how sensitive the issue. Auden pours out to me his dreams, his hopes, his fears, his daily concerns."

"And receives in return?"

"My unstinted and eternal devotion. What else? But Auden is deeply troubled at the moment. He is worried that the President is being led astray by unscrupulous women."

"I'm sure you agreed with that. Did Auden Travis name names?"

"Of course—after a little innocent coaxing on my part. The person most under Auden's skin is another aide, Yasmin Silvers. She's actually a relative of mine, a second cousin's child. Do you know her?"

"Enough to talk to. Not well."

"Auden doesn't know that I gave Yasmin the referral to help her get her job at the White House, and I don't want him to. I sense a personal jealousy there. He's convinced that Steinmetz wants to fuck her."

"The delectable Yasmin. Who wouldn't?"

"I wouldn't, to name one. Auden wouldn't, to name another. But the woman Auden is more worried about is Tricia Goldsmith. Which means that it's your ball. Did you talk to her?"

"Of course. We had lunch together, the night after she dined with the President."

"How did that go?"

"For the first half hour, very proper and sedate. Anyone at the next table would have seen a social lunch between two old friends. You have to understand Tricia as well as I do before you can have any idea how much she longs to be First Lady. She missed it once, because of some wrong information she was given. I told her that if she plays along with us, she'll get what she wants this time. Guaranteed? she asked. Guaranteed, I said. You should have seen her face. I thought she was having an orgasm on the spot. She said that the dinner with Saul 'couldn't have gone better.' Reading between the lines, she had him drooling and panting and climbing up the curtains. He's as hot for her as ever."

"Excellent." Lopez paused in his pacing. "Then they had sex?"

"No. He was ready, she could see it and feel it. But she thought she ought to hold out until he made her some sort of commitment. Keep him on the boil. She told him that she was a married woman, even though Joseph Goldsmith has apparently gone off to La-la-land." She saw Lopez's face. "You don't like that, do you?"

"I do not." Lopez towered over her, a frown on his broad brown face. "Now you have me worried. In my experience it doesn't work like that. Tricia should have snagged him when she had the chance. She ought to be having sex with him as often as he can manage it. Keeping him drained, it's the only safe way. Believe me, Sarah, I know."

He went to the window and stared toward a White House

hidden by federal buildings. The upper level of the Capitol vibrated to a harder gust of wind.

"I don't like this." With no one but Sarah to see him, he made no effort to hide his intelligence. "How do we know who else is chasing Steinmetz? How do we know that Yasmin Silvers isn't in his office right this minute, offering him a piece of her hot young ass?"

Nick Lopez was half right. As he was speaking, Yasmin was indeed in the President's office. But Saul was not present. And although Yasmin was breathing fast, it was from nervousness, not sexual arousal.

She told herself that what she was doing was legitimate, that she had permission directly from Saul himself. Back at Indian Head he had agreed that she could try to find out why Tricia Goldsmith had walked out on him before the election. He had also agreed—reluctantly—that she could tell people that the investigation was being done for the White House.

Did it matter that she would be using a telcom line from within Saul's private office? He would be out until about eleven, and so would Auden Travis. The response times here were so much faster.

She had entered Saul's office only ten minutes earlier, but she had been up and working for many hours. Awakened at two in the morning by the sounds of the storm, she had gone to her office rather than lying grieving for Raymond. With the vastly diminished telcom service, she had waited endlessly—often futilely—for data base connections to go through. Many denied her access. Even so, she had exhausted the obvious possible connections between Saul Steinmetz and Tricia Goldsmith. It was time for the more subtle connections.

The President's office, she knew, could key into every national data base. Why settle for anything less?

She examined her scattered notes. It was like a version of an old game. Pick a person, A. Pick another person, B. Now can you name another person, C, who provides a direct link between A and B? In the case of Yasmin and Saul Steinmetz, for example, there had been a connection before she came to the White House: her lying, rapist relative, Senator Lopez. The thought of him, and of poor Raymond, made her feel sick.

She went back to gnaw on the problem. In the case of Tricia Goldsmith and Saul Steinmetz, a particular time and place were involved. The connection had to exist two and a half years ago, and logically it was on the West Coast. Saul said he had been in Oregon, meeting with his advisers. Tricia had been in California, meeting with—whom?

There was no information. Just what Saul had told her that Tricia had been staying with people who were old friends from the time of her first marriage, when she had been Patsy Leighton.

Yasmin dug into the data bases using the limited query systems and cursed the inadequacies of both. A month ago this exercise would have been easy, everything in the world cross-referenced. Today she was poking and hopping and hoping.

Tricia Goldsmith ≡ Patsy Leighton, wife of software czar Rumford Leighton. Here it came, a spreading family tree of the Leightons by birth and marriage. The display was inadequate to show the full array. The results had to be printed, agonizingly slowly. Yasmin collected a dozen output sheets and scanned them for familiar names.

Nothing.

Try the other end. Saul Steinmetz's political supporters. They were, judging from their printed descriptions, a rich and powerful group. A careful inspection revealed no overlap with the Leighton clan. Leightons were Dexter supporters, not Centrists. Try again. Here were the guests at political rallies and dinners that Saul had attended during the relevant time period. The records were spotty. Again they told Yasmin nothing.

The handlers, then, those specialists who commissioned Saul's opinion polls and interpreted the results. What about them? Another half-dozen sheets, more confusing than ever. Yasmin was tired, and even the names of the polling research companies began to sound unreal. There were scores of them. Almost every one of them seemed to have done something connected with the Steinmetz presidential campaign. She scanned them, intrigued by the company names. Brybottle and Marchpane, Gluff and Aspinall, Quip Research—jokes a specialty? Crossley and Himmelfarb, Lamb and Love. Thomas, Jacko, and Nelly, the retired vaudeville team. Male and Middle.

Yasmin paused. Something was nagging at the edge of her attention, but she couldn't bring it into focus. She went on, printing lists of campaign contributors for the relevant time period, but her mind was no longer on what she was doing. What was it, what had she missed?

The buzzer by her right hand sounded, so loudly that she jumped and knocked half her papers to the ground. She thought that no one knew she was here.

She pressed the access pad.

"Yes?"

"I need to speak with the President. It's urgent."

"He's not here at the moment."

She waited for the question: "So what are you doing in his private office?" But the woman at the other end said only, "This is Moira Suomita, the State Department Acting Director of International Space Activities. To whom am I speaking?"

"This is Yasmin Silvers. I am an aide to President Steinmetz." It still gave her a thrill to say those final words.

"I see." The woman sounded more starchy than impressed. "I was told that this line gave direct access to the President's office. I will call back."

She was gone, and Yasmin was not sorry. There were more important things to do. Instead of retrieving the papers from the floor, she took the rest of them from the desk and sank to her hands and knees. She laid the convoluted Leighton family tree on the floor, with the campaign pollsters next to it. It took a while, but eventually she saw it. George Crossley, married at one time to Rumford Leighton's sister Anita Leighton, now divorced. Crossley and Himmelfarb, pollsters. Location, Palo Alto. When Saul was up in Oregon, Tricia was in San Francisco. Palo Alto was no more than twenty or thirty miles away.

Coincidence? No way to tell. Crossley and Himmelfarb listed no first names.

She queried the corporate and association listings. Crossley and Himmelfarb, the name was there, but the footnote showed that it had ceased operations more than a year ago.

Tax records? George Jarvis Crossley and Michaela Scarlatti Himmelfarb, principals. No outstanding tax obligations. No current address, but IDs for both people. Presumably George Crossley ≡ George Jarvis Crossley.

Yasmin looked at the clock. The morning was speeding away. Less than an hour, and Saul Steinmetz would be here. By then she needed a lot more than this to justify her invasion of the President's office.

Ten-fifteen, so it was seven-fifteen on the West Coast. Early, but not too early. She moved the printer out of the way, tagged George Jarvis Crossley's ID, and made the call.

It buzzed and buzzed. Just when she was ready to give up, a woman's voice came on the line.

"Mm?" She sounded barely awake.

"This is Yasmin Silvers. I'm calling from President Steinmetz's office."

"What?"

"President Steinmetz's office. The White House. Our ID should be on your telcom unit. I would like to speak with George Jarvis Crossley."

"Wait a minute."

Yasmin had to wait a good deal longer than that. She could hear muttered argument in the background, and finally a new and uneasy voice.

"This is George Crossley."

"Of Crossley and Himmelfarb, the poll research group?"

"That organization no longer exists. It was dissolved more than a year ago."

Was Yasmin imagining the guarded tone in Crossley's voice? And why didn't he ask what she wanted? Calls didn't come from the White House every day.

"I realize that the company is no longer in business. I wanted to ask about a survey conducted a couple of years ago. Do you remember a poll in connection with the election campaign of President Steinmetz?"

"We performed several such polls."

"This would have been on or about"—Yasmin consulted the calendar of events that she had constructed—"August 10, 2023."

"That's a long time ago. I don't recall any specific poll."

Maybe he had a bad memory. Maybe he was always so reserved and noncommittal. It was time to risk a long shot. "I fully understand, Mr. Crossley. It's hard to think in terms of dates rather than events. But this poll was completed just a few days before you had dinner in San Francisco with some of the Leighton family members."

There was silence. Yasmin could almost see the thinking going on at the other end. Why this call? What is the White House after? What do they already know?

"I do recall it. Vaguely."

"That's good. This particular poll concerned the election chances of then-candidate Steinmetz under certain operating assumptions regarding his marital status. Do you recall discussing the results of that poll with anyone in the Leighton group?"

"Professional ethics would never allow me to discuss the results of any poll we conducted with anyone other than the sponsor." The reply came with the speed and flat intonation of a standard response.

"This particular poll showed that candidate Steinmetz's chances of being elected were negligible. It preceded another poll making different assumptions and showing a quite different result. Was Tricia Chartrain/Leighton at the dinner party in question? And did you speak with her?"

"I don't remember. You say there was another poll?"

"Not performed by your group. This was done by Quip Research, of Denver."

"I didn't hear about that." Some surprise in the voice. Then, again, "Professional ethics would never allow me to discuss the results of any poll we conducted with anyone other than the sponsor. I must go." Yasmin was listening to a dead line.

He *had* spoken to Tricia, no doubt about it. He had told her that Saul was going to lose. Tricia wanted to keep going up the social ladder, she had no time for losers.

But how could you prove that? Crossley had hung up once, try again and he wouldn't even talk.

Ten thirty-five. Time for desperate measures.

While the call went through to Michaela Himmelfarb's ID, Yasmin wondered what she was going to say to her.

"Hello." A light, lively voice. "This is Michaela. Is that caller ID a joke?"

"No. This is the White House. I'm Yasmin Silvers, and I'm an aide to President Steinmetz. I have a question for you that may sound odd. Before I ask it, I want to assure you that your answer won't get you into trouble, no matter what you say."

"You're saying, trust me? Now where have I heard that line before? But go on."

"When you and George Crossley ran Crossley and Himmelfarb, do you remember that you did a poll asking about the chances of Saul Steinmetz being elected? One that concluded he didn't have a chance."

"Of course I remember. Look, if you're saying we screwed up in our analysis because he *was* elected, that's not true. The poll we did made certain assumptions that didn't apply in the actual campaign."

"Like the assumption that candidate Saul Steinmetz was married to Tricia Chartrain, who was once Patsy Leighton?"

"Patsy Leighton, and Patsy Stennis, and Patsy Beacon, and I don't recall how many others. Even before the poll, I could have told you her effect on the results. She was political poison."

"And George Crossley knew it, too, before the poll?"

"I doubt it. George has the political savvy of a wombat. He's a statistician, and a damned good one. Now, me, I wouldn't know a t-test from a tea bag, but I do understand political realities. So the two of us made a pretty fair team."

"He was related to the Leightons. He had dinner with a group of them soon after your poll, and the chances are good that Tricia—Patsy Leighton—was there. Do you think he might have talked to her about your poll?"

"I see where you're going. Give me a minute."

"Do you need to talk to him? I don't think he'd talk to me."

"No. I'm just trying to decide if what I'm going to say might get me or George into trouble. I don't see how. That poll and the whole election are ancient history. Here's what I think. I think George may well have told them that we had done this important piece of work. I mean, a poll for a candidate who was dating Patsy Leighton, and she's there at the time—that was a juicy bit of news. And old George gets a bit pompous when he's fizzed. I can imagine him, sitting there all smug and pointing out how such confidential matters could of course not be revealed to anyone."

" 'Professional ethics would never allow me to discuss the results of any poll we conducted with anyone other than the sponsor.' "

"I see you already talked to him. Now, I wouldn't know Patsy Leighton if I passed her in the street. But I have read her background, before we did that poll and after. As I recall, she broke up with Saul Steinmetz soon after the poll, and pretty soon she married some guy back east."

"Joseph Goldsmith."

"Loaded?"

"Lots of it. Old money, tons of prestige."

"Which makes my point for me. Patsy is a real operator when it comes to men. If she got George on his own at that party, and if she wanted information from him . . ."

"She would have got it."

"She'd have sucked him in, chewed him up, spit him out in pieces, and left him smiling. But she screwed up, didn't she? If she'd ignored the poll, bided her time, and hung on to Saul Steinmetz, she could have been First Lady."

"Don't use that past tense. She's taking another shot at him."

"That makes sense. He's the President now. Marrying her wouldn't have the same impact. But I finally have the picture at your end. Steinmetz wants to know exactly what happened the last time around."

"The President doesn't know about any of this. I don't think he suspects Tricia of anything. He doesn't even know I'm making this call."

"Well, why are you?" There was a pause. "Now I *really* get it. What did you say your name was?"

"Yasmin. Yasmin Silvers."

"Good luck, Yasmin. I don't know you, and I never met Patsy Leighton. But I'll tell you this, she's tough competition. I hope you can keep her away from him."

"I'm going to try. You've helped me a lot." The buzzer at Yasmin's side began again with its irritating tone.

"I hope I have. But remember, it was all hearsay."

"In Washington, hearsay's the same as gospel truth. Thank you, Michaela."

"Glad to help."

"Mind if I call you again?" The buzzer was still going; whoever was on the other end was determined.

"Do it. Keep me posted, Yasmin. I'll be rooting for you."

"Good-bye now. I've got to pick up this other call, it won't go away." Yasmin jabbed at the access pad. "Yes?"

"I need to speak with the President. Urgently." It was the starchy woman again. Moira what's-her-name.

"He's still not here." Yasmin glanced at the clock. "Maybe in half an hour—"

"Too late. This is Moira Suomita. I was forced to make a decision. Are you able to take a message for the President?"

"Yes." Yasmin made her private evaluation. *State Department Acting Director of International Space Activities.* The right title for a jumped-up bureaucrat with an exaggerated idea of her own worth. After Supernova Alpha there were no international space activities.

Yasmin said mildly, "I will make sure that the President gets your message as soon as he returns."

"This is a matter of great importance. Can you record what I am saying?"

"No. The recording systems are not yet back on-line."

"Then I will dictate. Make sure you get it exactly right. Have pencil and paper ready."

"I will." Yasmin waited, prepared for some piece of bureaucratic trivia. How did such people get the direct line to the President's office? The main thing was, Yasmin now knew exactly why Tricia had walked out on Saul. Six months before the election, George Crossley had shown Tricia what looked like conclusive evidence that Saul would lose the presidential race. Crossley had not had access to, and had not seen, the *other* poll, the one that showed Saul would win if he didn't marry Tricia before the election—and could marry her after it. Tricia had no time for losers. Her interest in Saul was zero if he were not President. But she had jumped ship too soon. Now, of course, he *was* President, so he was back in her sights.

But Michaela's other words. *Good luck, Yasmin . . . she's tough competition.* Michaela thought that she, Yasmin, wanted Saul—and was she right?

"Are you ready?" Moira Suomita, impatient and showing it. "What's taking you so long?"

"Sorry. I'm ready, I was waiting for you."

"Very well. Early this morning, my office received a most amazing call." Moira Suomita spoke with a pause after every word. "Are you writing this down?"

"Yes. You can speak faster if you like."

"I prefer not to. The call purported to come from two members of the international Mars expedition."

"But they all died, on attempted reentry." Yasmin's response was automatic.

"That was what I had been told. Please do not interrupt. The call came from Woodridge, Virginia. The speaker identified herself as Celine Tanaka, which is in fact the name of one of the Mars expedition. She described an astonishing sequence of events: a return to Earth using jury-rigged orbiters, which killed three of the seven crew members. An emergency landing, and capture by members of the religious sect known as the Legion of Argos. And an escape, by just two members, Tanaka herself and Wilmer Oldfield. He is a citizen of Australia, but apparently lacks suitable entry credentials to the United States. He was not cooperative. I asked many questions, despite the callers' impatience."

Yasmin could imagine. Survivors of the first Mars expedition! Heroes, the first people to set foot on the red planet, names to ring through world history. And this woman droned on about identification—their grandmother's maiden name, or their date and place of birth.

"I was unable to detect inconsistencies in their stories," Moira Suomita went on. "I therefore arranged for them to travel to Washington. However, after I had done so, I referred to my notes concerning the original plans for the returning Mars expedition. They call for an immediate notification of the President and, if he so desires, a meeting with the crew members. In view of the great change in circumstances since Supernova Alpha, I would like to know if those instructions still apply."

Bureaucrat, bureaucrat.

"Of course the President wants to see them. As soon as possible."

"Do you have authority to confirm that?"

Of course I don't. "Certainly."

"Then please do so, before noon if possible. When Tanaka and Oldfield arrive, I will inform you at once. It will be some time today."

Moira Suomita was off the line. *Before noon.* Yasmin glanced again at the clock. Eleven already. The President due, her notes all over his desk, the printer moved from its usual position, sheets of output scattered on the floor.

Let him be late. Let him be late. Just this once.

She grabbed her notes and stuck them away in a folder. The printer went back in place—not exactly, but close enough.

Yasmin was on her knees scooping up random handfuls of printout sheets when the door opened. Saul stood on the threshold, staring down at her.

"Well. Pardon me." He closed the door while Yasmin scrambled to her feet. He came toward her until his face was only a foot from hers.

"I mean, pardon me for walking into my own office without knocking. I'll listen to your explanation as soon as you're ready. But I'll tell you now, Yasmin, it had better be a good one."

38

From the secret diary of Oliver Guest.

My house is a three-bedroom brick rambler. Its one oddity, to external eyes, would probably be the disproportionately large lot size for so unpretentious a structure. The building sits in the middle of two acres of land.

The large garden had been woefully neglected. My hybrid climbing roses, so carefully bred and so lovingly tended, now straggled over the lattice frames and fought for lebensraum with wild honeysuckle. The flower beds had become weed beds. The clematis, buddleia, and wisteria were overgrown and infested with tent caterpillars.

I observed all this with mingled annoyance and satisfaction. Since there was no sign of recent cultivation, I had hopes that the house itself might have remained equally undisturbed.

The front and back doors were secured by new locks and plastered with yellow stickers: JUDICIAL CONTROL BOARD, DO NOT ENTER. *I had no keys of any kind, for locks old or new. One enters long-term judicial sleep naked, not accompanied by wallet, watch, and personal knickknacks. In any case, electronic keys were now presumably useless.*

"The kitchen window," I said. "I've done it before. The latch doesn't work."

Seth nodded. I led us around to the back of the house. On the way I paused at the herb and vegetable garden. It, too, was a wilderness of weeds. I went to the warmest corner, a patch of sun-warmed brick by the chimney posi-

tioned to catch day-long sun. The old box tortoise was still there, drowsing away the hours and years. I went across and picked up Methuselah, trying not to let my excitement show. No matter what had happened inside the house, my backup storage was intact. The complete genetic code of every one of my darlings was stored safely away here, in the form of introns added to Methuselah's own DNA. Given equipment and time, I would be able to separate them and reconstruct them exactly.

"If you don't mind, Doc," Seth said, "I'm not real big on turtles. Unless you're proposing to eat that thing, put it down and let's get inside."

I replaced Methuselah on his warm, dry patch. Not warm and dry for long, I suspected, because dark storm clouds were racing in from the south. Together Seth and I pried the window open and he helped me through. He had become more alert than ever, and his hand hovered at the gun at his belt. Perhaps he suspected that on my home turf I would attempt violent action.

He could not have been more wrong. At the moment, all my attention was focused on the condition of the house. Every counter and flat surface of the kitchen bore a reassuring layer of dust. The small dining room and living room were the same, mute testimony of long neglect. It occurred to me that my house had presented the judicial control board with an unusual problem. The living areas bore no evidence of my illegal pastime, and the lab in the basement served quite legitimate research needs. However, many prospective renters might imagine otherwise. Easier, then, for the judicial control board to leave the place vacant, until memories of Oliver Guest had weakened and faded.

My interest, however, lay not in kitchens and bedrooms. It centered on the lower levels.

Seth was climbing cautiously in through the window when I descended the steps leading to the basement. Pressing the light switch produced no result. Either power was off for the whole neighborhood or the judicial control board had reasonably decided that an empty house needs no electricity. An eerie light creeping in through dusty window wells gave evidence of the coming storm. It was just enough to reveal the benches, with their untidy equipment and incomplete experiments. Things had been moved around and presumably examined, but I saw nothing missing. I had everything here that I needed to satisfy the telomere monitoring needs of Seth and his companions.

But my own needs took precedence. Had the presence of the subbasement level been discovered? I moved toward the cupboard, at the back of which the doubly concealed door was located.

I had a premonition of bad news as soon as I saw the cupboard door. It was open. I went inside. The inner door was open also, the staircase beyond it visible in the gloom. I went down slowly, brushing away cobwebs and trying to suspend judgment. Seth dogged my heels. He had no idea what lay below. He just wanted to know—instantly, immediately, at once—if equipment to permit telomere monitoring was still in the lab.

I had observed the critical rules of concealment. The subbasement had its own supply of water and electricity, delivered and metered separately from the rest of the house. An array of fullerene batteries provided backup. When I touched the switch, fluorescent bulbs lit up at once.

The lab was revealed in all its bleak, horrible inadequacy. Every monitor was disconnected, its wires ripped loose. Every nutrient container had been drained. Hoses, severed at both ends, writhed along the floor like headless gray snakes. Worst of all, the clone tanks were all empty. Their delicate glass viewing ports had been shattered.

I could go no farther. The events of the past twenty-four hours, coupled with this anticipated but no less dreadful shock, were too much for me. I sat down on the bottom step and hid my face in my hands.

"You all right?" Seth had stopped. Still wary, he was three or four steps behind me.

"They are vandals." I could hear the shake in my voice, but I could not control it. "Ten years' hard work, wantonly destroyed in a few minutes. What sort of travesty of judicial control is this? What perversion of justice was at work here? The law is quite clear. The property of a person in judicial sleep is not to be abused or disposed of. But look what they have done to my lab—tanks and feeds smashed, equipment stolen, supplies poured down the drain. How dare *they do such a thing?"*

Seth edged his way around me and went to peer in through the broken front of one of the clone tanks.

"With all due respect, Doc, when it came to your rights I don't think they were high on anybody's list. You were s'posed to be iced down for six hundred years. Nobody expected you'd be back an' bitchin' about the state of this place. I sure didn't. I got a question, though. Was there anybody in these tanks?"

"No."

It was close enough to the truth. The clones in the tanks had been in a vestigial stage when I was arrested. No police officer had recognized them for what they were, otherwise the subbasement would not have been trashed and the nutrient supplies turned off. Also, their existence would have surely, no matter how irrelevantly, been introduced as evidence in my trial.

While I sat silent, Seth wandered around the long room. He examined everything and finally came back to stand in front of me. "Are you tellin' me that because all this is busted, you can't make anything to help me an' my buddies?"

He placed his hand on his gun. Only later did I realize that I was at that moment in great personal danger. If I could not help Seth, he would be better off getting rid of me at once.

"Oh, no, no," I said. "Not at all."

I hardly noticed him. My eye and mind were wandering the room, wondering if anything could be saved or salvaged. Reluctantly, I decided that it could not. My hope of continuing my clone work was over, at least for the time being.

I stayed slumped over, exhausted and despairing. Would I ever have the heart to start all over again? I was not sure. Then, like a sunrise, the faint light of optimism crept into my brain. Look at things positively. I faced not defeat, but delay. My darlings were safely hidden away inside Methuselah; they could stay there for years or decades. And Seth had it right. Nobody, myself included, had expected me to be alive and awake as early as 2026. Of course, if I wanted to prolong that desirable condition and know true freedom from pursuit, my "death" would have to be arranged. Did the authorities know by now that my body drawer at the Q-5 Syncope Facility was empty? Even with the supernova playing games with weather and everything else, at some point my absence would be noticed. The hunt would then be on—unless I was believed dead and gone.

"If you can, how will you do it?" Seth asked.

"Do what?" My thoughts were so far away, I imagined that he was reading my mind.

"Help me and my friends with the telomod therapy."

"I can do that easily enough," I said. "All the things that we need for the telomere work are up on the next level. But look at this.*" I gestured angrily around me. "The mindless destruction and the wanton savagery, you would think that after ten thousand years of civilization—"*

"Yeah, yeah, yeah. You're all broke up, don't need to tell me about it again. I got another question for you. You must have known that the telomod therapy has other effects than curing cancer. The second step, with the telomerase stimulators, rejuvenates. It might let somebody live forever. So why didn't you take it yourself?"

"It might let somebody live forever. On the other hand, it might produce an unexpected side effect and kill anybody who tried it. You and your group are pioneers. You certainly made the right decision, given your circumstances. Telomod risks are better than death. But I'm not sick. My plan would be to wait for thirty or forty years, see what happens to the test groups, and then *undergo the treatment. Remember what Hippocrates didn't say:* First, do no harm—especially to yourself.*"*

He laughed. "I'll second that. Come on. Let's get back up there. The other half of that saying is: Do some good—to yourself.*"*

He started toward the stairs, then paused. "We got power down here. We got lights. We got"—he went across to a faucet and tested—"running water."

"Tanks, not external supply. And the batteries will run down in a few days without recharge."

"Even so. Better we work down here than up there in the dark. Eat here, too—if we had food."

"I have—I had*—lots of it, up in the kitchen. Unless those swine . . ."*

How could I change so quickly, from blind despair to eager thoughts of food?

Easily. I was extremely hungry. Forget what the media said about me. I am human, as fully human as anyone else. At my trial, I in fact quoted in my own defense the words of the Roman poet Terence Africanus: "I am human, and I embrace to me everything that is human."

It was not a great success. The courtroom went utterly silent. I think maybe the translation I used was a poor one.

I followed Seth upstairs into the kitchen, to see what we could find in the way of dried and canned foods.

It was clear as soon as we arrived upstairs that, food or not, we were in for the night. My poor little house shook to great blasts of wind and driving torrents of rain. The afternoon was so dark that I was reduced to groping in the kitchen cabinets and passing the cans and packages that I found to Seth so he could take them to the window and read them.

This room had, so far as I could tell, not been pillaged by the judicial horde. There was far more food than we could eat or, indeed, be patient enough to examine. We settled for the first half-dozen items and carried them downstairs to where we had heat and water.

Soup, beans, oatmeal, tuna, olives, and pineapple juice, in that order, are better than they sound. Seth and I ate steadily, and stared at each other. When we were finished, he stood up.

"I'm not going to suggest starting work tonight, because I think neither one of us is up to it. I'm going to leave you down here and lock the door at the top. If you want pillows and blankets, better come up and get them now."

"There's no bathroom down here," I said.

He gestured to the sink and headed for the stairs. I followed him, and we did not speak again as I helped myself to a load of musty blankets and pillows. When I went back below to the subbasement level, I was more than ready to call it a day.

I made myself a bed, and as I lay down I reviewed the situation.

Seth's caution was perfectly natural, and in his place I would have acted no differently. He had brought me all the way from the Q-5 Syncope Facility to my own house, and no one else—not even his two companions—knew where we were.

My need for him was over. He was a burden to me, and he knew it. On the other hand, his need for me was as great as ever. The modification of equipment here in my lab to take care of the modest telomere monitoring needs of Seth and his friends was simple—for me. For him, it would be quite impossible.

I was, therefore, from that one point of view in a much superior position. He certainly knew it. He, on the other hand, had both a gun and a knife, and he was at the moment far stronger than I. He also, though this was an asset whose worth was difficult to evaluate, knew far more about the Supernova Alpha world than I. From those points of view, he held the better position. We both knew that.

What else? Well, if I didn't develop the tests to monitor his telomeres, and after a while he became convinced that either I could not or would not do it, then all he had to do was open the door and shout, "Oliver Guest. I have Oliver Guest in here." But so long as I was developing those tests, that was the last thing on earth that he would do.

Of course, when he had the test methods and materials, he would no longer need me at all. At that point he would be eager to have me arrested again, no matter what he told me. Only in that way would his own safety be assured.

I know all this; and he knows all this. And I know he knows it. And on, through the infinite regression.

I snuggled into the pillow, which carried with its mustiness a faint gardenia smell reminding me of LaRona. I was over my ghastly disappointment when I saw what those police-state barbarians had done to my cloning facility. I had no clone of myself, but I would find some other answer when Seth and I reached our unknown destination. I always had, and I always would. Somewhere, somehow, I would build again.

I see it clearly. My darlings rise from their dead

ashes. They grow as I want them to grow, learn as I want them to learn, clear of the encumbrances of dreadful unhealthy diets and half-witted parents and siblings. I make only one genetic change. They remain fourteen forever; and I possess them at that golden age—forever.

Giddy with that splendid vision of the future, I want to remain awake longer. It is much against my will that I quickly descend into profound, and regrettably vision-free, sleep.

39

By noon, Saul's day felt as though it should be ending. It had begun with a call in the darkest predawn hour.

"Mr. President?" A stranger's voice, on Saul's private bedside telcom.

"Yes." He peered at the illuminated display. Four-ten. Someone on the White House staff had made the decision to put this call through. It must be World War Three, at least. Except that every conceivable enemy was in economic and technological chaos. "Who is calling?"

"This is Dr. Evelyn Macabee, director of the Ben Ezra Sunglow Center. Mr. President, I'm sorry to have to tell you that Mrs. Hannah Steinmetz has suffered a serious stroke."

"When?"

"Shortly after two o'clock this morning."

Dr. Macabee was reassuringly calm and direct. How many calls like this had she made? Hundreds? Thousands? "Should I come down there?"

"I do not recommend it. Mrs. Steinmetz is unable to speak or see and the left side of her body is paralyzed, but her condition is stable. I will inform you at once if there is a significant change. Do you have questions or special instructions in the event of rapid deterioration?"

"What's the prognosis?"

"I cannot yet offer a meaningful one. We are conducting tests at the moment. They are somewhat hindered because the SQUIDs and OMRs were knocked out by the supernova. I will call again this evening. Do you have any special instructions?"

It was the second time she had asked that. Saul knew exactly what it meant: *If your mother's condition worsens, when should we stop trying?*

Thou shalt not kill, but need not strive, officiously to keep alive.

That would be Mother's own view. She was "stable," but stable how? A stability with loss of speech and sight and mobility, the things that make life worth living.

Saul forced the words out. "We want no extreme measures for life support."

"Thank you, Mr. President. Mrs. Steinmetz is ninety-two years old. I feel sure that you are making the right decision."

"Keep me informed."

"Of course."

Saul closed the line and lay back on the pillow. Polite, tidy, efficient. Logical. At the end of life the Gordian knot of existence, so complicated in youth and middle age, straightened and simplified. And, at last, was cut.

He would make sure that an aircraft was ready at all times to fly him to Florida. More than that, neither he nor anyone else in the world could do.

After such a call, sleep would not return. And at seven-thirty he had a top-secret briefing in the basement War Room. Finally he abandoned the effort. He alerted the switchboard that he was up and about, showered, dressed, and wandered through darkened rooms to his office. Breakfast was waiting when he arrived. Amazing. Did someone in the White House kitchen prepare meals twenty-four hours a day on the off chance that the President would ask for one?

He sat down at the web controller in the corner. To this point came all his global feeds. Before Supernova Alpha he could watch, in real time, events in almost every city in the world. Now, like Mother, he was blind.

Or almost blind. The light for the White House security system was blinking. There seemed little point in watching places he could walk to in a minute, but he flicked idly from floor to floor. Quiet, empty rooms, calls being taken from around the country and the world, guards drowsing over cups of coffee.

The surprise came from an unexpected place. In a room on the second floor, the two visitors who had removed Oliver Guest from the syncope facility were having sex.

Saul switched displays at once—this wasn't a security issue, and they clearly had no idea the room was monitored. But in that moment he had noticed their faces. Faces were his thing, they said far more than words. The two were sharing feelings that went beyond physical sensation. What he read was sorrow and comfort and reassurance. As the display roamed on through the rest of the floor, Saul remembered that closeness.

He arrived for the briefing fifteen minutes early, but the War Room was set up and the other participants were present and waiting. *When you are President, other people's time is yours.* Meetings begin when you are ready, and end when you say so. There is, of course, an unfortunate corollary. *When you are President, almost all your time is spent on someone else's problems.*

The agenda called for General Grace Mackay to lead the presentation. She provided a thirty-second introduction and handed over to Madeleine Liebchen.

The move from Indian Head to Washington had done nothing to improve the blond doctor's social skills. Saul received a scowl of recognition, followed at once by the opening words, "The first chart provides an estimate of military strength, by country and category, as of January 1, 2026."

No welcoming smile, no morning greeting—but also no posturing and no waffle. Half his cabinet could use a lesson from Madeleine Liebchen on the effective use of time. Saul hunched down in his seat, concentrated, and tried to absorb the torrent of facts. He had a reputation as a quick study. He didn't care what the assortment of staff colonels thought, but he was damned if he'd look like a monkey in front of Grace Mackay and La Belle Dame Sans Merci.

The meeting was scheduled to last for one hour. Madeleine Liebchen, presumably on orders from Grace Mackay, spoke her final word precisely on the thirty-five-minute mark. Long before that, Saul was feeling a profound discomfort. Not because he had not understood the briefing, but because he had.

"That's it?" he said, when she gave him a final scowl and sat down.

"Unless you have questions." General Mackay spoke with a straight face. Saul was not fooled. *Unless?* She knew he would have a thousand. She had deliberately left lots of time in the hour.

"I'm going to tell you what I heard," he said slowly, "and you can tell me when I go wrong.

"Our earlier estimates of this country's military strength were too pessimistic. We are helped today by four main factors—two of which I would normally deplore. First, our deep sea and deep underground resources were shielded from EMP effects and survived intact. Second, our military bases, for reasons of historical pride and respect for the past, hung on to weapons superseded by newer technology. Third, a continuing interservices rivalry produced great redundancy of fighting equipment. And fourth, intelligence community information storage, in protected Prospero environments, illegally duplicated and maintained many civilian data bases."

General Mackay said, "That is correct, sir." Dr. Liebchen raised one blond eyebrow.

Saul took that for assent and continued, "On the other hand, our earlier estimates of foreign war-fighting potential were made in the absence of facts. Now that we have those facts from overseas, we see reduced foreign capacity in every area, civilian and military. A few days ago, Dr. Liebchen told me that on the basis of her analysis—which she made single-handed—our relative strength in the world had improved by forty percent. You are now telling me that is much too conservative. A better number is more than a hundred percent. As a country we are over *twice as strong*, relatively speaking, as we were before Supernova Alpha."

"Yes, sir."

"Thank you. I have no questions." Saul stood up. His three security guards stood up with him. "I need to think about all this."

"It's good news, Mr. President," Grace Mackay volunteered.

"It may be. But remember: 'Democracy is the worst form of government except all those other forms that have been tried.' "

She looked at him uncertainly. "Disraeli?"

A fair guess, given Saul's interests. But Madeleine Liebchen gave the general a glance of infinite pity and said sharply, "No, Grace. Winston Churchill."

Saul continued out of the room. Sometime he would like to be present when those two were working together. When they were not bickering, they clearly *did* work together—and he suspected they did so with mutual respect and admiration. How long had he known General Mackay before he had dared to call her Grace?

Humans—present company not excepted—were strange animals.

But Grace Mackay and Madeleine Liebchen, without meaning to do so, had presented Saul with a terrible problem. They had no idea what he meant when he made his final remark. But he did. The overwhelming military and industrial strength of the United States was the worst situation, except for all the other options. It pointed the way to awful possibilities. Sarah Mander and Nick Lopez, and however many others in Congress they had recruited to their ideas, had a real case. If any moment in history offered the chance of maximizing the country's influence and power in the world, here it was. *It could be done.* That was the terrifying message of the briefing.

Next on Saul's agenda was a meeting with his agriculture commission. He made the right noises and nodded in all the right places, but his mind was elsewhere. Pax Americana. An American global outreach, industrial, political, and where necessary, military. It was immoral, but could you stop it? When you were on the wrong side of the argument, you could delay but you could not prevent.

The agriculture session was important, but he was delighted when it ended and he was free to escape.

Yasmin, groveling on the floor of his private office, completed the morning's surrealism. She clutched a mess of papers to her chest and stared at him with tawny, nervous eyes.

"I found out about Tricia." She held printed pages out toward him. "I know what she was doing, why she left you."

It took a few moments to realize that she was talking two years and not two nights ago. As Yasmin revealed what she had discovered, his spirits sank. The third blow of the day. His mother; the evidence that a global Pax Americana was possible technically, if not morally; and now this.

Yasmin might think she had proof beyond doubt about Tricia. Maybe she did. She was surely excited, relishing the description of her detective work. But Saul was not ready to accept her conclusion. Not ready to *believe* it. The passion, the heady excitement for each other, Tricia's absorption in everything he did, all that could not be faked. But—she had married Rumford Leighton and Bobby Beacon and Willis Chartrain and Joseph Goldsmith. Had they, too, enjoyed Tricia's blazing passion and focused affection?

It wasn't something Saul wanted to think about right now. He was relieved when Yasmin told him about the Mars expedition, throwing it in almost as a by-the-way. He forgot his own troubles.

"They *survived*? They made it all the way to Earth, when we thought that was impossible."

"So Moira Suomita at the State Department says."

She held out the paper on which she had recorded the message. Saul ignored it.

"Where are they now?"

"On their way to Washington."

"Excellent. I don't want them going to State, though, I want them here. I'd like you to get on over there, change things so they come to the White House first, and bring the whole bunch of them here with you."

"Yes, sir. Sir, they didn't all survive."

"How many?"

"Three died during orbiter reentry. Four made it back to a safe landing—but apparently two of those are being held prisoner."

"They landed somewhere abroad?"

"No, sir. They landed in Virginia. But they were captured by members of the Legion of Argos."

"*Damn* that woman and her crazy organization. They pop up all over the place. Go over to State anyway, bring the survivors."

He read Yasmin's sudden discomfort, and went on, "If you think they'll give you a hard time over there, ask General Mackay to go with you. They hate her guts, and after their last runaround they're terrified of her."

"Yes, *sir*."

"And while you're gone, I'll see what I can do to get the other two crew members freed."

As Yasmin left, Saul collapsed into the seat in front of the web controller. It seemed days since he had left it. How did you free members of the Mars crew from the grasp of the Legion of Argos? If you were ruthless and determined you invoked a domestic version of the Pax Americana. You found out where the prisoners were held, and went in with maximum firepower.

And if the prisoners were killed during the liberation process? Well, tough.

We had to destroy the village in order to save it. Another century, another President, another continent. But that particular disaster would not happen on Saul Steinmetz's watch. You'd have to kill him first.

I have brought myself by long meditation to the conviction that a human being with a settled purpose must accomplish it, and that nothing can resist a will which will stake even existence upon its fulfillment.

Now that *was* Benjamin Disraeli. It all came down to purpose and will. Saul saw only one problem. What purpose and will didn't tell you, unfortunately, was *how* to do something that must be done.

40

From the secret diary of Oliver Guest.

Seth Parsigian, I surmise, is a good chess player and a better poker player. I do not mean by this, better than I am. But in the first two days at my house, we both knew who held the high cards.

Consider.

He was totally dependent on me to produce a telomere monitoring system, without which his long-term survival was doubtful. Until that work was completed, he dared not kill or injure me. He could, of course, starve and abuse me in order to force my cooperation, but even here his power was limited. I had to be well enough to work.

I, on the other hand, daily gained in strength and confidence. Soon I would reach a point where I could vanish into the faceless multitude rendered homeless and hopeless by Supernova Alpha. I could begin a new life, if not in this country, then abroad. Travel itself might be more difficult, but travel controls and restrictions would surely be less.

All these facts, obvious to an intelligence far less acute than Seth Parsigian's, revealed themselves not in words but in acts. When I was working I could turn my back on him, fully confident that he would do nothing to harm or impede me. For him, on the other hand, constant vigilance was a necessity.

How was such continuous overview possible? The man was tough, but he was human. He had to sleep.

His solution was simple. The subbasement, from which there was no exit but the stairs, became my living quarters. I was locked down there all night, alone. It was the most frustrating situation in the world. Had the clone tanks been in working order, I would have been free to do with them anything I liked. As it was I was obliged to live for twenty-two hours a day with their gutted, useless shells in plain view, and think of what might have been.

Three times a day I ascended to the upper level of the house. There we would eat, go outside into the open air, and stroll around the big yard. Under Seth's watchful eye (and gun) I inspected and deplored the forsaken condition of my garden. I was careful to show no special interest in Methuselah, though it would probably have made no difference had I done so. Seth was, as he said, not big on turtles.

I moved all the equipment that I needed down one floor to the subbasement. There I had light and power and running water. And there I began work. Seth didn't need to be present, but of course he could not bear to stay away. He sat on the stairs, gun in hand, and watched my efforts.

I did not tell him this, but for those first couple of days he needed no gun. I had my compulsions, even as he had his. He had posed a challenging problem, in the central area where my own ego lies: How does one make an efficient device for telomere inspection, without genome scanners or anything else involving microchip technology?

After I had set up my microscope, ultra-centrifuge, electron capture detectors, and projection screen, I turned to Seth.

"As a first step, we are going to inspect the current state of your telomeres. For that, I need two things."

"Anything that helps, you got it."

I handed him two vials. "I require a skin fragment, from anywhere in your body. It can be small, all we need are a few cells. And we must have a semen sample."

Seth looked at the vials doubtfully. "Let me make sure I got this right, before I go an' do somethin' dumb. You want me to jerk off in this little jar?"

"Exactly."

"Mind if I ask why?"

"Not at all. During telomod therapy you were given

two drugs. The first inhibited the telomerase enzyme. Without that, the telomeres at the ends of your chromosomes shortened every time a cell divided. The cancer cells in your body divided a number of times, rapidly, and then died. Next you were given a drug that stimulated *the production of telomerase. This rebuilt the telomeres in your cells. Do you now need inhibitor or stimulant? I do not know. But once I have samples of both your germ cells and your normal body cells, I will use the information to calibrate the present condition of your telomeres."*

I again held out the vials, and this time Seth took them. "Suppose I'd been a woman?"

"Then I would have needed an ovum. Think yourself lucky."

He retreated upstairs, and returned within a few minutes. "Here. Scientists, they take the fun out of everythin'."

Without molecular-level manipulators—another casualty of the supernova—it took a while to separate and display a single cell of each kind. While I worked, I marveled at the prodigality of Nature. The skin cell looming large on the projection screen contained the complete genetic code for Seth Parsigian. His body held a hundred trillion such cells. From any one, a copy of Seth's body could be grown. Here was lavish redundancy, on a scale incomprehensible to humans.

The skin cell on the screen was suspended in a dichroic solution. That allowed me to color-code and zoom in on the chromosomes, and then amplify further the end section of one. I froze the display at a level of magnification where the individual molecules of the nucleotide bases could be seen.

"Look at that," I said. "There you have a telomere. One of yours, but of course any vertebrate animal's telomere would look the same."

It helps when you have seen something a thousand times before. Seth was staring at a display of the end units of a DNA molecule's curved double helix, but I could see from the expression on his face that to him it was a meaningless jumble of blurry dots. In fact, adenine, guanine, thymine, and cytosine molecules have quite different struc-

tures, and their electron density distributions as seen by a scanning probe microscope are readily distinguished by an experienced eye.

"See," I said. "We start from the end there. The same sequence repeats, over and over. T-T-A-G-G-G. And again. T-T-A-G-G-G. When you were born, that would repeat about eight hundred times. The number of repeating sequences gets less all your life. Now let's count." Under my control, the scanning probe traveled steadily along the molecular chain. I was counting out loud, for Seth's benefit rather than my own. I already saw the general picture.

"I hope you're not expectin' me to learn to do that," Seth said. "All those gizmos look the same to me."

We were moving along the chromosome into the subtelomeric region. The regular repeating pattern T-T-A-G-G-G was breaking down.

I froze the display again. "Let me make a guess," I said. "You were due to be given a shot of telomerase stimulator in less than two months."

"How'd you know that?"

"The telomere is quite a bit shorter than it should be. Not dangerously so, but it needs rebuilding. Now let's check the sperm cell."

It was of course haploid, containing only one half of his genetic code. The other half required for a complete diploid individual came from the mother. However, each chromosome of the sperm was intact. Its telomere should have been completely rebuilt, which meant that the nucleotide sequence ought to repeat about fifteen hundred times.

This time I did not bother to count for Seth's benefit. I could see where random elements began to enter the sequence. The telomere was far too short, no more than a few hundred repetitions of the same pattern of the six nucleotide bases.

"So I'm in trouble," Seth said when I explained to him what we were looking at.

"Not at all. You just need to monitor this for yourself and learn when you need a telomerase inhibitor or stimulator."

"I already told you, everythin' looks the same to me.

It's one big garbage can. I'd never learn to read it, and there's no way I could carry all this display stuff around with me."

"You won't have to do either of those things." I had made my point that he was dependent on me—more than ever, because he was close to needing treatment. "I'm going to package a set of wet chemistry tests for you. Then all you'll need to do is run through them with a skin sample and a semen or menstrual blood sample, and from the output you'll know what treatment you need. Making telomerase inhibitor and telomerase stimulator isn't hard for any biochemical supply house. I'll write that out for you."

"Great."

I went across to where he was sitting. "But before I start," I said, "I think we need to talk."

He didn't gape or frown or offer some other bogus pretense of lack of understanding. As I say, in his own disgusting way Seth Parsigian deserved lots of respect.

"I've been thinkin' that, too," he said. "Of course, before it was worth talkin' I needed to see evidence that you could do something for me. Now you've just given me that."

"Should I summarize how things stand, or will you?"

"Let me take a stab at my side, then you have a go at yours. Why don't you sit down—over there. I'd hate to have to shoot you."

From where I stood in front of him, I could, just conceivably, have made a dive for the gun. He was not to know that such a move on my part was most unlikely. My skin already contains a satisfactory number of apertures.

I went to sit down on a stool by the bench, and he continued, "Let's talk about what I want. I think that one's easy. I want the package you say you know how to make, something enough to last me a couple of years 'til things start gettin' back to normal, an' somethin' like the Institute's back in business. Actually, I want at least three of them packages. And I want you to explain exactly how to work 'em, so I can tell the other two."

"Really?"

"Yeah. You surprised? You shouldn't be. I could never have got to the Q-5 facility and yanked you out of

there without help. We got common interests, me and the other Lazarus Club members. We're all different, an' I got my own life to live, but chances are good that I'll need their help again. I scratch their backs, they scratch mine. You have a problem with that?"

"Not in the slightest. The real tragedy of the commons is that it need never have happened. A logical basis for group-level altruism in terms of individual genetic advantage was provided more than forty years ago."

"That right? I guess it didn't make it yet to West Virginia, 'cause I've no idea what you're talkin' about. Anyway, now you know what I want. What do you want?"

I had to be careful. Some of what I wanted was absolutely none of his business. It was also more than he could possibly offer.

"I want to vanish. I want to disappear from the face of the Earth, as completely as if I had never existed. As a matter of fact, that was my plan had I not been caught and sentenced. Some distant isle, some quiet beach."

"That right?" His tone implied not skepticism, but indifference. That I was speaking the exact truth was not relevant.

"Now, of course, the matter is much more difficult. I know that I will be hunted. It may not happen at once, but it will surely happen. When the time comes, I cannot afford to have left a trail. After you and I separate, I don't want you to know where I'm going. I don't want anyone *to know where I'm going."*

"That's fine with me. I don't work for judicial control, it's not my job to do theirs for 'em. But we hafta work out the mechanics. Once you make me the telomod kits, you're a free man. But if you don't want me to know where you are, I can't just leave you here."

"Of course not."

"So what do we do?"

"The place that you're going to meet your two friends. Where is it?"

My fishing was no more successful than it had been a few days earlier. Seth smiled and said, "I don't recognize a need to know there, as my old spook buddies tend to say. Why are you askin'?"

"Is it in a city, or somewhere off in the country?

That's all I want to know. If it's in the city, I don't want to go there. If it's out in the wilderness, that would be fine with me. I'd give you your telomod kits and take off from there."

"Could be. Let me think about that."

"I assume that we would require ground transportation."

It was more fishing on my part, but Seth's casual, "Don't worry your head none about that. I'll find whatever we need," told me that the information was not particularly useful.

"Let me think about it," he said. "It might work, you goin' with me. I'll be back at dinnertime, and we can talk things over some more."

How much mutual trust did we have? Let me put it this way: he backed up the stairs.

He had, quite reasonably, gone away to consider the dangers and advantages of my proposal. One danger, of course, was that I might cheat him by providing a telomod therapy kit that either did nothing or led to positive damage. Another possibility was death. I might find a way to kill him and his two fellow patients, thereby eliminating any chance that they would assist the judicial authorities in pursuing me.

The advantage, from his point of view, was that his two friends—I use the term loosely—would have an opportunity to explore the telomod therapy kits, and to ask me questions about its use. He would have two more people to help watch me. Finally, he would be on the territory of his choice, whereas my knowledge of this house presently offered me tactical superiority. If deadly violence were to be committed, he was like me. He would think it better to give than to receive.

I sat down to do my own serious pondering. In the language of chess, we were well into the middle game, and now we were defining our positions as we approached the endgame.

Did I understand Seth well enough to know how many moves ahead he thought, and what kind of traps he was apt to set?

How far inside me did he see? I have always felt

myself to be rather inscrutable, but it is just the kind of self-confidence which can so easily prove fatal.

According to Lord Macaulay, Man is so inconsistent a creature that it is impossible to reason from his beliefs to his conduct. I have never been persuaded of that. I certainly do not think that it applies either to me or to Seth Parsigian.

41

The President of the United States was not as Celine had imagined him. Saul Steinmetz was smaller, older, and too pale. He seemed almost unbelievably weary as they came into his office. But his eyes were warm and understanding, and when he smiled at you it lit up his face.

"Not quite the return that you deserved, or that I'd hoped you'd have," he said. "No big parade down the Mall, no bands and medals and dinners and speeches. Well, we'll get to that eventually. Welcome home."

He waved to the sideboard by the wall of his office. "Something to drink?"

The next half minute of conversation left Celine confused. It was all small talk, about things like weather and Washington. The President made no mention of the worldwide devastation caused by the supernova, and he showed little interest in the Mars expedition itself.

So why were they here?

Saul Steinmetz made it clear at last, with a quiet, "Now, tell me about your return to Earth. Tell me in particular what you know about Pearl Lazenby and the Legion of Argos."

In spite of his easy manner, he didn't waste much time. Three people had been ushered out of his office as Celine and Wilmer came in. Half a dozen more waited stoically in the antechamber.

The woman general and the beautiful young aide who had brought them to the White House stayed. Celine knew that General Grace Mackay was the Secretary of Defense, but the aide's name rang no bells. However, she sat down with the others without being invited. Yasmin Silvers was obviously an insider.

Celine gave her description of the failed reentry that had killed Zoe Nash, Ludwig Holter, and Alta McIntosh-Mohammad. She emphasized that the data from the first orbiter had been key to the second orbiter's survival. She caught the wag of the finger that Steinmetz gave to Yasmin Silvers, and realized that the aide was taking notes. Something would be done to memorialize the three dead crew members.

The President showed less interest in the story of the *Clark*'s successful reentry, until the orbiter made its emergency landing and the surviving crew members were met by followers of the Legion of Argos. Then he leaned forward and asked, "The head of the Legion—Pearl Lazenby. Did you meet her?"

"Several times."

"I don't know if you realize this, but she was sentenced to many centuries of judicial sleep for multiple terrorist actions. Her followers removed her from the syncope facility less than two weeks ago. What are your impressions of her?"

"Enormously dangerous." Celine repeated Jenny Kopal's estimate that the Legion of Argos had more than a hundred thousand followers armed and ready to act. "They're her absolute slaves. Anything she tells them to do, they do. As soon as she gives the word, they'll start a 'holy cleansing.' If you're not white, then you'll be doomed."

"Jews, too, for a bet. We're on everybody's hit list. When is this supposed to happen?"

"Any moment. That's why we felt we had to escape and give a warning."

"Do you think she believes what she tells her followers?"

"Absolutely. She sees visions. When that happens, she becomes the Eye of God and therefore infallible. When she's not the Eye of God, you think you're talking to a nice and persuasive lady. That's one reason she's so scary."

"Anyone can say they see visions. Did you hear any of her prophecies?"

"That's the other disturbing thing. She prophesied her own 'resurrection'—her escape from the syncope facility."

"Wishful thinking."

"But it happened. And she predicted Supernova Alpha, or at least something you could easily interpret as that. Floods and fires and dust storms, freak weather and the collapse of technology."

"Typical apocalyptic prophecies. Anything specific?"

"Yes. She claims to have predicted the date when it would happen."

"Which puts her streets ahead of any of my advisers." Saul Steinmetz turned to Wilmer, who was sitting eyeing the weather satellite displays on the wall opposite. "Did you meet her, too?"

"Yes."

When that seemed to be the full extent of his answer, Celine added, "Dr. Oldfield spent much more time with Pearl Lazenby than I did."

"Oh?" Saul turned his full attention to Wilmer. "Why was that?"

Wilmer frowned and rubbed the bald spot on the top of his head. "I dunno. I guess I got fed up with her prophecies, because it seemed like what she was telling us was a load of old cobblers. So I gave her a few prophecies of my own to chew on. She seemed to like 'em. She kept asking me back for more."

"You do prophecies, too?" Saul spoke to Wilmer, but his eyes were on Grace Mackay and Yasmin Silvers. *What sort of nut have you brought in here with you?*

Wilmer grinned. "Nah. What I gave her was science. Pearl Lazenby doesn't know the difference. I told her about global disasters that are going to happen half a century from now. They aren't predictions, they are guaranteed effects of Supernova Alpha. But she believes they are prophecies."

"The supernova is going to have an effect on Earth, fifty years in the future?"

"Fifty years, give or take ten years. Depends on particle speeds. A huge effect. I told her that, too."

"Why don't you tell me—the whole thing."

"You mean nobody's briefed you on it before?"

Saul looked at General Mackay. She nodded. "Yes, sir, they have. Weeks ago, just after the gamma pulse. Dr. Vronsky. He did it twice."

"And I suspect I didn't understand a word he said."

"It didn't matter at the time, sir. You had more urgent priorities."

"I'm not sure that's true." Saul turned again to Wilmer. "Go ahead. Keep it simple."

"It *is* simple," Wilmer said. Celine jabbed him in the ribs with her elbow. "All right. Simple. Alpha Centauri goes supernova. It shoots out a lot of stuff, visible radiation and gamma rays and particles. And I mean a *lot* of stuff. Enough to fry any planets it might have. We're lucky enough to be far away, we survive. We get the visible light, then a few weeks later the gas shell around the star ruptures and we get the gamma pulse. If Earth had been lucky the gammas would have squirted out in some other direction and missed us. But they didn't. They zapped Earth and the EMP wiped out most of the electronics."

"Fifty years," Saul prompted.

"I'm getting there. Everything that hit us so far was traveling at the speed of light. Gamma rays, visible light, neutrinos. But that's only a small fraction of the energy that a supernova releases. A lot more energy comes out as high-energy *particles.* And a particle can't travel as fast as light."

"Why not?"

"Well, I'm talking about a particle with mass. A zero mass particle, like a neutrino, travels at the same speed as light. In fact, it has to. But when an ordinary particle is accelerated to a high velocity, up close to light speed, relativity takes over. The amount of energy that you need to accelerate a particle relativistically becomes—"

"Dr. Oldfield, I hate to interrupt. Blame it on a defective education, but when two particular words appear in a briefing, I know that from that point on I'm not going to understand a thing. One of them is *relativity.* The other is *entropy.* I concede it, a particle can't travel as fast as light. What then?"

"Well, it travels slower than light. In the case of particles blown out of a supernova, the actual speed falls into a range. The peak of the velocity distribution, as I calculate it, falls right about eight and a half percent of light speed. Which gives the result that I mentioned."

He paused, gave the top of his head a last rub, and sat back.

"Finish it, Wilmer," Celine said grimly. "I've told you a hundred times. Dot the *i*'s and cross the *t*'s."

"What? Oh." Wilmer turned back to Saul. "The Alpha Centauri system is one and a third parsecs away from Earth. That's four point thirty-four light-years. So a particle that travels at eight and a half percent of light speed will take a little more than fifty-one years to get here. There's slop in the calculation, so half a century is about as good an estimate as you can get."

"Do you know what the effects will be, when the particles hit us?"

"No. I don't think anybody does. But I'll put it in energy terms. Earth—and the whole solar system—will be hit with at least ten times as much energy as we received from the visible and gamma radiation."

" 'In the long run, we are all dead.' That takes on a new meaning. Could it wipe out life on Earth?"

"Oh, I very much doubt that. Single-celled and oceanic forms will presumably survive. But it might make life impossible for humans."

"Actually, that tends to be my primary concern. Sponges and oysters will have to look after themselves." Saul turned to Grace Mackay. "See if you can find Dr. Vronsky, would you, and ask him to join us. And, Yasmin, tell the people waiting for me that I have to cancel."

"They include the French Ambassador, sir. You know what he's like. He will not be pleased."

"Life is tough all over. Give him a bottle of California wine, that should silence him one way or another. Dr. Oldfield, you paint a bleak picture. Is there anything at all that can be done to prepare ourselves for what's coming?"

"Many things. And fortunately, we have plenty of time. If you are interested only in human survival, dirt and rock provide excellent protection. It's not much of an answer, but we could follow Pearl Lazenby's example and move underground."

"Triumph of the Mole People. *'Then will I headlong run into the earth.'* I don't like that answer at all, it didn't work for Faust. What else?"

"I don't like it, either. The best solution is to stop the particle storm from hitting us."

"How would you propose to do that? Move the Earth?"

"No. Build a shield. Out in space."

"Wait a minute, Wilmer." Celine could see he was getting fired up, and the President's eyes were popping. Another man, a heavily built stranger with prominent brow ridges, had entered the room with General Mackay, but it was not the time to stop for introductions. She went on, "You never talked about this to any of us."

"That's because nobody ever asked me what we might be able to do." Wilmer turned again to Saul. "It sounds impossible at first, because the shield would have to be so big—about ten thousand miles across, and placed right between Earth and Alpha Centauri. But it's not nearly as bad as it sounds. You wouldn't make a *solid* shield. The good thing about the particles on their way here is that almost all of them are ionized—they carry charges. So you can divert them with an electromagnetic field. The shield I'm talking about can be a mesh of superconducting wires, thin as gossamer but carrying currents. Shape it correctly, and the rain of particles slide right around the lines of force. They don't hit the shield, and they don't hit the Earth."

The man by the door said, "What about momentum transfer?"

Wilmer nodded. "A valid question. I don't know the answer, but maybe we could balance it against gravitational forces."

"I think the forces would sum rather than cancel. Maybe use solar radiation pressure?"

"Dr. Vronsky," Saul interrupted. "Are you saying that this idea is technically feasible?"

The newcomer frowned. "*Technically* feasible? Assuredly. Admittedly, there are a thousand details to be worked out, but the technical problems are not the difficult ones. Engineering is another matter. A shield of this kind would require a space construction effort many thousands of times greater than has ever before been attempted."

"And thousands of times more expensive."

"Assuredly. It would call for global cooperation, and global resources."

"That's my department. I'd like you and Dr. Oldfield to begin at once with the 'engineering details.' " Saul stood up. He held out his hand to Wilmer, and then to Celine. "You've not had much of a welcome to Washington. If it's any consolation, no one in my whole life has ever given me as much to think about in so short a meeting. I will feel honored if you can have dinner with me at the White House tomorrow."

It was a dismissal, no matter how cordial. Somehow Celine was outside the door, with Wilmer at her side.

He said, "I didn't get the chance to tell him about the other possible ways you could protect from the supernova particle storm."

"No, you didn't. And I'll tell you another thing, you're not going to talk about them tomorrow night. How often do you get a chance for dinner with the President?"

"And the other thing, about Supernova Alpha."

"The fact that it's impossible, according to current theories? I don't think you'll get far with him on that one. You don't get far with *me*."

"You don't understand. It's not just close to impossible or

marginally impossible. It's flat-out, throw-away-all-of-physics impossible."

"So what are you suggesting?"

"That it wasn't a natural event. That something gave Alpha Centauri a helping hand."

"Wilmer." Celine sighed. "Let's put our problems in a stack. First priority: try and get the world here back to normal. Second priority: worry about what will happen fifty years from now. And you know what? There's only room in my stack for two problems at a time."

"If somebody or something could cause a star to go supernova—"

"Not today, sweetheart. Not with me, at least. Try it on Dr. Vronsky." Celine went to the window. "As for me, I'm going outside there. Want to come with me?"

"Sure. But the President told us—I mean, Dr. Vronsky is probably keen to begin work. I mean—"

"That's all right." Celine stretched up to give him a kiss on the cheek. "I was just checking, to see if you were back to normal. You are. You go play games with Dr. Vronsky."

"But what about you?"

"I'll be fine. I'm going to walk in the sunshine, and I'm going to daydream that I'm safe home on Earth, and I'm going to imagine that all my responsibilities are over. And then I'm going back to being the same insecure, nervous worrier that I always wanted to be."

Yasmin hung back when the others left. Saul gave her an odd look, but he didn't tell her to leave. Since the night at Indian Head they had yet to redefine their relationship.

"I suppose it's none of my business, sir. But I wondered what you did with the information about Tricia Goldsmith."

"Do you honestly believe that it's none of your business?"

"I suppose I don't. Or I wouldn't dare ask you."

"In that case, I'll tell you. I haven't done a thing—not even run a check on why Crossley and Himmelfarb went out of business. But I've thought about it more than you would believe." He stared at her steadily. "You're smart, and hardworking, and ambitious, Yasmin. You may have what it takes to go all the way in politics. Would you like to find out if you do?"

"Yes, sir. Unless I have to do something, well, you know—"

"Nothing illegal—though in politics it wouldn't be a first.

You told me you'd like to learn all I know. I'm going to give you that chance. There will be a meeting here tomorrow afternoon. It's probably going to be the most difficult session in my life."

"Do you want me to attend it?"

"You can't. That would be an absolute impossibility. I want you to watch and listen, and we'll talk about it afterward. I'll have a secret camera here in this office."

"Won't whoever you meet with expect that?"

"I'm sure they will. It won't make any difference. I'll be the one making the pitch, they'll mostly be listening."

"Very good, sir. Is that all?"

"Send Auden in. I need to have a word with him, too."

"Yes, sir." Yasmin began to walk out, but she hesitated at the door. "You know, if there's any way that I can help you to deal with Tricia, I'll do it gladly."

"Don't tempt me." He smiled. "Not yet, at any rate. There's too much going on."

"It's an open offer." Yasmin walked through to the outer office. Auden Travis stood by his desk with a distressed expression on his face. He was holding a telcom receiver. She said, "Are you all right, Auden?"

"No, I'm not. I was, until half a minute ago. I just got a call. The President's mother died twenty minutes ago. I'll have to tell him."

"He wants to see you anyway. Shall I tell the crew at Andrews to prepare Air Force One?"

"Better do that. Say, for a takeoff in half an hour."

Yasmin looked after Auden as he left. She was upset by the news, as he was, but her first shameful reaction had been a different one. *I hope Saul gets back by tomorrow afternoon, so I can be in on that special private meeting.*

Is that what it takes to go all the way in politics? Ambition first, everything else back in the pack?

And if it is, would any sane human want *to have what it takes?*

42

Auden Travis had been in a huge hurry. He stared at Art and Dana as though he had never seen them before in his life. Then he frowned and said: "Oh, yes. On the street south of the White House. Be there by eight forty-five. There's a small change, but they're expecting you. You'll have to tell the driver where you want to be dropped off, I wasn't sure."

Art and Dana had been up since seven, but couldn't find Auden or anyone else until it was past eight-thirty. They rushed away at once. By the time they passed the White House checkout points and were through the south gate, a far-off church bell had struck the quarter hour.

They surveyed the street. A dozen vehicles were parked there, but nothing remotely like a cement truck. Dana was saying, "Do you think it went without us?" when a frail, birdlike man in a dark green uniform and peaked cap came up behind her and said, "You the two for Harrisburg?"

He looked as though a random gust of wind would be enough to send him airborne. Dana turned. "Yes. Except that we want to be dropped off near Thurmont."

He pointed his sharp nose at her and cupped a hand to his ear. "Eh? Damned implant don't work no more."

"We want to be dropped off near Thurmont."

"Eh?"

"THURMONT. WE HAVE TO GET OFF AT THURMONT."

"Ah. You are the ones, then. Let's get moving. There was a change of plans, see, I'm supposed to be up in Harrisburg by midday. In a pig's ear."

He led them to a long, sleek limousine with tinted windows.

"This?" Art said.

"Eh? Oh, yes. I know it's old, and it drives like a barge. But once we're out on the open road you'll see it goes just fine."

"This is luxury," Dana said. "We thought we'd be riding in with a load of cement."

She and Art climbed into the back. The wall between the rear compartment and the driver had space for a bar and entertainment unit, now both long vanished. The seats were comfortable, but the brown fabric covers were old and worn.

So, it seemed, was the engine. They moved away in a cloud of blue smoke that a year ago would have made the pollution monitors of the city's AVC system spring into action and turn off the offending vehicle's engine. Today the limousine rolled on unimpeded. The only obstacles to progress were the traffic cops, unused to controlling with hand signals a flow of improvised methods of transportation that ranged from handcarts to bulldozers. Art noticed that every driver of a motor vehicle seemed to be eighty years old.

The weather had become bright and pleasant after the storm of the previous night, and the gusty wind had little effect on the heavy car. But the signs of recent devastation were everywhere: burned-out buildings, shattered storefronts, hulks of useless vehicles waiting to be towed away, ominous body-sized areas marked off on roads and sidewalks. In spite of everything, people were on the streets in increasing numbers. It was enough to suggest that, in this area at least, the worst effects of Supernova Alpha were over. Recovery was finally on the way.

Art and Dana sat, side by side and silent, all the way through the northern suburbs and up onto I-270. Finally she sighed and said, "All right, I know I talked too much last night. I shouldn't have gone on and on that way, and I'm sorry."

Art turned and stared. "Do you mean about your son? I didn't mind at all. I knew how hard it was for you to tell me what he did, and why he's hiding out down south under a false name. But it just made me feel closer to you. I liked that. It wouldn't be fair if you had to listen to me, and I didn't listen to you. And I did my own share of talking—more than I ever have to anyone."

"But now you're wishing you hadn't."

"I'm not."

"I think you are. You haven't said two words to me in over an hour. And your face says you're upset."

"I am. But it's not with you. I thought last night was wonderful, all of it. I'm worried about today. What will happen when we get to Catoctin Mountain Park?"

"I've been relying on you to answer that. I've never been there, and it's your home ground. You don't think Seth and Oliver Guest will already be up there, do you?"

"I doubt it. They would have to have traveled awful fast. But even if they're not there, we have to answer some questions. I guess I'm having second thoughts. When we were at the Treasure Inn, it seemed obvious. We had to wake Oliver Guest, so he could tell us how to continue our treatments. I hope he does that. But suppose he comes through, and we get what we want. What are we going to do with Oliver Guest *afterward*?"

"I don't know." Dana looked forward. The glass partition between the front and back of the car was intact, and the driver was unlikely to hear her even if she screamed. Even so, she lowered her voice. "We can't just let him go. We'll have to turn him in to the authorities."

"I agree. But what will Oliver Guest have to say about that? He must have thought about it. He knows that whether he helps us or not, his only real hope is to escape and hide. We can't protect him forever. He may be crazy, but he's not stupid. I'm beginning to think *we* were crazy, waking him up."

"So what do you want to do?"

"A couple of things. First of all, I don't want you there when I go to my house. Suppose that Oliver Guest went there with Seth, then found some way to overpower him? He could be there now, waiting to dispose of us, too."

He knew before he finished speaking that he had made a mistake. Dana's face changed from concerned to furious.

"What century do you think you're in, Art Ferrand? You've got this poor helpless little female, so the big strong man has to make sure she stays out of danger. Is that it? Well, your way of thinking was old-fashioned before I was born—before *you* were born. You're not Sir Galahad, and I'm not the Lady of Shalott."

"Sir Lancelot. You're mixing knights."

"Fuck the knights. You know what I mean. I had as much to do with pulling Oliver Guest out of cold storage as you did. If there's danger ahead, I helped make it."

"All right." Art held up his hands. "I surrender. It's just that I care what happens to you. I've got a personal interest in seeing that parts of you don't get damaged."

"That's fair. It works both ways. I'm not finished with you, either. But it doesn't mean you protect me. It means we *share* dangers, and protect each other."

"I think it means we try to avoid danger. When we can't, you want to be in with me every step of the way. I accept that—even if I don't really like it. But I still don't want to head straight to my house. We might find out when it's too late that Oliver Guest has killed and eaten Seth and has a booby trap waiting so we can be dessert."

"So what's the answer? Do you have one?"

She was much calmer. Art risked a hand (*friendly*, not protective) on her knee, and it wasn't smacked away. "Funnily enough I do have an answer, though I didn't two minutes ago. We don't go straight to my house."

"Where do we go?"

"Somewhere close by. And we enlist reinforcements."

Joe Vanetti and Ed O'Donnell were surprisingly restrained in their reactions. Joe, at one point in Art's description of his actions over the past two weeks, said, "You dumb shit." Ed confined himself to shaking his head and staring at Dana's calves. They were spattered with mud from the mile walk along a sticky dirt road, but Art didn't think that the mud was the main object of interest.

He was almost done with his story—minimizing the dangerous and experimental nature of the telomod therapy itself—when Ed's wife, Helen, appeared. She greeted Art, was introduced to Dana, and rounded on Ed. "They've been here an hour, and you've never offered them a bite to eat?"

"They've got a drink."

"And you think that's the same thing, you drunken Irish sot? Come on, dear"—to Dana—"we'll be through to the back kitchen, and leave these daft devils to talk. They're worse than animals. When there's women around the men won't feed themselves, and if *we* don't feed them they turn on us."

Ed waited until they were gone, then said, "That's it. Your friend's in for the third degree. By the time Helen's done with her, Dana's back teeth will be counted and numbered. She won't have a secret mole or birthmark left."

"He knows where those are already." Joe nodded toward Art. "Look at the man. Did you ever see such a picture of mindless sexual satisfaction?"

"Ah, don't be hard on him. It's been a long time coming."

Ed and Joe, not for the first time, spoke as though Art were not in the room.

"Only he's trying to make up for it all at once," Ed went on. "It's a miracle he's not gone blind."

"She must be the blind one."

"Not only that, you can see that it agrees with him. He looks healthier. How long's it been since you had your leg over, Art?"

"What do you think of Dana?" Art, with mass murderers half a step behind or maybe ahead of him, interrupted with a more important question.

"She's great," Joe said. "Sweet and sexy and sensible. Just what you need—what you've needed for all these years. Though I can't think what she's doing hanging around with you." Ed nodded agreement, and Joe went on, "And why you'd talk a nice, sane woman like that into the maddest scheme I've ever heard of, that's beyond me. Oliver Guest, for God's sake. And by the sound of it, your friend Seth Parsigian's as bad or worse. Why didn't you go the whole way and take Frankenstein along to wake up Dracula?"

No point in telling Joe and Ed that Dana had been as keen on the idea as he was—or that Seth had pushed both of them. No point in mentioning that nothing in the past couple of weeks had been normal, not even here. On the trek up to the house, Art had noticed three ominous crosses on top of piles of dirt, a few hundred yards off the main road. Catoctin Mountain Park seemed quiet, but Supernova Alpha had left its marks of violence everywhere, not just in the cities.

"All right, so I was an idiot." Art refused the offer of another drink. "I can admit that, and it doesn't help me. Here's my problem: I don't know if Seth and Oliver Guest are dead or alive. I don't know where they are, and I don't know what they're doing. What I do know is that Seth has my address. He got that, and the location of my house, from one of the maps I had. I want to go to my place and find out if they're already there. If they're not, I'll stay in my house—"

"Terrible idea," Ed said, and Joe nodded agreement. "Suppose Oliver Guest has done away with friend Seth," Ed continued, "and he arrives in the middle of the night. Don't you think, to make sure you don't cause trouble, he'd decide it's simplest to blow you and your whole house away?"

"He has no way to do that." But Art knew that was a poor assumption. He didn't know what Guest might be able to do. Or Seth, for that matter.

"You check the place," Ed went on, "and you keep it under observation. But you don't leave yourself a sitting duck."

"But I have to stay—"

"Here. You and Dana have to stay here."

"No. I don't want you involved. It could put you in danger."

"Then you shouldn't have come here at all." Ed stood up. "Let's go over to your place, see what's happening there. Joe?"

"What do you think? Rifles?"

"I guess so. Shotguns have too much spread. Semiautomatics, I'd say." Ed turned to Art. "See, we don't want to spoil your need to look brave and manly to your girlfriend. You can go up to your house by yourself. But we'll keep you covered."

"What about Dana?"

"She'll stay here, of course, safe with Helen."

"You think so?" Art stood up also. "Fine. I'm going to let the two of you explain that to her."

The approach to Art's cabin revealed no sign of a wheeled vehicle and no footsteps. The ground was drying, but any car or a person of normal weight would have broken through the thin crust of dried mud.

That was only partial reassurance. You could get to the building a hundred different ways, straight across the fields and up the hill, or down from the mountain park. Art walked cautiously toward his own front door. He had left it just a couple of weeks ago, two weeks going on years.

Dana was not with him. To Art's great irritation, when Ed and Joe suggested that she stay behind with Helen, she had meekly agreed. She had also stuck her tongue out at him.

The door looked exactly as it ought to, locked and with the little red tag on the left side in the I AM *OUT* position. Art didn't have his keys. They were in a toolbox on the tractor he had ridden south, which was now God-knows-where. He stooped down to retrieve the spare from under the foot-scraper, aware as he straightened up that two rifles were lined up on the house. He suspected that they were aimed at the door, which meant right at his back.

He breathed deep, inserted the key into the lock, and pushed the door open. Everything seemed exactly the way that he had left it—even the plate and dirty coffee cup on the table. He took a step inside.

All quiet.

He turned and waved. Joe walked slowly toward the house,

his finger on the rifle's trigger and the safety off. Ed came along thirty steps behind, covering him.

There were few places where anyone or anything could hide. Inside a minute, Art could nod and say with confidence, "I'm sure. They haven't been here yet."

"So what do we do now?" Ed asked. He held the gun easily, a man who often carried his rifle or shotgun hour after hour, ready to aim and shoot and kill game that might be gone and out of sight in a fraction of a second. Joe was outside again, standing watch.

"Well, I wish you'd done it before you came in." Art looked at the trail of mud that the other two had carried in on their boots. "I'll have to clean this mess up. But one thing I'm not going to do is lock the place. I don't want my door smashed in."

"It's nice to see you have your priorities in order. You don't mind being turned into chopped chicken liver, so long as your house stays intact and the floor's not dirty."

"I think that you two should go back home, Ed. I'll stay and keep an eye on this place."

"Very rational. So you stay here how long. And you eat when? And you sleep when? And when it rains like mad or gets freezing cold, you do what? You sure as hell can't stay *inside* this house and wait for Frank and Drac to arrive."

"I don't want you and Joe, or Dana or Helen or Anne-Marie, exposed to danger."

"I see no reason why we should be. Seth Parsigian knows about this place, but he doesn't know where me and Joe live. He doesn't even know we exist. He's not going to do a local home survey when he gets here, he has other things on his mind."

Art hesitated. What Ed said seemed to make sense, even though he was, in his wife's words, a drunken Irish sot, and in his best friend Joe's words, as witless and confused as a freshly fucked owl.

"We can't just ignore this house, Ed. Either Seth, or Oliver Guest, or both of them, will be here at some point."

"We don't ignore it. We come here every day—twice a day—and we do what we just did. You inspect it, with plenty of firepower as backup. Your friend and Dr. Guest may be tough customers, and they may get nasty; but I doubt they win many arguments with bullets."

It was logical, and Art could suggest nothing better. But it felt wrong. Ed didn't know Seth, and to all of them here at Catoctin

Mountain, Oliver Guest was little more than a name and an unpleasant legend.

The sense of uneasiness lasted while he cleaned mud from the floor, carefully closed the front door, and walked with the other two back toward Ed's house. The strong gusts of morning wind had ended. The afternoon had become hot and leaden, depressing Art's spirits and dulling his mind.

He comforted himself with the knowledge that no matter what happened, Dana and his friends could not be harmed.

43

From the secret diary of Oliver Guest.

Chance, as Louis Pasteur famously remarked, favors the prepared mind.

Actually, my hero among nineteenth-century medical researchers is not the Frenchman Pasteur, flamboyant and ebullient, but his methodical, painstaking, physically unprepossessing German contemporary and rival, Robert Koch. Koch it was, not Pasteur, who in rigorous Teutonic fashion established the procedural rules for modern bacteriology and virology, those tunes to which all serious research workers even today must dance.

However, Pasteur's well-known comment encourages a converse statement: Chance can transform or undo the most careful planning.

I had proof of this when Seth Parsigian and I headed for the place where we were to meet his colleagues. He had provided the method of transportation, an ugly box of a car that in its distant heyday must have been a sports utility vehicle. There was something that looked like dried blood on the passenger seat, concerning which I made no comment.

I loaded into the rear compartment a dozen boxes, complaining of their weight and of my own physical weakness. He offered no sympathy. I expected none, even had the weakness been genuine. As I packed the boxes, I explained what they were. When I said "test kit" I did not mean some tidy package or sealed plastic unit, where the press of a button popped final results up on a display. For that type of innately digital analysis, microchips would be an absolute essential. What I could provide used old-fashioned chemical tests, with reagents and precipitates and the comparison of colors. The work was not difficult, but it could be messy. And as soon as we reached our destination (but not before) I promised that I would reveal to Seth and his colleagues the sequence of tests to be performed, and their interpretations.

We both knew the other significance of that coming revelation. Once Seth knew how to do the tests, my vulnerability would increase enormously. As the endgame began, I was in danger of losing my queen. I knew—and he knew—that I needed a countermove.

He stared at me strangely when, with the car loaded and ready to go, I went back into the garden and collected Methuselah. "I won't have a chance to come back and get him later," I explained as I placed the box tortoise, appropriately, in with the other boxes in the rear compartment.

You won't have much use for turtles where you'll be going, *his look said. But of course, he could not suggest that to me. We were still playing the game of mutual trust and goodwill, assisted on his part by a loaded gun.*

He told me to drive. He would navigate. That was when I learned he had never before visited our destination.

So whose house was it? As we drove north I became increasingly apprehensive. I saw everything with heightened senses. Remember, this was my first opportunity to observe the effects of Supernova Alpha in a normal setting. My experience to date had been the emergence from the syncope facility, a bizarre river journey, and days of confinement within my own house and garden.

I drove slowly and carefully. The antique car would not go fast, and Seth did not need to remind me that police interest in our vehicle, for whatever reason, offered worse dangers for me than for him.

Our stately progress offered plenty of opportunity for observation. Seth's occasional descriptions of the past two months had suggested to me a world shattered and shaken by the supernova. I had no reason to doubt what he said, and certainly what I saw on the highway offered much evidence to support his view. Hardly a car or truck was familiar, and the changes were not those that I might have reasonably expected after five years in judicial sleep. The vehicles had a jerry-built look to them, things of rags and patches.

On the other hand, they moved. And their drivers, except for an air of antiquity that matched the cars, seemed perfectly cheerful. Their manner said, we have faced the worse effects of the supernova; they're over, and we're going to beat this thing.

Some, of course, would not make that statement. I saw burned-out wreckage of old accidents, still uncleared. Someone had placed wreaths at three roadside points, where blackened earth showed the first sprouts of new green. As we progressed farther north, off to the left of the highway I saw the tail of a crashed aircraft, jutting into the red afternoon sky like a giant silver memorial to the dead.

As we left the finished roads and began to ascend a gravel track, the evidence of death became more immediate. Our car passed three crosses formed from cut saplings. The soil of the graves that they marked was ruddy and newly turned. They could be no more than a few days old.

I don't think that Seth even noticed them. His attention was on his map.

"Turn left at the top," he said. "And that's it."

That's what? My apprehension mounted. I drove at a snail's pace along the rough dirt road, until a small wooden house came into view, set back into the hillside.

"Stop a few yards short." Seth was studying the house, but at the same time managed to keep one eye—and his gun—on me. "Then we'll go take a look."

"What about the telomere monitoring materials?"

"They can stay in the car. They'll keep awhile, an' I don't see raccoons an' deer takin' too much interest in 'em."

Which meant that Methuselah had to stay there, too. I made sure the doors and windows were closed before at Seth's bidding I stepped out of the car and walked in front of him toward the house.

I mentioned that my sense of observation had been heightened from the moment we left my home. Now I saw

Seth in the same supersensitive mood. In front of the house, he made me stop.

"No car tracks. Nobody has driven this way. But lots of boot marks. Recent. And both ways." He motioned me forward again.

I noticed that one set of imprints was identical to those of the boots I had been wearing when I awoke at the syncope facility. That didn't tell me much, and I did not mention it to Seth. In any case, I could see three different sizes and style of footprint. Not one of them looked like a woman's shoe.

It was at this point that, as I remarked, chance seemed ready to undo my plans. I had been prepared for three people: Seth, and his two still-anonymous colleagues. My hope was to dispose of them, and to vanish. No one else would have any idea where to look for me.

Now I faced an uncertain number of adversaries. At a minimum there were three men and one woman, plus Seth. Disposing of all of them, however desirable, seemed impossibly difficult. That was even more the case since the woman had not been at the house, and she could be anywhere. She would be able to direct others here. My earlier hope, for their death and my disappearance, had been destroyed.

Chance favors the prepared mind. I looked even more closely at everything. We entered the house, me a step ahead of Seth.

"This gets a bit annoyin'," he said, when we were both in the dim interior. He had a gift for understatement. "They've been here, sure as shootin'. Door not locked, footprints all over the place outside. But where the hell are they? It'll be dark in another couple of hours."

He did not expect an answer from me, so I was free to form my own impressions of the house. As Seth said, there were footprints outside, and not inside. But in places near the entrance, the wooden boards of the floor were slightly damp. Someone had recently been cleaning there. At the same time, the interior had the clammy, unused feel of a building unoccupied for weeks or months. A plate sat on the table, and the cup next to it contained a dried-out brown material. I bent over and sniffed. "Coffee," I said to Seth. "But not made today—or yesterday, either." When

I straightened up I held hidden in my hand a little paring knife from the table. It was sharp enough but of no use as a weapon. The blade was barely an inch long.

"I don't think so," Seth said. "Put it back."

Apparently he saw everything, even when he didn't seem to be looking. I laid the little knife back on the table. Then I walked in front of him as we carried out an inspection of every part of the house.

"Not a thing," Seth said at the end of it. "Not a sign, not a note, not even a callin' card—not that I'd expect them to leave one, because for all they know, you might have arrived without me."

Not a sign, *he said, meaning not a sign of the owner, but I very much disagreed with that. I saw many signs. The house was sturdy and built of wood throughout. Although it was furnished with electric power, I also saw propane tanks, an oil stove, and kerosene heaters. The little bathroom had an old-fashioned hand razor and men's aftershave lotion. The pantry was amply stocked with dried foods. The owner, whoever he might be, had apparently been rehearsing for Supernova Alpha long before the star exploded.*

We ate a quick and simple meal, lighting the gas stove with matches that Seth found in a kitchen cupboard and using it to cook rice. The combination of boiled rice and canned sardines tasted execrable, but neither of us complained. As we finished eating, Seth stood up.

"Sorry about this, but I got no choice. I need to take a look around, see if I can find out where they are. I wouldn't recommend you take off an' run while I'm gone, though, 'cause if you do I'll be after you 'til I find you. I really need to know how to use them telomod kits. But just in case you did feel like runnin', we'll rule out any crazy ideas like that." He walked across and picked up a coil of rope from a storage cupboard in the corner, came back, and gestured to me. "Go on through there."

We went into the bedroom. It faced east, and already the room was dark and gloomy. The bed, as I had already noted, had solid iron rails at foot and headboard. While he tied me, hands and feet, I waited for a moment when I might be able to grab the gun. It never came. Seth was too smart and too wary.

He stepped back, studied his efforts, and retied a couple of the knots. "There. That should do us. I don't know how long I'll be, but I'll come back soon as I can. I told you, it won't do no good to get loose an' run, even if you can. I'd be right after you 'til I found you. I need to know how to run them tests. An' don't go callin' for help, neither. Other people won't look after you near as good as I do."

I forced myself to wait for three minutes after he left. Then I stretched. It would do no good to pull directly on the ropes, that would only make the knots tighter. I had to get my hands around the top bed rail and pull on that directly.

Chance favors the prepared mind. I must stop repeating that cliché, or I will become a bore.

However, in this case it is relevant. The exercises that I had performed at night, quietly, locked away in the subbasement of my house, were both boring and unpleasant; now they also proved to have been necessary.

I stretched, grabbed, and heaved until my joints cracked. A bed, even a well-constructed one, is not designed to withstand such deliberate force. The headboard bent toward me, giving at the place where bolts secured it to the bed frame.

It did not come loose at a first effort; nor did I expect it to. I alternated pulling and pushing, relying on the fact that the bed was an old one. I did not know if the frame was wood or metal. If the former, the bolts would chew their way through it; if the latter, the bolts would themselves weaken from continued bending.

Both my vocation and my avocation had taught me patience. The ten minutes of hard work that it took before the headboard came free of the bed frame were rather less than I had expected.

I could not do the same thing with the foot of the bed. What I could do, with some effort, was lift the headboard, my hands still bound to it, right over my body, so that I could bend far enough to get my fingers to the knots on the ropes at my ankles. Seth had tied them tightly, but I had plenty of incentive. After another five minutes I could walk, still dragging the headboard, through to the kitchen where the paring knife lay on the tabletop.

Half a minute of awkward work, and I was free. And now came the hardest moment of all. My instincts told me to grab Methuselah from the car and run, far and fast. It was night, and the chance that Seth or anyone else would be able to catch me was small.

My instincts said that, but they were animal instincts. They were not the correct response for a thinking, analytical mind. I needed not only immediate freedom, I needed freedom from later pursuit.

That called for the use of valuable time, during which Seth might return, alone or with an unknown number of others. It also required that I perform a task both slightly distasteful and physically demanding.

I examined the garden tools in the lean-to by the house. I selected two, either of which could do the job. Then I headed to the car, opened it, and removed Methuselah. It was important to make as little noise as possible, so I pushed the door to but did not slam it. Carrying Methuselah and tools, I set off down the dirt track toward the main road.

Methuselah proved to be easy. The remains of a rusted barrel sat by the track, a couple of hundred yards from the house. I put Methuselah down inside it. The rim was only six inches high, but box tortoises are not given to athletic feats. He would make no effort to leave until he became hungry. I walked on.

It was two more hours before I could return to the house. By that time I was truly as tired as I had pretended to be earlier in the day. This had been a period of unrelenting and continuous effort, sustained by adrenaline and driven by the need to finish as quickly as possible.

The house was silent and empty as I crept through into the bedroom and thankfully placed my burden on the bed. Then the headboard went back to its original position. Finally, I had to make one more decision. Gas, or oil?

Gas has the disadvantage that it calls for judgment. I might easily blow myself up, along with everything else. So it was oil that I poured liberally onto the floor.

While I allowed time for the boards to saturate, I made one more trip to the car. I reached into one of the boxes in the rear compartment, removed half a dozen sheets of paper, and placed them prominently where no one looking into the car could possibly miss them.

Then it was back into the house, for one final brief act. I paused before I performed it. Had I omitted anything? If so, I certainly could not think what it might be.

True, I had not managed to dispose of Seth, an aspiration of mine since our first meeting. But as Longfellow remarks, life is real, life is earnest. It cannot all be simple pleasures.

I made my way down the hill again to collect Methuselah. It was beginning to rain, and I felt weary. All the same, there was joy in my heart and a spring in my step.

44

The conversion of the big cargo plane into Air Force One was a technical success, but a practical failure. Cargo simply does not have the same needs as humans. One of those needs is warmth. The plane's interior was not temperature-controlled, and trying to warm it with the available electrical power was like heating a barn with a candle. When Saul stepped out of the aircraft and into the waiting limousine, he felt frozen and semihuman.

Part of the problem was psychological. His mother's death had been looming closer for three years, ever since the time of her first and minor stroke. The prognosis after the recent stroke had been dismal. Her life had reduced to a misery of sightless, immobile existence, from which he saw her death as a merciful release. In spite of all that, her end still came as a surprise and a defeat.

What was it in the human brain that could see all the evidence of decline, accept it intellectually, and still be shocked viscerally by the final extinction of life?

Saul leaned back as the limousine rolled west into the city. He glanced at his watch. Almost nine o'clock. His meeting with Nick Lopez and Sarah Mander would begin in just over half an hour. Seldom had he felt less up to any challenge.

He went first to his bedroom and ran hot water over his hands. They trembled constantly, and they had almost no feeling in them. He had been awake for thirty-four of the past thirty-eight hours. He examined his face in the mirror. Except for a darkness under the eyes, he looked perfectly normal. That was just as well. Bad enough that he understood his condition, without Lopez and Mander becoming aware of it.

He went to find Auden Travis and Yasmin Silvers, who didn't

know if the meeting was on or off but had stayed on duty in case. He installed them together in an observation room whose display would show the scene in his office. From their shocked expressions, neither knew in advance that the other was also going to be watching the meeting. That was exactly as he intended.

He had ten minutes left when he reached his office. He didn't feel the slightest bit hungry, but he had eaten nothing since midday. From the credenza behind his desk he took two bars of milk chocolate and a packet of potato chips. After eating half a chocolate bar, he went across and poured himself a strong scotch and water.

A perfectly balanced dinner, and Dr. Forrest Singer should be proud of him. Something from each of the five food groups: fat, salt, sugar, caffeine, and alcohol.

When Sarah Mander and Nick Lopez appeared together at the open door of his office, Saul was feeling a lot better.

"Mr. President." After they had expressed their condolences for the loss of Saul's mother, Lopez stared curiously over to the corner of the office. "There's something new in here, but I can't quite say what."

"Sit down, Nick. You, too, Sarah. I think what you're noticing is actually something missing. It's the Disraeli Persona. I've retired it."

Sarah Mander sat down in a flow of flowered print skirt. "Really?" She was as fresh and elegant as Saul felt old and battered. "I thought Queen Victoria's favorite was your favorite, too."

"He was. He is. But I managed without him after Supernova Alpha, and I discovered something rather strange. The advice he gave me when the Persona was not working seemed rather better than the advice he offered me when it was. I think he was of his times. As we must be for ours."

They were outwardly relaxed and inwardly wary. As they should be. He had offered them no agenda for the meeting.

"Occasionally, though," Saul went on, "I still use Disraeli's words. Here is something he said: *'Life is too short to be little.'* That is why I have decided to accept your idea of a Pax Americana. I must congratulate you. You realized, long before I did, that this country, because of Supernova Alpha, is in a unique position of power and influence in the world. The idea that we should exert that power is not merely logical, it is essential to the continued existence of this country. And, in fact, of the world."

Now he had them baffled. With luck he also had them off balance. He went on, "Before I get to that, I want your opinions on a rather different problem. What do you know about Pearl Lazenby?"

"The Eye of God," Lopez said at once. "The Legion of Argos."

"But not anymore." Sarah Mander's perfect brow wrinkled. "Wasn't she sentenced years ago to perpetual judicial sleep?"

Saul nodded. "She was. Not perpetual in principle, but in practice you're quite right. She was sentenced to serve over six hundred years. But the supernova got into the act. Control of the syncope facility where she was stored broke down, and her followers came in and rescued her. Now she's promising a 'holy cleansing' of the whole country—starting with Washington. They apparently have over a hundred thousand people under arms, and they're all set to march this way. My question is, how do you think we ought to handle the situation?"

Nick Lopez spoke at once. "Delicately. You can stop them easily with the Army. But the PR would be terrible."

"So you have to use a small specialized team, and take out the leader." Sarah Mander went on as though she was continuing Lopez's remark. It confirmed Saul's impression. Regardless of what the House Minority and Senate Majority Leaders thought of each other personally, when it came to political instincts they were identical twins.

"Without her the rest of the organization is nothing," Lopez said. "Capture her, but whatever you do don't kill her. Otherwise you'll have a martyr on your hands."

"And *bad* trouble. All of which I'm sure is obvious to you." Sarah Mander arched her eyebrows at Saul. "Leaving only the question, why are you asking us?"

"I want to be sure that we all agree on the approach to small things, before we go on to large ones. I believe that the three of us are going to be working together extremely closely over the next few years. Perhaps the next few decades. We have to understand each other." Saul spoke again partly to keep them off balance, but they were professionals. Little could be read from their faces. He doubted that was true of the two secret observers.

He went on, "By the way, I have instructed General Mackay to do exactly what you propose. Pearl Lazenby is to be captured by a minimal strike team. Deaths and injuries within the Legion of Argos are to be avoided wherever possible, and the life of Pearl Lazenby herself is not to be taken, no matter what the circumstances.

"But now, to the larger issue. I said that I wished to follow through on your suggestion of a Pax Americana. That may be the wrong term. A better one might be a *dux Americana*. We have to lead the world in an unprecedented global effort. If we fail, then nothing else that anyone does for the next half century will make any difference. Humans are likely to become extinct. We have not seen the last of Supernova Alpha. What we have experienced so far is a small first wave of what will hit us later.

"I don't expect you to believe this without proof. In the next several days, if you are willing, I will arrange for that proof to be presented to you. Nor do I expect you to make an instant decision to cooperate completely with me. I will tell you only one thing. In this matter, anyone who is not with me is by definition against me. That will have several consequences. In your case, Nick, it will mean that Auden Travis will no longer be working on my staff. He is an extraordinarily dedicated and competent aide. But from now on, you and I must share a common goal. Otherwise he cannot stay."

Nick Lopez opened his mouth, and closed it again without speaking.

"And you, Sarah. I know about General Mackay and Secretary Munce, and I am sure there are many others. You will no longer seek to recruit or suborn members of my administration."

"Yes, sir." Sarah Mander stared at him. "Mr. President—Saul—something major has happened to you. And I don't mean the loss of your mother, which is something I've been through myself and I know how hard it is."

"It has indeed, Sarah. I'm hoping that it will happen to you, too, and to Nick as well."

"What is it?"

"It's this." Saul walked over to the side table and came back carrying decanter, glasses, and ice. Without asking, he poured three drinks. "I listened yesterday to somebody who told me that unless there is an all-out global industrial effort—my words, not his, he doesn't think geopolitically—unless that happens, our civilization will at best come crashing down to the Dark Ages. At worst, no one will be around to worry about that or anything else. Humans will go the way of the dinosaurs, and our nemesis, like theirs, will come from beyond the Earth. I believed what he told me. And I decided that I had a choice. I could either sit back and be remembered, if there's anybody left to remember anything, as the man who had a chance to save humanity from destruction and did nothing. Or I might be remembered as the totally unreasonable, obsessive, remorseless single-issue bastard who tried to force the whole world to share his point of view. I asked myself, What was I in politics for? Comfort and privilege, or immortality?

"I am asking you the same question. I made my decision. I'm hoping you'll make yours. There has to be more to life than patronage and pensions. If you're with me, you'll get everything that I can give you. Power, and trust, and more work than you thought the world contained. But if I find you're in this for the wrong reasons, I'll break you. I'll destroy anyone, House or Senate, man or woman, citizen or foreigner, who gets in the way. We're going to rule the world, but only because we *have* to rule the world. We have no choice."

"*Ich kann nicht anders.* Like Martin Luther." Nick Lopez said, then glanced at Sarah Mander. "Don't tell anyone I speak German, it would ruin my image." He turned to Saul. "I don't know if this makes sense, Mr. President, but it's the absolute truth. I think I'm frightened of you."

Saul looked into Lopez's brown eyes, and knew that he was not lying. He nodded. "I'm frightened of myself, Nick. *I have brought myself by long meditation to the conviction that a human being with a settled purpose must accomplish it, and that nothing can resist a will which will stake even existence upon its fulfillment.* That's not me speaking, that's Benjamin Disraeli. But for the first time in my life, I understand what he meant. I'm going to do this, or I'm going to die trying. Sarah?"

"I want to hear the evidence—a person can be absolutely sure of something, and still be wrong. But I agree with Nick on one thing. You've changed, Saul Steinmetz. You scare me, too. And I'm the original dragon lady; I don't scare easily."

"You'll hear the evidence, Sarah, anytime you're ready for it. If you can see a reason why it's wrong, you come and tell me. I'll be glad to hear it."

Saul held out his hand. It was perfectly steady. "I've said what I wanted to say. I respect greatly the political skills and abilities of both of you. In the past I do not think that they have been exercised to the full. I hope that they will be in the future."

The farewell handshakes were brief and formal, but Saul sensed a difference in them. He could not analyze it, and he did not try to do so. Instead, after the two had left he turned off most of the office lights and went to stand at the window. It was ten o'clock, and the last evening flights were arriving at National Airport. There were more of them every night. Slowly, little by little, the country was edging back to normal.

But it was his job to make the country and the world believe that normal was no longer good enough.

How well did people do, facing a threat still fifty years in the future? Did they say, not my problem, it's going to happen after my time? In fifty years, he would be dead or over a hundred years old.

Tonight's meeting was the merest beginning. The real work would start tomorrow, on the international front. He had to persuade every other country that cooperation was not a choice, it was a survival necessity. Sarah Mander and Nick Lopez were not typical. Regardless of their personal morality and mean prejudices, they had the intellect to see and grasp the large picture, the long term.

The lights in the office were low, and the reflection in the window was a pale ghost flickering across the room. He turned, slowly and wearily. It was Yasmin. He had been expecting her.

She stood for a few seconds in front of him, then said in a low, anguished voice, "You made me watch on purpose. You knew what you were going to do."

"Yes, that's quite true." Finally, he was able to do what for so long he had been unable to do: act on impulse, without thinking. He reached out, pulled Yasmin forward, and allowed her to bury her face against his chest.

"That man, that bastard, that awful, perverted, two-faced, lying *murderer*." Her voice sounded close to tears, but she went on, "He killed my brother. And you—you asked him, that man—"

"I did, didn't I? I asked him to work with me. Work with me closely, become part of my inner circle, share my trust."

"It was just awful. If it weren't for him, Raymond would still be alive. And Auden, he thinks the sun rises and sets on that dreadful man, that fucking hypocrite. He was so excited, so delighted."

"You told Auden about Lopez?"

"No. There was no point. Auden loves Lopez, he'd never believe me."

"Good. You're quite right about that. He wouldn't believe you."

"Why did you do it? I mean, why did you ask me to sit and watch that? You knew how I'd feel. You're heartless."

Saul held her by the shoulders and pushed her away from his chest, so that he could look into her eyes.

"I'm a politician, Yasmin. Isn't that what you told me, you wanted to learn to do what I do? Well, this is one of the toughest lessons. Politics is the art of accommodation, the science of the possible. If I refuse to work with everyone I dislike, how far do you think I'll get? You told me you wanted to find out if you had what it takes to go all the way. There's only one way to find out a thing like that. Didn't you realize it would get unpleasant?"

"Of course I did." She was under control, tight control. "I knew there would be compromises and odd partnerships. Sleeping with the enemy. But *that* enemy, Nick Lopez."

"You get to choose your friends, Yasmin. You don't get to pick your enemies. Do you think I *like* Nick Lopez and Sarah Mander?"

"You seem to."

"Then you have to give me credit for being a good politician. I don't like them—but I recognize their abilities, and if they'll give me their support for what I need to do, I want them on my side."

"But if I stay with you, and work for you—"

"Then, yes, you're quite right. You'll probably have to work with Nick Lopez. It goes with the territory. You work with *anyone*. Can you do it, or can't you? If you can't, the sooner you realize that, the better for both of us."

"You mean, if I can't deal with Lopez, I'm fired?"

"I'll say it again. I mean that you—and me—have to be able to work with *anybody*, anyone at all, if that's what it takes to get the job done."

"Oh, Saul. I don't know if I can. He killed my brother."

"No, he didn't. Your brother stabbed Nick Lopez. I know what Lopez did to Raymond, but your brother is dead because of what *he* did."

She was rummaging around in the pocket of her skirt.

"On the little table," Saul said. "Next to the desk."

"Thank you." She went across, took a tissue, and blew her nose. "I'm sorry. It was such a shock, seeing Lopez. I had no idea who you were going to meet."

"I knew that. I also know something else."

"What?"

"That it will never get any worse for you than this. I could bring a thousand people into my office, and say I wanted you to work with them, and you'd never again have so strong an emotional reaction, so strong a reason to say no. Think of it this way, Yasmin. If you can handle Lopez, you can handle anyone at all."

"If."

"Can you?"

"I guess. The shock's over now. If I see him again, it won't be as bad. And I really don't want to leave. I love this job."

"So do I. Politics is an odd business. You know what they say about wrestling with pigs?"

She managed a faint smile. "You mean, 'Don't do it, you get dirty, and the pigs like it.' "

"That's it. Well, it's the same with politics. If you don't like the game, you should never even consider it."

"I do like it. Most of it. Almost all of it."

"Even if you have to save the world?"

"I can stand that. I can stand anything." Yasmin took a deep breath. "I can stand Nick Lopez."

"That's what I want to hear. I think we ought to call it a day now, before you have a chance to change your mind. I feel as though I've forgotten what a bed looks like. There's nothing that won't wait until tomorrow."

"Oh, no." Yasmin was reaching for her pocket again. "Auden or I were supposed to give this to you the second you got back, but we got sidetracked because of the meeting."

"What is it?"

"It's a message. From Tricia Goldsmith. She'll be in Washington again, the day after tomorrow. She wants to know if you're free for dinner."

"Then I'd better call her, hadn't I?"

"You're not going to do it, are you? I mean, you're not going to have dinner with her?"

"Yes, I am. If she wants to, I will certainly have dinner with her." Saul waited just long enough, and added, "And so will you, if you are willing. You'll come with me as my companion. I'm over her, Yasmin. I want you to see that for yourself."

"She'll flame out. So you *did* check what I told you about Crossley and Himmelfarb. And you told me you hadn't."

"I didn't. And I don't give a damn about Crossley, or Himmelfarb, or Crossley and Himmelfarb, or who did and didn't say what and to whom when Tricia and I broke up before the election. That's all history. I need to start running. The country, and for the next term. With what's left in this term, I certainly can't get more than a good start on what has to be done."

"You should. Run again, I mean. Definitely."

In spite of Saul's declaration that they were leaving, they still stood in front of the window. He turned to her. "I'll need a new campaign slogan."

"You certainly will. The last one was lousy. You need something that reminds people that the President needs enormous powers if he's to carry out the global job you're tackling."

"Do you have ideas? Practical ones?"

"I might." Yasmin slipped her arm into Saul's. "I'll work on it. 'End White House impotence.' What do you think of that?"

45

Helen cooked an outstanding dinner, venison and pork with broad beans and potatoes and spinach and applesauce. Joe brought over a special wine, "wine I paid money for." It was like an evening on Catoctin Mountain before Supernova Alpha, made better for Art by Dana's presence. But a couple of things spoiled it.

First, the window was in the wrong part of the room, so he couldn't see his house. He kept glancing in that direction, as though the wall might have suddenly become transparent. Finally Dana leaned across, took his hand, and said, "I wanted to go with you, you know. But Helen hadn't been told anything, and she saw your faces and the guns. I couldn't leave her here. I had to stay and explain. When this is all over, I want you and me to go in your house and not come out for a week."

The other worrying factor was Ed. He kept his rifle by his side all the time, even when they were eating dinner. Art didn't ask, but he was willing to bet that the safety catch was not on.

The women were making a deliberate attempt to cheer everybody up. Helen said, "Why, now that you two are here I can give six-person dinner parties, something I've wanted to do for years. I'd have done it tonight if I'd known."

"Anne-Marie's up in Lantz with her cousin," Joe said. "We'll do it next week."

The assumption was clear: Art had Dana with him, so there was no possible reason why he would ever want to go back "down there" as Helen put it, with a strong suggestion that Route I-270 led a traveler to the gates of hell. Or to Washington, which in her view was not much different.

"We won't be here," Art said. "Not next week."

"Why ever not?"

"We have things to do. I promised to give a personal report." He did not add "to the President," but went on, "And I think those two idlers"—he pointed to Joe and Ed—"ought to go with us."

"What the hell for?" Joe asked. "They're all rogues down there."

"And you're not? You're missing the point. Did you ever fly a C-5A?"

"Damn right. I could fly one with my eyes closed. A lovely plane, they don't make anything like that these days."

"Did you know that they're in regular use again, because none of the new equipment works anymore? I think one of them has been converted to become Air Force One. With your background, you could probably get a job as a pilot tomorrow. And, Dana, tell them about the drivers in Washington."

She inspected Joe and Ed carefully before she answered. "I'm not sure today's drivers in D.C. would think you two were old enough to get a license. You look like teenagers compared with most of them."

"And anybody who can drive without an AVC in the car is in demand," Art added. "If you can drive a stick shift, or know how to install a carburetor in place of a chip-based fuel injection system—" He stopped. "No, Ed!"

Out of the corner of his eye he had noticed the gun barrel coming up, at the same time as he saw the dark face peering in at the window.

"Don't shoot, it's Seth." He waved, to indicate that Seth should go around to the front door. "How the hell did he know where we were?"

He pulled the door open. "Where's Guest?"

"He's safe and sound," Seth said, and then to Ed, "I'd rather you aimed that thing someplace other than my gut. I'm one of the good guys."

The rifle was trained squarely on Seth's navel. Ed lowered it to point at the floor. "Pardon me. You just don't look like one of the good guys."

Seth's clothes and face were filthy, and mud coated his legs up past the knees. "That's 'cause I've been fartin' an' fandango-in' around this place looking for you all. It don't help none that it's startin' to rain out there. I didn't see the light from this window 'til three minutes back. See, I could tell that Art had been in his house today, but he didn't leave no word where he was goin' when he left."

"We didn't want your friend Oliver dropping in." Joe took one good look at Seth and poured not the wine he had paid money for, but a big shot of Ed's moonshine. "Here."

Seth took the glass, drained it in one gulp, and rolled his eyes. "Jeez. That don't take prisoners, do it? Look, the main thing is, Guest came up with what we need."

"The treatment?" Dana asked.

"You got it. We'll be able to keep goin' with the telomods. He worked up a wet chemistry method, and the test kits are in the car we came here in. He still hasn't told me how to use any of this stuff, an' I'm sure that's gonna be his big bargainin' chip. So the sooner we get back over to your house—"

"Hold it," Ed interrupted in a strange, hoarse voice. He had been looking not at Seth in the doorway, but past him. "What's that?"

He and Art crowded Seth backward. "That's my house!" Art shouted. "It's on fire."

"An' Guest's inside—tied to the bed, he can't get out." Seth started as though he was going to run, then swung around. "You got a car or anythin', ready to go? Otherwise, he's a goner."

"The tractor." Ed turned as flames from the burning house roared to double their height. "In the barn—but it only carries one, and it's not fast."

"Forget it." Seth was already on the move. "Come on."

The fire was a beacon to draw them on, but it did nothing to light up the muddy road. Seth moved out ahead, with Dana not far behind. Art decided that if he was ever going to ruin his knee completely, this was the time. He ran full tilt along the dark path. Rain made the mud more than usually treacherous, but he had walked this way a hundred times. He had the advantage of knowing the twists and turns. By the time they reached the house he had passed Dana and was only a few yards behind Seth.

They skidded to a halt twenty yards short of the building. Orange flames were shooting from the roof and licking out of two of the windows. Art could feel the heat on his face.

"We can't go in there," he said. "We can't do anything."

Seth shook his head and ran forward. He got to within ten feet of the front door when a cloud of red-hot sparks gushed out over the transom. He turned and came reeling back, gasping for air.

The heat from the burning house was increasing. Raindrops

turned to puffs of steam as they hit the slate roof. "The tank," Art cried. "The propane will blow. We have to get away."

He took Dana by the arm and started along the road. Joe, Ed, and Helen were approaching. He waved them away. As he did so Dana pulled free from his grasp and turned back.

"Come on, Seth," she cried. "You can't do anything."

Seth had not run. He was a dark figure against the burning house. Flames were spewing out of the walls. As the front door cracked and burst open, Seth shook his head and ran to the car. There was no place to turn it without driving closer to the house. Art heard the engine race, then the car came zooming crazily backward, almost hit Dana, and veered at the last moment into a thicket of rhododendrons.

Art ran across to yank open the driver's door. "What the hell do you think you're doing?"

Seth was panting, leaning over, pulling at something in the rear compartment. He emerged with his arms full of boxes and a batch of papers.

"The telomod kits." He nodded toward the load of boxes. "I told you, we left them in the car. It was too close to the house. But this should be far enough—"

The explosion was a vivid flash of red and white. The sound was a flat, heavy thump. Moments later, burning debris from the house showered all around them. Art cowered back, shielding his face with his forearm. Seth dropped the papers that he was holding. A blast of hot air blew them along the ground. Dana, standing farther back, dived and managed to trap them on the muddy ground.

Art stared at the ruin of his house. The front wall tilted inward at a crazy angle. The chimney stood intact, but all around it roof slates were cracking in the heat. Each one as it split threw off random sputters of red sparks. Flames poured from the bedroom window, and the whole structure was beginning to settle. Nothing inside could possibly have survived.

He felt a hand on his shoulder. It was Joe. "Come on. Let's get back to Ed's place. Don't even think of trying to go in there. It's not worth dying for objects."

Joe hadn't heard Seth's shout before they started running to the burning house. Art turned to him. "You don't understand, Joe. I'm not worried about my things—I've got spares at my house in Olney. But Oliver Guest was inside there."

"Then I say it again. You don't go in. That murdering sod's the last person to risk your life for."

"He was tied up and helpless."

"Good. He *deserved* to die like that. And good riddance." Joe walked away.

Art went across to Dana and took her hand. In silence, the group moved slowly along the path. The rain fell steadily. By the time they reached Ed's house they were soaked, and the fire behind them was beginning to burn lower. Art took a last look back. The cabin was settling in the downpour, in gouts of blue flame and dying spurts of red-hot ash.

They went inside. Without being asked, Ed poured drinks of moonshine for everyone. Seth set the test kit boxes carefully on a table at the entrance. Dana brushed mud from the batch of wet papers and took a casual look at the top sheet. After a moment she frowned and read more carefully. Finally she went across to where Seth was sitting.

"I thought you said Guest didn't tell you how to use the test kits."

"He didn't." Seth was drinking fast, and too much. "Unless we can figure it out for ourselves—pretty long shot—we're nowhere."

Dana held out a sheet. "But this *is* the description of how to use the test kit. You can see, the first test is described here, how to do it and how to interpret it. The other pages give the same thing for the other tests."

"Gimme a look at that." Seth grabbed the sheets in a filthy hand and bent over them. After a couple of minutes he scowled and shook his head. "Ain't that the damnedest. You're right, this is the whole shebang. He never told me he'd written it out."

"I think he intended to use this when he bargained with us for his own future. Naturally, he wouldn't say ahead of time that he'd documented everything. But there it is."

Art had been listening in on the conversation. "Let me take a look."

He skimmed the first couple of pages, not reading as carefully as Dana. Seth waited until he looked up, then said, "Well?"

"It's the document we need. But this is all too pat."

"That's what I thought. Too neat."

"What do you mean?" Dana asked. "Isn't this just what we want?"

"It is. And it ties everything up." Art handed the sheets back to Dana. "Guest is officially dead, so the government doesn't hunt for him. We have the telomod test kits, and we know how to use them, so *we* don't have to look for him. Everybody lives happily ever after."

"Including old Ollie," Seth added. "Tell you what, tomorrow morning we go over to your house. No good doin' it now, everything's too hot to touch. But I'll make a bet with you. We won't find a body in the bedroom. We won't see a sign of one, there or anywhere else."

By morning the rain had eased to a thin drizzle. Before breakfast, Art, Seth, and Dana were heading over to the cabin. They had slept in Joe's house, which had more space. It also had more dogs. Dana had been wakened by three of them soon after dawn, as they wandered in to scratch and sniff at the interesting new female scent. She had thrown them out of the bedroom, but remained up. Art soon joined her. He couldn't sleep. Seth was up already. For all Art knew, he had been awake all night.

The burnt-out house had been reduced to a chaos of wet ash with an intact chimney protruding at one end. Everything was red-hot beneath the sodden upper layer of gray.

It was easy enough to find the bed. The iron headboard and footboard were intact and upright, sticking up from a cluster of fallen roof slates.

"See," Seth said. "Nothin'."

He had a straight sapling that he had cut on the way over. Now he reached in from outside and raked the long stick across the mess next to the headboard.

"Nothin'," he repeated. "Hey, wait a minute."

The sapling had run across an uneven hump. He moved it a couple of feet, and poked again.

"Son of a bitch. What's that?"

Something irregular in shape lay between headboard and footboard. It was impossible to tell what it was without direct examination. The three walked gingerly forward, hearing the sizzle as their shoes went through the crust of ash to the still-smoldering layers beneath.

"My feet are starting to burn," Dana said. "Can we pull the whole thing out? Unless it's too hot to hold."

Working together, they dragged the remains of the bed onto bare ground. The iron end parts fell away as they went, creating showers of black ash and hot sparks. Slate fragments and patches of ash dropped off the object that lay on the bed. Once they were clear of the ruins of the house, Seth and Art carefully removed the rest of the debris.

What came into sight was unmistakable. A human body lay faceup on the charred bed, most of its flesh burned away to reveal blackened bones.

"Well, how about that," Seth said softly. He stood looking down at the skeleton. "I said I'd take bets, an' I was wrong. Dr. G., I guess I owe you an apology."

"Or maybe you don't. Oliver Guest was a genius, but even a genius can't think of everything." Art squatted onto his haunches, staring at the scorched head with its naked cranium and empty eye sockets. He reached down and carefully removed something from the corpse's grinning mouth. "When Guest was sentenced to judicial sleep, he was stored away naked. We know, because we found him that way."

He held up what he had taken out of the mouth, showing Dana and Seth a partially melted object made of plastic and metal. "They put him into judicial sleep for six centuries. What do you think the chances are that they'd have stuck him into the syncope facility wearing dentures?"

They stared at what Art was holding, then at the burned body. Finally Dana said, "Who?"

"I doubt we'll ever know." Art tossed the melted dental bridge back into the ashes. "I'd like to believe that Guest found a corpse somewhere. There are plenty around, we saw signs all the way here."

"Or maybe he dug one up," Seth said cheerfully. "But knowin' old Ollie, it's more likely that's number nineteen on his little list. Look on the bright side, though—it could easily have been one of us."

Each of them straightened, turned, and scanned the trees and bushes.

"Come on." Art took Dana's hand. "Let's get back to Ed and Joe. For once in my life I'll feel safer with a few more guns around."

46

As the full moon slid behind clouds and darkness became absolute, Celine gave it one last try.

"I know the layout of the corridors and the feel of the place. You don't. It could make all the difference."

"I realize that, ma'am." The captain, no more than five years younger than Celine, treated her with the deference appropriate to some great and venerable head of state. "Your help in bringing us here and your description of what we are likely to find underground were really important. But you don't know how to use any of this."

He gestured around them. He, Celine, and nine black-clad strike team members were sitting in a vehicle that from the outside might be taken as a standard and old-fashioned electric van. Inside, gas masks, gas bombs, rifle mortars, and suits of body armor lined the walls. Four small screens showed black and white images. Two displayed the terrain using thermal infrared and active microwave sensors. The third observed in visible wavelengths, and was at the moment dark. The fourth was a general purpose television. Once it would have picked up any of ten thousand channels. Now there was one channel only, and that was dedicated to official government broadcasts and announcements.

"I wouldn't have to know how to use everything," Celine said. "You would do all that. I would just help you to find your way in the underground tunnels."

"Yes, ma'am. I know you are keen to help. But let me ask you this. You trained for many years before you went to Mars. What would you have said if, the day you left, someone without any training came along and told you they wanted to go along, too? My team has worked together for six years in this type of exercise. We know each other, we trust each other."

When Celine said nothing, he went on, "And there's one other reason, ma'am, why we don't want you along. This one sounds selfish, and maybe it is. But it's true. You went to Mars and you made it back. You're a legend. How do you think we'd feel, all of us, if you went along and somehow we got you killed? We'd never get over that."

Celine admitted defeat. This was supposed to be a neat surgical operation, fast in and fast out, with minimum violence and no casualties. But the Mars expedition had provided the ultimate proof that, plan as you liked, things went wrong.

"Will you do me one favor?" she asked. "I'd like to know what's going on. Can you show me the controls for the display units?"

"Glad to do that, ma'am." The captain nodded to one of his companions. The woman came forward and showed how each sensor could be controlled in look direction, focus, magnification, contrast, saturation level, and sensitivity. It was crude, it was cumbersome, and it had to be done manually. With the failure of the chips, none of the old taken-for-granted automatic features worked.

Celine made a practice run. Under her control, the visible wavelength display at maximum sensitivity showed a faint gray ghost of a scene. Outside, dawn was approaching.

Zero hour.

The strike team adjusted their equipment, picked up gas cylinders and projectors, and prepared to leave. With their black body armor, goggles, helmet communication antennae, and long-muzzled gas masks, they were like strange mutant insects. The captain had a final word with the driver. "Two hours. If we're not back, or you don't have radio contact at that time, you're on your own. Use your best judgment."

"Yes, sir." The driver checked his headset.

"Good luck," Celine added.

"Thank you, ma'am." The captain fixed his mask in position and slipped quietly out of the open rear of the vehicle.

Celine turned to the display controls. The microwave and thermal infrared channels showed the group snaking their way downhill toward the little schoolroom. As usual, her mind threw off half a dozen questions. What would the strike team do if the elevators were no longer in service? Would Pearl Lazenby, worried about Celine and Wilmer's escape, have moved her headquarters? What were the chances of an ambush, somewhere belowground? Were Jenny and Reza safe, or had they been sacrificed to atone for their help in the escape? Had they been tortured, to tell whatever they might know? The rules of civilized behavior did not apply to the Legion of Argos. The strike team did not care about Reza and Jenny, their whole focus was on the rapid capture of Pearl Lazenby.

The group reached the school. Celine watched them vanish inside. After that came the frustration of a view with nothing to offer but the gradual brightening of dawn outside the van.

She turned to the driver. "Are they all right?"

He gave the shrug of a man who had been through this sort of thing many times. "So far, so good. They've reached the elevators. We may lose radio contact once they go deep underground. Unfortunately, that's when it gets interesting."

He was deliberately casual, but Celine noticed that he did not take his eyes off his own monitor. It showed the same scene as hers. But suppose that the Legion of Argos came from some other direction?

She went to the open rear of the van, stepped outside, and looked around. All she saw was a peaceful morning of late spring. She returned to her seat and turned on the television that picked up general broadcasts. Apparently it was too early in the day. The little screen showed nothing but a test pattern.

"A few more minutes." The driver had observed her actions. "Then we'll get the channel news."

Presumably, that would come on the hour. But by then, the strike team would be well on the way to success or failure.

Celine tried to estimate times. Say, five or six minutes to descend. Another five to advance, cautiously, and determine the situation. The neural gas was supposed to make a person unconscious in seconds, quickly enough that there would be no time to use a gun. Then, say, five more minutes to take bearings and hurry along to Pearl Lazenby's private quarters. Would she be asleep, or awake—or there at all? In any case there would be more gas, followed with luck by a quick retreat carrying her body. Then into the elevator, and back to the surface.

Clean, tidy, efficient. Every task looked like that—until you came to carry it out. Then you discovered dirt, mess, and muddle.

She turned to the driver. "Any word?"

"They've left Grossman at the top with a radio. The rest are in the elevator. Don't worry, he'll report as soon as there's anything worth saying—unless he loses contact when they get down there and approach Lazenby's quarters."

Which would be the most crucial time. Naturally.

On the television set in front of Celine, the test pattern vanished and was replaced by the Great Seal of the United States. A disembodied voice bade her good morning and informed her that this was America.

But then, of more interest: ". . . the major speech made yesterday evening by the President."

Celine and the strike force had been on the way here and otherwise engaged. She had asked Wilmer to attend and note what was said, but she didn't have much hope. Wilmer heard what he wanted to hear. Anyway, he and Dr. Vronsky, along with a dozen other scientists, were too busy playing with semirigid body dynamics and space construction methods to notice much of anything. Celine kept one eye on the external scene monitors and turned most of her attention to the television.

President Saul Steinmetz was standing at a lectern. On the black-and-white image his face was pale and his eyes sat deep in their sockets. Somehow he seemed to have grown taller since her meeting with him, and the familiar voice was firm and commanding.

"This nation and the world have over the past two months been through very difficult times. Supernova Alpha caused tragedy on the largest scale, for which no nation was prepared and from which no nation emerged unscathed. Now everyone, here and through the whole world, faces the enormous problem of rebuilding. I feel sure that it will come as a surprise to most of my fellow citizens, as it did to me, to learn that this country was one of the luckiest ones in terms of the supernova's effects. But that is true. Our friends abroad were far less fortunate."

The camera scanned the crowded hall to show the audience of Senators and House members, then returned to the people standing directly behind the President. Celine recognized the new Vice President, Brewster Callaghan. Next to him on his left was the House Minority Leader, Sarah Mander, and on the right the Senate Majority Leader, Nick Lopez. Next to Lopez was the young male aide that Celine had met when she visited the White House. In front of Lopez stood the strikingly beautiful young woman who had accompanied Celine and Wilmer from the State Department to the White House. Yasmin Silvers presented her profile, because her eyes remained fixed on the President.

"A unique tragedy," Saul Steinmetz was continuing, "which we will certainly never forget. However, tragedy is not our business. Our business is the future. And now it is my duty to deliver a warning to us all. In the future—*all* our futures—half a century away, lies an event which without action on our part will kill every member of the human race. If humanity is to survive, we must undertake an enterprise of unprecedented size, difficulty, and duration. This Grand Design must be the construction of a vast shield, out in space, which can divert deadly follow-on radiation from Supernova Alpha. In order to build such a shield, the combined resources of the whole globe—"

"Getting a message," the driver interrupted. "Our man at the top thinks we got problems down below. Signal interrupted. He's trying to make contact again."

"They failed?"

"Don't know that, but apparently it's not going clean. Keep quiet a minute, let me listen."

Celine stared at the displays. They showed the same morning scene, with the schoolhouse sitting peaceful at the bottom of a gentle incline. The van was suddenly uncannily quiet, except for Saul Steinmetz's voice continuing from the television.

"—at once, and with not a day to lose. Therefore, I am arranging an immediate series of meetings with the heads of governments all around the world. In those meetings, I propose that this country pledge its manpower and materials to the rebuilding of the infrastructure and industry of other less fortunate nations. Let me remind you that such an act is not without precedent. Eighty years ago, in one of this nation's finest hours, we rebuilt the economies of those who had recently been our adversaries in the most bitter war in human history. Surely we will do no less now, for our friends. And, in return, we will ask their total commitment to a project which will save the world. Before seeking the support of other nations, however, all of us here must first be convinced that this action is necessary and indeed inevitable. To that end, I have arranged for a series of briefings, to begin tomorrow morning. The first ones will demonstrate both the danger and the need for action. Then the scale of the operation will be outlined—"

"Shit." The driver dragged off his headset and hurried to the rear of the van, for a direct view of the schoolhouse. "It's looking bad. We have casualties. They're on the way back up, but they didn't have time to disable the other elevators. I'm going to join Grossman and give them fire cover. You stay here and get in the driver's seat. If you see anything coming out and it's not our own people, don't wait and don't watch. Take off in the van and don't stop 'til you reach Washington."

He was already in full body armor. Without waiting to hear Celine's response he dropped his helmet into position and jumped off the open rear of the van.

She took one step toward the empty driver's seat, and paused. If the long years of the Mars expedition had taught her one thing above all others, it was that you did not abandon a teammate in trouble. Not ever, not for any reason. At the moment she was a part of the Pearl Lazenby capture team—she was even responsible for its existence. There was just one important difference: the others had to obey the commands of their team leader; she did not.

She went to the side wall of the van, inspected the body armor suits, and took down the one that seemed closest to her size. It took a minute to climb into it, but her experience with spacesuits helped a lot.

The choice of weapons was more difficult. She hated the idea of killing anyone, but gas bombs might be useless if the Legion of Argos followers had their own gas masks.

Finally she hooked three gas grenades to her belt and picked up an automatic rifle. The gun's advanced capabilities had been dumbed down a lot by the gamma pulse, but that suited her just fine. It was now a simple single-shot point-and-shoot projectile weapon, with a hundred-round ammo cartridge.

Celine carefully climbed from the open rear of the van and walked down the hill. The schoolhouse at the bottom seemed astonishingly normal and neat. It was hard to imagine violence taking place in or underneath it.

She recalled Eli's cold, unblinking face and the belts of live ammunition around his chest. She began to walk faster. Soon she was at the door of the schoolroom, and still no sound came from within.

She looked inside, past the broken glass window. The driver and the radioman Grossman stood side by side, guns raised. They were covering two of the three elevators.

The driver had seen her arrive, and he gestured angrily at her to leave. She ignored him. An elevator was on its way up—no, *two* were rising in the shafts, she could hear the creak of their cables.

The big question: Who was inside them?

Apparently her companions had no more idea than she did. The third elevator sat silent, but their guns veered between the other two.

She heard a final rattle of cables. The door of one elevator slid open. She held her rifle at the ready. Two people in body armor staggered forward. They were carrying a long object swaddled in light-colored material.

"Take this and get out of here." She recognized the captain's voice, hoarse and strained. "Grossman, you and I cover."

The driver grabbed the end of the burden thrust at him by the captain and started with the other man up the hill. Celine, ready to turn with them, saw from the corner of her eye that the door of the second elevator was sliding open. Grossman and the captain stood right in front of it. They began to shoot, but gray-clad soldiers at the back of the elevator were shielded by those in front. Celine saw a black oval fly through the air to explode right at Grossman's neck. His head vanished. Celine felt a hail of shrapnel on her armor and saw the captain blown backward—injured, dead, or stunned, she could not tell.

She grabbed a gas grenade from her belt and threw it forward in the same movement. The gray fog of the explosion filled the air. When it cleared, no one in the elevator was left standing.

Celine turned to where the captain lay. She was relieved to see him struggling to his knees. As she moved to help him, she heard the rumble of an ascending elevator. The third one was on its way.

The captain was dazed. Given a choice, he might have stayed to tackle the next arrivals. Celine didn't give him the option. She took his arm and steered him up the hill.

The driver and his companion had reached the van with their burden. They looked her way and shouted a warning. Celine did not stop, but she turned her head. Forty yards behind her, boiling out of the schoolroom like angry ants from a nest, came a score and more of people wearing Legion of Argos uniforms. They were all carrying rifles.

Celine didn't wait to find out what they would do with them. She staggered the last few steps to the van and helped the driver to hoist the half-conscious captain inside. As she put her own knee wearily on the tailgate she heard the slap of sharp impacts on the vehicle's side.

"Good," the driver said. "We got her. But don't stand there unless you're tired of life."

"How do you know we got her? What's happening?"

"Because they didn't shoot at you. The only way that makes sense is if we have their precious leader, and they're hoping to put this van out of action. They know we'd never get her away from them on foot if they disable it."

"Can they do that?"

"Not a prayer." The driver was back in his seat, hands on the wheel and foot on the throttle. "The body and tires of this baby are fullerene-reinforced to hell and gone. They'd need armor-piercing shells to do us any damage. But come on, ma'am. Get your ass on board, and let's move out of here."

As Celine placed her other knee onto the tailgate she caught a glimpse on the television of President Steinmetz saying forcefully, "—and survive the time of maximum danger." Surely, that program had finished hours ago. It seemed more like days.

She heard a bullet hum a few inches above her head. As she ducked, the engine roared and the van rocketed forward. She almost fell out of the back, but saved herself by a frantic grab at the cloth bundle. It slid backward a foot toward the rear of the van.

"Hey, don't give her back." The captain had removed his helmet and gas mask. He had a bloody nose, but seemed back to full consciousness. "We don't want to lose her after all our trouble getting her."

The cloth had come partly loose from the tug that Celine had given it. She looked, and realized that it held Pearl Lazenby, tight-wrapped and unconscious. As Celine stared at her face the eyes slowly opened. The captain waved a gas bomb a few inches away from them.

"Try one funny move, ma'am, and you get this. It will put you out for four or five hours, and next time you won't feel so good when you wake up."

Pearl Lazenby did not speak. She took a deep breath, closed her eyes, and appeared to go to sleep.

"What happened down there?" Celine said. "It was supposed to be no violence and no casualties."

"Of course it was." The captain was feeling his right cheek, which was riddled with tiny slivers of metal. "It's always supposed to be no violence and no casualties."

"But you lost people."

"Yeah. But some of them may not be dead, even though they're still down below. We needed to make a fake attack. Turned out that the lady here didn't rely on her own powers of prophecy to tell her when trouble might be coming, so she kept an armed guard around her quarters. Jake and Nancy and Sid lured them out of the way, and then the rest of us could go in." The captain stared hard at Celine. "Didn't I tell you to stay here in the van?"

"Yes."

"So?"

"You don't leave team members behind. Not where I come from."

"I understand that. Nor do we, though it may not look that way to you. Our people all know the deal. *First* we complete the mission—that's to deliver Sleeping Beauty here. *Then* we go back after Nancy and Jake and Sid—with lots and lots of reinforcements."

"I had two friends in there—Jenny Kopal and Reza Armani—did you . . ."

"I know about them, ma'am. Mars expedition members, too. I really wish I could have done something. But we had orders, straight in, straight out, and a single target. I'm very sorry."

"Captain, really." Pearl Lazenby's eyes had opened again, and she struggled to a sitting position. "With whom do you imagine you are dealing? Barbarians?"

To Celine's surprise, he blushed and looked down at his boots. "I don't know, ma'am. What I've heard—"

"—is utter nonsense. Jenny Kopal and Reza Armani are perfectly safe. Reza, I am delighted to say, is now one of our most loyal and capable members. As for Jenny Kopal, I would like to think that she, too, will become a convert to our cause. But if she does not, and if she wishes to leave, I will order that to happen. I made it clear to everyone in the Legion of Argos that the Mars expedition members were honored guests, to be treated as such." Pearl Lazenby looked reproachfully at Celine. "You and Dr. Oldfield were included in that category. It disappointed me grievously when you chose to leave—and destroyed our property into the bargain."

Celine found herself saying "I'm sorry" before she realized how preposterous that was. Here sat the woman who demanded a "holy cleansing" of everyone who was not white and did not accept her views.

"I'm sorry," Celine said, and continued, "but I regard you as the most dangerous and misguided person I have ever met."

Pearl Lazenby smiled beatifically, "And I regard you, my child, as someone to be pitied because you were shown truth and did not recognize it." Her eyes no longer looked at Celine or at anything else in the van. The bright gray irises seemed to film over. When she spoke, it was in a voice slower and deeper than before.

"Your departure from the Legion of Argos produced a great change in the world. That transformation continues, and it will continue for many years. I see ahead half a century of turmoil, of unceasing labor, of forced and unholy unions. Nature's natural divisions will fail, pure blood will be tainted with impure, God's domain will be invaded as never before. And at the end, at the end . . ."

She paused. The van raced on through the spring morning, while those inside became totally silent. The television in the background babbled on, but no one was listening to it.

At last Pearl Lazenby continued, "At the end, disaster. In that final hour of chaos, the Eye of God will rise again. And we will triumph."

Celine could feel the power, reaching out beyond the woman's body. She didn't know about the strike force members, but she could resist it. What she could not do was explain how Pearl Lazenby knew what was going on, now in Washington and soon around the world. Had Wilmer talked to her of the need for the great shield, of the size of the project, of the inevitable and massive global cooperation, of the implied social and racial mixing?

Or had Pearl Lazenby been listening with eyes closed to the television speech, still going on in the background? Saul Steinmetz had outlined what must be done, now he was introducing other speakers to give the Grand Design their personal endorsements. Celine saw Senator Lopez, with his broad and amiable face, shaking Saul's hand and smiling into the cameras.

Global cooperation; and, as part of it, a space development program that dwarfed the Mars expedition to insignificance. Building the shield would evolve an infrastructure in space strong enough to open the whole solar system to humans. Celine's dream.

But: *At the end, disaster. In that final hour of chaos, the Eye of God will rise once more. And we will triumph.*

Pearl Lazenby might well be right. Celine shivered. She could imagine a hundred ways that a gigantic, long-term international effort could fail. It would be a technological, sociological, and political tour de force. There was no model for its success. The rebuilding of Europe and Japan after the Second World War didn't even come close, in either scale or duration. Saul Steinmetz must know that as well as anyone.

"Are you all right, ma'am?" The captain had seen her shiver, and he was looking at her anxiously.

"I'm fine." Celine forced a smile. "I was just thinking that there's a lot of work ahead, that's all."

His young face cleared. "Oh, I'm sure you'll do it, ma'am. I mean, you went to Mars and back. Nothing could ever be as big a job as that."

It suggested a new way to look at things. Not that you had been to Mars and come back, therefore nothing in the rest of your life could ever approach that summit of achievement. But that the Grand Design guaranteed harder problems, bigger challenges, and worse dangers than anything you had met so far. The future would be no easier than the past, and it would probably be much more difficult.

And the Mars expedition?

Celine could feel within her a rising tension, the same shortness of breath as in the final hours preceding liftoff for Mars. It told her something that she would not mention to any other person: the Martian landing and return was not the greatest space exploit in human history.

It was an opening act before the main event.

EPILOGUE

From the secret diary of Oliver Guest.

Even Jove nods.

I do not know what mistake I made, and in a sense it does not matter. But, cursed as I am with a mind obliged to "wear itself and never rest," I cannot help wondering. What contingency did I fail to cover? Why was not my "perfect" disappearance a total success?

I can only offer as excuse my need to improvise action when I arrived with Seth Parsigian at Catoctin Mountain Park, and discovered that more people were involved than I had expected. I am not at my best when given little time to develop and consider alternatives.

Of course, I have not been recaptured. But I gather from the media that I am still officially alive, and therefore subject to potential pursuit.

It is, in one sense, quite unfair. I am an honorable man and I give fair value. Seth and his companions freed me from the syncope facility, and for that I was in their debt. The telomod therapy that I provided for them should work for at least three years, by which time other centers of treatment will surely be in operation. I left them full notes. I cited Otto Redman's name, over in England, my old colleague Bousson on the Canadian West Coast, and Akhtar Parvali in Iran. All of them have done significant work on telomod therapy, and at least one of them ought to have survived.

What more could be expected? My actions should have

been enough to earn my complete freedom, freedom in perpetuity.

It has not done so, but I will not complain. What though the field be lost? All is not lost.

I still have Methuselah. Hidden away within his introns lie my darlings' full genetic codes. He and I are safe in another country, where my little hobby is quite unknown. The temptation to indulge it again burgeons within me.

Meanwhile, the reconstruction, cloning, and training of my darlings must wait a little longer.

That can be endured. I know I will not wait forever.

ABOUT THE AUTHOR

Charles Sheffield has published forty books, the most recent being the novels *Tomorrow and Tomorrow; Putting Up Roots; Convergence: The Return of the Builders;* and *The Cyborg from Earth.*

He is a winner of the Nebula, Hugo, and John W. Campbell Memorial Awards.